THE CLOVEN FOOT

THE CLOVEN FOOT

MARY ELIZABETH BRADDON

WILDSIDE PRESS

Originally published in 1879.
Published by Wildside Press LLC.
wildsidpress.com

CHAPTER I.

THE HEIR PRESUMPTIVE.

The air was thick with falling snow, and the country side looked a formless mass of chilly whiteness, as the south-western mail train carried John Treverton on a lonely midnight journey. There were not many people in the train on that bleak night, and Mr. Treverton had a second-class compartment to himself.

He had tried to sleep, but had failed ignominiously in the endeavour, waking with a start, after five minutes' doze, and remaining broad awake for an hour at a time pondering upon the perplexities of his life, and hating himself for the follies that had made it what it was. It had been a very hard life of late, for the world had gone ill with John Treverton. He had begun his career with a small fortune and a commission in a crack regiment, and, after wasting his patrimony and selling his commission, he was now a gentleman at large, living as best he might, no one but himself knew how.

He was going to a quiet village in Devonshire, a far-away nook under the shadow of Dartmoor, in obedience to a telegram that told him a rich kinsman was dying, and summoned him to the death-bed. The day had been when he hoped to inherit this kinsman's property; not because the old man had ever cared for him, but because he, John, was the only relative Jasper Treverton had in the world; but that hope had vanished when the lonely old bachelor adopted an orphan girl to whom he was reported to have attached himself strongly. The *ci-devant* Captain had never seen this young person, and it is not to be supposed that he cherished very kindly feelings towards her. He had made up his mind that she was a deep and designing creature, who would, of course, play her cards in such a manner as to induce old Jasper Treverton to leave her everything.

'He never bore me or mine much goodwill,' John Treverton said to himself, 'but he might have left his money to me for want of anyone else to leave it to, if it hadn't been for this girl.'

During almost the whole of that dreary night journey he was meditating on this subject, half inclined to be angry with himself for having taken such useless trouble for the sake of a man who was not likely to leave him sixpence.

He was not an utterly bad fellow, this John Treverton, though his better and purer feelings had been a good deal blunted by rough contact with the world. He had a frank, winning manner, and a handsome face, a face which had won him the love of more than one woman, with little profit to himself. He was a man of no strong principle, and with a self-indulgent nature that had led him into wrong-doing very often during the last ten years of his life. He had an easy temper, a habit of looking at the pleasanter side of things so long as there was any pleasantness in them, and a chronic avoidance of all serious thought—qualities which do not serve to make up a strong character. But the charm of his manner was none the less because of this latent weakness of character, and he was better liked than many better men.

The train stopped at a little rustic station, forty miles westward of Exeter, about an hour after midnight—a dreary building with an open platform, across which the wind blew and the snow drifted as John Treverton alighted, the one solitary passenger to be deposited at this out-of-the-way place. He knew that the house to which he had to go was some miles from the station, and he applied himself at once to the sleepy station-master to ascertain if there were any possibility of procuring a conveyance at that time of night.

'There's a gig waiting for a gentleman from London,' the man answered, stifling a yawn. 'I suppose you are the party, sir.'

'A gig from Treverton Manor?'

'Yes, sir.'

'Thanks, yes; I am the person that is expected. Civil, at any rate,' John Treverton added to himself, as he walked off to the gig, wrapped to the eyes in his great coat, and with a railway rug across his shoulder.

He found a gig, with a rough-looking individual of the gardener species waiting for him in the snow.

'Here I am, my man,' he cried cheerily. 'Have you been waiting long?'

'No, sir. Miss Malcolm said as how you'd come by this train.'

'Miss Malcolm sent you for me, then?

'Yes, sir.'

'And how is Mr. Treverton to-night?'

'Mortal bad, sir. The doctors say as th' old gentleman hasn't many hours to live. And Miss Malcolm, she says to me, "Jacob, you're to drive home as fast as th' horse can go, for papa is very anxious to see Mr. John before he dies." She allus calls the old gentleman papa, you see, sir, he having adopted of her ten years ago, and

6

brought her up as his own daughter like ever since.'

They had jolted over the uneven stones of a narrow street, the high street of a small settlement which evidently called itself a town, for here, at a point where two narrow lanes branched off from the central thoroughfare, there stood a dilapidated old building of the town-hall species, and a vaulted market-place with iron railings and closely-locked gates shutting in emptiness. John Treverton perceived dimly through the winter darkness an old stone church, and at least three Methodist chapels. Then, all in a moment, the town was gone, and the gig was rattling along a Devonshire lane, between high banks and still higher hedges, above which rose a world of hill and moor, that melted far off into the midnight sky.

'And your master is very fond of this young lady, Miss Malcolm?' John Treverton inquired presently, when the horse, after rattling along for a mile and a half at a tremendous pace, was slowly climbing a hill which seemed to lead nowhere in particular, for one could hardly imagine any definite end or aim in a lane that went undulating like a snake amidst a chaos of hills.

'Oncommon, sir. You see, she's about the only thing he has ever cared for.'

'Is she as much liked by other people?'

'Well, yes, sir, in a general way Miss Malcolm is pretty well liked, but there is some as think her proud—think her a little set up as you may say, by Mr. Treverton's making so much of her. She's not one to make friends very easy; the young ladies in the village, Squire Carew's daughters, and such like, haven't taken to her as much as they might have done. I've heard my wife—as has been parlour-maid at the Manor for the last twenty years—say as much many a time. But Miss Malcolm is a pleasant-spoken young lady, for all that, to those she likes, and my Susan has had no fault to find with her. You see all of us has our peculiarities, sir, and it ain't to be supposed as Miss Malcolm would be without hers,' the man concluded in an argumentative tone.

'Humph!' muttered John Treverton. 'A stuck-up young lady, I dare say—and a deep one into the bargain. Did you ever hear who she was—what her position was, and so on—when my cousin Jasper adopted her?' he asked aloud.

'No, sir. Mr. Treverton has kept that oncommon close. He'd been away from the Manor a twelvemonth when he brought her home without a word of warning to any one in the house, and told his old housekeeper as how he'd adopted this little girl—who was an orphan—the daughter of an old friend of his, and that's all he ever said about her from that time to this. Miss Malcolm was about seven or eight year old at that time, as pretty a little girl as you could see—and she has grown up to be a beautiful young woman.'

Beautiful. Oh, this artful young person was beautiful, was she? John Treverton determined that her good looks should have no influence upon his opinions.

The man was quite willing to talk, but his companion asked no more questions. He felt, indeed, that he had already asked more than he was warranted in asking, and felt a little ashamed of himself for having done so. The rest of the drive, therefore, passed for the most part in silence. The journey had seemed long to John Treverton, partly because of his own impatience, partly on account of the numerous ups and downs of that everlasting lane, but it was little more than half-an-hour after leaving the station when they entered a village street where there was not a glimmer of light at this hour, except one solitary lamp shining feebly before the door of the general shop and post-office. This was the village of Hazlehurst, near which Hazlehurst Manor-house was situated. They drove to the end of this quiet street and along a high road bordered by tall elms which looked black against the night sky, till they came to a pair of great iron gates.

The man handed the reins to his companion, and then dismounted and opened these gates. John Treverton drove slowly into a winding carriage drive that led up to the house, a great red-brick mansion with many long, narrow windows, and a massive carved stone shell over the door, which was approached on each side by a flight of broad stone steps.

There was light enough from the stars for John Treverton to see all this as he drove slowly up to the hall door. His coming had evidently been awaited anxiously, as the door was opened before he had alighted from the gig, and an old man-servant peered out into the night. He opened the door wide when he saw John Treverton. The gardener—or groom, whichever he might happen to be—led the gig slowly away to a gate at the side of the house, opening into a stable yard. John Treverton went into the hall, which looked very bright and cheerful after his dreary drive—a great, square hall hung with family portraits and old armour, and with crimson sheep-skins and tawny hides of savage beasts lying about on the black and white marble pavement. There was a roomy old fireplace on one side of this hall, with a great fire burning in it, a fire which was welcome as meat and drink to a traveller this cold night. There were ponderous carved oak chairs with dark-red velvet cushions, looking more

8

comfortable and better adapted for the repose of the human frame than such chairs are wont to be, and at the end of the hall there was a great antique buffet adorned with curious bowls and bottle-shaped jars in Oriental china.

John Treverton had time to see these things as he sat before the fire with his long legs stretched out upon the hearth, while the old servant went to announce his arrival to Miss Malcolm.

'A pleasant old place,' he said to himself. 'And to think of my never having seen it before, thanks to my father's folly in having quarrelled with old Jasper Treverton, and never having taken the trouble to heal the breach, as he might have done, I dare say, with some slight exercise of diplomacy. I wonder whether the old fellow is very rich. Such a place as this might be kept up on a couple of thousand a year, but I have a notion that Jasper Treverton has six times as much as that.'

The old butler came downstairs in about five minutes to say that Miss Malcolm would be pleased to see Mr. Treverton, if he liked. His master had fallen asleep, and was sleeping more peacefully than he had done for some time.

John Treverton followed the man up a broad staircase with massive oak bannisters. Here, as in the hall, there were family portraits on the walls, and armour and old china in every available corner. At the top of this staircase was a gallery, lighted by a lantern in the roof, and with numerous doors opening out of it. The butler opened one of these doors and ushered John Treverton into a bright-looking, lamp-lit sitting-room, with panelled walls. A heavy green damask curtain hung before a door opening into an adjoining room. The mantelpiece was high, and exquisitely carved with flowers and cupids, and was ornamented by a row of eggshell cups and saucers, and the quaintest of Oriental teapots. The room had a comfortable, homelike look, John Treverton thought—a look that struck him all the more perhaps because he had no settled home of his own, nor had ever known one since his boyhood.

A lady was sitting by the fire, dressed in a dark-blue gown, which contrasted wonderfully with the auburn tints of her hair, and the transparent pallor of her complexion. As she rose and turned her face towards John Treverton, he saw that she was indeed a very beautiful young woman, and there was something in her beauty which took him a little by surprise, in spite of what he had heard from his companion in the gig.

'Thank God you have come in time, Mr. Treverton,' she said earnestly—an earnestness which John Treverton was inclined to consider hypocritical. What interest could she have in his arrival? What feeling could there be between them but jealousy?

'I suppose she feels so secure about the old man's will that she can afford to be civil,' he thought as he seated himself by the fireside, after two or three polite commonplaces about his journey. 'There is no hope of my cousin's recovery, I suppose?' he hazarded presently.

'Not the faintest,' Laura Malcolm answered, very sadly. 'The London physician was here for the last time to-day. He has been down every week for the last two months. He said to-day that there would be no occasion for him to come any more; he did not think papa—I have always called your cousin by that name—could live through the night. He has been less restless and troubled since then, and he is now sleeping very quietly. He may linger a little longer than the physician seemed to think likely; but beyond that I have no hope whatever.'

This was said with a quiet, restrained manner that was more indicative of sorrow than any demonstrative lamentation could have been. There was something almost like despair in the girl's look and tone—a dreary hopelessness—as if there were nothing left for her in life when the friend and protector of her girlhood should be taken from her. John Treverton watched her closely as she sat looking at the fire, with her dark eyes shrouded by their long lashes. Yes, she was very beautiful. That was a fact about which there was no possibility of doubt. Those large hazel eyes alone would have given a charm to the plainest face, and in this face there was no fault to be redeemed.

'You seem to be much attached to my cousin, Miss Malcolm,' Mr. Treverton said presently.

'I love him dearly,' she answered, looking up at him with those deep, dark eyes, which had a melancholy expression to-night. 'I have had no one else to care for since I was quite a child; and he has been very good to me. I should be something worse than ungrateful if I did not love him as I do.'

'And yet your life must have been a trying one, as the sole companion of an old man of Jasper Treverton's eccentric temper. I speak of him as I have heard him described by my father. You must have found existence with him rather troublesome now and then, I should think.'

'I very soon learnt to understand him, and to bear all the little changes in his humour. I knew that his heart was noble.'

'Humph!' thought John Treverton. 'Women can do these things

better than men. I couldn't stand being shut up with a crusty old fellow for a week.'

And after having made this reflection, he thought that no doubt Miss Malcolm was of the usual type of sycophants and interlopers, able to endure anything in the present for the chance of a stupendous advantage in the future, able to wait for the fruition of her hopes with a dull, grovelling patience.

'This appearance of grief is all put on, of course,' he said to himself. 'I am not going to think any better of her because she has fine eyes.'

They sat for a little time in silence; Laura Malcolm seemed quite absorbed by her own thoughts, and in no way disturbed by the presence of John Treverton. It was a proud face which he looked at every now and then so thoughtfully, not a lovable face by any means, in spite of its beauty. There was a coldness of expression, a self-contained air about Miss Malcolm which her new acquaintance was inclined to dislike. He had come to that house prepared to think unfavourably of her; had come there, indeed, with a settled dislike to her.

'I think it is to you I am indebted for the telegram that summoned me here?' he said by-and-by.

'Oh, no, not to me directly. It was your cousin's wish that you should be sent for—a wish he only expressed on Monday, though I had asked him many times if he would not like to see you, his only surviving relative. Had I known your address, or where a letter would reach you, I think I should have ventured to ask you to come down without his permission, but I had no knowledge of this.'

'And it was only the day before yesterday that my cousin spoke of me for the first time?'

'Only the day before yesterday. On every previous occasion he gave me a short, impatient answer, telling me not to worry him, and that he had no wish to see anyone, but on Monday he mentioned your name, and told me he wanted particularly to see you. He had no idea where you were to be found, but he thought a telegram addressed to your father's old lawyer would reach you. I sent the message as he directed.'

'The lawyer had some difficulty in hunting me out, but I lost no time after I got your message. I cannot, of course, pretend any attachment to a man whom I never saw in my life, but I am pleased that Jasper Treverton should have thought of me at the last, nevertheless. I am here to testify my respect for him, in a perfectly independent character, having not the faintest expectation of inheriting one shilling of his wealth.'

'I don't know why you should not expect to inherit his estate, Mr. Treverton,' Laura Malcolm answered, quietly. 'To whom else should he leave it, if not to you?'

John Treverton thought this question a piece of gratuitous hypocrisy.

'Why, to you, of course,' he replied, 'his adopted daughter, who have earned his favour by years of patient submission to all his whims and fancies. Surely you must be quite aware of his intentions upon this point, Miss Malcolm, and this affected ignorance of the subject is intended to hoodwink me.'

'I am sorry you should think so badly of me, Mr. Treverton. I do not know how your cousin has disposed of his money, but I do know that none of it has been left to me.'

'How do you know that?'

'I have been assured of it by his own lips, not once but many times. When he first adopted me he made a vow that he would leave me no part of his wealth. He had been treated with falsehood and ingratitude by those he had loved, and had found out their mercenary feelings about him. This had soured him a good deal, and he was determined—when he took me under his care out of motives of the purest charity—that he would have one person about him who should love him for his own sake, or not pretend to love him at all. He took an oath to this effect on the night he first brought me home to this house, and fully explained the meaning of that oath to me, though I was quite a child at that time. "I have had toadies and sycophants about me, Laura," he said, "until I have come to distrust every smiling face. Your smiles shall be true, my dear, for you shall have no motive for falsehood." On my eighteenth birthday he placed in trust six thousand pounds for my benefit, in order that his death should not leave me unprovided for, but he took occasion at the same time to remind me that this gift was all I must ever expect at his hands.'

John Treverton heard this with a quickened breath, and a new life and eagerness in the expression of his face. The aspect of affairs was quite altered by the fact of this oath sworn long ago by the eccentric old man. He must leave his money to some one. What if he should, indeed, leave it to him, John Treverton?

For some few minutes his heart beat high with a new hope, and then sank again suddenly. Was it not much more likely that Jasper Treverton would find some means of evading the letter of his vow, for the benefit of a beloved adopted daughter, than that he should bequeath his fortune to a kinsman who was a stranger to him?

'Don't let me be a fool,' John Treverton said to himself; 'there's not the faintest chance of any such luck for me, and I dare say this girl knows as much, though she is artful enough to pretend complete ignorance of the old man's designs.'

The butler came in presently to announce that supper was ready for Mr. Treverton in the dining-room below. He went downstairs in answer to this summons, after begging Miss Malcolm to send for him the moment the invalid awoke.

The dining-room was handsomely furnished with massive side-board and chairs of carved oak, the long, narrow windows draped with dark-red velvet. There was a fine old Venetian glass over the sideboard, and a smaller circular mirror above the old inlaid bureau that occupied the space between the windows opposite. There were a few good cabinet pictures of the Dutch school on the panelled walls, and a pair of fine blue-and-white Delft jars on the high carved oak chimney-piece. A wood fire burned cheerily in the wide grate, and the small round table on which the traveller's supper had been laid was wheeled close to the edge of the Turkey hearthrug, and had a very comfortable appearance in the eyes of Mr. John Treverton as he seated himself in one of the capacious oak chairs.

In his disturbed state of mind he had little inclination to eat, though the cook had prepared a cosy supper that might have tempted an anchorite; but he did justice to a bottle of excellent claret, and sat for some time, sipping his wine and looking about him thought-fully, now at the curious old silver tankards and rose-water dishes on the sideboard, now at the Cuyps and Ostades on the dark oak walls. To whom would all these things belong when Jasper Trever-ton was no more? Throughout the house there were indications of wealth that inspired an almost savage longing in this man's mind. What a changed life his would be if he should inherit only half of his cousin's possessions! He thought, with a weary sigh, of the wretched hand-to-mouth existence that he had led of late years, and then thought of the things that he would do if he came in for any share of the old man's money. He sat meditating thus until the servant came to tell him that Mr. Treverton was awake and had asked to see him. He followed the man back to the study, where he had found Miss Malcolm. The room was empty now, but the curtain was drawn aside from the door of communication, and he passed through this into Jasper Treverton's bedroom.

Laura Malcolm was seated at the bedside, but she rose as John entered, and slipped quietly away by another door, leaving him alone with his cousin.

'Sit down, John,' the old man said in a feeble voice, pointing to the empty chair by the bedside.

'It is rather late in the day for us two to meet,' he went on, after a brief pause, 'but perhaps it is better for us to see each other once before I die. I won't speak of your father's quarrel with me. You know all about that, I dare say. We were both in the wrong, very likely; but it has long been too late to undo that. I loved him once, God knows!—Yes, there was a day when I loved Richard Treverton dearly.'

'I have heard him say as much, sir,' John answered in subdued tones. 'I regret that he should have quarrelled with you; I regret much more that he should not have sought a reconciliation.'

'Your father was always a proud man, John. Perhaps I liked him all the better for that. Most men in his position would have courted me for the sake of my money. He never did that.'

'It was not in him to do it, sir. He had his faults, I have no doubt, but a sordid nature was not one of them.'

'I know that,' answered Jasper Treverton, 'nor have you ever sought me out, John, or tried to worm yourself into my favour. Yet I suppose you know that you are my sole surviving relative.'

'Yes, sir, I am quite aware of that.'

'And you have left me in peace, and have been content to take your chance. Well, you will find yourself none the worse off for having respected yourself and not worried me.'

John Treverton's face flushed, and the beating of his heart quickened again, as it had quickened when Laura Malcolm told him of his kinsman's vow.

'My death will make you a rich man,' returned Jasper, always speaking with a painful effort, and in so low a voice that John was obliged to bend over his pillow in order to hear him, 'on one condition—a condition which I do not think you will find it difficult to comply with.'

'You are very good, sir,' faltered the young man, almost too agitated to speak. 'Believe me, I had no expectation of this.'

'I dare say not,' replied the other. 'I took a foolish oath some years ago, and bound myself not to leave my fortune to the only creature I really love. To whom else should I leave it then, but to you—my next of kin? I know nothing against you. I have lived too remote from the world to hear its scandals, and I know not whether you have won good or evil repute among your fellow men; but I do know that you are the son of a man I once loved, and that it will be

14

in your power to carry out my wishes in the spirit, if not in the letter. The rest I trust to Providence.'

After having said this the dying man lay back upon the pillows, and remained silent for some minutes, resting after the exertion involved in so long a speech. John Treverton waited for him to speak again—waited with a tumultuous sense of gladness in his breast, looking round the room now and then. It was a spacious apartment, with handsome antique furniture, and panelled walls hung with old pictures, like those in the dining-room below. Dark-green velvet curtains were closely drawn before the three lofty windows, and in the spaces between them there were curious old cabinets of carved ebony, inlaid with silver. John Treverton looked at all these things, which seemed to be his already, after what the dying man had said to him. How different from the home he had left, the shabby-genteel London lodging, with its tawdry finery and decrepit chairs and tables!

'What do you think of my adopted daughter, John Treverton?' the old man asked presently, turning his dim eyes towards his cousin.

The younger man hesitated a little before replying. The question had taken him by surprise. His thoughts had been far away from Laura Malcolm.

'I think she is very handsome, sir,' he said, 'and I dare say she is amiable; but I really have had very little opportunity of forming any opinion about the young lady.'

'No, you have seen nothing of her as yet. You will like her better when you come to know her. I cannot doubt that. Her father and I were warm friends, once upon a time. We were at Oxford together, and travelled a good deal in Spain and Italy together, and loved each other well enough, I believe, till circumstances parted us. I need have no shame in owning the cause of our parting now. We loved the same woman, and Stephen Malcolm won her. I thought—whether rightly or wrongly—that I had not been fairly treated in the matter, and Stephen and I parted, never to meet as friends again till Stephen was on his death-bed. The lady jilted him after all, and he did not marry until some years later. When I heard of him next he was in reduced circumstances. I sought him out, found him in a pitiable condition and adopted his daughter—an only child—doubly orphaned. I cannot tell you how dear she soon became to me, but I had made an oath I would leave her nothing, and I have not broken that oath, dearly as I love her.'

'But you have made some provision for her future, sir?'

'Yes, I have striven to provide for her future. God grant it may be a happy one. And now call my servant, if you please, John. I have talked a great deal too much as it is.'

'Only one word before I call the man. Let me tell you, sir, that I am grateful,' said John Treverton, kneeling down beside the bed, and taking the old man's wasted hand in his.

'Prove it when I am gone, John, by trying to carry out my wishes. And now good-night. You had better go to bed.'

'Will you allow me to sit with you for the rest of the night, sir? I have not the least inclination to sleep.'

'No, no, there would be no use in your sitting up. If I am well enough to see you again in the morning I will do so. Till then, good-bye.'

The old man's tone was decisive. John Treverton went out of the room by a door that opened on the gallery. Here he found Jasper Treverton's valet, a grave-looking, grey-haired man, dozing upon a window seat. He told this man that he was wanted in the sick room, and then went to the study.

Miss Malcolm was still there, sitting in a thoughtful attitude, looking at the fire.

'What do you think of him?' she asked, looking up suddenly, as John Treverton entered the room.

'He does not seem to me so ill as I expected to see him from your account. He has spoken to me with perfect clearness.'

'I am very glad of that. He seemed a good deal better after that long sleep. I will ring for Trimmer to show you your room, Mr. Treverton.'

'Are you not going to bed yourself, Miss Malcolm? It is nearly three o'clock.'

'No. I cannot sleep during this time of suspense. Besides, he may want me at any moment. I shall lie down on that sofa, perhaps, a little before morning.'

'Have you been keeping watch like this many nights?'

'For more than a week; but I am not tired. I think when the mind is so anxious the body has no capability of feeling fatigue.'

'You will find the reaction very severe by-and-by, I fear,' Mr. Treverton replied; and Trimmer, the old butler, having appeared by this time with a candle, he wished Miss Malcolm good-night.

The room to which Trimmer led John Treverton was on the other side of the house—a large room, with a comfortable fire blazing on the hearth, and reflecting itself in a border of old Dutch tiles. Late as it was, Mr. Treverton sat by the fire thinking for a long time before he went to bed, and even when he did lie down under the shadow of the damask curtains that shrouded the gloomy-looking four-post bed, sleep kept aloof from him. His mind was busy with thoughts of triumph and delight. Innumerable schemes for the future—selfish ones for the most part—crowded and jostled each other in his brain. It was a feverish night altogether—a night which left him unrefreshed and haggard when the cold wintry light came creeping in between the window curtains, and a great clock in the stable yard struck eight.

A countryfied-looking young man, a subordinate of the butler's, brought the visitor his shaving water, and, on being questioned, informed him that Mr. Treverton the elder had passed a restless night, and was worse that morning.

John Treverton dressed quickly, and went straight to the study next the invalid's room. He found Laura Malcolm there, looking very wan and pale after her night's watching. She confirmed the young man's statement. Jasper Treverton was much worse. His mind had wandered towards daybreak, and he now seemed to recognise no one. His old friend the vicar had been with him, and had read the prayers for the sick, but the dying man had been able to take no part in them. The end was very near at hand, Laura feared.

Mr. Treverton stopped with Miss Malcolm a little while, and then wandered down to the dining-room, where he found an excellent breakfast waiting for him in solitary state. He fancied that the old butler treated him with a peculiar deference, as if aware that he was to be the new master of Treverton Manor. After breakfast he went out into the gardens, which were large, and laid out in an old-fashioned style; straight walks, formal grass-plats, and flower-beds of geometrical design. John Treverton walked here for some time, smoking his cigar and looking up thoughtfully at the great red-brick house with its many windows glittering in the chill January sunshine, and its air of old-world repose.

'It will be the beginning of a new life,' he said to himself. 'I feel myself ten years younger since my interview with the old man last night. Let me see—I shall be thirty on my next birthday. Young enough to begin life afresh—old enough to use wealth wisely.'

CHAPTER II.

JASPER TREVERTON'S WILL.

Jasper Treverton lingered nearly a week after the coming of his kinsman—a week that seemed interminable to the expectant heir, who could not help wishing the old man would make a speedy end of it. What use was that last remnant of life to him lying helpless on his bed, restless, weary, and for the greater part of his time delirious? John Treverton saw him for a few minutes once or twice every day, and looked at him with a sympathising and appropriate expression of countenance, and did really feel compassionately towards him; but his busy thoughts pressed forward to the time when he should have the handling of that feeble sufferer's wealth, and should be free to begin that new life, bright glimpses whereof shone upon his roving fancy like visions of paradise.

After six monotonous days, every one of which was exactly like the other for John Treverton, who smoked his solitary cigar in the wintry garden, and ate his solitary meals in the great dining-room with his mind always filled by that one subject—the inheritance which seemed so nearly within his grasp—the night came upon which Jasper Treverton's feeble hold of life relaxed altogether, and he drifted away to the unknown ocean, with his hand in Laura Malcolm's, and his face turned towards her, with a wan smile upon the faded lips, as he died. After this followed three or four days of wearisome delay, in which the quiet of the darkened rooms seemed intolerable to John Treverton, to whom death was an unfamiliar horror. He avoided the house in these days as much as possible, and spent the greater part of his time in long rambles out into the open country, leaving all the arrangements of the funeral to Mr. Clare, the vicar, who had been Jasper Treverton's closest friend, and a Mr. Sampson, an inhabitant of the village, who had been the dead man's solicitor.

The funeral came at last, a very quiet ceremonial, in accordance with Jasper Treverton's express desire, and the master of Treverton Manor was laid in the vault where many of his ancestors slept the last long sleep. There was a drizzling rain and a low, lead-coloured sky, beneath which the old churchyard looked unspeakably dismal;

but John Treverton's thoughts were far away as he stood by the open grave, while the sublime words of the service fell unheard upon his ear. To-morrow he would be back in London, most likely, with the consciousness of wealth and power, inaugurating that new life which he thought of so eagerly.

He went back to the house, where it was a relief to find the blinds drawn up and the dull gray winter light in the rooms. The will was to be read in the drawing-room—a very handsome room, with white-and-gold panelling, six long windows, and a fireplace at each end. Here Mr. Sampson, the lawyer, seated himself at a table to read the will, in the presence of Mr. Clare, the vicar, Laura Malcolm, and the upper servants of the Manor-house, who took their places in a little group near the door.

The will was very simply worded. It commenced with some bequests to the old servants, a small annuity to Andrew Trimmer, the butler, and sums varying from fifty to two hundred pounds to the coachman and women servants. There was a complimentary legacy of a hundred guineas to Thomas Sampson, and a bequest of old plate to Theodore Clare, the vicar. After these things had been duly set forth the testator went on to leave the remainder of his property, real and personal, to his cousin, John Treverton, provided the said John Treverton should marry his dearly-beloved adopted daughter, Laura Malcolm, within one year of his decease. The estate was to be held in trust during this interval by Theodore Clare and Thomas Sampson, together with all moneys therefrom arising. In the event of this marriage not taking place within the said time, the whole of the estate was to pass into the hands of the said Theodore Clare and the said Thomas Sampson, in trust for the erection of a hospital in the adjacent market town of Beechampton.

Miss Malcolm looked up with a startled expression as this strange bequest was read. John Treverton's face assumed a sudden pallor that was by no means flattering to the lady whose fate was involved in the singular condition which attached to his inheritance. The situation was an awkward one for both. Laura rose directly the reading of the will was finished, and left the room without a word. The servants retired immediately after, and John Treverton was left alone with the vicar and the lawyer.

'Allow me to congratulate you, Mr. Treverton,' said Thomas Sampson, folding up the will, and coming to the fireplace by which John Treverton was seated; 'you will find yourself a very rich man.'

'A twelvemonth hence, Mr. Sampson,' the other answered doubtfully, 'always provided that Miss Malcolm is willing to accept

19

me for her husband, which she may not be.'

'She will scarcely fly in the face of her adopted father's desire, Mr. Treverton.'

'I don't know about that. A woman seldom cares for a husband of any one else's choosing. I don't want to look a gift horse in the mouth, or to seem ungrateful to my cousin Jasper, from whom I entertained no expectations whatever a week or so ago: but I cannot help thinking he would have done better by dividing his property between Miss Malcolm and myself, leaving us both free.'

He spoke in a slow, meditative way, and he was pale to the very lips. There was no appearance of triumph or gladness—only an anxious, disappointed expression, which made his handsome face look strangely worn and haggard.

'There are not many men who would think Laura Malcolm an encumbrance to any fortune, Mr. Treverton,' said Mr. Clare. 'I think you will be happier in the possession of such a wife than in the enjoyment of your cousin's wealth, large as it is.'

'In the event of the lady's accepting me as her husband,' John Treverton again interposed doubtfully.

'You have an interval of a twelvemonth in which to win her,' replied the vicar, 'and things will go hard with you if you fail. I think I can answer for the fact that Miss Malcolm's affections are disengaged. Of course she, like yourself, is a little startled by the eccentricity of this condition. The position is much more embarrassing for her than for you.'

John Treverton did not reply to this remark, but there was a very blank look in his face as he stood by the fire listening to the vicar's and the lawyer's praises of his departed kinsman.

'Will Miss Malcolm continue to occupy this house?' he asked presently.

'I scarcely know what her wishes may be,' replied Mr. Clare, 'but I think it would be well if the house were placed at her disposal. I suppose that we as trustees would have power to make her such an offer, Mr. Sampson, with Mr. Treverton's concurrence.'

'Of course.'

'I concur most heartily in any arrangement that may be agreeable to the young lady,' John Treverton said, in rather a mechanical way. 'I suppose there is nothing further to detain me here. I can go back to town to-morrow.'

'Wouldn't you like to go over the estate before you return to London, Mr. Treverton?' asked Thomas Sampson. 'It would be just as well for you to see the extent of a property that is pretty sure to be your own. If you don't mind taking things in a plain way, I should be very much pleased by your spending a week or so at my house. There's no one knows the estate better than I do, and I can show you every rood of it.'

'You are very kind, Mr. Sampson. I shall be glad to accept your hospitality.'

'That's what I call friendly. When will you come over to us? This evening? We are all to dine together, I believe. Why shouldn't you go home with me after dinner? Your presence here can only embarrass Miss Malcolm.'

Having accepted the lawyer's invitation, John Treverton did not care how soon his visit took place, so it was agreed that he should walk over to 'The Laurels' with Mr. Sampson that evening after dinner. But before he went it would be necessary to take some kind of farewell of Laura Malcolm, and the idea of this was now painfully embarrassing to him. It was a thing that must be done, however, and it would be well that it should be done at a seasonable hour; so in the twilight, before dinner, he went up to the study, which he knew was Miss Malcolm's favourite room, and found her there with an open book lying on her lap and a small tea-tray on the table by her side.

She looked up at him without any appearance of confusion, but with a very pale, sad face. He seated himself opposite her, and it was some moments before he could find words for the simple announcement he had to make. That calm, beautiful face, turned towards him with a grave, expectant look, embarrassed him more than he could have imagined possible.

'I have accepted an invitation from Mr. Sampson to spend a few days with him before I go back to town, and I have come to bid you good-bye, Miss Malcolm,' he said at last. 'I fancied that at such a time as this it would be pleasanter for you to feel yourself quite alone.'

'You are very good. I do not suppose I shall stay here many days.'

'I hope you will stay here altogether. Mr. Sampson and Mr. Clare, the trustees, wish it very much. I do not think that I have much power in the affair; but believe me, it is my earnest desire that you should not be in a hurry to leave your old home.'

'You are very good. I do not think I could stay here alone in this dear old house, where I have been so happy. I know some respectable people in the village who let lodgings. I think I would rather remove to their house as soon as my trunks are packed. I have plenty to live upon, you know, Mr. Treverton. The six thousand pounds your cousin gave me yields an income of over two hundred a year.'

'You must consult your own wishes, Miss Malcolm. I cannot presume to interfere with your views, anxious as I am for your welfare.'

This was about as much as he would venture to say at this early stage of affairs. He felt his position indescribably awkward, and he wondered at Laura Malcolm's composure. What ought he to say or do? What could he say that would not seem dictated by the most sordid motive? What disinterested feeling could there ever arise between those two, who were bound together by their common interest in a great estate, who met as strangers to find themselves suddenly dependent upon each other's caprice?

'I may call upon you before I leave Hazlehurst, may I not, Miss Malcolm?' he asked presently, with a kind of desperation.

'I shall be happy to see you whenever you call.'

'You are very kind. I'll not intrude on you any longer this evening, for I am sure you must want quiet and perfect rest. I must go down to dinner with Mr. Sampson and the vicar—rather a dreary kind of entertainment I fear it will be. Good-bye.'

He offered her his hand for the first time since they had met. Hers was very cold, and trembled a little as she gave it to him. He detained it rather longer than he was justified in doing, and looked at her for the first time with something like tender pity in his eyes. Yes, she was very pretty. He would have liked her face better without that expression of coldness and pride, but he could not deny that she was beautiful, and he felt that any young man might be proud to win such a woman for his wife. He did not see his own way to winning her, however; and it seemed to him as if the fortune he had so built upon during all his reveries lately, was now removed very far out of his reach.

The dinner was not such a dismal feast as he had imagined it would be. People are apt to accustom themselves very easily to an old friend's removal, and the vicar and the lawyer seemed tolerably cheerful about their departed neighbour. They discussed his little eccentricities, his virtues and his foibles, in an agreeable spirit, and did ample justice to his claret, of which, however, Mr. Clare said he had never been quite so good a judge as he had believed himself to be. They sat for a couple of hours over their dessert, sipping some Burgundy of which Jasper Treverton had been especially proud, and John Treverton was the only one of the three who seemed troubled by gloomy thoughts.

22

It was ten o'clock when Mr. Sampson proposed an adjournment to his own abode. He had sent a little note home to his sister before dinner, telling her of Mr. Treverton's intended visit, and had ordered a fly from the inn, in which vehicle he and his guest drove to 'The Laurels,' a trim, bright-looking, modern house, with small rooms which were the very pink of neatness; so neat and new-looking, indeed, that John Treverton fancied they could never have been lived in, and that the furniture must have been sent home from the upholsterer that very day.

Thomas Sampson was a young man, and a bachelor. He had inherited an excellent business from his father, and had done a good deal to improve it himself, having a considerable capacity for getting on in life, and an ardent love of money-making. He had one sister, who lived with him. She was tolerably good-looking, in a pale, insipid way, with eyes of a cold light blue, and straight, silky hair of a nondescript brown.

This young lady, whose name was Eliza, welcomed John Treverton with much politeness. There were not many men in the neighbourhood of Hazlehurst who could have borne comparison with that splendid military-looking stranger, and Miss Sampson, who did not yet know the terms of Jasper Treverton's will, supposed that this handsome young man was now master of the Manor and all its dependencies. For his sake she had bestowed considerable pains on the adornment of the spare bedroom, which she had embellished with more fanciful pincushions, and ring-stands and Bohemian glass scent-bottles, than are consistent with the masculine idea of comfort. For his gratification also she had ordered a reckless expenditure of coals in the keeping up of a blazing fire in the same smartly-furnished chamber, which looked unspeakably small and mean to the eyes of John Treverton after the spacious rooms at the Manor-house.

'I know of a room that will look meaner still,' he said to himself, 'for this at least is clean and neat.'

He went to bed, and slept better than he had done for many nights, but his dreams were full of Laura Malcolm. He dreamt that they were being married, and that as she stood beside him at the altar her face changed in some strange, ghastly way into another face, a face he knew only too well.

CHAPTER III.

A MYSTERIOUS VISITOR.

The next day was fine, and Mr. Sampson and his visitor set out in a dogcart directly after breakfast on a tour of inspection. They got over a good deal of ground between an eight o'clock breakfast and a six o'clock dinner, and John Treverton had the pleasure of surveying many of the broad acres that were in all probability to be his own; but the farms which lay within a drive of Hazlehurst did not constitute a third of Jasper Treverton's possessions. Mr. Sampson told his companion that the estates were worth about eleven thousand a year altogether, besides which there was an income of about three thousand more accruing from money in the funds. The old man had begun life with only six thousand a year, but some of his land bordered closely on the town of Beechampton, and had developed from agricultural land into building land in a manner that had increased its value seven-fold. He had lived quietly, and had added to his estate year after year by fresh purchases and investments, until it reached its present amount. To hear of such wealth was like some dream of fairyland to John Treverton. Mr. Sampson spoke of it as if to all intents and purposes it were already in the other's possession. His sound legal mind could not conceive the possibility of any sentimental objection on the part of either the gentleman or the lady to the carrying out of a condition which was to secure the possession of that noble estate to both. Of course, in due time Mr. Treverton would make Miss Malcolm a formal offer, and she would accept him. Idiocy so abject on the part of either the gentleman or the lady as a refusal to comply with so easy a condition was scarcely within the limits of human folly.

Looking at the matter from this point of view, Mr. Sampson was surprised to perceive a certain air of gloom and despondency about his companion which seemed quite unnatural to a man in his position. John Treverton's eye kindled with a gleam of triumph as he gazed across the broad, bare fields which the lawyer showed him; but in the next minute his face grew sombre again, and he listened to the description of the property with an absent air that was inexplicable to Thomas Sampson. The solicitor ventured to say as much by-

24

and-by, when they were driving homeward through the winter dusk.

'Well, you see, my dear Sampson, there's many a slip between the cup and the lip,' John Treverton answered, with that light, airy tone which most people found particularly agreeable. 'I must confess that the manner in which this estate has been left is rather a disappointment to me. My cousin Jasper told me that his death would make me a rich man. Instead of this I find myself with a blank year of waiting before me, and with my chances of coming into possession of this fortune entirely dependent upon the whims and caprices of a young lady.'

'You don't suppose for a moment that Miss Malcolm will refuse you?'

John Treverton was so long before he answered this question that the lawyer presently repeated it in a louder tone, fancying that it had not been heard upon the first occasion.

'Do I think she'll refuse me?' repeated Mr. Treverton, in rather an absent tone. 'Well, I don't know about that. Women are apt to have romantic notions on the money question. She has enough to live upon, you see. She told me as much last night, and she may prefer to marry some one else. The very terms of this will are calculated to set a high-spirited girl against me.'

'But she would know that in refusing you she would deprive you of the estate, and frustrate the wishes of her friend and benefactor. She'd scarcely be so ungrateful as to do that. Depend upon it, she'll consider it her duty to accept you—not a very unpleasant duty either, to marry a man with fourteen thousand a year. Upon my word, Mr. Treverton, you seem to have a very poor opinion of yourself, when you imagine the possibility of Laura Malcolm refusing you.'

John Treverton made no reply to this remark, and was silent during the rest of the drive. His spirits improved, or seemed to improve a little at dinner, however, and he did his best to make himself agreeable to his host and hostess. Miss Sampson thought him the most agreeable man she had ever met, especially when he consented to sit down to chess with her after dinner, and from utter listlessness and absence of mind allowed her to win three games running.

'What do you think of Miss Malcolm, Mr. Treverton?' she asked, by-and-by, as she was pouring out the tea.

'You mustn't ask Mr. Treverton any questions on that subject, Eliza,' said her brother, with a laugh.

'Why not?'

'For a reason which I am not at liberty to discuss.'

'Oh, indeed!' said Miss Sampson, with a sudden tightening of her thin lips. 'I had no idea—at least I thought—that Laura Malcolm was almost a stranger to Mr. Treverton.'

'And you're quite right in your supposition, Miss Sampson,' answered John Treverton, 'nor is there any reason why the subject should be tabooed. I think Miss Malcolm very handsome, and that her manner is remarkable for grace and dignity—and that is all I am able to think about her at present, for we are, as you say, almost strangers to each other. As far as I could judge she seemed to me to be warmly attached to my cousin Jasper.'

Eliza Sampson shook her head rather contemptuously.

'She had reason to be fond of him,' she said. 'Of course you are aware that she was completely destitute when he brought her home, and her family were, I believe, a very disreputable set.'

'I fancy you must be mistaken, Miss Sampson,' John Treverton answered, with some warmth. 'My cousin Jasper told me that Stephen Malcolm had been his friend and fellow-student at the University. He may have died poor, but I heard nothing which implied that he had fallen into disreputable courses.'

'Oh, really,' said Miss Sampson; 'of course you know best and no doubt whatever your cousin told you was correct. But to tell the truth Miss Malcolm has never been a favourite of mine. There's a reserve about her that I've never been able to get over. I know the gentlemen admire her very much, but I don't think she'll ever have many female friends. And what is of so much consequence to a young woman as a female friend?' concluded the lady sententiously.

'Oh, the gentlemen admire her very much, do they?' repeated John Treverton. 'I suppose, then, she has had several opportunities of marrying already?'

'I don't know about that, but I know of one man who is over head and ears in love with her.'

'Would it be any breach of confidence on your part to say who the gentleman is?'

'Oh, dear, no. I found out the secret for myself, I assure you. Miss Malcolm has never condescended to tell me anything about her affairs. It is Edward Clare, the vicar's son. I have seen them a good deal together. He used to be always making some excuse for dropping in at the Manor-house to talk to Mr. Treverton about old books, and papers for the Archæological Society, and so on, and anybody could see that it was for Miss Malcolm's sake he spent so much of his time there.'

'Do you think she cared about him?'

'Goodness knows. There's no getting at what she thinks about

26

anyone. I did once ask her the question, but she turned it off in her cold, haughty way, saying that she liked Mr. Clare as a friend, and all that kind of thing.'

Thomas Sampson had looked rather uneasy during this conversation.

'You mustn't listen to my sister's foolish gossip, Treverton,' he said; 'it's hard enough to keep women from talking scandal anywhere, but in such a place as this they seem to have nothing else to do.'

John Treverton had taken his part in this conversation with a keener interest than he was prepared to acknowledge himself capable of feeling upon the subject of Laura Malcolm. What was she to him, that he should feel such a jealous anger against this unknown Edward Clare? Were not all his most deeply-rooted feelings in her disfavour? Was she not rendered unspeakably obnoxious to him by the terms of his kinsman's will?

'There's something upon that man's mind, Eliza,' said Mr. Sampson, as he stood upon the hearthrug, warming himself in a thoughtful manner before the fire for a few minutes, after his guest had gone to bed. 'Mark my words, Eliza, there's something on John Treverton's mind.'

'What makes you think so, Tom?'

'Because he's not a bit elated about the property that he has come into, or will come into in a year's time. And it isn't in human nature for a man to come into fourteen thousand a year which he never expected to inherit, and take it as coolly as this man takes it.'

'What do you mean by a year's time, Tom? Hasn't he got the estate now?'

'No, Eliza; that's the rub.' And Mr. Sampson went on to explain to his sister the terms of Jasper Treverton's will, duly warning her that she was not to communicate her knowledge of the subject to anyone, on pain of his lasting displeasure.

Thomas Sampson was too busy next day to devote himself to his guest; so John Treverton went for a long ramble, with a map of the Treverton Manor estate in his pocket. He skirted many a broad field of arable and pasture land, and stood at the gates of farmhouse gardens, looking at the snug homesteads, the great barns and haystacks, the lazy cattle standing knee-deep in the litter of a straw-yard, and wondering whether he should ever be master of these things. He walked a long way, and came home with a slow step and a thoughtful air in the twilight. About a mile from Hazlehurst he emerged from a narrow lane on to a common, across which there was a path leading to the village. As he came out of this lane he saw the figure of a lady in mourning a little way before him. Something in the carriage of the head struck him as familiar; he hurried after the lady, and found himself walking beside Laura Malcolm.

'You are out rather late, Miss Malcolm,' he said, not knowing very well what to say.

'It gets dark so quickly at this time of the year. I have been to see some people at Thorley, about a mile and a half from here.'

'You do a great deal of visiting among the poor, I suppose?'

'Yes, I have been always accustomed to spend two or three days a week amongst them. They have come to know me very well, and to understand me, and, much as people are apt to complain of the poor, I have found them both grateful and affectionate.'

John Treverton looked at her thoughtfully. She had a bright colour in her cheeks this evening, a rosy tint which lighted up her dark eyes with a brilliancy he had never seen in them before. He walked by her side all the way back to Hazlehurst, talking first about the villagers she had been visiting, and afterwards about her adopted father, whose loss she seemed to feel deeply. Her manner this evening appeared perfectly frank and natural, and when John Treverton parted from her at the gates of the Manor-house, it was with the conviction that she was no less charming than she was beautiful.

And yet he gave a short, impatient sigh as he turned away from the great iron gates to walk to The Laurels, and it was only by an effort that he kept up an appearance of cheerfulness through the long evening, in the society of the two Sampsons and a bluff, red-cheeked gentleman-farmer, who had been invited to dinner, and to take a hand in a friendly rubber afterwards.

John Treverton spent the following day in the dogcart with Mr. Sampson, inspecting more farms, and getting a clearer idea of the extent and nature of the Treverton property that lay within a drive of Hazlehurst. He told his host that he would be compelled to go back to town by an early train on the next morning. After dinner that evening Mr. Sampson had occasion to retire to his office for an hour's work upon some important piece of business, so John Treverton, not very highly appreciating the privilege of a prolonged *tête-à-tête* with the fair Eliza, put on his hat and went out of doors to smoke a cigar in the village street.

Some fancy, he scarcely knew what, led him towards the Manor-house; perhaps because the lane outside the high garden wall at the side of the house was a quiet place for the smoking of a meditative cigar. In this solitary lane he paced for some time, coming round to the iron gates two or three times to look across the park-like grounds at the front of the house, whose closely-shuttered windows showed no ray of light.

'I wonder if I could be a happy man,' he asked himself, 'as the master of that house, with a beautiful wife and an ample fortune? There was a time when I fancied I could only exist in the stir and bustle of a London life, but perhaps, after all, I should not make a bad country gentleman if I were happy.'

On going back to the lane after one of these meditative pauses before the iron gates, John Treverton was surprised to find that he was no longer alone there. A tall man, wrapped in a loose great-coat, and with the lower part of his face hidden in the folds of a woollen scarf, was walking slowly to and fro before a narrow little wooden door in the garden wall. In that uncertain light, and with so much of his face hidden by the brim of his hat and the folds of his scarf, it was impossible to tell what this man was like, but John Treverton looked at him with a very suspicious feeling as he passed him near the garden door, and walked on to the end of the lane. When he turned back he was surprised to see that the door was open, and that the man was standing on the threshold, talking to some one within. He went quickly back in order to see, if possible, who this some one was, and as he came close to the garden door he heard a voice that he knew very well indeed—the voice of Laura Malcolm.

'There is no fear of our being interrupted,' she said. 'I would rather talk to you in the garden.'

The man seemed to hesitate a little, muttered something about 'the servants,' and then went into the garden, the door of which was immediately shut.

John Treverton was almost petrified by this circumstance. Who could this man be whom Miss Malcolm admitted to her presence in this stealthy manner? Who could he be except some secret lover, some suitor she knew to be unworthy of her, and whose visits she was fain to receive in this ignoble fashion. The revelation was unspeakably shocking to John Treverton; but he could in no other manner account for the incident which he had just witnessed. He lit another cigar, determined to wait in the lane till the man came out again. He walked up and down for about twenty minutes, at the end of which time the garden door was re-opened, and the stranger emerged and walked hastily away, John following him at a respectable distance. He went to an inn not far from the Manor-house, where there was a gig waiting for him, with a man nodding sleepily over the reins. He jumped lightly into the vehicle, took the reins from the man's hands and drove away at a smart pace, very much to the discomfiture of Mr. Treverton, who had not been able to see his face, and who had no means of tracing him any further. He did, indeed, go into the little inn and call for soda-water and brandy, in order to have an excuse for asking who the gentleman was who had just driven away; but the innkeeper knew nothing more than that the gig had stopped before his door half-an-hour or so, and that the horse had had a mouthful of hay.

'The man as stopped with the horse and gig came in for a glass of brandy to take out to the gentleman,' he said, 'but I didn't see the gentleman's face.'

John Treverton went back to The Laurels after this, very ill at ease. He determined to see Miss Malcolm next morning before he left Hazlehurst, in order, if possible, to find out something about this mysterious reception of the unknown individual in the loose coat. He made his plans, therefore, for going to London by an afternoon train, and at one o'clock presented himself at the Manor-house.

Miss Malcolm was at home, and he was ushered once more into the study, where he had first seen her.

He told her of his intended departure, an announcement which was not calculated to surprise her very much, as he had told her the same thing when they met on the common. They talked a little of indifferent subjects; she with perfect ease of manner, he with evident embarrassment; and then, after rather an awkward pause, he began:—

'Oh, by the way, Miss Malcolm, there is a circumstance which I think it my duty to mention to you. It is perhaps of less importance than I am inclined to attach to it, but in a lonely country house like this one cannot be too careful. I was out walking rather late last night, smoking my solitary cigar, and I happened to pass through the lane at the side of these grounds.'

He paused a moment. Laura Malcolm gave a perceptible start, and he fancied that she was paler than she had been before he began to speak of this affair; but her eyes met his with a steady, inquiring look, and never once faltered in their gaze as he went on:—

'I saw a tall man, very much muffled up in an overcoat and neckerchief—with his face quite hidden, in fact—walking up and down before the little door in the wall, and five minutes afterwards I was surprised by seeing the door opened, and the man admitted to the garden. The secret kind of way in which the thing was done was calculated to alarm anyone interested in the inmates of this house. I concluded, of course, that it was one of the servants who admitted some follower of her own in this clandestine manner.'

He could not meet Laura Malcolm's eyes quite steadily as he said this, but the calm scrutiny of hers never changed. It was John Treverton who faltered and looked down.

'Some follower of her own,' Miss Malcolm repeated. 'You know, then, that the person who let this stranger into the garden was a woman?'

'Yes,' he answered, not a little startled by her self-possession. 'I heard a woman's voice. I took the trouble to follow the man when he came out again, and I discovered that he was a stranger to this place, a fact which, of course, makes the affair so much the more suspicious. I know that robberies are generally managed by collusion with some servant, and I know that the property in this house is of a kind to attract the attention of professional burglars. I considered it, therefore, my duty to inform you of what I had seen.'

'You are very good, but I can fortunately set your mind quite at rest with regard to the plate and other valuables in this house. The man you saw last night is not a burglar, and it was I who admitted him to the garden.'

'Indeed?'

'Yes. He is a relation of mine, who wished to see me without making his appearance here the subject of gossip among the Hazlehurst people. He wrote to me, telling me that he was about to travel through this part of the country, and asking me to give him a private interview. It suited his humour best to come to this place after dark, and to leave it unobserved, as he thought.'

'I trust you will not think me intrusive for having spoken of this subject, Miss Malcolm?'

'Not at all. It was natural you should be interested in the welfare of the house.'

'And in yours. I hope that you will believe that was nearer my thoughts than any sordid fears as to the safety of the old plate and pictures. And now that I am leaving Hazlehurst, Miss Malcolm, may I venture to ask your plans for the future?'

'They are scarcely worth the name of plans. I intend moving from this house to the lodgings I spoke of the other day; that is all.'

'Don't you think you will find living alone very dull? Would it not be better for you to go into a school, or some place where you could have society?'

'I have thought of that, but I don't fancy I should quite like the monotonous routine of a school. I am prepared to find my life a little dull, but I am very fond of this place, and I am not without friends

31

here.'

'I can quite imagine that. You ought to have many friends in Hazlehurst.'

'But I have not many friends. I have not the knack of forming friendships. There are only two or three people in the world whose regard I feel sure of, or who seem to understand me.'

'I hope your heart is not quite inaccessible to new claims. There is a subject which I dare not speak of just yet, which it might be cruel to urge upon you at a time when I know your mind is full of grief for the dead; but when the fitting time does come I trust I may not find my case quite hopeless.'

He spoke with a hesitation which seemed strange in so experienced a man of the world. Laura Malcolm looked up at him with the same steady gaze with which her eyes had met his when he spoke of the incident of the previous night.

'When the fitting time comes you will find me ready to act in obedience to the wishes of my benefactor,' she answered quietly. 'I do not consider that the terms of his will are calculated to secure happiness for either of us; but I loved him too dearly—I respect his memory too sincerely to place myself in opposition to his plans.'

'Why should not our happiness be secured by that will, Laura?' John Treverton asked, with sudden tenderness. 'Is there no hope that I may ever win your love?'

She shook her head sadly.

'Love very seldom grows out of a position such as ours, Mr. Treverton.'

'We may prove a happy exception to the general rule. But I said I would not talk of this subject to-day. I only wish you to believe that I am not altogether mercenary—that I would rather forego this fortune than force a hateful alliance upon you.'

Miss Malcolm made no reply to this speech, and after a few minutes' talk upon indifferent subjects, John Treverton wished her good-bye.

'She would accept me,' he said to himself as he left the house. 'Her words seemed to imply as much; the rest remains with me. The ice has been broken, at any rate. But who can that man be, and why did he visit her in such a secret, ignominious manner? If we were differently circumstanced, if I loved her, I should insist upon a fuller explanation.'

He went back to The Laurels, to bid his friends the Sampsons good-bye. The lawyer was ready to drive him over to the station, and made him promise to run down to Hazlehurst again as soon as he was able, and to make The Laurels his headquarters on that and all other occasions.

'You'll have plenty of love-making to do between this and the end of the year,' Mr. Sampson said, facetiously.

He was in very good spirits, having that morning made an advance of money to Mr. Treverton on extremely profitable terms, and he felt a personal interest in that gentleman's courtship and marriage.

John Treverton went back to town in almost as thoughtful a mood as that in which he had made the journey to Hazlehurst. Plan his course as he might, there was a dangerous coast ahead of him, which he doubted his ability to navigate. Very far away gleamed the lights of the harbour, but between that harbour and the frail bark that carried his fortunes how many shoals and rocks there were whose perils he must encounter before he could lie safe at anchor?

CHAPTER IV.

LA CHICOT.

About this time there appeared among the multifarious placard which adorned the dead walls and hoardings and railway arches and waste spaces of London one mystical dissyllable, which was to be seen everywhere.

Chicot. In gigantic yellow capitals on a black ground. The dullest eye must needs see it, the slowest mind must needs be stirred with vague wonder. Chicot! What did it mean? Was it a name or a thing? A common or a proper noun? Something to eat or something to wear? A quack medicine for humanity, or an ointment to cure the cracked heels of horses? Was it a new vehicle, a patent cab destined to supersede the world-renowned Hansom, or a new machine for cutting up turnips and mangold-wurzel? Was it the name of a new periodical? Chicot! There was something taking in the sound. Two short, crisp syllables, tripping lightly off the tongue. Chicot! The street arabs shouted the word as a savage cry, neither knowing nor caring what it meant. But before those six-sheet posters had lost their pristine freshness most of the fast young men about London, the medical students and articled clerks, the dapper gentlemen at the War Office, the homelier youths from Somerset House, the shining-hatted City swells who came westward as the sun sloped to his rest, knew all about Chicot. Chicot was Mademoiselle Chicot, premiere danseuse at the Royal Prince Frederick Theatre and Music-hall, and she was, according to the highest authorities on the Stock Exchange and in the War Office, quite the handsomest woman in London. Her dancing was distinguished for its audacity rather than for high art. She was no follower of the Taglioni school of saltation. The grace, the refinement, the chaste beauties of that bygone age were unknown to her. She would have 'mocked herself of you' if you had talked to her about the poetry of motion. But for flying bounds across the stage—for wild pirouettings on tiptoe—for the free use of the loveliest arms in creation—for a bold backward curve of a full white throat more perfect than ever sculptor gave his marble bacchanal, La Chicot was unrivalled.

She was thoroughly French. Of that there was no doubt. She

34

was no scion of the English houses of Brown, Jones, or Robinson, born and bred in a London back slum, and christened plain Sarah or Mary, to be sophisticated later into Celestine or Mariette. Zaïre Chicot was a weed grown on Gallic soil. All that there was of the most Parisian La Chicot called herself; but her accent and many of her turns of phrase belied her, and to the enlightened ear of her compatriots betrayed her provincial origin. The loyal and pious province of Brittany claimed the honour of La Chicot's birth. Her innocent childhood had been spent among the fig-trees and saintly shrines of Auray. Not till her nineteenth year had she seen the long, dazzling boulevards stretching into unfathomable distance before her eyes; the multitudinous lamps; the fairy-like kiosks—all infinitely grander and more beautiful than the square of Duguesclin at Dinan illuminated with ten thousand lampions on a festival night. Here in Paris life seemed an endless festival.

Paris is a mighty schoolmaster, a grand enlightener of the provincial intellect. Paris taught La Chicot that she was beautiful. Paris taught La Chicot that it was pleasanter to whirl and bound among serried ranks of other Chicots in the fairy spectacle of 'The Sleeping Beauty,' or the 'Hart with the Golden Collar,' clad in scantiest drapery, but sparkling with gold and spangles, with hair flowing wild as a Mænad's, and satin boots at two napoleons the pair, than to toil among laundresses on the quay. La Chicot had come to Paris to get her living, and she got it very pleasantly for herself as a member of the *corps de ballet*, a cypher in the sum total of those splendid fairy spectacles, but a cypher whose superb eyes and luxuriant hair, whose statuesque figure and youthful freshness did not fail to attract the notice of individuals.

She was soon known as the belle of the ballet, and speedily made herself obnoxious to the principal dancers, who resented her superior charms as an insolence, and took every occasion to snub her. But while her own sex was unkind, the sterner sex showed itself gentle to la belle Chicot. The ballet-master taught her steps which he taught to none other of the sisterhood under his tuition; he made opportunities for giving her a solo dance now and then; he pushed her to the front; and at his advice she migrated from the large house where she was nobody, to a smaller house in the students' quarter, a popular little theatre on the left bank of the Seine, amidst a labyrinth of narrow streets and tall houses between the School of Medicine and the Sorbonne, where she soon became everybody. *C'était le plus gentil de mes rats*, cried the ballet-master regretfully, when La Chicot had been tempted away. *Cette petite ira loin*, said the manager, vexed with himself for having let his handsomest coryphée slip through his fingers; *elle a du chien*.

At the Students' Theatre it was that La Chicot met with her fate, or in other words, it was here that her husband first saw her. He was an Englishman, leading a rather wild life in this students' quarter of Paris, living from hand to mouth, very poor, very clever, very badly qualified to get his own living. He was gifted with those versatile talents which rarely come to a focus or achieve any important result. He painted, he etched, he sang, he played on three or four instruments with taste and fancy, but little technical skill; he wrote for the comic papers, but the comic papers generally rejected or neglected his contributions. If he had invented a lucifer match, or originated an improvement in the sewing-machine, he might have carved his way to fortune; but these drawing-room accomplishments of his hardly served to keep him from starving. Not a very eligible suitor, one would imagine, for a young lady from the provinces who wished to make a great figure in life; but he was handsome, well-bred, with that unmistakable air of gentle birth which neither poverty nor Bohemianism can destroy, and in the opinion of La Chicot the most fascinating man she had ever seen. In a word, he admired the lovely ballet-dancer, and the ballet-dancer adored him. It was an infatuation on both sides—his first great passion and hers. Both were strong in their faith in their own talents and the future; both believed that they had only to live in order to become rich and famous. La Chicot was not of a calculating temper. She was fond of money, but only of money to spend in the immediate present; money for fine dresses, good dinners, wine that foamed and sparkled, and plenty of promenading in hired carriages in the Bois de Boulogne. Money for the future, for sickness, for old age, for the innumerable necessities of life, she never thought of. Without having ever read Horace, or perhaps ever having heard of his existence, she was profoundly Horatian in her philosophy. To snatch the pleasure of the day, and let to-morrow take care of itself, was the beginning and end of her wisdom. She loved the young Englishman, and she married him, knowing that he had not a napoleon beyond the coin that was to pay for their wedding dinner, utterly reckless as to the consequences of their marriage, and as ignorant and unreasoning in her happiness as a child. To have a handsome man—a gentleman by birth and education—for her lover and slave,—to have the one man who had ensnared her fancy tied to her apron-string for ever,—this was La Chicot's notion of happiness. She was a strong-minded young woman, who to this point had made her way in life unaided by relatives or friends, uncared for, uncoun-

36

selled, untaught, a mere straw upon the tide of life, but not without a fixed idea of her own as to where she wanted to drift. She desired no guardianship from a husband. She did not expect him to work for her, or support her; she was quite resigned to the idea that she was to be the breadwinner. This child of the people set a curious value upon the name gentleman. The fact that her husband belonged to a superior race made up, in her mind, for a great many shortcomings. That he should be variable, reckless, a creature of fits and starts, beginning a picture with zeal in the morning, to throw it aside with disgust in the evening, seemed only natural. That was race. Could you put a hunter to the same kind of work which the patient packhorse performs without a symptom of revolt? La Chicot hugged the notion of her husband's superiority to that drudging herd from which she had sprung. His very vices were in her mind virtues.

They were married, and as La Chicot was a person of some importance in her own small world, while the young Englishman had done nothing to distinguish himself, the husband came somehow to be known by the name of the wife, and was spoken of everywhere as Monsieur Chicot.

It was an odd kind of life which these two led in their meagrely-furnished rooms on the third floor of a dingy house in a dingy street of the students' quarter; an odd, improvident, dissipated life, in which night was turned into day, and money spent like water, and nothing desired or obtained out of existence except pleasure, the gross, sensual pleasures of dining and drinking; the wilder pleasure of play, and moonlight drives in the Bois; the Sabbath delights of free-and-easy rambles in rural neighbourhoods, beside the silvery Seine, on the long summer days, when a luxurious idler could rise at noon without feeling the effort too hard a trial; winding up always with a dinner at some rustic house of entertainment, where there was a vine-curtained arbor that one could dine in, and where one could see the dinner being cooked in a kitchen with a wide window opening on yard and garden, and hear the balls clicking in the low-ceiled billiard-room. There were winter Sundays, when it seemed scarcely worth one's while to get up at all, till the scanty measure of daylight had run out, and the gas was aflame on the boulevards, and it was time to think of where one should dine. So the Chicots spent the first two years of their married life, and it may be supposed that an existence of this kind quite absorbed Madame Chicot's salary, and that there was no surplus to be put by for a rainy day. Had La Chicot inhabited a world in which rain and foul weather were unknown, she could not have troubled herself less about the possibilities of the future. She earned her money gaily, and spent it royally; domineered over her husband on the strength of her superb beauty; basked in the sunshine of temporary prosperity; drank more champagne than was good for her constitution or her womanhood; grew a shade coarser every year; never opened a book or cultivated her mind in the smallest degree; scorned all the refinements of life; looked upon picturesque scenes and rustic landscapes as a fitting background for the riot and drunkenness of a Bohemian picnic, and as good for nothing else; never crossed the threshold of a church, or held out her hand in an act of charity; lived for herself and her own pleasure; and had no more conscience than the butterflies, and less sense of duty than the birds.

If Jack Chicot had any compunction about the manner in which he and his wife were living, and the way they spent their money, he did not give any expression to his qualms of conscience. It may be that he was restrained by a false sense of delicacy, and that he considered his wife had a right to do what she liked with her own. His own earnings were small, and intermittent—a water-colour sketch sold to the dealers, a dramatic criticism accepted by the director of a popular journal. Money that came so irregularly went as it came.

'Jack comes to have sold a picture!' cried the wife; 'that great impostor of mine has taken it into his head to work. Let us go and dine at the "Red Mill." Jack shall make the cost.'

And then it was but to whistle for a couple of light open carriages, which, in this city of pleasure, stand in every street, tempting the idler to excursionize; to call together the half-dozen chosen friends of the moment, and away to the favourite restaurant to order a private room and a little dinner, *bien soigné*, and one's particular brand of champagne, and then, hey for a drive in the merry green wood, while the *marmitons* are perspiring over their *casseroles*, and anon back to a noisy feast, eaten in the open air, perhaps, under the afternoon sunshine, for La Chicot has to be at her theatre before seven, since at eight all Bohemian Paris will be waiting, eager and open-mouthed, to see the dancer with wild eyes and floating hair come bounding on to the stage. La Chicot was growing more and more like a Thracian Mænad as time went on. Her dancing was more audacious, her gestures more electrical. There was a kind of inspiration in those wild movements, but it was the inspiration of a Bacchante, not the calm grace of dryad or sea-nymph. You could fancy her whirling round Pentheus, mixed with the savage throng of her sister Mænads, thirsting for vengeance and murder; a creature to be beheld from afar with wondering admiration, but a being to be shunned by

38

all lovers of peaceful lives and tranquil paths. Those who knew her best used to speak pretty freely about her in the second year of her wedded life, and her third season at the Théâtre des Etudiants.

'La Chicot begins to drink like a fish,' said Antoine, of the orchestra, to Gilbert, who played the comic fathers. 'I wonder whether she beats her husband when she has had too much champagne?'

'They lead but a cat-and-dog sort of life, I believe,' answered the comedian; 'one day all sunshine, the next stormy weather. Renaud, the painter, who has a room on the same story, tells me that it sometimes hails cups and saucers and empty champagne-bottles when the weather is stormy in the Chicot domicile. But those two are desperately fond of each other all the same.'

'I should not appreciate such fondness,' said the fiddler; 'when I marry it will not be for beauty. I would not have as handsome a wife as La Chicot if I could have her for the asking. A woman of that stamp is created to be the torment of her husband's life. I find that this Jack is not the fellow he used to be before he married. C'est un garçon bémolisé par le mariage.'

When the Chicots had been man and wife for about three years—a long apprenticeship of bliss or woe—the lady's power of attracting an audience to the little theatre in the students' quarter began visibly to wane. The parterre grew thin, the students yawned or talked to each other in loud whispers while the dancer was executing her most brilliant steps. Even her beauty had ceased to charm. The habitués of the theatre knew that beauty by heart.

'C'est cliché comme une tartine de journal,' said one. 'C'est connu comme le dôme des Invalides,' said another. 'Cela fatigue; on commence à se désillusionner sur La Chicot.'

La Chicot saw the decline of her star, and that lively temper of hers, which had been growing more and more impulsive during the last three years, took reverse of fortune in no good spirit. She used to come home from the theatre in a diabolical humour, after having danced to empty benches and a languid audience, and Jack Chicot had to pay the cost. She would quarrel with him about a straw, a nothing, on these occasions. She abused the students who stayed away from the theatre in roundest and strongest phraseology. She was still more angry with those who came and did not applaud. She upbraided Jack for his helplessness. Was there ever such a husband? He could not advance her interests in the smallest degree. Had she married any one else—one of those little gentlemen who wrote for the papers, for instance—she would have been engaged at one of the boulevard theatres before now. She would be the rage among the best people in Paris. She would be earning thousands. But her husband had no influence with managers or newspapers, not enough to get a puff paragraph inserted in the lowest of the little journals. It was desolating.

This upbraiding was not without its effect upon Jack Chicot. He was a good-tempered fellow by nature, prone to take life easily. In all their quarrels it was his wife who took the leading part. When the cups and saucers and empty bottles went flying, she was the Jove who hurled those thunderbolts. Jack was too brave to strike a woman, too proud to lower himself to the level of his wife's degradation. He suffered and was silent. He had found out his mistake long ago. The delusion had been brief, the repentance was long. He knew that he had bound himself to a low-born, low-bred fury. He knew that his only chance of escaping suicide was to shut his eyes to his surroundings, and to take what pleasure he could out of a disreputable existence. His wife's reproaches stung him into activity. He wrote half-a-dozen letters to old friends in London—men more or less connected with the press or the theatres—asking them to get La Chicot an engagement. In these letters he wrote of her only as a clever woman in whose career he was interested; he shrank curiously from acknowledging her as his wife. He took care to enclose cuttings from the Parisian journals in which the dancer's beauty and chic, talent and originality, were lauded. The result of this trouble on his part was a visit from Mr. Smolendo, the enterprising proprietor of the Prince Frederick Theatre, who had come to Paris in search of novelty, and the engagement of Mademoiselle Chicot for that place of entertainment. Mr. Smolendo had been going in strongly for ballet of late. His scenery, his machinery, his lime-light and dresses were amongst the best to be seen in London. Everybody went to the Prince Frederick. It had begun its career as a music-hall, and had only lately been licensed as a theatre. There was a flavour of Bohemianism about the house, but it only gave a zest to the entertainment. All the most notorious Parisian successes in the way of spectacular drama, all the fairy extravaganzas and demon ballets and comic operettas, were reproduced by Mr. Smolendo at the Prince Frederick. He knew where to find the prettiest actresses, the best dancers, the freshest voices. His chorus and his ballet were the most perfect in London. In a word, Mr. Smolendo had discovered the secret of dramatic success. He had found out that perfection always pays.

La Chicot's beauty was startling and incontestible. There could not be two opinions about that. Her dancing was eccentric and clever. Mr. Smolendo had seen much better dancing from more carefully-trained dancers, but what La Chicot wanted in training she made up for with dash and audacity.

'She won't last many seasons. She's like one of those high-stepping horses that knock themselves to pieces in a year or two,' Mr. Smolendo said to himself; 'but she'll take the town by storm, and she'll draw better for her first three seasons than any star I've had since I began management.'

La Chicot was delighted at being engaged by a London manager, who offered her a better salary than she was getting at the students' theatre. She did not like the idea of London, which she imagined a city given over to fog and lung disease, but she was very glad to leave the scene where she felt that her laurels were fast withering. She gave her husband no thanks for his intervention, and went on railing at him for not having got her an engagement on the boulevard.

'It is to bury myself to go to your dismal London,' she exclaimed; 'but anything is better than to dance to an assembly of idiots and cretins.'

'London is not half a bad place,' answered Jack Chicot, with his listless air, as of a man long wearied of life, and needing a stimulant as strong as aquafortis to rouse him to animation. 'It is a big crowd in which one may lose one's identity. Nobody knows one, one knows nobody. A man's sense of shame gets comfortably deadened in London. He can walk the streets without feeling that fingers are being pointed at him. It is all the same to the herd whether he has just come out of a penitentiary or a palace. Nobody cares.'

The Chicots crossed the Channel, and took lodgings in a street in the neighbourhood of Leicester Square, near which, as everyone knows, the Prince Frederick is situated. It was a dingy street, offering scanty attractions to the stranger, but it was a street which from the days of Garrick and Woffington had been favoured by actors and actresses, and Mr. Smolendo recommended the Chicots to seek a lodging there. He gave them the names of three or four householders who let lodgings to 'the profession,' and among these Madame Chicot made her choice.

The apartments which pleased her best were two fair-sized rooms on a first floor, furnished with a tawdry pretentiousness which would have been odious to a refined eye, and which was particularly offensive to Jack's artistic taste. The cheap velvet on the chairs, the gaudy tapestry curtains, the tarnished ormolu clock and candelabra, delighted La Chicot. It was almost Parisian, she told her husband.

The drawing-room and bedroom communicated with folding-doors. There was a little third room—a mere hole—with a window looking northward, which would do for Jack to paint in. That convenience reconciled Jack to the shabby finery of the sitting-room, the doubtful purity of the bedroom, the woe-begone air of the street, with its half-dozen dingy shops sprinkled among the private houses, like an eruption.

'How it is ugly, your London!' exclaimed La Chicot. 'Is it that all the city resembles this, by example?'

'No,' answered Jack, with his cynical air. 'There are brighter-looking streets, where the respectable people live.'

'What do you call respectable people?'

'The people who pay income-tax on two or three thousand a year.'

Jack inquired as to the other lodgers. It was as well to find out what kind of neighbours they were to have.

'I am not particular,' said Jack, in French, to his wife, 'but I should not like to find myself living cheek by jowl with a burglar.'

'Or a spy,' suggested Zaïre.

'We have no spies in London. That is a profession which has never found a footing on this side of the Channel.'

The landlady was a lean-looking widow, with a false front of gingery curls, and a cap that quivered all over with artificial flowers on corkscrew wires. Her long nose was tinted at the extremity, and her eyes had a luminous yet glassy look, suggestive of ardent spirits.

'I have only one lady in the parlours,' she explained, 'and a very clever lady she is too, and quite the lady—Mrs. Rawber, who plays leading business at the Shakespeare. You must have heard of her. She's a great woman.'

Mr. Chicot apologized for his ignorance. He had been living so long in Paris that he knew nothing of Mrs. Rawber.

'Ah,' sighed the landlady, 'you don't know how much you've lost. Her Lady Macbeth is as fine as Mrs. Siddons's.'

'Did you ever see Mrs. Siddons?'

'No, but I've heard my mother talk about her. She couldn't have been greater in the part than Mrs. Rawber. You should go and see her some night. She'd make your flesh creep.'

'And a respectable old party, I suppose,' suggested Jack Chicot.

'As regular as clockwork. Church every Sunday morning and evening. No hot suppers. Crust of bread and cheese and glass of ale left ready on her table against she comes home—lets herself in with her key—no sitting up for her. Chop and imperial pint of Guinness at two o'clock, when there ain't no rehearsal; something plain and simple that can be kept hot on the oven top, when the rehearsal's late. She's a model lodger. No perquisites, but pay as regular as the Saturday comes round, and always the lady.'

'Ah,' said Jack, 'that's satisfactory. How about upstairs? I suppose you've another pattern of commonplace respectability on your second floor?'

The landlady gave a faint cough, as if she were troubled with a sudden catching of the breath, and her eyes wandered absently to the window, where she seemed to ask counsel from the grey October sky.

'Who are your upstairs lodgers?' asked Jack Chicot, repeating his inquiry with a shade of impatience.

'Lodgers? No, sir. There's only one gentleman on my second floor. I have never laid myself out for families. Children are such mischievous young monkeys, and always tramping up and down stairs, or endangering their lives leaning out of winder, or leaving the street door open. And the damage they do the furniture! Well, nobody can understand that except them as have passed through the ordeal. No, sir, for the last six years I haven't had a child across my threshold.'

'I wasn't inquiring about children,' said Mr. Chicot; 'I was asking about your upstairs lodger.'

'He's a single gentleman, sir.'

'Young?'

'No, sir; middle-aged.'

'An actor?'

'No, sir. He has nothing to do with the theatres.'

'What is he?'

'Well, sir, he is a gentleman—everyone can see that—but a gentleman as has run through his property. I should gather from his ways that he must have had a great deal of property, and that he's run through most of it. He is not quite so regular in his payments as I could wish—but he does pay,—and he's very little trouble, for he's often away for a week at a time, the rent running on all the same, of course.'

'That would hardly matter to him if he doesn't pay it,' said Chicot.

'Oh, but he does pay, sir. He's dilatory, but I get my money. A poor widow like me couldn't afford to lose by the best of lodgers.'

'What is the gentleman's name?'

'Mr. Desrolles.'

'That sounds like a foreign name.'

'It may, sir, but the gentleman's English. I haven't in a general way laid myself out for foreigners,' said the landlady, with a glance at La Chicot, 'though this is rather a foreign neighbourhood.'

The lodgings were taken, and Jack Chicot and his wife began a new phase of existence in London. The life lacked much that had made their life in Paris tolerable—the careless gaiety, the brighter skies, the Bohemian pleasures of the French city—and Jack Chicot felt as if a dense black curtain had been drawn across his youth and all its delusions, leaving him outside in a cold, commonplace world, a worn-out, disappointed man, old before his time.

He missed the gay, happy-go-lucky comrades who had helped him to forget his troubles. He missed the drives in the leafy wood, the excursions to suburban dining-houses, the riotous suppers after midnight, all the merry dissipations of his Parisian life. London pleasures were dull and heavy. London suppers meant no more than eating and drinking too many oysters and too much wine.

Mr. Smolendo's expectations were fully realised. La Chicot made a hit at the Prince Frederick. Those flaming posters under every railway arch and on every hoarding in London were not in vain. The theatre was crowded nightly, and La Chicot was applauded to the echo. She breathed anew the intoxicating breath of success, and she grew daily more insolent and more reckless, spent more money, drank more champagne, and was more eager for pleasure, flattery, and fine dress. The husband looked on with a gloomy face. They were no longer the adoring young couple who had walked away arm-in-arm from the Mairie, smiling and happy, to share their wedding dinner with the chosen companions of the moment. The wife was now only affectionate by fits and starts, the husband had a settled air of despondency which nothing but wine could banish, and which, like the seven other spirits, returned with greater power after a temporary banishment. The wife loved the husband just well enough to be desperately jealous of his least civility to another woman. The husband had long ceased to be jealous, except of his own honour.

Among the frequenters of the Prince Frederick there was one who at this time was to be seen there almost nightly. He was a man of about five-and-twenty, tall, broad-shouldered, with strongly-marked features and the eye of a hawk; a man whose clothes were well worn, and whose whole appearance was slovenly, yet who looked like a gentleman; evidently uncared for, possibly destitute, but however low he might have sunk, a gentleman still.

He was a medical student, and one of the hardest workers at St.

Thomas's—a man who had chosen his profession because he loved it, and whose love increased with his labour. Those who knew most about him said that he was a man destined to make his mark upon the age in which he lived. But he was not a man to achieve rapid success, to distinguish himself by a happy accident. He went slowly to work, sounded the bottom of every well, took up every subject as resolutely as if it were the one subject he had chosen for his especial study, flung himself into every scientific question with the feverish ardour of a lover, yet worked with the steadiness and self-denial of a Greek athlete. For all the vulgar pleasures of life, for wine or play, for horse-racing, or riot of any kind, this young surgeon cared not a jot. He was so little a haunter of theatres, that those of his fellow-students who recognised him night after night at the Prince Frederick were surprised at his frequent presence in such a place.

'What has come to Gerard?' cried Joe Latimer, of Guy's, to Harry Brown, of St. Thomas's. 'I thought he despised ballet-dancing. Yet this is the third time I have seen him looking on at this rot, with his attention as fixed as if he were watching Paget using the knife?'

'Can't you guess what it all means?' exclaimed Brown. 'Gerard is in love.'

'In love!'

'Yes, over head and ears in love with La Chicot—never saw such a well-marked case—all the symptoms beautifully developed—sits in the front row of the pit and gazes the whole time she is on the stage—never takes his eyes off her—raves about her to our fellows—the loveliest woman that ever lived since the unknown young person who served as a model for the Venus that was dug up in a cave in the island of Milo. Fancy having known that young woman, and put your arm round her waist! Somebody did, I dare say. Yes, George Gerard is gone—annihilated. It's too pathetic.'

'And Mademoiselle Chicot is a married woman, I hear?' said Latimer.

'Very much married. The husband is always in attendance upon her. Waits for her at the stage door every night, or stands at the wing while she dances. La Chicot is a most correct person, though she hardly looks it. Ah! here comes Gerard. Well, old fellow, has the disease reached its crisis?'

'What disease?' asked Gerard, curtly.

'The fever called love.'

'Do you suppose I'm in love with the new dancer, because I drop in here pretty often to look at her?'

'I don't see any other motive for your presence here. You're not a play-going man.'

'I come to see La Chicot simply because she is quite the most beautiful woman in face and form that I ever remember seeing. I come as a painter might to look at the perfection of human loveliness, or as an anatomist to contemplate the completeness of God's work, a creature turned out of the divine workshop without a flaw.'

'Did you ever hear such a fellow?' cried Latimer. 'He comes to look at a ballet-dancer, and talks about it as if it were a kind of religion.'

'The worship of the beautiful is the religion of art,' answered Gerard, gravely. 'I respect La Chicot as much as I admire her. I have not an unworthy thought about her.'

Latimer touched his forehead lightly with two fingers, and looked at his friend Brown.

'Gone!' said Latimer.

'Very far gone!' replied Brown.

'Come and try the Dutch oysters, Gerard, and let us make a night of it,' said Latimer persuasively.

'Thanks, no. I must go home to my den and read.'

And so they parted, the idlers to their pleasure, the plodding student—the man who loved work for its own sake—to his books.

CHAPTER V.

A DISAPPOINTED LOVER.

Laura Malcolm remained at the Manor-house. Mr. Clare, the vicar, had persuaded her to relinquish her idea of going into lodgings in the village. It would be a pity to abandon the good old house, he argued. A house left to the care of servants must always suffer some decay; and this house was full of art treasures, objects of interest and of price which hitherto had been in Laura's charge. Why should she not stay in the home of her girlhood till it was decided whether she was to rule there as mistress, or to abandon it for ever?

'Your remaining here will not compromise your freedom of choice,' said Mr. Clare kindly, 'if you find before the end of the year that you cannot make up your mind to accept John Treverton as a husband.'

'He may not ask me,' interjected Laura, with a curious smile.

'Oh yes, he will. He will come to you in good time to offer you his heart and hand, you may be sure, my dear. It cannot be a difficult thing for any young man to fall in love with such a girl as you, and it seems to me that this John Treverton is very worthy of any woman's regard. I see no reason why your marriage should not be a love match on both sides, in spite of my old friend's eccentric will.'

'I'm afraid that can never be,' answered Laura, with a sigh. 'Mr. Treverton will never be able to think of me as he might of any other woman. I must always seem to him an obstacle to his freedom and his happiness. He is constrained to assume an affection for me, or to surrender a splendid fortune. If he is mercenary he will not hesitate. He will take the fortune and me, and I shall despise him for his readiness to accept a wife chosen for him by another. No, dear Mr. Clare, there is no possibility of happiness for John Treverton and me.'

'My dear child, if you are convinced that you cannot be happy in this marriage, you are free on your part to refuse him,' said the vicar.

Laura's pale cheek crimsoned.

'That would be to doom him to poverty, and to frustrate his cousin's wish,' she answered, falteringly. 'I should hate myself if I could be so selfish as to do that.'

'Then, my dear girl, you must resign yourself to the alternative:

and if John Treverton and you are not as passionately in love as the young people who defy their parents and run away to Gretna Green to be married—or did when I was a young man—you may at least enjoy a sober kind of happiness, and get on as well together as the princes and princesses whose marriages are arranged by cabinet councils and foreign powers.'

'Do you know anything about Mr. Treverton?' asked Laura, thoughtfully.

'Very little. He is an only son—an only child, I believe. His father and mother died while he was a boy, and he became a ward in Chancery. He had a nice little property when he came of age, and ran through it nicely, after the manner of idle young men without friends to advise and guide them. He began his career in the army, but sold out after he had spent his money. I have no idea what he has been doing since—living by his wits, I'm afraid.'

So it was settled that Laura was to remain at the Manor-house, with so many of the old servants as would suffice to keep things in good order—the servants to be paid and fed at the expense of the estate, Laura to maintain herself out of her own modest income. She was a young lady of particularly independent temper, and upon this point she was resolute.

'The money is nobody's money at present,' she said. 'I will not touch a penny of it.'

Sad as were the associations of the house, dreary as was the blank left in the familiar rooms by the absence of one revered figure, dismal as was the silence which that voice could never break again, Laura was better pleased to stay in her old home than she would have been to leave it. Even the mute, lifeless things among which she had lived so long had some part of her love, some hold upon her heart. She would have felt herself a waif and stray in a stranger's house. Here she felt always at home. If the rooms were haunted by the shadow of the dead, the ghost was a friendly one, and looked upon her with loving eyes. She had never thwarted, or neglected, or wronged her adopted father. There was no remorse mingled with her grief. She thought of him with deepest sadness, but without pain.

The vicar was anxious that Miss Malcolm should have a companion. There were plenty of homeless young women—women of spotless reputation and genteel connections—who would no doubt have been delighted to be her unsalaried companion, for the sake of a pleasant home. But Laura declared that she wanted no companion.

'You must think me very empty-minded if you suppose I cannot endure my life without a young woman of the same age to sit opposite me and answer to all my idle fancies like an echo, or to walk out with me and help me admire the landscape, or to advise me what I should order for dinner,' she said. 'No, dear Mr. Clare, I want no companion, except Celia now and then. You will let her come and see me very often, won't you?'

'As often as you like, or as often as she can be spared from her parish work,' answered the vicar.

'Ah, you are all such hard workers at the Vicarage,' exclaimed Laura.

'Some of us work hard enough, I believe,' answered Mr. Clare, with a sigh. 'I wish my son could make up his mind to work a little harder.'

'That will come in good time.'

'I hope so, but I am almost tired of waiting for that good time.'

'He is clever and artistic,' said Laura.

'His cleverness allowed him to leave the University without a degree, and his artistic faculties will never help him to a living,' answered the vicar, bitterly.

This only son of the vicar's was a thorn in his side. Edward Clare was everybody's favourite, and nobody's enemy but his own. That was what the village said of him. He was good-looking, clever, agreeable, but he had no ballast. He was a feather to be blown by every puff of wind. He had never been able to discover the work which he had been sent into the world to do, but he had speedily found out the work for which he was not adapted. At the University he discovered that the curriculum of an English classical education was not fitted to the peculiar cast of his mind. How much better he could have done at Heidelberg or Bonn! But when he made this discovery he had wasted three years at Oxford, and had cost his father something very close to a thousand pounds.

The vicar wanted his only son to go into the Church, and Edward had been educated with that view, but after failing to get his degree, Edward found out that he had a conscientious repugnance to the Church. His opinions were too broad.

'A man who admires Ernest Renan as warmly as I do has no right to be a parson,' said Edward, with agreeable frankness; so poor Mr. Clare had to submit to the disappointment of his most cherished hopes, because his son admired Renan.

After having made up his mind upon this point Edward stayed at home, read a good deal in a desultory way, wrote a little, sketched a little in fine weather, fished, shot, and dawdled away life in the pleasantest manner, finding his days never so sweet as when they were spent at the Manor-house.

Jasper Treverton had warmly esteemed the vicar, and he had liked the son for the father's sake. Edward had always been welcome at the Manor-house while the old man lived, and as Edward's sister was Laura Malcolm's chosen friend, it was natural that the Oxonian should be very often in Laura's society.

But now his visits to the good old house where he had felt himself so completely at home, the library in which he had read, the garden in whose formal walks he had delighted to smoke, were suddenly restricted. Miss Malcolm had given him to understand, through his sister, that she considered herself no longer at liberty to receive him. Her friendship for him was in no wise lessened, but it would not do for him to drop in at all hours, or to spend half his afternoons in the library, as in the days that were gone.

'I don't see why there should be such restrictions among old friends,' said Edward, with an injured air. 'Laura and I are like sister and brother.'

'Very likely, Ned, but then, you see, everybody knows you and Laura are not brother and sister, and I think there are a good many people in Hazlehurst who think that you feel something a good deal stronger than brotherly regard for her. If she and I were drowning, I know which of us you would try to save.'

'*You* can swim,' growled Edward, remembering Talleyrand's famous answer. 'Well, I suppose I must submit to fate. Miss Malcolm no doubt considers herself engaged to the mysterious heir, who does not seem in any hurry to begin his courtship. If old Treverton had bequeathed such a chance to me I should have seized upon my opportunity without an instant's hesitation.'

'I admire the delicacy which prompts Mr. Treverton to keep in the background just at first,' said Celia.

'How do you know that it is delicacy which restrains him,' exclaimed Edward. 'How do you know that it is not some entanglement—some degrading connection, perhaps—or at any rate a previous engagement of some kind which ties his hands, and hinders his advancement with Laura? No man, unless so constrained, would be besotted enough to neglect such an opportunity, or to hazard his chances of success. If he offends Laura, she is just the kind of girl to refuse him, fortune and all.'

'I don't think she would do that, except upon very serious grounds,' said Celia. 'Laura has a strong sense of duty, and she believes it her duty to her adopted father to assist in carrying out his wishes. I believe she would sacrifice her own inclination to that duty.'

'That's going far,' said Edward, discontentedly. 'I begin to think that she has fallen in love with this fellow, meteoric as was his appearance here.'

'He stayed nearly a fortnight,' remarked Celia, 'and Laura saw him several times. I don't mean to say that she is in love with him. She has too much common sense to fall in love in that rapid way—but I am sure she does not dislike him.'

'Oh, when love begins common sense ends. I dare say she is in love with him. Hasn't she told you as much now, Celia? Girls like to talk about such things.'

'What do you know about girls?'

'Oh, nothing. I've got a sister who is one of the breed; a model always at hand to draw from. Come, now, Celia, be sisterly for once in your life. What has Laura told you about John Treverton?'

'Nothing. She is particularly reserved upon the subject. I know that it is a painful one for her, and I rarely approach it.'

'Well, he is a lucky dog. I never hated a fellow so much. I have an instinctive idea that he is a scoundrel.'

'Are not instinctive ideas convictions that jump with our own inclinations?' speculated Celia, philosophically. 'I am heartily sorry for you, Ned dear, for I know you are fond of Laura, and it does seem hard to have her willed away from you like this. But seriously now, would you be pleased to marry her with no better portion than her own little income?'

'Six thousand in Consols,' said Edward, meditatively. 'That would not go very far with a young man and woman of refined tastes. We might love each other ever so dearly, and be ever so happy together, but I'm afraid we should starve, Celia, and that our children's only inheritance would be their legal claim on their own parish. I thought that wicked old man would leave her handsomely provided for.'

'You had no right to think that, knowing that he had pledged himself to leave her nothing.'

'Oh, there would always have been a way of evading that. I call his will absolutely shameful—to force a high-spirited girl to take a husband of his choosing—a fellow whom he had never seen when he made the stipulation.'

'He took care to see young Mr. Treverton before he died. I dare say if he had not been favourably impressed he would have altered his will at the last moment.'

This conversation took place nearly four months after Jasper

Treverton's death. The hedgerows were growing green; the birds had eaten the last of the crocuses; the violets were all in bloom in the shrubbery borders, the grass grew fast enough to require weekly shearing, and the Manor-house garden was a pleasant place to walk in, full of budding trees and opening blossoms, and the songs of birds, telling each other rapturously that spring had come in earnest, and that winter days and a stony-hearted, frost-bound earth were things of the past.

Edward Clare believed himself the most ill-used of young men. He was good-looking—nay, according to the general judgment of his particular circle, remarkably handsome; he was cleverer and more accomplished than most young men of his age and standing. If he had done nothing as yet to distinguish himself it was not for lack of talent, he told himself complacently. It was only because he had never yet put his shoulder to the wheel. He did not consider that duty strongly called upon every man to do his uttermost part in the labour of moving that mighty wheel. A clever young man, like himself, might stand on one side and watch other fellows toiling at the job, knowing that he could do it ever so much better if he only cared to try.

Four years ago, when he first went to Oxford, he had made up his mind that he was to be Laura Malcolm's husband. Of course Jasper Treverton would leave her a handsome fortune, most likely his entire estate. There must be a dozen ways of evading that ridiculous oath. The old man might make over his property to Laura by deed of gift. He might leave it to trustees for her use and benefit. In some manner or other she would be his heiress. Edward felt very sure of that, seeing as he did Jasper's deep love of his adopted daughter. So when he found himself falling in love with Laura's sweet face and winning ways, the young Oxonian made no struggle against Cupid, the mighty conqueror. To fall in love with Laura was the high road to fortune, infinitely better than Church or Bar. But he was in no hurry to declare himself—he was not an impulsive young man; slow and cautious rather. To make Laura an offer and be rejected would mean banishment from her society. He thought she liked him, but he wanted to be very sure as to the strength of her feelings before he declared himself her lover. His position as her friend was too advantageous to be lightly hazarded.

CHAPTER VI.

LA CHICOT HAS HER OWN WAY.

Slowly, reluctantly, Winter crawled away to his hidden lair, and made room for a chilly, uncomfortable spring. It had been the longest, dullest winter that Jack Chicot had ever lived through. He did not wonder that the Continental idea associated London fog and suicide in a natural sequence. Never had he felt himself so inclined to self-destruction as in the foggy December afternoons, the bleak January twilights, when he paced the dull grey streets under the dull grey sky, smoking his solitary cigar, and thinking what a dismal ruin he had made of himself and his life; he who had entered upon the bustling scene of manhood ten years ago, with such bright hopes, such an honourable ambition, such an arrogant confidence in the future as the bringer of all good things.

Now where was he? What was he? The husband of La Chicot, a being in himself so worthless, so aimless and obscure that no one ever took the trouble to inquire his real name. His wife's name—the name made notorious by a ballet-dancer, the goddess of medical students and lawyers' clerks—was good enough for him. In himself and by himself he was nothing. He was only the husband of La Chicot, a woman who drank like a fish and swore like a trooper.

It was a sorry pass for a man to have come to in whom the sense of shame was not utterly dead. Perhaps it was something to be remembered in Jack Chicot's favour that at this time of his life, when despair had fastened its claw upon his aching heart, when love and liking had given place to a mute and secret abhorrence, he was not cruel or harsh to his wife. He never said hard or bitter things to her: so long as he had any lingering belief in her capability of amendment he remonstrated with her on the folly of her ways, always temperately, often with much kindness: and when he saw that reform was hopeless he held his peace and did not upbraid her.

She had never done him that kind of wrong which honour forbids a husband to forgive. So far she had been true to him, and loved him, in her maudlin way, flying at him like a fury when she was betwixt sobriety and intoxication, calling him her angel, or her cat, or her cabbage, with imbecile tenderness, when she was comfortably tipsy. He who had quarrelled with her a good deal before he began to hate her, could now endure her utmost violence and keep calm. He dared not give the reins to passion. It might carry him—he knew not whither. He felt like a man standing on the edge of a black gulf, blindfolded, yet knowing that the pit was there. One false step might be fatal. He had been luckier in this gloomy London than in his much-regretted Paris, so far as the exercise of his own small talents went. He had obtained a regular engagement as draughtsman on one of the comic journals, and his caricatures, pencilled on a wood block while his heart ached with misery and his head burned with fever, amused the idle youth of London with reminiscences of Cham and Gavarni. By the use of his pencil he contrived to earn something like two pounds a week, more than enough for his own wants; so La Chicot could spend every sixpence of her salary on herself, an arrangement which suited her temper admirably. She had a bottle of champagne in her dressing-room every night, and finished it before she went on for her great pas. So long as she abstained from brandy this meant sobriety. She was a woman of limited ideas, and as in San Francisco champagne is 'wine' par excellence, no meaner liquor being deemed worthy of the noble name, so, with La Chicot, champagne was the only wine worth drinking. When she felt that its sustaining power was insufficient she fortified it with brandy, and then La Chicot was a creature to be shunned.

Winter lingered late that year. Though the green banks of every country lane and every hollow of the leafless woodland were starred with primroses and spangled with dog-violets, wintry winds were still wracking the forest trees, and whistling shrill among the London chimney-pots.

March had come in like a lion, and continued to roar and bluster in leonine fashion to the very verge of April. A dry, dusty, bitter March, dealing largely in death and shipwreck. A villainous March, better calculated to inspire thoughts of suicide than even the fogs and creeping mists of November.

But even this miserable March came to an end at last. The London season had begun. La Chicot was attracting not only medical students and lawyers' clerks, the Stock Exchange and the War Office, but the fine flower of the aristocracy—the topmost strawberries in the basket—the Brobdingnagian Guardsmen, whose gloves were numbered nine and a half at the little hosier's in Piccadilly, the dainty foplings who wore a lady's six and three-quarters with four buttons, and who were beings of so frail and effeminate a type that a whisper through the telephone might blow them to the utmost ends of the earth. These opposite species, the athletics and the æsthetics, the hammer throwers, bicycle riders, boating men, hunting men, and pugilists, and the china collectors, art lunatics, and tame-cat section of society, met and mingled in the stalls at the Prince Frederick, and resembled each other in nothing except their appreciation of La Chicot.

Mr. Smolendo produced a new ballet early in April, a ballet which was as ridiculous and generally imbecile in plot and purpose as most of its kind, but which for scenery, dresses, and effects was supposed to surpass anything that had ever been accomplished at his theatre. Everything in this ballet tended to the glorification of La Chicot. She was the central figure, the cynosure: every crest was lowered to give prominence to hers, principal dancers were her handmaidens, a hundred ballet-girls prostrated themselves before her throne, a hundred and fifty auxiliaries, specially engaged for this great spectacle, licked the dust beneath her feet. The final tableau, which was to cost Mr. Smolendo more money than he could calculate, was an apotheosis of La Chicot, a beautiful, bold, half-tipsy peasant, going to heaven on a telescopic arrangement of iron. It was a wonderful sight. The athletics called it 'no end of jolly.' The æsthetics described it as 'unspeakably touching.'

This final tableau was supposed to represent the coral caves of the Indian Ocean. La Chicot was a mermaid who lured mariners to their doom beneath the wave. She lived in a jewelled cavern, a hall sparkling and shining with sapphires and emeralds and lapis-lazuli, all flooded with rainbow light, where she and her sister mermaidens, golden, glittering, and scaly, danced perpetually. Then came the end, and she floated upward through an ocean of blue gauze, in a moving frame of rosiest coral.

The ironwork upon which she mounted was a somewhat complicated piece of machinery, a telescope in three parts, requiring nice adjustment on the part of the stage carpenter. It was perfectly safe if properly worked; but a hitch, the slightest carelessness in the working, would be perilous, and might be fatal.

'I don't like that business by any means,' said Jack Chicot, when he saw his wife ascending to the sky borders, in the dust and gloom of rehearsal, clad in her practising petticoats, and with a lace-bordered handkerchief tied under her chin, like a coquettish nightcap. 'It looks dangerous. Can't you dispense with it, Smolendo?'

'Impossible; it's the great feature of the scene. Perfectly safe, I assure you. Roberts is the best carpenter in London.'

Mr. Smolendo's people were always the best. He had a knack

of getting first-rate talent in every line, from his prima donna to his gasman.

'He seems clever, but rather a queer-tempered man, I hear.'

'Talent is always queer-tempered,' answered Smolendo, lightly. 'Amiability is the redeeming virtue of fools.'

Mr. Chicot was not convinced. He took his wife aside presently in a grove of dingy wings and side pieces, and entreated her to refuse that ascent in the coral bower.

'*Pas si bête,*' she answered, curtly. 'I know what suits me. I shall look lovely in that coral frame with my hair down. You needn't be frightened, my friend. *Pas de danger.* Or, if I should be killed—come, I don't think that would break your heart. It's a long time since you've left off caring for me as much as that.'

She snapped her fingers under his nose, with one of those little audacious movements of hers which were infinitely fascinating—to strangers. Jack Chicot shuddered visibly. Yes, it was horribly true. Her death would be his release from bondage. Her death? Would he know himself, believe in his own identity, if she were gone, and he was free to walk the world again, his own master, with hopes and ambitions of his own, bearing his own name, not ashamed to look mankind in the face, no longer known as the husband of La Chicot?

He persuaded her earnestly to have nothing to do with the iron-work that had been made to bear her to the theatrical skies. Why should she run such a risk? Any ballet-girl would do as well, he argued.

'Yes, and the ballet-girl would show off her good looks, and get all the applause. I am not such a fool as to give her the chance. Don't waste your breath in talking about it, Jack. I mean to do it.'

'Of course,' he said bitterly. 'When did you ever renounce a caprice to please me?'

'Perhaps never. I am a creature of caprices. It was a caprice that made me marry you, a caprice that made you marry me, and now we are both honestly tired. That's a pity, isn't it?'

'I try to do my duty to you, my dear,' he answered gravely, with a sigh.

La Chicot had her own way, naturally, being one of those women who, once having taken their bent, are no more to be diverted than a mountain torrent which the rains have swollen. The new ballet was a success; the final tableau was a triumph for La Chicot. She looked lovely, in an attitude more perfect than anything that was ever done in marble—her round white arms lifted above her head, flinging back the loose branches of coral, her black hair covering her like a mantle. That long rich hair was one of her chief beauties—something to be remembered where all was beautiful.

The machinery worked splendidly. Jack was at the wings the first night, anxious and watchful. A fragment of conversation which he heard just behind him while the coral bower was rising, did not tend to reassure him.

'It's all very well to-night,' said one of the scene-shifters to his mate, 'they're both sober; but when she's drunk, and he's drunk, God help her.'

Jack went to Mr. Smolendo directly the curtain was down.

'Well,' cried the manager, radiant, 'a screaming success. There's money in it. I shall run this three hundred nights.'

'I don't like that ascent of my wife's. I hear that the man who works the machinery is a drunkard.'

'My dear fellow, these men all drink,' answered Smolendo, cheerfully. 'But Roberts is a treasure. He's always sober in business.'

Again Jack tried the effect of remonstrance with his wife, just as vainly as before.

'If you weren't a fool you would make Smolendo give me an extra five pounds a week on account of the danger, instead of worrying me about it,' she said.

'I am not going to make the safety of your life a question of money,' he answered; and after this there was no more said between them on the subject of the coral bower, but that speech of the scene-shifter's haunted Jack Chicot.

'When she is drunk.' The memory of that speech was bitter. Though his wife's habits had long been patent to him, it was not the less galling to think that everyone—the lowest servant in the theatre even—knew her vices.

Towards the end of April, Chicot and his wife had a serious quarrel. It arose out of a packet which had been left at the stage door for the dancer—a packet containing a gold bracelet, in a morocco case, bearing the name of one of the most fashionable and expensive jewellers at the West End. There was nothing to show whence the offering came; but on a narrow strip of paper, nestling under the massive gold band, there was scrawled in a mean little, foreign-looking hand:—

'Homage to genius.'

La Chicot carried the gift home in triumph and exhibited it to her husband, clasped upon her round white arm, a solid belt of gold, flat, wide, and thick, like a fetter, severely simple, an ornament for the arm of a Greek dancing-girl.

'You will send it back, of course,' said Jack, frowning at the thing.

'But, my friend, where should I send it?'

'To the jeweller. He must know his customer.'

'I am not so stupid. There can be no harm in accepting an anonymous gift. I shall keep it, of course.'

'I did not think you had fallen so low.'

Upon this La Chicot retorted insolently, and there were very hard words spoken on both sides. The lady kept the bracelet, and the gentleman went next day to the jeweller who had supplied it, and tried to discover the name of the purchaser.

The jeweller was studiously polite, but he had no memory. Jack Chicot minutely described the bracelet, but the jeweller assured him that he sold a dozen such in a week.

'I think you must be mistaken,' said Chicot; 'this is a bracelet of very uncommon form. I never saw one like it,' and then he repeated his description.

The jeweller shook his head with a gentle smile.

'The style is new,' he said, 'but I assure you we have sold several exactly corresponding to your description. It would be quite impossible to recall——'

'I see,' said Chicot; 'you would not like to disoblige a good customer. I dare say you know what the bracelet was meant for. Such shops as yours could hardly thrive unless they were indulgent to the vices of their patrons.'

And after launching that shaft Mr. Chicot left the shop.

He returned to his lodgings to pack a small portmanteau, and then went off to take his own pleasure. What need had such a wife as his of a husband's care? She would not accept his advice, or be ruled by him. She had chosen her road in life, and would follow it to the fatal end. Of what avail was his weak arm to bar the path? To this daughter of the people, with her deadened conscience and indomitable will, that interposing arm was no more than a straw in her way.

'Henceforth I have done with her,' he said to himself. 'The law could desire no stronger divorce between us than this which she has made. And if she does me wrong the law shall part us. I will have no mercy.'

While he was packing his portmanteau an idea flashed into his mind. It was a horrible notion, and his cheek paled at the first aspect of it, but he took it to his heart nevertheless.

He was going away, for an indefinite time, perhaps. He would set a watch upon his wife. Her audacity, her insolence, had aroused the darkest suspicions. A woman who thus openly defied him must be capable of anything.

'Whom can I trust?' he asked himself, pausing in his preparations, on his knees before the open portmanteau. 'The landlady, Mrs. Evitt? No, she is sly enough, but she has too long a tongue. A glass of grog would loosen that tongue of hers at any time, and she would betray me to my wife. It must be a man. Desrolles. Yes, the very man. He has all the qualities of the trade.'

Chicot locked his portmanteau, strapped it, and carried it out on to the landing. Then he ran up to the second floor, and knocked at the door of the front room.

'Come in,' said a languid voice, and Jack Chicot went in.

The room smelt of brandy and stale cigars. It was shabbier and tawdrier than the sitting-room on the first floor—a sordid copy of that sordid original. There was the same attempt at finery, tarnished ormolu, gaudy chintz curtains and chair-covers, where roses and lilies were almost effaced by dirt. The cheap tapestry carpet was threadbare, a desert of arid canvas, with here and there an oasis of faded colour, which hinted at the former richness of the soil. The windows were clouded with London grime and London smoke, and lent an additional gloom to the chilly sky and the dingy street upon which they looked. The cracked and bulging ceiling was brown with the smoke of ages. Dirt was the pervading impression which the room left upon the stranger's mind.

On a rickety old sofa lay the present proprietor of the apartment, dozing gently at noontide, with the *Daily Telegraph* slipping from his loosened grasp. The remains of a bachelor breakfast, a half-empty eggshell, a fragment of toast, and a cracked coffee-cup, indicated that he had but lately taken his morning meal.

He lifted himself lazily from the crumpled pillow, and confronted his visitor with a prolonged and audible yawn.

'Dear boy!' he exclaimed, 'what an untimely hour! What has happened that you are astir so early?'

He was not a common-looking man. He was tall, broad, and deep of chest, with lean, muscular arms, an aquiline nose, large and somewhat prominent eyes, bloodshot and tarnished by long years of evil experience, thin iron-gray hair, worn unduly long to conceal its scantiness, a complexion of a dull leaden hue, stained with patches of bistre—the complexion of a man to whom fresh air was an unusual luxury—thin lips, a high, narrow forehead. He wore a threadbare frock coat, closely buttoned, a frayed black satin stock, gray trousers, tightly strapped over well-worn boots, boots that had begun their career as dress boots.

Despite the shabbiness of his attire the man looked every inch a gentleman. That he was a gentleman who had fallen about as low as gentle breeding can fall, outside the Old Bailey, there was no doubt. Vice had set its mark upon him so deeply that the brand of crime itself could scarcely have done more to separate him from respectability. A man must have been very young indeed, and utterly unlearned in the experience of life, who would have trusted Mr. Desrolles in any virtuous enterprise. But Jack Chicot showed himself by no means wanting in penetration when he pitched upon Mr. Desrolles as a likely instrument for doing dirty work. He was the material of which the French *mouchard* is made.

'I've been worried, Desrolles,' answered Jack, dropping wearily into a chair.

'My dear fellow, the normal condition of life is worry,' replied Desrolles, languidly. 'The wisest of Jews knew all about it. Man was born to trouble as the sparks fly upward. The most that philosophy can suggest is to take trouble easily, as I do. All the Juggernaut cars of life have gone over me, but I am not crushed.'

The tone was at once friendly and familiar. Jack Chicot and the second-floor lodger had become acquainted very soon after the Chicots' advent in Cibber Street. They met each other on the stairs, first smiled, then nodded, then loitered to discuss and generally to anathematise the weather, then went a little further, and talked about the events of the day—the shocking murder recorded in the morning paper—the fire down Millwall way—the chances of war, or disturbances in the political atmosphere. By-and-by Jack Chicot asked Desrolles into his room, and they played a hand or two at écarté—first-rate players both—for three-penny points. Soon the écarté became an institution, and they played two or three times a week, while La Chicot was standing on the tips of her satin-shod toes, and enchanting the gilded youth of the capital. Jack found his acquaintance a man of infinite resources and wide experience. He had begun life in a good social position, had—according to his own account—distinguished himself as a soldier under such men as Gough and Hardinge; and had descended slowly, step by step, to be the thing he was. That gradual descent had carried him through scenes so strange and varied that his experiences of all that is oddest and worst in life would have made a book as big as 'Les Misérables.' And the creature knew how to talk. He never told the same story twice. Jack sometimes fancied this must be because he invented his stories upon the spot, and forgot them immediately afterwards. The man was no pretender to virtues which he did not possess, but rather advertised his vices. The only redeeming qualities he affected were a recklessness in money matters, which he appeared to consider generosity, and a rough-and-ready notion of honour, such as is supposed to obtain among thieves. Jack tolerated, despised, and allowed himself to be amused by the man. If he had been a king he would have liked such a fellow to lounge beside his throne, dressed in motley, flinging Rabelaisian witticisms in the smug faces of the courtiers.

'What's the particular trouble to-day, Jack?' asked Desrolles, selecting a meerschaum from the litter on the mantelpiece, and lazily filling the blackened bowl. 'Financial, I conclude.'

'No. I am anxious about my wife.'

'The natural penalty for marrying the handsomest woman in Paris. What's the mischief you're afraid of?'

'She has received a present from an anonymous admirer; and because it is anonymous, she imagines she is justified in receiving it.'

'Where's the harm?'

'You ought to see it. The anonymous gift is the thin end of the wedge. The giver will see my wife dancing with his bracelet on her arm, and will believe her as venal as the girl who sold Rome for the same kind of gewgaw. He will follow up his first offering with a second, and then will come letters, anonymous at first, perhaps, like the bracelet, but when by insidious flattery he has smoothed the way to dishonour, he will declare himself—and then——'

'Unless your wife is a better woman than you believe her, there will be danger. Is that what you mean?' asked Desrolles calmly, slowly puffing at his meerschaum.

'No,' said Chicot, reddening indignantly. He had not fallen low enough to hear his wife maligned, though he hated her. 'No. If my wife were a woman to be led away by temptation of that kind, she and I would have parted long ago. But I don't want to leave her exposed to the pursuit of a scoundrel. She and I have quarrelled about this trumpery bracelet, and I am going to leave her for a few days, till we are both in a better temper. I don't want to leave her unprotected, with some silky rascal lying in wait for her between her lodgings and the theatre. I want some one, a man I can trust——'

'To keep an eye upon her while you're away,' said Desrolles. 'My dear fellow, consider it done. Madame Chicot and I are excellent friends. I admire her; and I think she likes me. I will be her slave and her guardian in your absence; a father, with more than a father's devotion.'

'She must not know,' exclaimed Jack.

'Of course not. Women are children of a larger growth, and must be treated as such. The pills we give them must be coated with sugar, the powders concealed in raspberry jam. I will make myself so agreeable to Madame Chicot that she will be delighted to accept my escort to and from the theatre; but I will keep her anonymous admirer at a distance as thoroughly as the fiercest dragon that ever kept watch over beauty.'

'A thousand thanks, Desrolles. You won't find me ungrateful. Good-bye.'

'Are you going across the Channel?'

Mr. Chicot did not say where he was going, and Desrolles was too discreet to push the question. He was a man who boasted sometimes, when drink had made him maudlin, that, whatever had become of his morals, he had never lost his manners.

Jack Chicot left a brief pencilled note for his wife:—

'DEAR ZAÏRE,—Since we get on so badly together, a few days' separation will be good for both of us. I am off to the country for a breath of fresh air. I sicken in the odour of gas and stale brandy. Take care of yourself for your own sake, if not for mine.—Yours, 'J. C.'

CHAPTER VII.

'A LITTLE WHILE SUCH LIPS AS THINE TO KISS.'

It was midwinter when Jasper Treverton died. Spring had come in all her glory—her balmy airs and sultry noontides, stolen from summer; her variety and wealth of wood and meadow blossoms; her snowy orchard bloom, tinted with carnation; her sweetness and freshness of beauty—a season to be welcomed and enjoyed like no other season in the changing year; a little glimpse of Paradise on earth between the destroying gales of March and the fatal thunderstorms of July. Spring had filled all the lanes and glades round Hazlehurst with perfume and colour when John Treverton reappeared in the village, as unexpectedly as if he had dropped from the skies.

Eliza Sampson was destroying the aphids on a favourite rose tree, handling them daintily with the tips of her gloved fingers, as if she loved them, when Mr. Treverton appeared at the little iron gate, carrying his own portmanteau. He, the heir of all the ages, and of what signified much more in Miss Sampson's estimation, an estate worth fourteen thousand a year.

'Oh,' she cried, 'Mr. Treverton, how could you? We would have sent the boy to the station.'

'How could I do what?' he asked, laughing at her horrified look.

'Carry your own portmanteau. Tom will be so vexed.'

'Tom need know nothing about it, if it will vex him. The portmanteau is light enough, and I have only brought it from the "George," where the 'bus dropped me. You see I have taken your brother at his word, Miss Sampson, and have come to quarter myself upon you for a few days.'

'Tom will be delighted,' said Eliza.

She was meditating how the dinner she had arranged for Tom and herself could be made to do for the heir of Hazlehurst Manor. It was one of those dinners in which the economical housekeeper delights, a dinner that clears up every scrap in the larder, and leaves not so much as a knuckle-bone for the predatory 'follower,' male or female, the cook's hungry niece, or the housemaid's young man. A little soup, squeezed, as by hydraulic pressure, out of cleanly picked bones and odd remnants of gristle; a dish of hashed mutton, a very small hash, fenced round with a machicolated parapet of toasted bread; a beefsteak pudding with a kidney in it, boiled in a basin the size of a breakfast-cup. This latter savoury mess was intended to gratify Tom, who was prejudiced against hashed mutton, and always pretended that it disagreed with him. For *entremets sucrés* there were a dish of stewed rhubarb and a mould of boiled rice, wholesome, simple, and inexpensive. It was a little dinner which did honour to Miss Sampson's head and heart; but she felt that it was not good enough for the future lord of Hazlehurst, a gentleman out of whom her brother hoped to make plenty of money by-and-by.

'I'll go and see about your room while you have a chat with Tom in the office,' she said, tripping lightly away, and leaving John Treverton on the lawn in front of the drawing-room windows, a closely-shorn piece of grass about fifty feet by twenty-five.

'Pray don't give yourself any trouble,' he called after her; 'I'm used to roughing it.'

Eliza was in the kitchen before he had finished his sentence. She was deep in consultation with the cook, who would have resented the unannounced arrival of any ordinary guest, but who felt that Mr. Treverton was a person for whom people must be expected to put themselves about. He had given liberal vails, too, after his last visit, and that was much in his favour.

'We must have some fish, Mary,' said Eliza, 'and poultry. It's dreadfully dear at this time of year, and Trimpson does impose so, but we must have it.'

Trimpson was the only fishmonger and poulterer of Hazlehurst, a trader whose stock sometimes consisted of a pound and a half of salmon, and a single fowl, long-necked and skinny, hanging in solitary glory above the slate slab, where the salmon steak lay frizzling in the afternoon sun, which shone full upon Trimpson's shop.

'Well, miss, if I was you, I'd have a pair of soles and a duck to follow, with the beefsteak pudding for a bottom dish,' suggested cook; 'but, lawks, what's the good of talking? we must have what we can get. But I saw two ducks in Trimpson's window this morning when I went up street.'

'Put on your bonnet, Mary, and run and see what you can do,' said Eliza. And then, while Mary ran off, without stopping to put on her bonnet, Miss Sampson and the housemaid went upstairs together and took out lavender-scented linen, and decorated the spare room with all those pin-trays, china candlesticks, and pomatum pots, which went into retirement when there was no company.

'Of course he has come to make her an offer,' mused Eliza, as she lingered to give a finishing touch to the room, after the house-maid had gone downstairs.

'He has waited a proper time after the old gentleman's death, and now he has come down to ask her to marry him, and I dare say they will be married before the summer is over. It will be rather awkward for her to throw off such deep mourning all at once, but that's her own fault for going into crape, just as if Mr. Treverton had really been her father! I put it down to pride.'

Miss Sampson had a knack of finding motives for all the acts of her acquaintance, and those motives were rarely of the best.

John Treverton's chat with Mr. Sampson did not last more than ten minutes, friendly, and even affectionate, as was the lawyer's reception.

'I see you're busy,' said Treverton; 'I'll go and have a stroll in the village.'

'No, upon my honour, I was just going to strike work. I'll come with you if you like.'

'On no account; I know you haven't half finished. Dinner at six, as usual, I suppose. I'll be back in time for a talk before we sit down.'

And before Mr. Sampson could remonstrate, John Treverton was gone. He wanted to see what Hazlehurst Manor was like in the clear spring light, framed in greenery, brightened with all the flowers that bloom in early May, musical with thrush and blackbird, noisy with the return of the swallows. Never had he so longed to look upon anything as he longed to-day to see the home of his ancestors, the home which might be his.

He walked quickly along the village street. Such a quaint little street, with never one house like another; here a building bulging forward, with bow windows below and projecting dormers above; there a house retiring modestly behind a patch of garden; further on an inn set at right angles with the highway, its chief door approached by a flight of stone steps that time had worn crooked. Such a variety of chimneys, such complexities in the way of roofs and gables; but everywhere cleanliness and spring flowers, and a purer air than John Treverton had breathed for a long time. Even this queer little village street, with its dozen shops and its half-dozen public-houses was very fair and pleasant in his town-weary eyes.

When he left the street he entered a noble high-road, bordered on each side by a row of fine old elms, which made the turnpike road an avenue worthy to be the approach to a king's palace. The Manor-house lay off this road, guarded by tall gates of florid iron tracery, manufactured in the Low Countries two hundred years ago. He stopped at the gates to contemplate the scene, looking at it dreamily, as at something unreal—a picture that was fair but evanescent, and might vanish as he gazed.

Between the gates and the house the ground undulated gently. It was all smooth sward, too small for a park, too irregular for a lawn. A winding carriage-road, shadowed with fine old trees, skirted the green expanse, and groups of shrubs here and there adorned it, rhododendrons, laurels, bay, deodaras, cypresses, all the variety of ornamental conifers. Two great cedars made islets of shadow in the sunny grass, and a copper beech, a giant of his kind, was just showing its dark brown buds. Beyond stood the Manor-house, tall, and broad, and red, with white stone dressings to door and windows, and a noble cornice, a house of Charles the Second's reign, a real Sir Christopher Wren house, massive and grand in its stern simplicity.

John Treverton roused himself from his waking dream and rang the bell. A woman came out of the lodge, looked at him, dropped a low curtsey, opened the gate, and admitted him without a word, as if he were master there. In her mind he was master, though the trustees paid her wages. It was an understood thing in the household that Mr. Treverton was going to marry Miss Malcolm and reign at Hazlehurst Manor.

He walked slowly across the smooth, well-kept grass. Everything was changed and improved by the altered season. House and grounds seemed new to him. He remembered the flower-garden on the left of the house, the cheerless garden without a flower, where he had walked in the bleak winter mornings, smoking his solitary cigar; he remembered the walled fruit-garden beyond, to which he had seen that strange guest admitted under cover of darkness.

The thought of that night scene in the winter disturbed him even to-day, despite the apparent frankness of Laura's explanation.

'I suppose there is a mystery in every life,' he said, with a sigh; 'and, after all, what can it matter to me?'

He had heard nothing of the change in Miss Malcolm's plans, and supposed the house abandoned to the care of servants. He was surprised to see the drawing-room windows open, flowers on the tables, and a look of domesticity everywhere. He went past the house and into the flower-garden, a garden of the Dutch school, prim and formal, with long, straight walks, box borders, junipers clipped into obelisks, a dense yew hedge, eight feet high, with arches cut in it to give admittance to the adjoining orchard. The beds and borders were a blaze of red and yellow tulips, which shone out against the verdure of the close-shorn bowling-green and the tawny hue of the gravel, and made a feast of vivid colour, like the painted windows of a cathedral. John Treverton, who had not seen such a garden for years, was almost dazzled by its homely beauty.

He walked slowly to the end of the long path, looking about him in dreamy contentment. The sweet, soft air, the sunshine—just at that quiet hour of the afternoon when the light begins to be golden—the whistling of the blackbirds in the shrubbery, the freshness and beauty of all things, steeped his soul in a new delight. His life of late had been spent in cities, fenced from the beauty of earth by a wilderness of walls, the glory of heaven screened by smoke, the air thick and foul with the breath of men. This placid garden scene was as new to him as if he had come straight from the bottom of a mine.

Presently he stopped, as if struck with a new thought, looked straight before him, and muttered between clenched teeth:—

'I shall be a fool if I let it slip from my hand.'

'It' meant Hazlehurst Manor, and the lands and fortune thereto belonging.

He was standing within a few yards of the yew-tree hedge, and just at this moment the green arch opposite him became the frame of a living picture, and that a lovely one.

Laura Malcolm stood there, bareheaded, dressed in black, with a basket of flowers upon her arm—Laura, whom he had no idea of meeting in this place.

The western sky was behind her, and she stood, a tall, slim figure in straight, black drapery, against a golden background, like a saint in an early Italian picture, an edge of light upon her chestnut hair making almost an aureole, her face in shadow.

For a few moments she paused, evidently startled at the apparition of a stranger, then recognised the intruder, and came forward and offered him her hand frankly, as if he had been quite a commonplace acquaintance.

'Pray forgive me for coming in unannounced,' he said; 'I had no idea I should find you here. Yet it is natural that you should come sometimes to look at the old gardens.'

'I am living here,' answered Laura. 'Didn't you know?'

'No, indeed. No one informed me of the change in your plans.'

'I am so fond of the dear old house and garden, and the place is so full of associations for me, that I was easily induced to stay when Mr. Clare told me that it would be better for the house. I am a kind of housekeeper in charge of everything.'

'I hope you will stay here all your life,' said Treverton quickly, and then he coloured crimson, as if he had said something awful.

The same crimson flush mounted almost as quickly to Laura's pale cheeks and brow. Both stood looking at the ground, embarrassed as a schoolboy and girl, while the blackbirds whistled triumphantly in the shrubbery, and a thrush in the orchard went into ecstasies of melody.

Laura was the first to recover.

'Have you been staying long at Hazlehurst?' she asked, quietly.

'I only came an hour ago. My first visit was to the Manor, though I expected to find it an empty house.'

Another picture now appeared in the green frame—a young lady with a neat little figure, a retroussé nose, and an agreeably vivacious countenance.

'Come here, Celia,' cried Laura, 'and let me introduce Mr. Treverton. You have heard your father talk about him. Mr. Treverton, Miss Clare.'

Miss Clare bowed and smiled, and murmured something indefinite. 'Poor Edward!' she was thinking all the while. 'This Mr. Treverton is awfully good-looking.'

'Awfully' was Miss Clare's chief laudatory adjective; her superlative form of praise was 'quite too awfully,' and when enthusiasm carried her beyond herself she called things 'nice.' 'Quite too awfully nice,' was her maximum of rapture.

As she rarely left Hazlehurst Vicarage, and knew in all about twenty people, it is something to her credit that she had made herself mistress of the current metropolitan slang.

'I suppose you are staying at the Sampsons?' she said. 'Mr. Sampson is always talking of you. "My friend Treverton," he calls you, but I suppose you won't mind that. It's rather trying.'

'I think I can survive even that,' answered John, who felt grateful to this young person for having come to his rescue at a moment when he felt himself curiously embarrassed. 'Mr. Sampson has been very kind to me.'

'If you can only manage to endure him he is an awfully good-natured little fellow,' said Miss Clare with her undergraduate air. She modelled her manners and opinions upon those of her brother, and was in most things a feminine copy of the Oxonian. 'But how do you contrive to get on with his sister? She is quite too dreadful.'

'I confess that she is a lady whose society does not afford me unqualified delight,' said John, 'but I believe she means kindly.'

'Can a person with white eyelashes mean kindly?' inquired Celia, with a philosophical air. 'Has not Providence created them like that as a warning, just as venomous snakes have flat heads?'

'That is treating the matter rather too seriously,' said John. 'I don't admire white eyelashes, but I am not so prejudiced as to consider them an indication of character.'

'Ah,' replied Celia, with a significant air, 'you will know better by-and-by.'

She was only twenty, but she talked to John Treverton with as assured a tone as if she had been ages older than he in wisdom and experience of life.

'How pretty the gardens are at this season!' said Treverton, looking round admiringly, and addressing his remark to Laura.

'Ah, you have only seen them in winter,' she answered; 'perhaps you would like to walk round the orchard and shrubberies?'

'I should, very much.'

'And after that we will go indoors and have some tea,' said Celia. 'You are fond of tea, of course, Mr. Treverton?'

'I confess that weakness.'

'I am glad to hear it. I hate a man who is not fond of tea. There is that brother of mine appreciates nothing but strong coffee without milk. I'm afraid he'll come to a bad end.'

'I am glad you think tea-drinking a virtue,' said John, laughing.

And then they all three went under the yew-tree arch, into the loveliest of orchards—an orchard of seven or eight acres—an orchard that had been growing a century and a half; pears, plums, cherries, apples; here and there a walnut tree towering above the rest; here and there a gray old medlar; a pool in a corner overshadowed by two rugged old quinces; grass so soft, and deep, and mossy; primroses, daffodils; pale purple crocuses; the whole bounded by a sloping bank on which the ferns were just unfolding their snaky, gray coils, and revealing young leaves of tenderest green, under a straggling hedge of hawthorn, honeysuckle, and eglantine.

Here among the old gnarled trunks, and on the hillocky grass, Mr. Treverton and the two young ladies walked for about half-an-hour, enjoying the beauty and freshness of the place, in this sweetest period of the balmy spring day. Celia talked much, and John Treverton talked a little, but Miss Malcolm was for the most part silent. And yet John did not think her dull or stupid. It was enough for him to look at that delicate, yet firmly-modelled profile, the thoughtful brow, grave lips, and calm, dark eyes, to know that neither intellect nor goodness was wanting in her whom his kinsman had designed for his wife.

'Poor old man,' he thought, 'he meant to secure my happiness without jeopardising hers. If he could have known—if he could have known!'

They returned to the garden by a different arch; they visited the hot-houses, where the rose-hued azaleas and camellias made pyramids of vivid colour; they glanced at the kitchen garden with its asparagus-beds and narrow box-edged borders, its all-pervading odour of sweet herbs and wallflowers.

'I am positively expiring for want of a cup of tea,' cried Celia. 'Didn't you hear the church clock strike five, Laura?'

John remembered the six o'clock dinner at The Laurels.

'I really think I must deny myself that cup of tea,' he said. 'The Sampsons dine at six.'

'What of that?' exclaimed Celia, who never would let a man out of her clutches till stern necessity snatched him from her. 'It is not above ten minutes' walk from here to The Laurels.'

'What an excellent walker you must be, Miss Clare. Well, I'll hazard everything for that cup of tea.'

They went into a pretty room, opening out of the garden, a room with two long windows wreathed round with passionflower and starry white clematis—the clematis montana, which flowers in spring. It was not large enough for a library, so it was called the book-room, and was lined from floor to ceiling with books—a great many of which had been collected by Laura. It was quite a lady's collection. There were all the modern poets, from Scott and Byron downwards, a good many French and German books—Macaulay, De Quincey, Lamartine, Victor Hugo—a good deal of history and belles-lettres, but no politics, no science, no travels. The room was the essence of snugness—flowers on mantelpiece and tables, basket-work easy chairs, cushions adorned with crewel-work, delightful little tables (after Chippendale), and on one of the tables a scarlet Japanese tea-tray, with the quaintest of old silver teapots, and cups and saucers in willow-pattern Nankin ware. Laura poured out the tea, while Celia began to devour hot buttered cake, the very look of which suggested dyspepsia; but to some weak minds earth has no more overpowering temptation on a warm spring afternoon than hot buttered cake and strong tea with plenty of cream in it.

John Treverton sat in one of the low basket arm-chairs—such chairs as they make in Buckinghamshire and Oxfordshire—and drank tea as if it were the elixir of life. He had a strange feeling as he sat in that chair by the open window, looking across the beds of tulips, above which the bees were humming noisily—a feeling as if his life were only just beginning; as if he were a child in his cradle, dimly conscious of the dawning of existence; no burdens on mind or conscience; no tie or encumbrance; no engagement of honour or faith; a dead blank behind him; and before him life, happiness, the glory and freshness of earth, love, home, all things which fate reserves for the man born to good luck.

This dream or fancy of his was so pleasant that he let it stay with him while he drank three cups of tea, and while Celia rattled on about Hazlehurst and its inhabitants, giving him what she called a social map of the country, which might be useful for his guidance during the week he proposed to spend there. He only roused himself when the church clock chimed the three-quarters, and then he pulled himself out of the basket chair with a jerk, put down his cup and saucer, and wished Laura good-bye.

'I shall have to do the distance in ten minutes, Miss Clare,' he said, as he shook hands with that vivacious young lady.

'I'm afraid I ought to have said ten minutes for a bicycle,' replied Celia; 'but the Sampsons won't mind waiting dinner for you, and I don't suppose the delay will hurt their dinner.'

'It will be nearer for you through the orchard,' said Laura.

So John Treverton went through the orchard, at the end of which there was a gate that opened into a lane leading to the high-road. It was the same lane that skirted the walled fruit-garden, with the little door that John had seen mysteriously opened that winter night. The sight of the little wooden door made him curiously thoughtful.

'I'll never believe that there was anything approaching guilt in that mystery,' he said to himself. 'No, I have looked into those lovely eyes of hers, and I believe her incapable of an unworthy thought. Some poor relation, I dare say—a scamp whom she would have been ashamed of before the servants, so she received him secretly; doubtless to help him with money.'

* * * *

'What an extraordinary girl you are, Laura!' said Celia, draining the teapot. 'Why did you never tell me that John Treverton was so perfectly lovely?'

'My dear Celia, how am I to know what constitutes your idea of perfect loveliness in a young man? I have heard you praise so many, all distinctly different. I told you that Mr. Treverton was gentleman-like and good-looking.'

'Good-looking!' cried Celia. 'He is absolutely perfect. To see him sitting in that chair drinking tea and looking dreamily out of the garden with those exquisite eyes of his! Oh, he is quite too awfully nice. Do you know the colour of his eyes?'

'I have not the slightest idea.'

'They are a greeny-gray—a colour that changes every minute, a tint between blue and brown; I never saw it before. And his complexion—just that olive paleness which is so positively delightful. His nose is slightly irregular in line, not straight enough to be Grecian, and not curved enough to be aquiline—but his mouth is awfully nice—so firm and resolute-looking, yet lapsing now and then into dreamy thought. Did you see him lapse into dreamy thought, Laura?'

Miss Malcolm blushed indignantly; vexed, no doubt, at such foolishness.

'Really, Celia, you are too ridiculous. I can't think how you can indulge in such absurd raptures about a strange man.'

'Why not about a strange man?' asked Celia, with her philosophical air. 'Why should the perfections of a strange man be a forbidden subject? One may rave about a landscape; one may be as enthusiastic as one likes about the stars or the moon, the sea, or a sunset, or even the last popular novel? Why must not one admire a man? I am not going to put a padlock upon my lips to flatter such an absurd prejudice. As for you, Laura, it is all very well to sit there stitching at that faded blackberry leaf—you are putting too much brown in it, I am sure—and looking the image of all that is demure. To my mind you are more to be envied than any girl I ever heard of, except the Sleeping Beauty in the Wood.'

'Why should I be envied?'

'Because you are to have a splendid fortune and John Treverton for your husband.'

'Celia, I shall be so grateful to you if you will be quite silent on that subject, supposing that you can be silent about anything.'

'I can't,' said Celia frankly.

'It is by no means certain that I shall marry Mr. Treverton.'

'Would you be so utterly idiotic as to refuse him?'

'I would not accept him unless I could believe that he really liked me—better than any other woman he had ever seen.'

'And of course he will; of course he does,' cried Celia. 'You know, as a matter of personal inclination, I would much rather you should marry poor Edward, who adores the ground you walk upon, and, of course, adores you much more than the ground. But there is a limpness about Ted's character which makes me fear that he will never get on in the world. He is a clever young man, and he thinks that he has nothing to do but go on being clever, and write verses for the magazines—which even I, as his sister, must confess are the weakest dilution of Swinburne—and that Fame will come and take him by the hand, and lead him up the steps of her temple, while Fortune will meet him in the portico with a big bag of gold. No, Laura, dearly as I love Ted, I should be sorry to see you sacrifice a splendid fortune, and refuse such a man as John Treverton.'

'There will be time enough to debate the question when Mr. Treverton asks me to marry him,' said Laura gravely.

'Oh, that will come upon you all in a moment,' retorted Celia, 'when you won't have me to help you. You had better make up your mind beforehand.'

'I should despise Mr. Treverton if he were to make me an offer before he knew a great deal more of me than he does now. But I forbid you to talk any more of this, Celia. And now we had better go and walk in the orchard for half-an-hour, or you will never be able to digest all the cake you have eaten.'

'What a pity digestion should be so difficult, when eating is so easy,' said Celia.

And then she went dancing along the garden paths with the airy lightness of a nymph who had never known the meaning of indigestion.

Once more John Treverton drove round his late kinsman's estate, and this second time, in the sweet spring weather, the farms, and homesteads, the meadows where the buttercups were beginning to show golden among the grass, the broad sweeps of arable land where the young corn was growing tall—seemed to him a hundredfold more fair than they had seemed in the winter. He felt a keener longing to be the master of all these things. It seemed to him as if no life could be so sweet as the life he might lead at Hazlehurst Manor, with Laura Malcolm for his wife.

The life he might lead——if——

What was that 'if' which barred the way to perfect bliss?

There was more than one obstacle, he told himself gloomily, as he paced the elm avenue on the London road, one evening at sunset, after he had been at Hazlehurst more than a week, during which week he had seen Laura very often.

There was, among many questions, the doubt as to Laura's liking for him. She might consider herself constrained to accept him, were he to offer himself, in deference to the wish of her adopted father; but could he ever feel sure that she really cared for him, that he was the one man upon earth whom she would choose for her husband?

A flattering whisper which crept into the ear of his mind, like a caressing breath of summer wind gently fanning his cheek, told him that he was already something nearer and dearer to this sweet girl than the ruck of mankind; that her lovely hazel eyes took a new light and colour at his coming, that their beauty was shadowed with sadness in the moment of parting from him; that there were tender, broken tones of voice, fleeting blushes, half smiles, sudden droop-ings of darkly-fringed eyelids, and many other more subtle signs, that told of something more than common friendship. Believing this, what had he to do but snatch the prize?

Alas! between him and the light and glory of life stood a dark, forbidding figure, a veiled face, an arm sternly extended to stop the way.

'It is not to be thought of,' he said to himself. 'I honour her too much—yes, I love her too well. The estate must go, and she and I must go on our several ways in the wilderness of life—to meet by chance, perhaps, half-a-century hence, when we have grown old, and hardly remember each other.'

It was to be his last evening at Hazlehurst, and he was going to the Manor-house to bid Laura and her friend good-bye. A very sim-ple act of politeness, assuredly, yet he hung back from the perfor-mance of it, and walked slowly up and down under the elm trees, smoking a meditative cigar, and chewing the cud of fancies which were mostly bitter.

At last, just when the topmost edge of the sinking sun dropped below the dark line of distant woods, John Treverton made up his mind there was no more time to be lost, if he meant to call at the Manor-house that evening. He quickened his pace, anxious to find Laura in the garden, where she spent most of her life in this balmy spring weather. He felt himself more at ease with her in the garden than when he was brought face to face with her within four walls. Out of doors there was always something to distract attention, to give a sudden turn to the conversation if it became embarrassing to either of them. Here, too, it was easier to escape Celia's searching eye, which was so often upon them indoors, where she had very lit-tle to occupy her attention.

He went in at the lodge gate, as usual unquestioned. All the old servants agreed in regarding him as the future owner of the estate. They wondered that he asserted himself so little, and went in and out as if he were nobody. The way to the old Dutch garden was by this time very familiar to him. He had been there at almost every hour of the day, from golden noon to gray evening.

As he went round by the house he heard voices, a man's voice among them, and the sound of that masculine voice was not welcome to his ear. Celia's shrill little laugh rang out merrily, the sky-terrier yapped in sympathy. They were evidently enjoying themselves very much in the Dutch garden, and John Treverton felt as if their enjoyment were an affront to him.

He turned the angle of the house, and saw the group seated on a little lawn in front of the book-room windows; Laura and Celia in rustic chairs, a young man on the grass at their feet, the dog dancing round him. John Treverton guessed at once that the young man was the Edward, or Ted, about whom he had heard Celia Clare so often discourse; the Edward Clare who, according to Miss Sampson, was in love with Laura Malcolm.

Laura half rose to shake hands with her guest. Her face at least was grave. *She* had not been laughing at the nonsense which provoked Celia's mirth. John Treverton was glad of that.

'Mr. Clare, Mr. Treverton.'

Edward Clare looked up and nodded—a rather supercilious nod, John thought, but he did not expect much friendliness from the vicar's son. He gave the young man a grave bow, and remained standing by Laura's chair.

'I hope you will forgive my late visit, Miss Malcolm,' he said. 'I have come to wish you "good-bye."'

She glanced up at him with a startled look, and he fancied—yes, he dared to fancy—that she was sorry.

'You have not stopped long at Hazlehurst,' she said, after a palpable pause.

'As if any one would who was not absolutely obliged,' cried Celia. 'I can't imagine how Mr. Treverton has existed through an entire week.'

'I assure you that I have not found my existence a burden,' said John, addressing himself to Celia. 'I shall leave Hazlehurst with deep regret.'

He could not for worlds, in his present mood, have said as much to Laura.

'Then you must be one of two things,' said Celia.

'What things?'

'You must be either a poet, or intensely in love. There is my brother here. He never seems tired of roaming about Hazlehurst. But then he is a poet, and writes verses about March violets, and the first leafbuds on the willows, and the reappearance of the May-fly, or the return of the swallow. And he smokes no end, and he reads novels to an extent that is absolutely demoralizing. It's dreadful to see a man dependent upon Mudie for getting through his life,' exclaimed Celia, making a face that expressed extreme contempt.

'I am not a poet, Miss Clare,' said John Treverton, quietly; 'yet I confess to having been very happy at Hazlehurst.'

He stole a glance at Laura to see if the shot told. She was looking down, her sweet, grave face pure and pale as ivory in the clear evening light.

'It's very civil of you towards the parish to say as much,' said Edward with a veiled sneer, 'and it is kind of you to shrink from wounding our feelings as aborigines, but I am sure you must have been ineffably bored. There is positively nothing to do at Hazlehurst.'

'I suppose that's why the place suits you, Ted?' observed Miss Clare innocently.

The conversation had an uncomfortable tone which was quite out of harmony with the soft evening sky, and shadowy garden, where the flowers were losing their colour as the light declined. John Treverton looked curiously at the man he knew to be his rival.

He saw a man of about six-and-twenty, of the middle height, slim almost to fragility, yet with a compactness of form which indicated activity and possibly strength. Gray eyes inclining to blue, long lashes, delicately-pencilled eyebrows, a fair complexion, low, narrow brow, and regular features, a pale brown moustache, more silky than abundant, made up a face that was very handsome in the estimation of some people, but which assuredly erred on the side of effeminacy. It was a face that would have suited the velvet and brocade of one of the French Henry's minions, or the lovelocks and jewel-broidered doublet of one of James Stuart's silken favourites.

It would have been difficult to imagine the owner of that face doing any good or great work in the world, or leaving any mark upon his time, save some petty episode of vanity, profligacy, and selfishness in the memoirs of a modern St. Simon.

'Anything new in the evening papers?' asked Mr. Clare, with a stifled yawn.

The languid inquiry followed upon a silence that had lasted rather too long to be pleasant.

'Sampson had not got his *Globe* when I left him,' answered John Treverton; 'but in the present stagnation of everything at home and abroad I confess to feeling very little interest in the evening papers.'

'I should like to have heard if that unlucky dancer is dead,' said Celia.

John Treverton, who had been standing beside Laura's chair like a man lost in a waking dream, turned suddenly at this remark.

'What dancer?' he asked.

'La Chicot. Of course you have seen her dance. You happy Londoners see everything under the sun that is worth seeing. She is something wonderful, is she not? And now I suppose I shall never see her.'

'She's a very handsome woman, and a very fine dancer, in her particular style,' answered Treverton. 'But what did you mean just now when you talked about her death? She is as much alive as you and I are; at least I know that her name was on all the walls and she was dancing nightly when I left London.'

'That was a week ago,' said Celia. 'Surely you saw the account of the accident in this morning's *Times*? There was nearly a column about it.'

'I did not look at the *Times*. Mr. Sampson and I started early this morning for a long round. What was this accident?'

'Oh, quite too dreadful!' exclaimed Celia. 'It made my blood run cold to read the description. It seems that the poor thing had to go up into the flies, or the skies, or something, hooked on to some moveable irons—a kind of telescopic arrangement, you know.'

'Yes, yes, I know,' said Treverton.

'Well, of course that would be awfully jolly as long as it was safely done, for she must look lovely floating upwards, with the limelight shining on her; but it seems the man who had the management of the iron machine got tipsy, and did not know what he was doing, so the irons were not properly braced together, and just as she was near the top the thing gave way and she came down headlong.'

'And was killed?' asked John Treverton breathlessly.

'No, she was not killed on the spot, but her leg was broken—a compound fracture, I think they call it, and she was hurt about the head, and the paper said she was altogether in a very precarious state. Now I have noticed that when a newspaper says that a person is in a precarious state, the next thing one hears of that person is that he or she is dead; so that I shouldn't at all wonder if La Chicot's death were in the evening papers.'

'What a loss to society!' sneered Edward Clare. 'I think you are the most ridiculous girl in the world, Celia, to interest yourself in people who are as far off your groove as if they were the inhabitants of the moon.'

'*Homo sum*,' said Celia, proud of a smattering of Latin, the crumbs that had fallen from her brother's table, 'and all the varieties of mankind are interesting to me. I should like to have been a dancer myself, if I had not been a clergyman's daughter. It must be an aw-fully jolly life.'

'Delightful,' exclaimed Edward, 'especially when it ends abrupt-ly through the carelessness of a drunken scene-shifter.'

'I must say good-night and good-bye,' said John Treverton to Laura. 'I have my portmanteau to pack ready for an early start to-morrow morning. Indeed, I am inclined to go by the mail to-night. It would save me half-a-day.'

'The mail leaves at a quarter past ten. You'll have to look sharp if you travel by that,' said Edward.

'I'll try it, at any rate.'

'Good-night, Mr. Treverton,' said Laura, giving him her hand.

The lively Celia was not going to let him depart with so cold a farewell. He was a man, and, as such, eminently interesting to her.

'We'll all walk to the gate with you,' she said; 'it will be better for us than sitting yawning here, watching the bats skimming across the flower-beds.'

They all went, and it happened somehow, to John Treverton's tremulous delight, that Laura and he were side by side, a little behind the other two.

'I am sorry you are obliged to leave so soon,' said Laura, anxious to say something vaguely civil.

'I should go away more happy than I can tell you if I thought my going could make you sorry.'

'Oh, I did not mean in such a particular sense,' she said, with a little laugh. 'I am sorry for your own sake that you have to leave the country, just when it is so lovely, and to go back to smoky London.'

'If you knew how I hate that world of smoke and all foul things, you would pity me with the uttermost compassion your kind heart can feel,' he answered, very much in earnest. 'I am going from all I love to all I detest; and I know not how long it may be before I can return; but if I should be able to come quickly will you promise me a kindly welcome, Laura? Will you promise to be as glad of my return as I am sorry to go to-night.'

'I cannot make any such bargain,' she said gently, 'for I cannot measure your sadness to-night. You are altogether a mysterious per-son; I have not even begun to understand you. But I hope you may come back soon, when our roses are in bloom and our nightin-gales are singing, and if their welcome is not enough for you I will promise to add mine.'

There was a tender playfulness in her tone which was unspeakably sweet to him. They were quite alone, in a part of the carriage-drive where the trees grew thickest, the shadow of chestnut leaves folding them round, the low breath of the evening wind whispering in their ears. It was an hour for tender avowals, for unworldly thoughts.

John Treverton took Laura's hand, and held it unreproved.

'Tell me that you do not hate the memory of my cousin Jasper because of that absurd will,' he said.

'Could I hate the memory of one who was so good to me, the only father I ever knew?'

'Say then that you do not hate me because of my cousin's will.'

'It would be very unchristianlike to hate you for an act of which you are innocent.'

'No doubt, but I can imagine a woman hating a man under such circumstances. You take away your hand. Yes, I feel convinced that you detest me.'

'I took away my hand because I thought you had forgotten to let it go,' said Laura, determined not to be too serious. 'Will it really make you more satisfied with yourself if I tell you that I heartily forgive my adopted father for his will?'

'Infinitely.'

'And that, in spite of our ridiculous position towards each other, I do not quite—hate you.'

'Laura, you are making me the happiest of men.'

'But I am saying very little.'

'If you knew how much it is to me! A world of hope, a world of delight, an incentive to high thoughts and worthy deeds, a regeneration of body and soul.'

'You are talking wildly.'

'I am wild with gladness. Laura, my love, my darling.'

'Stop,' she said suddenly, turning to him with earnest eyes, very pale in the dim light, now completely serious. 'Is it me or your cousin's estate you love? If it is the fortune you think of, let there be no stage-play of love-making between us. I am willing to obey your cousin—as I would have obeyed him living, honouring him and submitting to him as a father—but let us be true and loyal to each other. Let us face life honestly and earnestly, and accept it for what it is worth. Let us be faithful friends and companions, but not sham lovers.'

'Laura, I love you for yourself, and yourself only. As I live, that is the truth. Come to me to-morrow penniless, and tell me that Jasper Treverton's will was a forgery. Come to me and say: "I am a pauper like yourself, John, but I am yours," and see how fond and glad a welcome I will give you. My dearest, I love you truly, passionately. It is your lovely face, your tender voice, yourself I want.'

He put his arm round her, and drew her, not unwilling, to his breast, and kissed her with the first lover's kiss that had ever crimsoned her cheek.

'I like to believe you,' she said softly, resting contentedly in his arms.

This was their parting.

CHAPTER VIII.

'DAYS THAT ARE OVER, DREAMS THAT ARE DONE.'

There was excitement and agitation in Cibber Street, Leicester Square, that essentially dramatic, musical, and terpsichorean nook in the great forest of London. La Chicot had narrowly escaped death. It had been all but death at the moment of the accident. It might be absolute death at any hour of the night and day that followed the catastrophe. At least this is what the inhabitants of Cibber Street told each other, and they were one and all as graphic and as full of detail as if they had just left La Chicot's bedside.

'She has never stirred since they laid her in her bed,' said the shoemaker's wife, at the dingy shop for ladies' boots, two doors from the Chicot domicile; 'she lies there like a piece of waxwork, pore thing, and every five minutes they takes and wets her lips with a feather dipped in brandy; and sometimes she says "more, more," very weak and pitiful!'

'That looks as if she was sensible, at any rate,' answered the good woman's gossip, a letter of lodgings at the end of the street.

'I don't believe it's sense, Mrs. Bitters; I believe it's only an inward craving. She feels that low in her inside that the brandy's a relief to her.'

'Have they set her leg yet?'

'Lord love you, Mrs. Bitters, it's a compound fracture, and the swelling ain't begun to go down. They've got a perfessional nurse from one of the hospitals, and she's never left off applying cooling lotion, night or day, to keep down the inflammation. The doctor hasn't left the house since it happened.'

'Is it Mr. Mivart?'

'Lor, no; it's quite a stranger; a young man that's just been walking the orspital, but they say he's very clever. He was at the Prince Frederick when it happened, and see it all; and helped to bring her home, and if she was a duchess he couldn't be more careful over her.'

'Where's the husband?' asked Mrs. Bitters.

'Away in the country, no one knows where, for she hasn't sense to tell 'em, pore lamb. But from what Mrs. Evitt tells me, they was never the happiest of couples.'

'Ah!' sighed Mrs. Bitters, with an air of widest worldly experience, 'dancers and such like didn't ought to marry. What do they want with 'usbands, courted and run after as they are? Out every night too, like Tom cats. 'Ow can they make a 'ome 'appy?'

'I can't say as I ever thought Mr. Chicot 'ad a 'appy look,' assented the shoemaker's wife. 'He's got a way of walking with his eyes on the ground and his hands in his pockets, as if he didn't take no interest in life.'

Thus, and in various other manners, was the evil fate of La Chicot discussed in Cibber Street and the surrounding neighbourhood. Everybody was interested in her welfare. If she had been some patient domestic drudge, a devoted wife and mother, the interest would have been mild in comparison, the whole thing tame and commonplace. But La Chicot—whose name was on the walls in capitals three feet high, whose bold, bright face smiled on the foot passenger at every turn in the road—La Chicot was a personage, and whether she was to draw the lot of life or death from fate's mysterious urn was a public question.

It had been as the scene-shifter had shrewdly prophesied. She had been drunk, and the stage-carpenter had been drunk, and the result had been calamity. There had been a perennial supply of champagne in La Chicot's dressing-room during the last week, thanks to the liberality of an anonymous admirer, who had sent a three-dozen case of Rœderer, pints—fascinating little gold-tipped bottles that looked as innocent as flowers or butterflies. La Chicot had an idea that a pint of champagne could hurt nobody. Of a quart she opined, as the famous glutton did of a goose, that it was too much for one and not enough for two.

She naturally suspected that the anonymous champagne came from the unknown giver of the bracelet, but she was not going to leave the case unopened on that account. It was very pleasant to have an admirer who gave so freely and asked nothing. Poor fellow! It would be time enough to snub him when he became obtrusive. In the meanwhile she accepted his bounty as unquestioningly as she received the gifts of all-bounteous nature—the sun that warmed her, the west wind that fanned her cheek, the wallflowers and primroses at the street corners that told her spring was abroad in the land.

Yet she was a woman, and, therefore, naturally curious about her nameless admirer. Her splendid eyes roamed among the faces of the audience, especially among the gilded youth in the stalls, until they alighted on a countenance which La Chicot believed likely to be the one she sought. It was a face that watched her with a grave attention she had seen in no other countenance, though all were attentive—a sallow face, of a Jewish type, black eyes, an almost death-like pallor, a firmly-moulded mouth, the lips too thick for beauty, black hair, smooth and sleek.

'That is the man,' La Chicot said to herself, 'and he looks inordinately rich.'

She stole a glance at him often after this, and she always saw the same expression in the pallid Israelitish face, an intensity she had never seen in any other countenance.

'C'est un homme à parvenir,' she told herself; 'si ça était guerrier il aurait vaincu un monde, comme Napoléon.'

The face fascinated her somehow, or, at all events, it made her think of the man. She drank his champagne with greater gusto after this, and on the night after her discovery, the weather being unusually sultry for the season, she drank two bottles in the course of her toilet. When she went down to the wings, glittering with silvery tinsel, clad in a cloud of snowy gauze, she could hardly stand; but dancing was a second nature with her, and she managed to get through her solos without disgrace. There was a certain wildness, an extra audacity, a shade too much of that peculiar quality which the English call 'go,' and the French call 'chic,' but the audience at the Prince Frederick liked extremes, and applauded her to the echo.

'By Jove, she's a wonderful woman!' exclaimed Mr. Smolendo, watching her from the prompter's entrance. 'She's a safe draw for the next three seasons.'

Ten minutes afterwards came the ascent through the coral caves. The ironwork creaked, groaned, trembled, and then gave way. There was a shrill scream from the dancer, a cry of horror from the men at the wings, and La Chicot was lying in the middle of the stage, a confused heap of tumbled gauze and silver, silent and unconscious, while the green curtain came down with a run.

It was late on the night after the accident when Jack Chicot came home. He found his wife lying in a dull stupor, as the gossips had described her, life sustained by the frequent administration of brandy. The woman was as near death as she could be without being ready for her grave. A stranger was sitting by her bedside when Jack went into the room, a young man with a gravity of face and manner which was older than his years. The nurse was on the other side of the bed, applying a cooling lotion to La Chicot's burning forehead. The leg had been successfully set that afternoon, by one of the cleverest surgeons in London, and was suspended in a cradle under the light coverlet.

Jack went to the bedside and bent over the motionless figure, and looked at the dull, white face.

'My poor Zaïre, this is bad,' he murmured, and then he turned to the stranger, who had risen and stood beside him. 'You are the doctor, I suppose?'

'I am the watch-dog, if you like. Mr. Smolendo would not trust my inexperience with so delicate an operation as setting the broken leg. It was a terrible fracture, and required the highest art. He sent for Sir John Pelham, and everything has been done well and successfully. But he allowed me to remain as surgeon in charge. Your wife's state is perilous in the extreme. I fear the brain is injured. I was in the theatre when the accident happened. I am deeply interested in this case. I have lately passed my examination creditably, and am a qualified practitioner. I shall be glad if you will allow me to attend your wife—under Pelham, of course. It is not a question of remuneration,' the young man added hurriedly. 'I am actuated only by my professional interest in Madame Chicot's recovery.'

'I have no objection to my wife's profiting by your generous care, provided always that Sir John Pelham approves your treatment,' answered Chicot, in a calmer tone than George Gerard expected from a man who had just come home after a week's absence to find his wife in peril of death. 'Do you think she will recover?'

This question was asked deliberately, with intense earnestness. Gerard saw that the eyes which looked at him were watching for the answering look in his own eyes, waiting as for the sentence of doom.

That look set the surgeon wondering as to the relations between husband and wife. A minute ago he had wondered at Chicot's coldness—a tranquillity that seemed almost indifference. Now the man was all intensity. What did the change mean?

'Am I to tell you the truth?' asked Gerard.

'By all means.'

'Remember I can give you only my opinion. It is an obscure case. The injury to the brain is not easily to be estimated.'

'I will take your opinion for what it is worth. For God's sake be candid.'

'Then in my opinion the chances are against her recovery.'

Jack Chicot drew a long breath, a strange shivering sigh, which the surgeon, clever as he was, knew not how to interpret.

'Poor thing!' said the husband, after a brief silence, looking down at the dull, blank face. 'And three years ago she and I came out

84

of the Mairie very happy, and loving each other dearly! *C'est dommage que cela passe si vite.'*

These last words were spoken too low for Gerard to hear. They were a brief lament over a love that was dead.

'Tell me about the accident,' said Jack Chicot, sitting down in the chair Gerard had vacated. 'You were in the theatre, you say. You saw it all.'

'I did, and it was I who picked your wife up. I was behind the scenes soon enough for that. The panic-stricken wretches about were afraid to touch her.'

Gerard told everything faithfully. Jack Chicot listened with an unchanging face. He knew the worst that could be told him. The details could make little difference.

'I said just now that in my opinion the chances were against your wife's recovery,' said Gerard, full of earnestness, 'but I did not say the case was hopeless. If I thought it were, I should not be so anxious to undertake the care of your wife. I ask you to let me watch her because I entertain the hope—a faint hope at present, I grant—of curing her.'

Jack Chicot gave a little start, and looked curiously at the speaker.

'You must be tremendously in love with your profession, to be so anxious about another man's wife?' he said.

'I am in love with my profession. I have no other mistress. I desire no other!'

'Well, you may do all you can to snatch her from the jaws of death,' said Chicot. 'Let her have her chance, poor soul. That is only fair. Poor butterfly! Last night the star of a crowded theatre, the delight of every eye; to-night to lie thus, a mere log, living and yet dead. It is hard.'

He walked softly up and down the room, deep in thought.

'Do you know I implored her to refuse that ascent?' he said. 'I had a foreboding that harm would come of it.'

'You should have forbidden it,' said the surgeon, with his fingers on the patient's wrist.

'Forbidden! You don't know my wife.'

'If I had a wife she should obey me.'

'Ah! that's a common delusion of bachelors. Wait till you have a wife, and you will tell a different story.'

'She will do for to-night,' said Gerard, taking up his hat, yet lingering for one long scrutiny of the white, expressionless face on the pillow. 'Mrs. Mason knows all she has to do; I will be here at six to-morrow morning.'

'At six! You are an early riser.'

'I am a hard worker. One is impossible without the other. Good-night, Mr. Chicot; I congratulate you upon your power to take a great trouble quietly. There is no better proof of strong nerve.'

Jack fancied there was a hidden sneer in this parting compliment, but it made very little impression upon him. The perplexity of his life was big enough to exclude every other thought. 'You had better go to bed, Mrs. Mason,' he said to the nurse. 'I shall sit up with my wife.'

'I beg your pardon, sir, I could not feel that I was doing my duty if I indulged myself with a night's rest while the case is so critical; by-and-by I shall be thankful to get an hour's sleep.'

'Do you think Madame Chicot will ever be better?'

The nurse looked down at her white apron, sighed gently, and as gently shook her head.

'We always like to look at the bright side of things, sir,' she answered.

'But is there any bright side to this case?'

'That rests with Providence, sir. It is a very bad case.'

'Well,' said Jack Chicot, 'we must be patient.'

He seated himself in the chair by the bedside and remained there all night, never sleeping, hardly changing his attitude, sunk to the bottom of some deep gulf of thought.

Day came at last, and soon after daybreak came George Gerard, who found no change either for better or worse in his patient, and ordered no change in the treatment.

'Sir John Pelham is to be here at eleven,' he said. 'I shall come at eleven to meet him.'

The great surgeon came, made his inspection, and said that all was going on well.

'We shall make her leg sound again,' he said, 'I have no fear about that; I wish we were as certain about the brain.'

'Do you think the brain is seriously hurt?' asked Chicot.

'We can hardly tell. The iron struck her head as she fell. There is no fracture of the skull, but there is mischief of some kind—rather serious mischief, I fear. No doubt a good deal will depend on care and nursing. You are lucky to have secured Mrs. Mason; I can highly recommend her.'

'Frankly, do you think my wife will recover?' asked Chicot, questioning Sir John Pelham to-day as earnestly as he had questioned George Gerard last night.

86

'My dear sir, I hope for the best; but it is a bad case.'

'That must mean that it is hopeless,' thought Chicot, but he only bowed his head gently, and followed the surgeon to the door, where he tried to slip a fee into his hand.

'No, no, my dear sir, Mr. Smolendo will arrange that little matter,' said the surgeon, rejecting the money, 'and very properly too, since your wife was injured in his service.'

'I would rather have paid her debts myself,' answered Chicot, 'though Heaven knows how long I could have done it. We are never very much beforehand with the world. Oh, by the way, how about that young man upstairs, Mr. Gerard? Do you approve his treatment of the case?'

'Very much so; a remarkably clever young man—a man who ought to make rapid way in his profession.'

Sir John Pelham gave a compassionate sigh at the end of his speech, remembering how many young men he had known deserving of success, and how few of them had succeeded, and thinking what a clever and altogether commendable young man he must himself have been to be one of the few.

After this Jack Chicot allowed Mr. Gerard to prescribe for his wife with perfect confidence in the young man's ability. Sir John Pelham came once a week, and gave his opinion, and sometimes made some slight change in the treatment. It was a lingering, wearying illness, hard work for the nurse, trying work for the watcher. The husband had taken upon himself the office of night nurse. He watched and ministered to the invalid every night, while Mrs. Mason enjoyed four or five hours' sleep. Mr. Smolendo had suggested that they should have two nurses. He was willing to pay for anything that could ameliorate the sufferer's condition, though La Chicot's accident had almost ruined his season. It had not been easy to get a novelty strong enough to replace her.

'No,' said Jack Chicot, 'I don't want to take more of your money than I can help; and I may as well do something for my wife. I'm useless enough at best.'

So Jack went on drawing for the comic periodicals, and worked at night beside his wife's bed. Her mind had never awakened since the accident. She was helpless and unconscious now as she had been when they brought her home from the theatre. Even George Gerard was beginning to lose heart, but he in no way relaxed his efforts to bring about a cure.

In the day Jack went for long walks, getting as far away from that close and smoky region of Leicester Square as his long legs would take him. He tramped northward to Hampstead and Hendon, to Highgate, Barnet, Harrow; southward to Dulwich, Streatham, Beckenham; to breezy commons where the gorse was still golden, to woods where the perfume of pine trees filled the warm, still air; to hills below which he saw London lying, a silent city, wrapped in a mantle of blue smoke.

The country had an inexpressible charm for him at this period of his life. He was not easy till he had shaken the dust of London off his feet. He who a year ago in Paris had wasted half his days playing billiards in the entresol of a *café* on the Boulevard St. Michel, or sauntering the stony length of the boulevards from the Madeleine to the Chateau d'Eau—was now a solitary rambler in suburban lanes, choosing every path that led him furthest from the haunts of men.

'You are always out when I come in the daytime, Mr. Chicot,' said Gerard, one evening, when he had called later than usual and found Jack at home, dusty, tired after his day's ramble. 'Is not that rather hard on Madame Chicot?'

'What can it matter to her? She does not know when I am here; she is quite unconscious.'

'I am not so sure of that. She seems unconscious, but beneath that apathy there may be some struggling sense of outward things. It is my hope that the mind is there still, under a dense cloud.'

The struggle was long and weary. There came a day on which even George Gerard despaired. The wound in the leg had been slow to heal, and the pain had weakened the patient. Despite all that watchful nursing could do, she had sunk to the lowest ebb.

'She is very weak, is she not?' asked Jack, that summer afternoon—a sultry afternoon late in June, when the close London street was like a dusty oven, and faint odours from stale strawberries and half-rotten pineapples on the costermonger's barrows tainted the air with a sickly sweetness.

'She is as weak as she can be and live,' answered Gerard.

'You begin to lose faith?'

'I begin to fear.'

As he spoke he saw a look of ineffable relief flash into Jack Chicot's eyes. His own eyes caught and fixed that look, and the two men stood facing each other, one of them knowing that the secret of his heart was discovered.

'I fear,' said the surgeon, deliberately, 'but I am not going to leave off trying to save her. I mean to save her life if it is in human power to save it. I have set my heart upon it.'

'Do your utmost,' answered Chicot. 'Heaven is above us all. It must be as fate wills.'

'You loved her once, I suppose?' said Gerard, with searching eyes still on the other's face.

'I loved her truly.'

'When and why did you leave off loving her?'

'How do you know that I have ever done so?' asked Chicot, startled by the audacity of the question.

'I know it as well as you know it yourself. I should be a poor physician for an obscure disease of the brain if I could not read your secret. This poor creature, lying here, has for some time past been a burden and an affliction to you. If Providence were to remove her quietly, you would thank Providence. You would not lift your hand against her, or refuse any aid you can give her, but her death would be an infinite relief. Well, I think you will have your wish. I think she is going to die.'

'You have no right to talk to me like this,' said Chicot.

'Have I not? Why should not one man talk freely to another, uttering the truth boldly. I do not presume to judge or to blame. Who among us is pure enough to denounce his brother's sin? But why should I pretend not to understand you? Why affect to think you a loving and devoted husband? It is better that I should be plain with you. Yes, Mr. Chicot. I believe this business is going to end your way, and not mine.'

Jack stood looking gloomily out of the open window down into the dingy street, where the strawberry barrow was moving slowly along, while the costermonger's brassy voice brayed out his strange jargon. He had no word to answer to the surgeon's plain speaking. The accusation was true. He could not gainsay it.

'Yes, I loved her once,' he said to himself presently, as he sat by the bedside after George Gerard had gone. 'What kind of love was it, I wonder? I felt my life a failure, and had abandoned all hope of ever getting back into the beaten tracks of respectability, and it seemed to me to matter very little what I did with my life, or what kind of woman I married. She was the handsomest woman I had ever seen, and she was fond of me. Why should I not marry her? Between us we could manage to live somehow, *au jour le jour*, from hand to mouth. We took life lightly, both of us. Those were pleasant days. Yet I look back and wonder that I could have lived in the gutter and revelled in it. How even a gentleman can sink when once he ceases to respect himself? When did I first begin to be weary? When did I begin to hate her? Never till I had met ——. Oh, Paradise, which I have seen through the half-opened gate, shall I verily be free to enter your shining fields, your garden of gladness and delight?'

He sat by the bed in thoughtful silence, till the nurse came in to take his place, and then he went out into the dusty streets, and walked northward in search of air. He had promised the nurse to be back at ten o'clock, when she could have her supper and go to bed, leaving him in charge for the night. This was the usual routine.

'All may be over when I go home to-night,' he said to himself, and it seemed to him as if the past few years—the period of his married life—were part of a confused dream.

It was all over now. Its follies and its joys belonged to the past. He could look back and pity his wife and himself. Both had been foolish, both erring. It was done with. They had come to the last page of a volume that was speedily to be closed for ever. He could forgive, he could pity and deplore all that foolish past, now that it was no longer to fetter the future.

He rambled far that day—he was lighter of foot—the atmosphere out of London was clearer, or it seemed clearer, than usual. He walked to Harrow, and lay on the grass below Byron's tomb, looking dreamily down at the dim world of London.

It was after eleven when he got back to Cibber Street. The public house at the corner was closed, the latest of the gossips had deserted their door-steps. He looked up to the first-floor windows. La Chicot's bed had been moved into the front room, because it was more cheerful for her, the nurse said; but it was Mrs. Mason and not La Chicot who looked out of the window. The sickly yellow light shone through the dingy blind, just as it always did after dark. There was nothing to indicate any change. But all things would be the same, no doubt, if death were in the room.

As Jack stood on the door-step feeling in his pockets for the key, the door opened, and Desrolles, the second-floor lodger, came out.

'I am going to see if I can get a drop of brandy at the Crown and Sceptre,' he said, explanatorily; 'I've had one of my old attacks.'

Mr. Desrolles was a sufferer from some chronic complaint which he alluded to vaguely, and which necessitated frequent recourse to stimulants.

'The Crown and Sceptre is closed,' said Jack. 'I've some brandy upstairs; I'll give you a little.'

'That's uncommonly good-natured of you,' said Desrolles. 'I should have a night of agony if I couldn't get a little brandy somewhere. How late you are!'

'I've walked further than usual. It was such a fine evening.'

'Was it really? Hereabouts it was dull and grey. I thought we were going to have a thunderstorm. Local, I suppose. I've got some good news for you.'

'Good news for me. The rarity of the thing will make it welcome.'

'Your wife's better, decidedly better. I looked in two hours ago to inquire. The nurse thinks she has taken a turn. Mr. Gerard was here at eight, and thinks the same. It's wonderful. She rallied in an extraordinary manner between three and five o'clock, took her nourishment with an appearance of appetite for the first time since she has been ill. Mrs. Mason is delighted. Wonderful, isn't it?'

'Very wonderful!' exclaimed Jack Chicot; and who shall tell the bitterness of heart with which he turned from the shining vision of the future—the vision that had been with him all that evening, back to the dreary reality of the present.

He found Mrs. Mason elated. She had never seen a more marked change for the better.

'She's as weak as a new-born infant, poor dear,' she said of her patient, 'but it's just as if life was coming gently and slowly back, like the tide coming in over the sands when it has ebbed as low as ever it can ebb.'

The improvement continued steadily from that hour. The brain, so long clouded, awakened as from sleep. Zaïre recovered her strength, her senses, her beauty, her insolence and audacity. Before September she was the old 'Chicot;' the woman whose portrait had flaunted on all the walls of London. Mr. Smolendo was in raptures. The broken leg was as sound as ever it had been. La Chicot would be able to dance early in November. A paragraph announcing this fact had already gone the round of the papers. Another paragraph, more familiar in tone, informed the town that Madame Chicot's beauty had gained new lustre during the enforced retirement of her long illness. Mr. Smolendo knew his public.

CHAPTER IX.

'AND ART THOU COME! AND ART THOU TRUE!'

It was late in November, and the trees were bare in the grounds of Hazlehurst Manor. The grand old mansion wore its air of grave dignity, under the dull grey skies of late autumn, but the charms and graces of summer had gone, and there was a shade of melancholy in the stillness of the house and garden, and that pleasant enclosure, too big for a meadow, and too small for a park, over which the rooks swept like a black cloud at evensong, going screaming home to their nests in the tall elms behind the house.

In this dreary season of the year Laura Malcolm was living quite alone at the Manor-house. Celia Clare had been invited to spend a month with a well-to-do aunt at Brighton, and Brighton in the winter season represented the highest form of terrestrial bliss that had ever come within Celia's experience. She had vague dreams of Paris, as of a city that must far surpass even Brighton in blissfulness; but she had no hope of seeing Paris, unless, indeed, she were to get married, when she would insist on her husband taking her there for the honeymoon.

'Of course, the poor creature would do anything I told him then,' said Celia; 'it would be different afterwards. I dare say when we had been married a year he would try to trample on me.'

'I can't imagine any one trampling upon you, Celia,' said Laura, laughing.

'Well, I think I should make it rather difficult for him. But all men are tyrants. Look at papa, for instance; the best of men, with a heart of gold; but let the cook make a failure, and he goes on all dinner-time like the veriest heathen. Oh, they are altogether an inferior breed, believe me. There is your young man, Laura—very handsome, very gentlemanlike, but as weak as water.'

'Whom do you mean by my young man?' asked Laura.

'You know, or you would not blush so violently. Of course I mean John Treverton, your future husband. And, by-the-bye, you are to be married within a year after old Mr. Treverton's death. I hope you have begun to order your trousseau.'

'I wish you would not talk such nonsense, Celia. You know very well that I am not engaged to Mr. Treverton. I may never be engaged to him.'

'Then what were you two talking about that night under the chestnuts, when you lingered so far behind us?'

'We are not engaged. That is quite enough for you to know.'

'Then if you are not engaged you ought to be. That is all I can say. It is ridiculous to leave things to the last moment, if you are ever so sure of each other. Old Mr. Treverton died early in January, and it is now late in November. I feel quite uncomfortable about going away and leaving your affairs in such an unsatisfactory state.'

Celia, who was the most frivolous of beings, affected a talent for business, and assumed an elder sister air towards Laura Malcolm that was pleasant in its absurdity.

'You need not be uneasy, Celia. I can manage my own affairs.'

'I don't believe you can. You are awfully clever, and have read more books than I have ever seen the outside of in the whole course of my life. But you are not the least little bit practical or business-like. You run the risk of losing this dear old house, and the estate that belongs to it, as coolly as if it were the veriest trifle. I begin to be afraid that you have a sneaking kindness for that worthless brother of mine.'

'You need have no such fear. I feel kindly towards your brother for auld lang syne, and because I think he likes me——'

'As well as he can afford to like anybody, taking into account the small residue of affection that remains over and above his great re-gard for himself,' interjected Celia, contemptuously.

'But I have no feeling for him warmer than a commonplace friendship. I never shall have.'

'Poor Ted! I am sorry for his sake, but I am very glad for yours.'

Celia went off to Brighton radiant with three trunks and two bonnet-boxes, and the Manor-house sank suddenly into silence and gloom. Celia's small frivolities were often troublesome, but her perennial gaiety of temper had pleasantly enlivened the spacious un-peopled house. Her fun was a mere school-girl's fun, perhaps, at best, but it was genuine, the spontaneous outcome of animal spirits and a happy disposition. Celia would have chatted as merrily over a cup of tea and a herring in a garret at five shillings a week, as amidst the fleshpots of Hazlehurst Manor. She was a joyous, im-provident, idle creature, with the unreasoning love of life for its own sake which makes a Neapolitan beggar happy in the sunshine, and an English gipsy contented under the low arch of his canvas tent, on the patch of waste grass by the wayside, whence he may be driven at any moment by a relentless constable.

Celia was gone, and Laura had ample leisure for serious meditation. In the first few days she was glad to be alone, to be free to think her own thoughts, to have no fear of encountering the keen glance of Celia's penetrating eyes; not to see that canary head, perched on one side with an air of insufferable knowingness. Then, after a little while, a deep melancholy crept over her spirits, a bitter sense of disappointment, which she could not banish from her mind.

She had never forgotten that long leave-taking in the avenue. Surely, if anything could mean an engagement, the words spoken then, the kiss taken then, meant the most solemn engagement. Yet since that night six months had passed and John Treverton had made no sign. And in all that time his image had but rarely been absent from her thoughts. Day after day, hour after hour, she had expected to see him enter the garden unannounced, as when she had seen him from the yew tree archway, standing looking quietly round him at the spring flowers and the smiling sunny lawn, where the shadows of the trees came and went like living things, where the earliest bees were humming, and the first of the butterflies skimming over beds of red and yellow tulips.

She had seen him every day during his last visit to the Sampsons, and that one week of friendly companionship had brought them very near together. In all that time he had said no word about the curious position which they occupied towards each other, and she had admired the delicacy of mind to which she ascribed this reticence. It seemed to her that no word ought to be said till the final word which fulfilled Jasper Treverton's wish and united their two destinies for ever. And Laura saw no reason why that word should not be spoken in due time. She fancied that John Treverton liked her. He was somewhat fitful in his spirits during that week of sun and shower, variable as the weather; at times wildly gay, capping Celia's maddest joke with one still madder; on other occasions lapsing into gloom, which provoked Celia to protest that he must have committed a murder in his early youth, and that the memory of his crime was haunting him.

'Just like Eugene Aram,' she had said; 'now positively, Laura, he is like Eugene Aram; and I feel convinced that somebody's bones are bleaching in a cave ready to be put together like the pieces of a puzzle, and to appear against him at the predestined moment. Don't marry him, Laura, I'm sure there is some dreadful burden on his conscience.'

They had been infinitely happy together in the most artless fashion, with the unthinking gladness of children whose calculations never travel beyond the present moment. Perhaps it was the delicious April weather, which spread a warm glaze of sunny yellow over the earth, and bathed the young leaves in vivid light, and painted the sky an Italian blue, and set the blackbirds and throstles singing from an hour before sunrise to an hour after sundown. This might in itself be enough for happiness. And then there was youth, a treasure so rich that none of us have ever learned to measure its value till we have lost it; when we look back and lament it, as perhaps, after all is said, the dearest of all those dear friends we have buried; for was it not this which made those others so deeply dear?

Whatever the cause, those three, and more especially those two, had been happy. And yet after that week of innocent intimacy, after that parting kiss, John Treverton had remained away for more than half a year, and not by so much as a letter had he assured Laura that she still held a place in his heart and mind.

She thought of him now with bitterest self-reproach. She was angry with herself for having let her heart go out to him, for having made the tacit engagement involved in that farewell kiss.

'After all it is only the fortune he cares about,' she said to herself, 'and after my foolishness that night he fancies himself so secure of me that he can stay in London and enjoy life in his own way, and then come and claim me at the last moment, just in time to fulfil the conditions of his cousin's will. He is making the most of his last year of liberty. He will have no more of me than the law obliges him to have. The year has nearly gone, and he has given me one little week of his society. A cool lover, certainly. A hypocrite, too, for he puts on looks and tones that seemed like deepest, strongest love. A gratuitous hypocrisy,' pursued Laura, lashing herself to sharper scorn, 'for I implored him to be frank with me. I offered him a loyal, friendly alliance. But he is a man, and I suppose it is man's nature to be false. He preferred to declare himself my lover, forgetting that his conduct would belie his words. I will never forgive him. I will never forgive myself for being so easily deceived. The estate shall go to the hospital. If he were here to-morrow, kneeling at my feet, I would refuse him. I know the hollowness of his pretended love. He cannot fool me a second time.'

She had never been vain of her beauty. The secluded life she had led with her adopted father had left her simple as a cloistered nun in all her thoughts and habits. Edward Clare had told her that she was lovely, many times, and had praised her loveliness in his verses, with all the affectation, and some of the license of that new school of poets of which he was an obscure member; but Laura had received all

95

such praises as the effervescence of the poet's frothy intellect rather than as a just tribute to her charms. Now, full of anger against John Treverton, she looked in her glass one winter night and wondered if she were really beautiful.

Yes, if the Guido in the dining-room below was beautiful—if features of purest modelling, dark hazel eyes, and a clear complexion faintly flushed with delicate carnation—if sculptured eyelids darkly fringed, a mouth half sad, half scornful, and dimples that showed momentarily in the mockery of a self-contemptuous smile—if these meant beauty, Laura Malcolm was assuredly beautiful. She was too true an artist not to know that this was beauty which smiled at her bitterly from the darkness of the glass.

'Perhaps I am not his style,' she said, with a little laugh. 'I have heard Edward Clare say that of girls I have praised. "Yes, she is very well, but not my style," as if Providence ought to have had him in view whenever it created a pretty woman. "Not my style," Edward would drawl languidly, as much as to say, "and therefore a failure."'

Every idea of John Treverton now remaining in Laura's mind was a thought of bitterness. She was so angry with him that she could not give him credit for one worthy act or one honourable feeling. As nearly as a soul so generous could hate did she now approach to the sin of hatred.

This was her mood one day in the beginning of December, indeed, it had been her mood always for the last three months; but in the leisure of her late solitude her anger had intensified. This was her mood as she walked in the garden, in the cold sunshine, looking at the pale prim faces of the fading chrysanthemums,—the perky china asters lending the last touch of bright colour to the dying year—the languorous late roses, flaunting their sickly beauty, like ball-room belles who refused to bow their heads to the sentence of time. It was a morning of unusual mildness: the arrow-point of the old-fashioned vane pointed south-west; the leaves of the evergreen oaks were scarcely ruffled by the wind; the tall Scotch firs, red and rugged columns topped by masses of swart foliage, stood darkly out against a calm, clear sky.

This garden was Laura's chief delight in her loneliness. God had gifted her with that deep and abiding love of nature, which is perhaps one of His richest gifts. They who possess it can never be utterly joyless.

She had walked in garden and orchard for more than an hour, when she came back by the old yew tree arch, and just in the spot where she had seen him more than half a year ago, she saw John Treverton standing again to-day.

What an unstable thing is a woman's anger against the man she loves! Laura's first feeling at sight of John Treverton was indignation. She was on the point of receiving him with crushing politeness, of freezing him with coldest courtesy, when she perceived that he looked ill and careworn, and was gazing at her with eyes full of yearning tenderness. Then she forgot her wrongs in one moment, and went up to him and gave him her hand, saying gently,—

'What have you been doing with yourself all this time?'

'Knocking about London, doing very little good for myself or any one else,' he answered frankly.

Then he seemed to lose himself in the delight of being with her. He walked by her side, saying never a word, only looking at her with fond, admiring eyes; as if she had come upon him suddenly, like a revelation of hitherto unknown loveliness and delight.

At last he found a voice, but not for any brilliant utterance.

'Are you really just a little glad to see me again?' he asked. 'Remember, you promised me a welcome.'

'You have been in no haste to claim the fulfilment of my promise. It was made more than six months ago. You have had other welcomes in the meanwhile, no doubt, and have forgotten all about Hazlehurst Manor.'

'The Manor-house, and she who occupies it, have never been absent from my thoughts.'

'Really; and yet you have stayed away so long. That looks rather like forgetfulness.'

'It was not forgetfulness. There have been reasons—reasons I cannot explain.'

'And do they no longer exist?'

'No,' he gave a long sigh, 'they are at an end now.'

'You have been ill perhaps,' speculated Laura, looking at him with a solicitude she could not wholly conceal.

'I have been far from well. I have been working rather harder than usual. I have to earn my bread, you know, Laura.'

'Have you any profession now that you have left the army?' asked Laura.

'I left the army six years ago. I have managed to live by my own labour since that time. My career has been a chequered one. I have lived partly by art, partly by literature, and have not succeeded in winning a name in either profession. That does not sound a brilliant account, does it? Its only merit is truth. I am nobody. Your generosity and my cousin Jasper's will may make me somebody. My fate depends on you.'

This was hardly the tone of a lover. It was a tone that Laura's pride would have resented had she not inwardly believed that John Treverton loved her. There is a subtle power in the love which keeps silence mightier than all love's eloquence. A hand that trembles when it touches another, one swift look from loving eyes, a sigh, a tone, will tell more than an oration. John Treverton was the most reticent of lovers, yet his reserve did not offend Laura.

They went into the grave old house together, and sat down to luncheon, *tête-à-tête*, waited upon by Trimmer, the old butler, who had lived more than thirty years with Jasper Treverton, and had lifted Laura out of the carriage when his master brought her to the manor a delicate child, looking wistfully round at strange objects with wide-opened eyes.

'They looked just for all the world like man and wife,' said Trimmer, when he went back to his pantry, 'and I hope before long it'll be that. They'll make a fine couple, and I'm sure they're fond o' one another already.'

'It isn't in Miss Laura to marry a man she wasn't fond of, not for all the fortunes in Christendom,' retorted Mrs. Trimmer, who had been cook and housekeeper nearly as long as her husband had been butler.

'Well, if I was a young woman I'd marry a'most anybody rather than I'd lose such a 'ome as Hazlehurst Manor,' answered Trimmer. 'I ain't a money-grubber, but a good 'ome ain't to be trifled with. And if they don't marry, and the estate goes to build a norsepital, what's to become of you and me? Some folks in our position would be all agog for setting up in the public line and making our fortunes, but I've seen more fortunes lost than won that way, and I know when I'm well off. Good wages paid reg'lar, and everything found for me, is all I ask.'

After luncheon Laura and John went for a walk in the grounds. A mutual inclination led them to the shrubbery where they had parted that April night. The curving avenue of good old trees made a pleasant walk even at this season, when not a green leaf was left, and the ragged crows' nests showed black amidst the delicate tracery of the topmost branches. The air was even milder than in the morning. It might have been an afternoon early in October. John Treverton stopped in front of the rugged trunk of the great chestnut under which Laura and he had parted. The young leaves had made a canopy of shade that night; now the big branches stood out dark and bare, stained with moss and weather. The grass at the foot of the tree was strewn with green husks and broken twigs, dead leaves and shining brown nuts.

'I think it was at this spot we parted,' said John. 'Do you remember?'

'I have a vague recollection that it was somewhere about here,' Laura answered, carelessly.

She knew the spot to an inch, but was not going to admit as much.

He took her hand, and drew it gently through his arm, as if they were starting upon a pilgrimage somewhere, then bent his head and kissed the delicate bare hand—a lovely tapering hand that could only belong to a lady, a hand which was in itself something for a lover to adore.

'Darling, when are we to be married?' he asked softly, almost in a whisper, as if an unspeakable shyness took hold of him at that critical moment.

'What a question!' cried Laura, with pretended astonishment. 'Who has ever talked about marriage? You have never asked me to be your wife.'

'Did I not? But I asked you if you were angry with your adopted father for his will, and you said No. That was as much as to say you were content we should gratify the good old man's wish. And we can only do so by becoming man and wife. Laura, I love you more than I can ever say, and loving you as I do, though I am conscious of many shortcomings—yes, though I know myself in many respects unworthy to be your husband—a pauper—unsuccessful—without name or fame—less than nobody—still, darling, I fall upon my knees here, at your feet; I, who never knelt to a woman before, and have too seldom knelt to my God, and sue to you in *forma pauperis*. Perhaps in all England there lives no man less worthy to be your husband, save for the one merit of loving you with all his heart and soul.'

He was kneeling before her, bareheaded, at the foot of the old chestnut tree, among the rugged roots that curved in and out amidst the grass. Laura bent down, and touched his forehead with her lips. It was hardly a kiss. The sweet lips fluttered on his forehead for an instant and were gone. No butterfly's wing was ever lighter.

'I will take you, dear,' she said gently, 'with all your faults, whatever their number. I have a feeling that I can trust you—all the more, perhaps, because you do not praise yourself. We will try to do our duty to each other, and to our dead benefactor, and to use his wealth nobly, shall we not, John?'

'*You* will use it, nobly, love; you can do nothing that is not noble,' he answered, gravely.

He was pale to the lips, and there was no gladness in his look, though it was full of love.

CHAPTER X.

ENGAGED.

John Treverton stayed at the Manor-house till after dark, alone with his betrothed, and happier than he had ever been in his life. Yes, happy, though it was with a desperate happiness as of a child plucking wild flowers on the sunny edge of an abyss. He must have been something less or more than human if he had not been happy in Laura Malcolm's company to-day, as they sat by the fire in the gloaming, side by side, her head leaning against his shoulder, his arm round her waist, her dark eyes hidden under drooping lids as they gazed dreamily downward at the smouldering logs; the room lit dimly by the fire-glow, grotesque shadows coming and going on the wall behind them, like phantom forms of good or evil angels hovering near them as they sat face to face with fate, the one unconscious of all danger, the other reckless and defiant.

Now that the word had been spoken, that they two were pledged to each other to the end of life, Laura let her heart go out to her lover without reserve. She was not afraid to let him see her fondness. She did not seek to make her love more precious to him by simulated coldness. She gave him all her heart and soul, as Juliet gave herself to Romeo. Lips that had never breathed a word of love, now murmured sweetest words in his ear; eyes that had never looked into a lover's eyes, gazed and lost themselves in the depths of his. Never was lover more innocently or unreservedly adored. If he had been boastful or self-assertive, Laura's pride would have taken alarm. But his deep humility, and a shadow of melancholy which hung over him even when he seemed happiest, asked for her pity; and a woman is never better pleased with her lover than when he has need of her compassion.

'And do you really love me, Laura?' he asked, his face bent over the beautiful head which seemed to have found so natural a resting-place upon his shoulder. 'If there had been no such thing as my cousin Jasper's will, and you and I had met in the outside world, do you think I am the man your heart would have chosen?'

'That is too abstruse a question in metaphysics,' she answered, laughingly. 'I only know that my heart chose you, and that papa's will—I must call him by the old name—did not influence my choice. Don't you think that is quite enough for you to know?'

'It is all I desire to know, my loveliest. Or not quite all. I should like to know—out of mere idle curiosity—when you first began to think me not altogether despicable.'

'Do you want the history of the case from the very beginning?'

'From the eggs to the apples, from the very first instant when your heart began to beat a little more kindly for me than for all the rest of the world.'

'I will tell you——'

She paused, and looked up at him with a smile of innocent coquetry.

'Yes, dearest.'

'When you have told me the history of your life, from the instant when I became more to you than the common herd of women.'

His first answer was a deep sigh.

'Ah, dear love, my case was different. I struggled against my passion.'

'Why?'

'Because I felt myself unworthy of you.'

'That was foolish.'

'No, dear, it was wise and right. You are like a happy child, Laura; your past is a blank page, it has no dark secrets——'

He felt her trembling as he spoke. Had his words frightened her? Did she begin to divine the dangers that hemmed him around?

'Dearest, I don't want to alarm you; but in the past experience of a man of my age there is generally one page he would give ten years of his life to cancel. I have a dark page. Oh, my love, my love, if I felt myself really worthy of you my heart would hardly hold my happiness. It would break with too great a joy. Men's hearts have so broken. When did I begin to love you? Why, on the night I first entered this house—the cheerless winter night, when I came, like the prodigal son, weary of the husks and the stye, vaguely yearning for some better life. Your thrilling eyes, your grave, sweet smile, your tender voice, came upon me like the revelation of a new world, in which womanhood meant goodness and purity and truth. My senses were as yet unmoved by your beauty; my mind reverenced your goodness. You were no more to me than a picture in a gallery, but you thrilled my soul as the picture might have done; you awakened new thoughts, you opened a door into heaven. Yes, Laura, admiration, reverence, worship, those began on the first night. Before I left Hazlehurst, worship had warmed into passionate love.'

'Yet you stayed away from January to April!'

'My absence was one long conflict with my love.'

'And from April to December—after——'

'After you had shown me your heart, dear love, and I knew that you might be mine. That last absence needed a more desperate courage. Well, I came back, you see. Love was stronger than wisdom.'

'Why must it be unwise for us to love each other?'

'Only because of my unworthiness.'

'Then we will forget your unworthiness, or, if your modesty likes better, I will love you and your unworthiness too. I do not suppose you a faultless paragon, John. Papa told me that you had been extravagant and foolish. You will not be extravagant and foolish any more, will you, dear, when you are a sober married man?'

'No, love.'

'And we will both strive to do all the good we can with our large fortune.'

'You shall be the chief disposer of it.'

'No, no, I would not have it so on any account. You must be lord and master. I shall expect you to be quite the ideal country squire, the sun and centre of our little universe, the general benefactor. I will be your prime minister and adviser, if you like. I know all the poor people for ten miles round, on our estate, and on other people's land. I know their wants and their weaknesses. Yes, John, I think I can help you in doing much good; in making improvements that will not ruin you, and will make the lives of the labouring people much happier.'

> *'Being your slave, what should I do but tend*
> *Upon the hours and times of your desire?*
> *I have no precious time at all to spend,*
> *Nor services to do, till you require,'*

quoted John, tenderly. 'Can I ever be happier than in obeying you?'

'Do you know that it will be a great happiness to me not to leave the Manor,' said Laura, presently. 'You must not think me mercenary, or that I value a big house and a large fortune. It is not so, John. I could live quite contentedly on the income papa left me, more than contentedly, in a cottage with you; but I love the Manor for its own sake. I know every tree in the grounds, and have watched them all growing, and sketched and painted them until I almost know the form of every branch. And I have lived so long in these old rooms that I doubt if any other rooms would ever look like home. It is a dear old house, is it not, John? Will you not be very proud when you are the master of it?'

'I shall be very proud of my wife when I can dare to call her mine. That will be pride enough for me,' answered John, drawing her a little nearer to his heart. 'And now, I suppose I ought to go and see Sampson, and tell him that everything is definitely settled. When are we to be married, love? My cousin died on the 20th of January. We ought not to delay our marriage longer than the end of this month.'

'Let us be married on the last day of the month,' said Laura. 'It is the most solemn day in all the year. We shall never forget the anniversary of our wedding if it is on that day.'

'I should never forget it in any case,' answered John Treverton. 'Let it be on that day, love. The closing year shall unite me to you for life. I shall see Mr. Clare to-night, and arrange everything.'

They were a long time saying 'Good-bye,' and just at the last John Treverton suggested that Laura should put on her hat and jacket and walk to the gates with him, so the first 'Good-bye' was wasted trouble. They were a long time walking to the gates, and the early winter night had come, and the stars were shining when they reluctantly parted. Laura tripped along the avenue with as light a foot as Juliet's when she came to the friar's cell to be married; John Treverton went slowly down the road towards Hazlehurst village, with his head bent upon his breast, and all the joy faded out of his face.

He found Mr. Sampson and his sister just sitting down to dinner, and was welcomed with enthusiasm by both.

'Upon my soul, you're a most extraordinary fellow,' exclaimed the lawyer, after a good deal of handshaking. 'You run off in no end of a hurry, promising to come back in a week or two at latest, and for six months we see no more of you; and you don't even favour your family solicitor with a line to say why you don't come. There are not many men in England who would play fast and loose with such chances as yours. Your cousin, when he made that curious will of his, told me you had been wild, but I was not prepared for such wildness as this.'

'Really, Tom,' remonstrated Miss Sampson, blushing the salmon pink peculiar to sandy-haired beauty, 'you have no right to talk to Mr. Treverton like that.'

'Yes, I have,' answered Sampson, who prided himself on his open manner—his 'bonnomy,' as he called it; 'I have the right given me by a genuine interest in his affairs—the interest of a friend rather than a lawyer. You don't suppose it's for the sake of the six-and-eightpences I take so much upon myself, Lizzie? No, it is because I have a sincere regard for my old client's kinsman, and a disinterested anxiety for his welfare.'

'I think you may make your mind easy about me,' said John, without any appearance of elation; 'I am going to be married on the last day of this month, and I want you to prepare the settlement.'

'Bravo!' cried Tom Sampson, flourishing his napkin; 'I'm almost as glad as if I'd backed the winner of the double event and woke up to find myself worth twenty thousand pounds. My dear fellow, I congratulate you. The Hazlehurst property is a good eight thousand a year. There's three thousand in ground rents in Beechampton, and your dividends from railways and consols bring your income to a clean fourteen thousand.'

'If Miss Malcolm were penniless, I should be as proud of winning her as I am now,' said John, gravely.

'That's a very gentlemanlike way of looking at it,' exclaimed the lawyer, as much as to say, 'We know all about it; you are bound to say that kind of thing.'

Miss Sampson looked down at her plate, and felt that appetite was gone for ever. It was foolishness, no doubt, to feel so keen a pang; but girlhood is prone to foolishness, and Eliza Sampson had not yet owned to thirty. She had known from the first that John Treverton was to marry Laura Malcolm, and yet she had allowed herself to indulge in secret worship at his shrine. He was handsome and attractive, and Miss Sampson had seen so few young men who were either one or the other, that she may be forgiven for fixing her young unhackneyed affection on the first distinguished stranger who came within the narrow orbit of her colourless life.

She had lived under the same roof with him; she had handed him his coffee in the morning, his tea—ah, how carefully creamed and sugared!—in the evening. She had studied his tastes, and catered for him with unfailing care. She had played Rosellen's Reverie in G for his delectation every evening during his two visits. She had sung his favourite ballads, and if her voice sometimes failed her on the high notes, she made up in pathos what she wanted in power. These things are not easily to be forgotten by a youthful mind fed upon three-volume novels, and naturally prone to sentiment.

'Our wedding will be a very quiet affair,' said John Treverton, presently; 'Laura wishes it to be so, and I am of her mind. I shall be glad if you will kindly refrain from talking about it to anyone, Sampson, and you too, Miss Sampson. We don't want to be objects of interest in the village.'

'I will be as dumb as a skin of parchment,' answered the lawyer, 'and I know that Eliza will be the soul of discretion.'

Eliza looked up shyly at their guest, her white eyelashes quivering with emotion.

'I ought to congratulate you, Mr. Treverton,' she faltered, 'but it is all so sudden, so startling, that I can hardly find words.'

'My dear Miss Sampson, I know your friendly feeling towards me,' John answered, with tranquil good-nature.

Oh, how cool he was, how cruelly indifferent to her feelings! And yet he ought to have known! Had Rosellen's Reverie, with the soft pedal down, said nothing?

Later in the evening John Treverton and his host smoked their cigars *tête-à-tête* in Mr. Sampson's office, beside the comfortable hearth, by which the lawyer was fonder of sitting than in his sister's highly decorated drawing-room, among the starched antimacassars, and chairs that were not to be sat on, and foot-stools that were intended for anything rather than the accommodation of the human foot. This unsociable habit of spending his evenings aloof from the family circle Mr. Sampson excused on the plea of business.

The two men sat opposite each other for some time in friendly silence, John Treverton gravely meditative, Mr. Sampson in an agreeable frame of mind. He was congratulating himself on the prospect of retaining his position as agent for the Treverton Estate, which profitable stewardship must have been lost to him if John Treverton had been so besotted in his folly as to forfeit his heritage by refusing to comply with the conditions of his kinsman's will.

'I want fully to understand my position,' said John, presently. 'Am I free to make what settlement I please upon my future wife?'

'You are free to settle anything which you at present possess,' answered the lawyer.

'My present possessions amount to something less than a five-pound note.'

'Then I don't think we need talk about a marriage settlement. By the terms of your cousin's will his estate is to be held in trust for a twelvemonth. If within that time you shall have married Miss Malcolm, the estate will pass into your possession at the end of the year. You can then make a post-nuptial settlement, on as liberal a scale as you please; but you cannot give away what you do not possess.'

'I see. It must be a post-nuptial settlement. Well, you may as well take my instructions at once. You can rough-draft the settlement, submit your draft to counsel, have it engrossed and ready for execution upon the day on which I pass into possession of the property.'

'You are in a desperate hurry,' said Sampson, smiling at his client's grave eagerness.

'Life is full of desperate uncertainties. I want the welfare of the woman I love to be assured, whatever fate may be mine.'

'That is a generous forethought rare in lovers. However intensely they may love in the present, their love seldom takes the form of solicitude for the beloved one's future. Hence generation after generation of penniless widows and destitute children. After me the deluge, is your lover's motto. Well, Mr. Treverton, what do you propose to settle on your wife in this post-nuptial deed?'

'The entire estate, real and personal,' answered John Treverton, quietly.

Mr. Sampson dropped his cigar, and sat transfixed, an image of half-amused astonishment.

'This bangs Banagher;' he exclaimed, 'you must be mad.'

'No, I am only reasonable,' answered Treverton. 'The estate was left to me nominally, to Laura Malcolm actually. What was I to the testator? A blood relation, truly, but a stranger. At the time he made that will he had never seen my face; what little he had ever heard of me must have been to my disadvantage; for my life has been one long mistake, and I have given no man reason to sing my praises. What was Laura to him? His adopted daughter, the beloved and the affectionate companion of his declining years; his faithful nurse, his disinterested slave. Whatever love he had to give must have been given to her. She had grown up by his hearth. She had sweetened and cheered his lonely life. He left his estate to me, in trust for her; so that he might keep his oath, and yet leave his wealth where his heart prompted him to bestow it. He found in me a convenient instrument for the carrying out of his wishes; and I have reason to be proud that he was not unwilling to trust me with such a charge, to give me the being he held dearest. I shall settle the whole of the estate on my wife, Sampson. I consider myself bound in honour to do so.'

Mr. Sampson looked at his client with a prolonged and searching gaze, a slow smile dawning on his somewhat stolid countenance.

'Don't be offended at my asking the question,' he said. 'Are you in debt?'

'I don't owe sixpence. I have lived a somewhat Bohemian life, but I have not lived upon other people's money.'

'I am glad to hear that,' said Sampson, selecting a fresh cigar from a comfortably-filled case, 'because if you imagine that by such a settlement as you propose you could escape the payment of any debts now existing you are mistaken. A man can make no settlement to the injury of his creditors. As regards future liability the case would be different, and if you were deeply involved in commerce, a speculator, I could understand your desire to shift the estate from your own shoulders to your wife's. But as it is——'

'Can't you understand something not strictly commercial?' exclaimed John Treverton, waxing impatient. 'Can't you understand that I want to obey the spirit as well as the letter of my cousin Jasper's will? I want to make his adopted daughter the actual mistress of the estate, in the same position she would have naturally occupied had he never made that foolish vow.'

'In so doing you make yourself a pensioner on her bounty.'

'So be it. I am content to occupy that position. Come, my dear Sampson, we need not argue the question any further. If you won't draw up the form of settlement I want, I must find a lawyer who will.'

'My dear sir,' cried Tom Sampson, briskly, 'when a client of mine is obstinately bent upon making a fool of himself, I always see him through his folly. He had better make a fool of himself in my hands than in anyone else's. I do not suffer by the loss of his business, and I am vain enough to believe that he suffers less than he would if he took his business to any other office. If you have quite made up your mind, I am ready to rough-draft any form of settlement you dictate; but I am bound to warn you that the dictation of such a settlement is a qualification for Bedlam.'

'I will risk even as much as that. Nobody need know anything about the settlement but you and I, and, later, my wife. I shall not speak of it to her until it is ready for execution.'

Mr. Sampson, in a chronic state of wonder, took half a quire of slippery blue foolscap, and began his draft, with a very squeaky quill pen and a large consumption of ink. Simple and uniform as the gift was which John Treverton wished to make to his wife, the transfer of it required to be hedged round and intertwined with so much legal phraseology that Tom Sampson had consumed his half-quire of foolscap before he came to the end of the draft. The estate had to be scheduled, and every homestead and labourer's cottage had to be described in a phrase of abstract grandeur, as 'all that so and so, commonly known as so and so,' and so forth, with almost maddening iteration. John Treverton, smoking his cigar, and letting his thoughts wander away at a tangent every now and then to regions that were not always paths of pleasantness, thought his host would never leave off driving that inexorable quill—the sort of pen to sign a death-warrant and feel none the worse for it—over the slippery paper.

'Come,' exclaimed Sampson, at last, 'I think that ties the estate up pretty tightly on your wife and her children after her. She can squander the income as she pleases, and play old gooseberry up to a certain point, but she can't put the tip of her little finger on the principal. And now you have only to name two responsible men as trustees.'

'I don't know two respectable men in the world,' said John, frankly.

'Yes, you do. You know the vicar of this parish, and you know me. Your cousin Jasper considered us worthy to be trustees to his will. You need hardly be afraid to make us trustees to your marriage settlement.'

'I have no objection, and I certainly know no better men.'

'Then we'll consider it settled. I'll send the deed to counsel by to-morrow's post. I hope you quite understand that this settlement will make you a pauper—wholly dependent upon your wife. If you were to throw yourself on the parish, she would have to maintain you. Bar that, she may use you as badly as she likes.'

'I am not afraid of her ill-usage.'

'Upon my honour and conscience,' mused Thomas Sampson, as he laid himself down to rest that night. 'I believe John Treverton is over head and ears in love with Miss Malcolm. Nothing but love or lunacy can explain his conduct. Which is it? Well, perhaps the line that divides the two is only a distinction without a difference.'

CHAPTER XI.

NO TROUSSEAU.

Laura was utterly happy in the brief interval between her betrothal and her wedding. She had given her love and trust unreservedly, feeling that duty and love went hand in hand. In following
the inclination of her heart she was obeying the behest of her benefactor. She had been very fond of Jasper Treverton, had loved him
as truly as ever daughter loved a father. It seemed the most natural process to transfer her love from the adopted father to his young
kinsman. The old man in his grave was the bond of union between
the girl and her lover.

'How pleased papa would have been if he could have known that
John and I would be so fond of each other,' she said to herself, innocently.

Celia Clare hurried back from Brighton, eager to assist her friend
at this momentous crisis of her life.

'Brighton was quite too delightful,' said Celia, 'but not for
worlds would I be absent from you at such a time. Poor soul, what
would you have done without me?'

'Dear Celia, you know how fond I am of you, but I think I could
really have managed to get married without your assistance.'

'Get married! Yes, but how would you have done it?' cried
Celia, making her eyes very round and big. 'You would have made a
most horrid muddle of it. Now, what about your trousseau? I'll wa-
ger you have hardly thought of it.'

'There you are wrong. I have ordered two travelling dresses, and
a handsome dinner dress.'

'And your collars and cuffs, your handkerchiefs, your peignoirs,
your camisoles,' pursued Celia, enumerating a string of articles.

'My dear child, do you suppose I have lived all these years without cuffs and collars, and handkerchiefs?'

'Laura, unless you have everything new you might just as well
not be married at all.'

'Then you may consider my marriage no marriage, for I am not
troubling myself about new things.'

'Give me carte blanche and leave everything to me. What is the use of my sacrificing Brighton just when it was more than too en-chanting, unless I can be of some use to you?'

'Well, Celia, in order that you may not be unhappy, I will give you permission to review my wardrobe, and if you find an alarming dearth of collars and handkerchiefs I'll drive you to Beechampton in the pony carriage, and you shall buy whatever you think proper.'

'Beechampton is hideously behind the age, disgustingly *démodé*, and your things ought to be in the latest style. I'll look through the advertisements in the *Queen*, and send to London for patterns. It is no use having new things if they are not in the newest fashion. One does not wear out one's cuffs and collars—they go out.'

'You shall have carte blanche, dear, if it will atone for the loss of Brighton.'

'My dearest girl, you know I would not desert you at such a cri-sis of your life for forty Brightons,' cried Celia, who had lofty ideas about friendship; 'and now about your wedding gown? That is the most important point of all.'

'It is ordered.'

'You did not mention it just now.'

'Did I not? I am going to be married in one of the gowns I or-dered for travelling, a mixture of grey silk and velvet, the jacket trimmed with chinchilla. I think it will be very handsome.'

Celia fell back in her chair as if she were going to faint.

'No wedding gown!' she cried; 'no trousseau, and no wedding gown! This is indeed an ill-omened marriage! Well may poor Ed-ward talk.'

Laura flushed indignantly at this last sentence.

'Pray what has your brother been saying against my marriage?' she asked, haughtily.

'Well, dear, you cannot expect him to feel particularly pleasant about it, knowing—as you must know—how he has gone on doting upon you, and hoping against hope, for the last three years. I don't want to make you unhappy, but I must confess that Edward has a very bad opinion of Mr. Treverton.'

'I daresay Mr. Treverton will manage to exist without Edward's good opinion.'

'He thinks there is something so utterly mysterious in his con-duct—something insulting to you in the fact of his holding himself aloof so long, and then coming back at the last moment, just in time to secure the estate!'

'I am the best judge of Mr. Treverton's conduct,' answered Lau-ra, deeply wounded. 'If I can trust him other people may spare themselves the trouble of speculating upon his motives.'

'And you can trust him?' asked Celia, anxiously.

'With all my heart and soul.'

'Then have a proper wedding gown,' exclaimed Celia, as if the whole question of bliss or woe were involved in that one detail.

When next Miss Malcolm met Edward Clare there was a coolness in her greeting which the young man could not mistake.

'What have I done to offend you, Laura?' he asked, piteously.

'I am offended with everyone who doubts the honour of my future husband,' she answered.

'I'm sorry for that,' he said, gloomily. 'A man cannot help his thoughts.'

'A man can hold his tongue,' said Laura.

'Well, I will be silent henceforth. Good-bye.'

'Where are you going?'

'Anywhere, anywhere out of the world; that is to say out of this little world of Hazlehurst. I think I am going to London. I shall take a lodging close to the British Museum, and work hard at literature. It is time I made my mark.'

Laura thought so too. Edward had been talking of making his mark for the last five years, but the mark as yet was a very feeble one.

Next day he was gone, and Laura had a sense of relief in his absence.

Celia stayed at the Manor-house during the time before the wedding. She was always in attendance upon the lovers, drove with them, walked with them, sat by the fire with them at the cheery, dusky afternoon tea time, when those mysterious shadows that looked like guardian angels came and went upon the walls. John Treverton seemed to have no objection to Celia's company, he rather courted it, even. He was not an ardent lover, Celia thought; and yet it would have been difficult to doubt that he was deeply in love. Never since that first evening had Laura's head rested against his breast, never since then had he given full and unrestrained utterance to his passion. His manner was full of reverent affection; as if he respected his betrothed almost too deeply to be lavish in the expression of warmer feeling; as if she stood so high above him in his thoughts of her that love was a kind of worship.

'I think I should like a more demonstrative lover,' said Celia, with a critical air. 'Mr. Treverton is so awfully serious.'

'And now that you have seen more of him, Celia, are you still inclined to think that he is mercenary; that it is the estate and not me he cares for?' asked Laura, with no fear as to the answer.

'No, dear, I honestly believe that he adores you, that he is dreadfully, desperately, almost despairingly, in love with you,' answered Celia, very seriously, 'but still he is not my style of lover. He is too melancholy.'

Laura had no answer to this objection. As the days had hurried on towards the end of this eventful year her lover's spirits had assuredly not grown lighter. He was full of thought, curiously absent-minded at times. She, too, grew grave in sympathy with him.

'It is such a solemn crisis of our lives,' she thought. 'Sometimes I feel as if all things could not go happily to the end, as if something must happen to part us, at the very last, on the eve of our wedding day.'

The eve of the wedding came, and brought no calamity. It was a very quiet evening. The lovers dined together at the vicarage, and walked to the Manor-house afterwards, alone with each other, almost for the first time since the night of their betrothal. Everything had been arranged for to-morrow's wedding! Such a quiet wedding! No one had been invited except Mr. Sampson and his sister. The vicar's wife was to be present, of course. She would in a manner represent the bride's mother. Celia was to be the only bridesmaid. They were to be married by licence, and no one in the village had as yet any inkling of the event. The servants at the Manor-house had only been told the date of the marriage within the last two days, and had been forbidden to talk about it; and as they were old servants, who had long learned to identify themselves with 'the family,' they were not likely to disobey Miss Malcolm's orders.

The house, always the perfection of neatness, had been swept and garnished for this important occasion. The chintz covers had been taken off the chairs and sofas in the drawing-room, revealing tapestry wreaths and clusters of flowers, worked by Jasper Treverton's mother and aunts in a period of almost awful remoteness. The housekeeper had been baking her honest old face in front of a huge kitchen fire, while she stirred her jellies, and watched her custards, and turned her game pie. There was to be a breakfast fit for the grandest wedding, though Miss Malcolm had told Mrs. Trimmer that a very simple meal would be wanted.

'You mustn't deny me the pleasure of doing my best, at such a time,' urged the faithful servant. 'I should feel it a reproach to me all the rest of my life if I didn't. There shan't be no extravagance, Miss, but I must put a pretty breakfast on the table. I'm so glad our barberry bushes bore well this year. The berries make such a tasty garnish for cold dishes.'

Mrs. Trimmer was roasting herself and her poultry in the spacious old kitchen, at ten o'clock at night, while John and Laura were coming from the vicarage, arm in arm, Laura strangely glad to have him all to herself for one little half hour, he vexatiously silent. Celia was at the Manor-house, laid up with a headache and a new novel. She had excused herself from the dinner in her usual flippant style.

'Give them my love, and say I was too seedy to come,' she said. 'Going to dine with one's parents is quite too slow. I dined with them on Christmas Day, you know; and Christmas Day at the vicarage has always been the quintessence of dulness. The thing I wondered at most, when I came of age, was how I ever could have lived through twenty-one of our Christmases.'

They were thus, by happy accident, as Laura thought, alone together; and, behold! the lover, the bridegroom of to-morrow, had not a word to say.

'John,' Laura began softly at last, almost afraid to break this gloomy silence, 'there is one thing you have not told me, and yet it is what most girls in my position would call a very important matter.'

'What is that, dearest?'

'You have never told me where we are to spend our honeymoon. Celia has been worrying me with questions about our plans, and I have found it difficult to evade her. I did not like to confess my ignorance.'

A simple and a natural question surely, yet John Treverton started, as at the sharpest thrust that Fate could have at him.

'My dearest love—I—I have really not thought about it,' he answered, stumblingly. 'We will go anywhere you like. We will decide to-morrow, after the wedding.'

'Is not that a rather unusual mode of proceeding?' asked Laura, with a faint laugh.

She was somewhat wounded by this show of indifference as to the very first stage in their journey through life. She would have liked her lover to be full of wild schemes, to be eager to take her everywhere—to the Engadine, the Black Forest, the English Lakes, Killarney, the Trossachs—all in a breath.

'Are not all the circumstances of our marriage unusual?' he replied gravely. 'There is only one thing certain, there is only one thing sweet and sacred in the whole business—we love each other truly and dearly. That is certain, is it not, Laura?'

'On my side quite certain.'

'And on my side quite as certain as that I live and that I shall die.

114

Our love is deep and fixed, rooted in the very ground of our lives, is it not, Laura? Nothing, no stroke of time or fate can change it.'

'No stroke of time or fate can change my love for you,' she said, solemnly.

'That is all I want to know. That is the certainty which makes my soul glad and hopeful.'

'Why should it be otherwise? Were there ever two people more fortunate than you and I. My dear adopted father dies, leaving a will that might have made us both wretched, that might have tempted you to pretend a love you could not feel, me to give myself to a man I could not love. But instead of any such misery as that, we fall in love with each other, almost at first sight, and feel that Providence meant us for each other, and that we could be happy together in the deepest poverty?'

'Yes,' said John, meditatively, 'it is odd that my cousin Jasper should have been so sure we should suit each other.'

'There is a Providence in these things,' murmured Laura.

'If I could but think so,' said her lover, rather to himself than to her.

CHAPTER XII.

AN ILL-OMENED WEDDING.

The last day of the year, nature's dullest, dreariest interval between the richness of autumn and the fresh young beauty of spring. Not a flower in the prim old Manor-house garden, save a melancholy tea-rose, that looked white and wan under the dull grey sky, and a few pallid chrysanthemums, with ragged petals and generally deplorable aspect.

'What a miserable morning!' exclaimed Celia, shivering, as she looked out of Laura's dressing-room window at the sodden lawn and the glistening yew-tree hedge, beyond which stretched a dismal perspective of leafless apple-trees, and the tall black poplars that marked the boundary of the home pastures, where the pretty grey Jersey cows had such a happy time in spring and summer.

Laura and her companion were taking an early breakfast—a meal at which neither could eat—by the dressing-room fire. Both young women were in a state of nervous agitation, but while one was restless and full of talk, the other sat pale and silent, too deeply moved for any show of emotion.

'Drip, drip, drip,' cried Celia, pettishly, 'one of those odious Scotch mists, that is as likely to last for a week as for an hour. Nice draggle-tail creatures we shall look after we have walked up that long churchyard path under such rain as this. Well, really, Laura, don't think me unkind for saying so, but I do call this an ill-omened wedding.'

'Do you?' said Laura, with a faint smile. 'Do you really suppose that it will make any difference to my future life whether I am married on a rainy day or on a fine one? I rather like the idea of going out of the dulness into the sunshine, for I know our wedded life will be full of sunshine.'

'How confident you are!' exclaimed Celia, wonderingly.

'What have I to fear? We love each other dearly. How can we fail to be happy?'

'That's all very well, but I should have been easier in my mind if you had had a wedding gown. Think how awkward it will be, by-and-by, when you are asked to dinner parties. As a bride you will be expected to appear in ivory satin and orange blossoms. People will hardly believe in you.'

'How many dinner parties are likely to be given within ten miles of Hazlehurst during the next six months?' asked Laura.

'Not many, I admit,' sighed Celia. 'One might as well live on the Gold Coast, or at some remote station in Bengal. Of course, papa and mamma will give a dinner in your honour, and Miss Sampson will ask you to tea. Oh, Miss Sampson's teas, with the tea and coffee handed round on an electro-plated salver, and Rosellen's Reverie in G on the cracked old piano, and *vingt et un* at the loo-table, and anchovy sandwiches, blanc-mange, and jelly to wind up the wild dissipations of the evening. Then there are the county families, bounded on the east by Sir Joshua Parker, and on the north by the Dowager Lady Barker. You will have stately calls from them. Lady Barker will regret that she has left off giving dinner parties since her lamented husband's death. Lady Parker will square accounts by sending you a card for a garden party next July.'

This conversation took place at half-past eight. At ten the two girls were dressed and ready to drive to the church. Laura looked lovely in her grey silk travelling dress, and grey Gainsborough hat, with its drooping ostrich plume.

'One thing I can honestly say, from the bottom of my heart,' exclaimed Celia, and Laura turned to her with a smile, expecting to hear something interesting; 'you have out and away the handsomest ostrich feather I ever saw in my life. You may leave it to me in your will if you like. I'm sure I took trouble enough to get it; and you ought to be grateful to me for getting your hat to match your gown so exactly.'

And now they are driving along the muddy road, between bare ranks of dark and dripping trees, and under as dull and colourless a sky as ever roofed in Hazlehurst. The old church, with its queer corners and darksome side-aisles, its curious gallery pews in front of the organ, something like boxes at a theatre, where the aristocracy sit in privileged retirement, its hatchments, its old-fashioned pulpit, reading-desk, and clerk's desk, its faded crimson cushions and draperies—a church which the restorer's hand has never improved, for whose adornment no devout ladies have toiled and striven, the dull old-world parish church of the last century—looked its darkest and gloomiest to-day. Not even the presence of youth and beauty could brighten and enliven it.

John Treverton, and Mr. Sampson, who was to give the bride away, were the last to arrive. The bridegroom was deadly pale, and the smile with which he met his bride, though full of fondest love, was wanting in gladness. Celia performed her duty as bridesmaid in a business-like way, worthy of the highest praise. Mr. Clare read the service deliberately and well, the pale bridegroom spoke out manfully when his time came; nor did Laura's low voice falter when she pronounced the words that sealed her fate.

The wedding breakfast was quietly cheerful. That the bridegroom should have very little to say, and that the bride should be pale and thoughtful, surprised no one. The vicar and the lawyer were in excellent spirits; Celia's lively tongue chimed in at every opportunity. Mrs. Clare was full of friendly anticipations about what the young couple would do when they settled down. The dull, damp morning had sharpened people's appetites, and there was a good deal said in praise of the game pie and the truffled turkey; while the old wines that had been brought forth, mantled in cobwebs, from the dark recesses of Jasper Treverton's cellar, were good enough to evolve faint flashes of wit from the most sluggish brain. Thus the wedding breakfast, which had the air of a small family gathering, went off pleasantly enough.

The bride and bridegroom were not to start on their travels till after dark. They were going northward by the mail, on their way to Dover.

Very little had been said about the honeymoon. It was only vaguely understood that John Treverton and his wife were going to the South of France. The vicar had to hurry off soon after breakfast, to read the funeral service over the coffin of a venerable parishioner, and the rest of the company took his departure as a signal to disperse. There was nothing to detain them. This marriage was not as other marriages. There were to be no evening revels, there was no dazzling array of wedding gifts to stare at and talk about. Laura had so few friends that her wedding presents could have been reckoned on the fingers of the little white hand that looked so strange and wonderful in her eyes, glorified with a brand new ring, a broad and solid band of gold, strong enough to wear till her golden wedding. The few guests felt that there was nothing more for them to do but to take their leave, with much reiteration of good wishes, and cheery anticipations of the festivities which were to enliven the old house, when the honeymoon should have waned.

And now all were gone; the brief winter day was closing, the new year was coming with hastening footsteps. Only the merest remnant of the old year remained. How silent the house was in the winter gloaming, silent with an almost death-like stillness! Laura and Celia had spun out their parting to the last moment, lingering together in the hall long after the rest had gone. Celia had so much to say, so many injunctions about cuffs and collars, and the time and seasons at which Laura was to wear her various gowns. And then there were little gushes of affection, hugs and squeezes.

'You won't care one iota for me now you've a husband,' murmured Celia.

'You know better, you silly girl. My marriage will not make the slightest difference in my feelings.'

'Oh, but it always does,' said Celia, with an experienced air. 'When a man marries, the friends of his bachelor days go to the wall; everybody knows that; and it's just the same thing with a girl. I expect to find myself nowhere.'

Laura declared she would always be true to friendship, and thus they parted, Celia running home by herself, with all her wedding finery smothered under a waterproof Ulster. The rain had ceased by this time, and there was the red gleam of a wintry sunset in the west.

The hall-door shut with a clang that echoed in the silence of the house, and Laura went slowly back to the drawing-room, wondering a little to find herself alone in the gloom of twilight on her wedding day. It was altogether so different from the ordinary idea of a wedding—this delayed departure, this uncomfortable interval between the festivity of the wedding breakfast and the excitement of the wedding journey.

She found the drawing-room empty. She had left John Treverton there with Mr. Sampson half an hour ago, when she went upstairs to assist in packing Celia in the waterproof, and now both were gone. The spacious room, splendid with an old-fashioned splendour, was lighted only by the fading wood fire. The white panelled walls and antique mirrors had a ghostly look; the shadowy corners were too awful to contemplate.

'Perhaps I shall find him in the study,' Laura said to herself. 'It is kettledrum time.'

She laughed softly to herself. How new, how strange it would be to sit down *tête à tête* at the oval tea-table, man and wife, settled in domesticity for life, no further doubt of each other or of their fate possible to either—the bargain made, the bond sealed, the pledge given, that could be broken only by death.

She went slowly through the silence of the house to the room at the end of the corridor, the little book-room opening into the flower garden. She opened the door softly, meaning to steal in and surprise her husband in some pleasant reverie, but on the threshold she stopped appalled, struck dumb.

He was sitting in an attitude of deepest dejection, his forehead resting on his folded arms, his face hidden. Sobs, such as but seldom come from the agonized heart of a strong man, were tearing the heart of John Treverton. He had given himself up, body and soul, to the passion of an unconquerable despair.

Laura ran to him, bent over him, drew her arm gently round his neck.

'Dearest, what is amiss?' she asked, tenderly, with trembling lips. 'Such grief, and on such a day as this! Something dreadful must have happened. Oh, tell me, love, tell me!'

'I can tell you nothing,' he answered, hoarsely, putting her arm away as he spoke. 'Leave me, Laura. If you pity me, leave me to fight my battle alone. It is the only kindness you can show me.'

'Leave you, and in such grief as this! No, John, I have a right to share your sorrow. I will not go till you have confided in me. Trust me, love, trust me. Whom can you trust if not your wife?'

'You don't know,' he gasped, almost angrily. 'There are griefs you cannot share—a depth of torture you can never fathom. God forbid that your pure young soul should ever descend into that black gulf. Laura, if you love, if you pity me—and indeed, dear love, I need all your pity—leave me now for a little while; leave me to finish my struggle alone. It is a struggle, Laura, the fiercest this weak soul of mine has ever passed through. Come back in an hour, dear, and then—you will know—I can explain some part, at least, of this mystery. In an hour, in an hour,' he repeated, with increasing agitation, pointing with a wavering hand to the door.

Laura stood for a moment or so, irresolute, deeply moved, her womanly dignity, her pride as a wife, hurt to the quick. Then, with a smile, half sad, half bitter, she softly quoted the gentle speech of Shakespeare's gentlest heroine:—

'Shall I deny you? No: Farewell, my lord.
Whate'er you be, I am obedient.'

And with those words she left him, full of painful wonder.

If she could have seen the agonized look he turned upon her as she left him; if she could have seen him start and shiver as the door closed upon her, and rise and rush to the door, and kneel down and press his lips upon the insensible panel her hand had touched, and beat his forehead against the dull wood in a paroxysm of despair, she might have better estimated the strength of his love and the bitterness of his grief.

She went to her own room, and sat wondering helplessly at this trouble and mystery that had come down like a sudden storm-cloud upon the brightness of her new life. What did it mean? Had all his professions of love been false? Had he bound himself to her for the sake of his cousin's fortune, despite all his protestations to the contrary? Did he love some one else? Was there some older, dearer tie that made this bond of to-day intolerable to him? Whatever the cause of his repentance, it was clear to Laura's mind that her husband of a few hours bitterly repented his marriage. Never surely had such deep humiliation fallen upon a woman.

She sat in the firelit dressing-room, looking straight before her, numbed and helpless in her grief and humiliation. Reflection could throw no new light upon her husband's conduct. What reason could he have for grief or regret, if he loved her? Never had fortune smiled more kindly upon man and wife than upon these two.

She looked back upon the days of their brief courtship, and remembered many things which favoured the idea that he had never really loved her, that he had been actuated by mercenary considerations alone. She remembered how cold a lover he had been, how seldom he had courted her confidence, how little he had told of his own life, how glad he had always seemed of Celia's company, frivolous and even fatiguing as that young lady's conversation was apt to be. It was all too clear. She had been duped and fooled by this man to whom she had so freely given her heart, from whom she had asked nothing but candour and plain dealing. She lived through that hour of waiting somehow. It was the longest hour she had ever known. Her maid came to attend to the fire, and light the candles on dressing-table and mantelpiece, and lingered a little, pretending to be busied about the trunks and travelling bags, expecting her mistress to talk to her, and then departed softly, to go back to the revellers in the housekeeper's room, where the atmosphere was heavily charged with tea and buttered toast, and to tell them how dull the bride looked, and how she had sat like a statue and said never a word.

'Who was it went out at the front door just now?' asked the old butler, looking up from a cup of tea which he had been gently fanning with his breath. 'I heard it shut to.'

'It must 'ave bin Mr. Treverton,' said Mary, Laura's maid. 'I met 'im in the 'all. I dessay he were goin' out to smoke his cigar. It was too dark for me to see his face, but he didn't walk as gay and light as a gentleman ought on his wedding day, to my mind,' added Mary, with authority.

'Well, I dunno,' remarked Mr. Trimmer, the butler, solemnly. 'Perhaps a wedding ain't altogether the comfortablest day in a man's life. There's too many eyes upon him. He feels as he's the objick of everybody's notice, and if he's a delicate-minded man it kind of preys upon him. I can quite understand Mr. Treverton's not feeling quite himself to-day. And then you see he comes into the estate by a fluke, as you may say, and he ain't got it yet, and he won't feel himself independent till the year's out, and the property is 'anded over to him.'

Mr. Trimmer did not drop his aspirates habitually, like Mary; he only let one slip now and then when he was impressive.

The hour was ended. For the last twenty minutes Laura had been sitting with her watch in her hand. Now she rose with her heart beating tumultuously, and went quickly down the wide old staircase, hastening to hear her husband's explanation of his extraordinary conduct. He had promised to explain.

Had she not been very foolish in torturing herself for this last hour with vain endeavours to fathom the mystery?

Had she not been still more foolish when she jumped at conclusions, and made up her mind that John Treverton did not love her? There might be twenty other reasons for his grief, she told herself, now that the hour of suspense was ended, and that she was going to hear his explanation.

She trembled as she drew near the door, and felt as if in another moment she might stumble and fall fainting on the threshold. She was approaching the most critical moment of her life, the very turning-point of her destiny. All must depend upon what John Treverton had to say to her in the next few minutes. She opened the door and went in, breathless, incapable of speech. She felt that she could ask him no questions, she could only stand there and listen to all he had to tell.

The room was empty, Laura could just see as much as that in the fitful glow of the fire; and then a jet of flame leaped suddenly out of the dimness like a living thing, and showed her a letter lying on the table. He had written to her. That which he had to tell was too terrible for speech, and he had, therefore, written. Hope and comfort died within her at the sight of that letter. She hurried back to her dressing-room, where she had left the candles burning, locked herself in, and then, standing, faint and still trembling, by the mantelpiece, she tore open the envelope and read her husband's letter.

'DEAREST AND EVER DEAREST,—

'When this letter is in your hands I shall have left you, in all probability for a long time, perhaps for ever. I love you as dearly, as fondly, as passionately as ever man loved woman, and the pain of leaving you is worse than the pain of death. Life is not so sweet to me as you are. This world holds no other delight for me but your sweet company, your heavenly love; yet I, the most miserable of men, must forego both.

'Dearest, I have done a shameful and perhaps a foolish act. I have committed a crime in order to bind your life with mine, somehow, in the rash hope that some day that bond may be made legal and complete. Two ends are served by this act of mine. I have won you from all other men—John Treverton's wife will have no suitor—and I have secured you the possession of your old home and your adopted father's fortune. His desire is at least realized by this sad and broken wedding of ours.

'Dearest love, I must leave you, because there is an old tie which forbids me as a man of honour to be more to you than I now am. Your husband in name; your defender and champion, if need were, before all the world; your adoring slave, in secret and in absence, to the day of my death. If Fate prove kind, this bond of which I speak will not last for ever. My fetters will fall off some day, and I shall return to you a free man. Oh, my love, pity and forgive me, keep a place in your heart for me always, and believe that in acting as I have acted I have been prompted by love alone. I shall not touch a sixpence of my cousin's fortune till I can come back to you, a free man, and receive wealth and happiness from you. Till then you will be sole mistress of Hazlehurst Manor, and all that goes with it. Mr. Sampson will tell you what settlement I have made—a settlement that will be duly executed by me upon the day on which I become the ostensible owner of my cousin Jasper's estate.

'My beloved, I can say no more; I dare reveal no more. If you deign to think at all of one who has so deceived you, think of me pityingly as the most deeply wretched of men. Forgive me if you can; and I dare even to hope for pardon from the infinite goodness of your nature. It is sweet to me in my misery to know that you bear my name—that there is a link between us that can never be broken, even though Fate should be cruel enough to part us for life. But I hope for better things from destiny; I hope for and look forward to a time when I shall sign myself with pride and gladness more intense than the pain I feel to-day, your loving husband, JOHN TREVERTON.'

She stood for some minutes pale as marble, with the letter in her hand, and then she lifted the senseless paper to her lips, and kissed it passionately.

'He loves me,' she cried involuntarily. 'Thank God for that. I can bear anything now I am sure of that.'

She believed implicitly in the letter. A woman with wider knowledge of the evil things of this world might have seen only a tissue of lies in these wild lines of John Treverton's; but to Laura they meant truth and truth alone. He had acted very wickedly; but he loved her. He had done her almost the deepest wrong a man could do to a woman; but he loved her. He had duped and fooled her, made her ridiculous in the sight of her friends and acquaintance; but he loved her. That one virtue in him almost atoned for all his crimes.

'There's not the least use in my trying to hate him,' she told herself, in piteous self-abasement, 'for I love him with all my heart and soul. I suppose I am a mean-spirited young woman, a poor creature, for I cannot leave off loving him, though he has treated me very cruelly, and almost broken my heart.'

She locked the letter in the secret drawer of her dressing-case, and then sat down on a low stool by the fire and wept very quietly over this new, strange sorrow.

'Celia was right,' she said to herself, by-and-by, with a bitter smile. 'It was an ill-omened marriage. She need not have taken so much trouble about my collars and cuffs.'

And then later she began to think of the difficulties, the absurdity of her position.

'Wife and widow,' she thought, 'with a husband who ran away from me on my wedding-day. How am I to account to the world for his conduct? What a foolish, miserable creature I shall appear.'

It came suddenly into her mind that she could not endure, not yet awhile, at any rate, to have to explain her husband's conduct—to give some reason for his desertion of her. Anything would be better than that. She must run away somewhere. She must leave the revelation to time. It would be easier for her to write to her old friend the vicar from a distance.

She could bear anything rather than to be cross-examined by Celia, who had always distrusted John Treverton, and who might be secretly elated at his having proved himself an impostor.

'I must go away at once,' she decided; 'this very night. I must go for my honeymoon alone.'

She rang, and Mary came quickly, flushed with tea, buttered toast, and the hilarity below stairs.

'What time is the carriage to come for us, Mary?' asked Mrs. Treverton.

124

'At a quarter to eight, ma'am. The mail goes at twenty minutes before nine.'

'And it is just half-past six. Mary, do you think you could get ready to go with me in an hour and a quarter?'

It had been arranged that Laura was to travel without a maid, much to the disappointment of Mary, who had an ardent desire to see foreign lands.

'Lor', ma'am, I haven't a thing packed; but I should dearly like to go. Do you really mean it?'

'I do mean it, and I shall be very much pleased with you if you'll contrive to pack your trunk in time to go with me.'

'I'll do it, ma'am,' cried Mary, clasping her hands in ecstasy, and then she tore downstairs like a mad thing to announce to the assembly in the housekeeper's room that she was going to France with her mistress.

'That's a sudden change,' said the butler. 'And where's Mr. Treverton all this time? He didn't ought to be out of doors in the dark, smoking his cigar, instead of keeping his wife company.'

'No more he didn't,' said Mary, with indignation; 'he ain't my notion of a 'usband, leaving her to mope alone on her wedding day, poor dear! It's my belief she'd been crying her eyes out just now, tho' she was artful enough to keep her face turned away from me while she spoke. I dessay she's made up her mind to take me abroad with her for company, because she feels she'll be dull and lonesome with 'im.'

'You'd better go and pack up your box,' said the housekeeper, 'and not stand gossiping there. What do you know of the ways of gentry, married or single, I should like to know? When you've been in service as long as I have you may talk.'

'Well, I'm sure,' cried Mary, indignantly, and then she expressed a hope that her soul was her own, even at Hazlehurst Manor.

Before half-past seven, Mary had packed her box, and had it conveyed to the hall. Mrs. Treverton's trunks and bags had also been brought down. At a quarter to eight the carriage drove up to the door, an old-fashioned landau in which Jasper Treverton used to take his daily airing, drawn by a pair of big horses that had begun life at the plough. Since the lamps had been lighted no one had seen the bridegroom. The tea-things had been taken into the book-room, and the urn had hissed itself to silence, but no one had come there to take tea. Laura only came downstairs when the carriage was at the door.

'Joe, run and look for Mr. Treverton,' cried the butler to his underling.

'Mr. Treverton will meet us at the station,' Laura said, hurriedly; and then she got into the carriage, and called to Mary to follow her.

'Tell Berrows to drive quickly to the station,' she told the butler, and at the first crack of the whip the overfed horses swung the big carriage round, as if they meant to annihilate the good old house, and went off along the avenue with the noise of a Barclay and Perkins dray.

'Well, I never did!' exclaimed the housekeeper. 'Fancy his meeting her at the station, instead of their going off together, sitting side by side, like true lovers.'

'I'm afraid there's not much true love about it, Martha,' said her husband, sententiously, and then, waxing familiar, he said, 'When you and me was married we didn't manage matters so did we, my lass?'

CHAPTER XIII.

THE SETTLEMENT.

Laura had been married three weeks and a day, and the new year was just three weeks old. It was a very ailing and ungenial year in this infantine stage of its existence. There had been hardly a day of pleasant weather since its birth, nothing but rain and sleet, and damp raw cold, and morning mists and evening fogs. It was not a good, honest, old-fashioned winter, such as we read of in story books, and enjoy about once in a decade. It was simply obnoxious, ill-conditioned weather, characteristic of no particular season.

It was just a day after the anniversary of Jasper Treverton's death, and Tom Sampson was meditating in a lazy, comfortable way, on his former client, as he sat by the office fire sipping his tea, which he had desired to be brought to him in his den, as he was so terribly busy. He had not dipped a pen in the ink yet, and it was half-past nine o'clock; but it was not for Eliza Sampson to know this. She was always taught to believe that when her brother spent his evenings in the office he was working severely—'double tides,' he called it. If she came in to look at him she found him scratching away violently with a quill that tore shrieking along the paper, like an express train rushing through a village station; and it was not for her to know that Thomas snatched up his pen and put on this appearance of industry when he heard her gentle footfall at his door. Domestic life is made up of such small secrets.

To-night Tom Sampson was in a particularly lazy humour. He was getting a rich man, not by large earnings, but by small expenditure, and life, which is an insoluble problem for many, was as easy for him as one of those nine elementary axioms in Euclid that seem too foolishly obvious to engage the reasoning power of the smallest schoolboy, such as—'if equals be taken from equals, the remainders are equal,' and so on. Tom was thinking that he ought to be thinking about marrying. He was not in love, and never had been since he exchanged his schoolboy jacket for a tail-coat; but he told himself that the time had come when he might prudently allow himself to fall in love. He would love not too well, but wisely.

'Lizzie is a good girl, and she knows my ways,' he said to himself, 'but she's getting old maidish, and that's a fault which will grow upon her. Yes, decidedly, it is time I thought of a wife. A man's choice is confoundedly limited in such a hole as this. I don't want to marry a farmer's daughter, though I might get a fine healthy young woman, and a tidy little bit of money, if I could please myself among the agricultural class; but Tom Sampson has his failings, and pride is one of 'em. I should like my wife to be a cut above me. There's Celia Clare, now. She's more the kind of thing I should fancy; plump and pretty, with nice, lively ways. I've had a little too much of the sentimental from poor Lizzie. Yes, I might do worse than marry Celia. And I think she likes me.'

Mr. Sampson's meditations were interrupted at this point by the sound of a footstep on the sloshy gravel walk outside his office door. There was a half-glass door opening into the garden, as well as the door opening from the passage, which was the formal approach for Mr. Sampson's clients. Only his intimates entered by the garden door, and he was unable to imagine who his late visitor could be.

'Ten o'clock,' he said to himself. 'It must be something particular. Old Pulsby has got another attack of gout in the stomach, perhaps, and wants to alter his will. He always alters his will when he gets a sharp attack. The pain makes him so savage that it's a relief to him to disinherit somebody.'

Mr. Sampson speculated thus as he undrew the bolt and opened the glass door. The man who stood before him was no messenger from old Pulsby, but John Treverton, clad in a white mackintosh, from which the water ran in little rills.

'Is it yourself or your ghost?' asked Sampson, falling back to let his client enter.

The question was not without reason. John Treverton's face was as white as his raiment, and the combined effect of the pale, haggard face and the long white coat was altogether spectral.

'Flesh and blood, my dear Sampson, I assure you,' replied the other coolly, as he divested himself of his mackintosh, and took up his stand in front of the comfortable fire, 'flesh and blood frozen to the bone.'

'I thought you were in the South of France.'

'It doesn't matter what you thought, you see I am here. Yesterday put me in legal possession of my cousin's estate. I have come to execute the deed of settlement. It's all ready of course?'

'It's ready, yes; but I didn't think you'd be in such a hurry. I should have thought you would have stopped to finish your honeymoon.'

128

'My honeymoon is of very little importance compared with my wife's future welfare. Come, Sampson, look sharp. Who's to witness my signature?'

'My sister and one of the servants can do that.'

'Call them in, then. I'm ready to sign.'

'Hadn't you better read the deed first?'

'Well, yes, perhaps. One can't be too careful. I want my wife's position to be unassailable as the summit of Mount Everest. You have taken counsel's opinion, and the deed will hold water?'

'It would hold the Atlantic. Your gift is so entirely simple, that there could be no difficulty in wording the deed. You give your wife everything. I think you a fool, so did the advising counsel; but that makes no difference.'

'Not a whit.'

John Treverton sat down at the office table and read the deed of settlement from the first word to the last. He gave to his dear wife, Laura Treverton, all the property, real and personal, of which he stood possessed, for her sole and separate use. There was a good deal of legal jargon, but the drift of the deed was clear enough.

'I am ready,' said John.

Mr. Sampson rang the bell for the servant, and shouted into the passage for his sister. Eliza came running in, and at sight of John Treverton's pale face screamed, and made as if she would have fainted.

'Gracious, Mr. Treverton!' she gasped, 'I thought there were oceans between us. What in mercy's name has happened?'

'Nothing alarming. I have only come to execute my marriage settlement, which I was not in a position to make till yesterday.'

'How dreadful for poor Mrs. Treverton to be left alone in a foreign land!'

John Treverton did not notice this speech. He dipped his pen in the ink and signed the paper, while Miss Sampson and Sophia, the housemaid, looked on wonderingly.

'Sophia, run and get a pair of sheets aired, and get the spare room ready,' cried Eliza, when she had affixed her signature as witness. 'Of course you are going to stop with us, Mr. Treverton?'

'You are very kind. No, I must get away immediately. I have a trap waiting to take me back to the station. Oh, by-the-way, Sampson, about that money you kindly advanced to me. It must come out of the estate somehow; I suppose you can manage that?'

'Yes, I think I can manage that,' answered Sampson modestly. 'Do you want any further advance?'

'No, the estate belongs to my wife now. I must not tamper with it.'

'And what's hers is yours of course. Well, I congratulate you with all my heart. You are the luckiest fellow I ever knew, bar none. A handsome wife, and a handsome fortune. What more can a man ask from Fate?'

'Not much, certainly,' said John Treverton, 'but I must catch the last up-train. Good-night.'

'Going back to the South of France?'

John Treverton did not wait to answer the question. He shook hands hastily with Eliza, and dashed out into the garden. A minute afterwards Mr. Sampson and his sister heard the crack of a whip, and the sound of wheels upon the high road.

'Did you ever see such a volcanic individual?' exclaimed the solicitor, folding up the deed of settlement.

'I am afraid he is not happy,' sighed Eliza.

'I am afraid he is mad,' said Tom.

CHAPTER XIV.

'YOU HAVE BUT TO SAY THE WORD.'

Mr. Smolendo was in his glory. In the words of his friends and followers he was coining money. He was a man to be cultivated and revered. A man for whom champagne suppers or dinners at Richmond were as nothing; a man for whom it was easier to lend a five-pound note than it is for the common ruck of humanity to advance half-a-crown. Flatterers fawned upon him, intimate acquaintances hung fondly upon him, reminding him pathetically that they knew him twenty years ago, when he hadn't a sixpence, as if that knowledge of bygone adversity were a merit and a claim. A man of smaller mind might have had his mental equilibrium shaken by all this adulation. Mr. Smolendo was a man of granite, and took it for what it was worth. When people were particularly civil, he knew they wanted something from him.

'The lessee of a London theatre is not a man to be easily had,' he said; 'he sees human nature on the ugliest side.'

Christmas had come and gone, the New Year was six weeks old, and Mr. Smolendo's prosperity continued without abatement. The theatre was nightly crowded to suffocation. There were morning performances every Saturday. Stalls and boxes were booked a month in advance.

'La Chicot is a little gold mine,' said Mr. Smolendo's followers.

Yes, La Chicot had the credit of it all. Mr. Smolendo had produced a grand fairy spectacle, in which La Chicot was the central figure. She appeared in half-a-dozen costumes, all equally original, expensive, and audacious. She was a fountain of golden water, draped exclusively in dazzling golden fringe, a robe of light, through which her finely-sculptured form flashed now and then, as the glittering fringe parted for an instant, like a revelation of the beautiful. She was a fishwoman in a scanty satin kirtle, scarlet stockings, and a high cap of finest Brussels lace. She was a bayadère, a debardeur, a wood nymph, an odalisque. She did not dance as she danced before her accident, but she was as beautiful as ever, and a trifle more impudent. She had learnt enough English to speak the lines of her part, and her accent gave a charm and a quaintness to the performance.

She sang a comic song with more chic than melody, and was applauded to the echo. The critics told her she had ascended to a higher grade in the drama. La Chicot told herself that she was the greatest woman in London, as well as the handsomest. She lived in a circle of which she herself was the centre. The circumference was a ring of admirers. There was no world beyond.

Something to this effect she told her fellow lodger, Mr. Desrolles, one grey afternoon in February, when he dropped in to beg a glass of brandy, in order to stave off one of those attacks he so often talked about. She was always particularly friendly with the 'Second Floor,' as it was the fashion of the house to call this gentleman. He flattered and amused her, fetched and carried for her, and sometimes kept her company when she was in too low spirits to drink alone.

'My good creature, you oughtn't to live in such a hole as this. Upon my soul, you ought not,' said Desrolles with an air that was half-protection, half-patronage.

'I know I ought not,' replied La Chicot. 'There is not an actress in Paris who would not call me stupid as an owl for my pains. *Que diable*, I sacrifice myself for the honour of a husband who mocks himself of me, who amuses himself elsewhere, and leaves me to fret and pine alone. It is too much. See then, Desrolles, it may be that you think I boast myself when I tell you that one of the richest men in London is over head and ears in love with me. See, here are his letters. Read them, and see how much I have refused.'

She opened a work-basket on the table, and from a chaos of reels of cotton, tapes and buttons, and shreds and patches, extracted half-a-dozen letters, which she tossed across the table to Desrolles.

'Do you leave your love-letters where your husband might so easily find them?' asked Desrolles, wonderfully.

'Do you suppose he would give himself the trouble to look at them?' she cried scornfully. 'Not he. He has so long left off caring for me himself, that he never supposes that anybody else can fall in love with me. Help yourself to that cognac, Monsieur Desrolles. It is the only safe drink in this miserable climate of yours; and put some coals on the fire, *mon bonhomme*. I am frozen to the marrow of my bones.'

La Chicot filled her glass by way of setting a good example, and emptied it as placidly as if the brandy had been sugar and water.

Desrolles looked over the letters she had handed him. They all went to the same tune. They told La Chicot that she was beautiful, and that the writer was madly in love with her. They offered her a carriage, a house in Mayfair, a settlement. The offers rose in value with the lapse of time.

'How have you answered him?' asked Desrolles, curious and interested.

'Not at all. I knew better how to make myself valued. Let him wait for his answer.'

'A man must be very hard hit to write like that,' suggested the gentleman.

La Chicot shrugged her statuesque shoulders. She was lovely even in her more than careless attire. She wore a long loose dressing-gown of scarlet cashmere, girdled with a cord and tassels, which she tied and untied, and twisted and untwisted in sheer idleness. Her massy hair was rolled in a great rough knob at the back of her head, ready to escape from the comb and slide down her back at the slightest provocation. The dead white of her complexion showed like marble against the scarlet robe, the dense hair showed raven black above the pale brow and large luminous eyes.

'Is he as rich as he pretends to be?' asked La Chicot, thoughtfully swinging the heavy scarlet tassel, and lazily contemplating the fire.

'To my certain knowledge,' said Mr. Desrolles, with an oracular air, 'Joseph Lemuel is one of the wealthiest men in London.'

'I don't see that it much matters,' said La Chicot, meditatively. 'I like money, but so long as I have enough to buy what I want, it's all that I care about, and I don't like that grim-looking Jew.'

'Compare a house in Mayfair with this den,' urged Desrolles.

'Where is Mayfair?'

Desrolles described the neighbourhood.

'A wilderness of dull streets,' said La Chicot, with a contemptuous shrug. 'What is one street better than another? I should like a house in the Champs Elysées—a house in a garden, dazzling white, all over flowers, with big, shining windows, and a Swiss stable.'

'A house like a toy,' said Desrolles. 'Well, Lemuel could buy you one as easily as I could buy you a handful of sugar plums. You have but to say the word.'

'It is a word that I shall never say,' exclaimed La Chicot, decisively. 'I am an honest woman. And then, I am too proud.'

Desrolles wondered whether it was pride, virtue, or rank obstinacy which made La Chicot reject such brilliant offers. It was not easy for him to believe in virtue, masculine or feminine. He had not travelled by those paths in which the virtues grow and flourish, but he had made intimate acquaintance with the vices. Since a certain interview with La Chicot's husband, in which he had promised to keep a paternal eye upon the lady, Mr. Desrolles had wound himself completely into the wife's confidence. He had made himself alike useful and agreeable. Though she kept her wealthy adorer at arm's length, she liked to talk of him. The hothouse flowers he sent her adorned her table, and looked strangely out of place in the tawdry, littered room, where yesterday's dust was generally left to be swept away to-morrow.

One thing La Chicot did not know, and that was that Mr. Desrolles had made the acquaintance of her admirer, and was being paid by Mr. Lemuel to plead his cause.

'You seem to be better off than you used to be, my friend,' she said to him one day. 'Unless I deceive myself, that is a new coat.'

'Yes,' answered the man of the world, without blushing. 'I have been dabbling a little on the Stock Exchange, and have had better luck than usual.'

Desrolles stirred the heaped-up coals into a blaze, and filled himself a third glass of cognac.

'It's as fine as a liqueur,' he said, smacking his lips. 'It would be a sin to dilute such stuff. By the way, when do you expect your husband?'

'I never expect him,' answered La Chicot. 'He goes and comes as he chooses. He is like the wandering Jew.'

'He is gone to Paris on business, I suppose!'

'On business or pleasure. I neither know nor care which. He earns his living. Those ridiculous pictures of his please both in London and Paris. See here!'

She tossed him over a crumpled heap of comic papers, English and French. Her husband's name figured in all, affixed to the wildest caricatures—scenes theatrical and Bohemian, sketches full of life and humour.

'To judge from those you would suppose he was rather a cheerful companion,' said La Chicot, 'and yet he is more dismal than a funeral.'

'He vents all his cheerfulness on his wood blocks,' suggested Desrolles.

Of late Jack Chicot had been a restless wanderer, spending very little of his life in the Cibber Street lodging. There was not even the pretence of union between his wife and him, and there never had been since La Chicot's recovery. They were civil to each other, for the most part; but there were times when the wife's tongue grew bitter, and her evil temper flashed out like a thin thread of forked lightning cleaving a dark summer sky. The husband was always civil. La Chicot could not exasperate him into retaliation.

'You hate me too much to lose your temper with me,' she said to him one day in the presence of the landlady; 'you are afraid to trust yourself. If you gave way for a moment you might kill me. The temptation would be too strong for you.'

Jack Chicot said never a word, but stood with his arms folded, smiling at her, heaven knows how bitterly.

One day she stung him into speech.

'You are in love with some other woman,' she cried. 'I know it.'

'I have seen a woman who is not like you,' he answered with a sigh.

'And you are in love with her.'

'For her unlikeness to you? That would be a charm, certainly.'

'Go to her. Go to your ——'

The sentence ended in a foul epithet—one of the poison-flowers of Parisian argot.

'The journey is too long,' he said. 'It is not easy to travel from hell to heaven.'

Jack Chicot had been once to the Prince Frederick Theatre since his wife's return to the stage. He went on the first night of the grand spectacular burlesque which had brought Mr. Smolendo so much money. He sat looking on with a grave, unchanging face, while the audience around him grinned in ecstasy; and when La Chicot asked his opinion of the performance, he openly expressed his disgust.

'Are not my costumes beautiful?' she asked.

'Very. But I should prefer a little less beauty and a little more decency.'

The rest of the audience were easier to please. They saw no indecency in the dresses. No doubt they saw what they had paid to see, and that contented them.

Never had woman more of her own way than La Chicot after that wonderful recovery of hers. She went where she liked, drank as much as she liked, spent every sixpence of her liberal salary on her own pleasure, and was held accountable by no one. Her husband was a husband only in name. She saw more of Desrolles than of Jack Chicot.

There was only one person who ever ventured to reprove or expostulate with her, and that was the man who had saved her life, at so large a sacrifice of time and care. George Gerard called upon her now and then, and spoke to her plainly.

'You have been drinking again,' he would say, while they were shaking hands.

'I have had nothing since last night, when I took a glass of champagne with my supper.'

'You mean a bottle; and you have had half a bottle of brandy this morning to correct the champagne.'

She no longer attempted to deny the impeachment.

'Well, why should I not drink?' she exclaimed, defiantly. 'Who cares what becomes of me?'

'I care: I have saved your life once, against long odds. You owe me something for that. But I cannot save you if you make up your mind to drink yourself to death. Brandy is a slow suicide, but for a woman of your temperament it's as certain as prussic acid.'

Upon this La Chicot would dissolve in maudlin tears. It was a pitiful sight, and wrung the student's heart. He could have loved her so well, would have tried so hard to save her, had it been possible. He did not know how heartless a piece of beautiful clay she was. He put down her errors to her husband's neglect.

'If she had been my wife, she might have been a very different woman,' he said to himself, not believing the innate depravity of anything so absolutely beautiful as La Chicot.

He forgot how fair some poisonous weeds are, how beautiful the scarlet berries of the nightshade look when they star the brown autumn hedges.

So La Chicot went her way triumphantly. There was no danger to life or limb for her in the new piece—no perilous ascent to the sky borders. She drank as much brandy as she liked, and, so long as she contrived to appear sober before the audience, Mr. Smolendo said nothing.

'I'm afraid she'll drink herself into a dropsy, poor thing,' he said compassionately one day to a friend at the Garrick Club. 'But I hope she'll last my time. A woman of her type could hardly be expected to draw for more than three seasons, and La Chicot ought to hold out for another year or so.'

'After that, the hospital,' said his friend.

Mr. Smolendo shrugged his shoulders.

'I never trouble myself about the after-career of my artists,' he answered pleasantly.

CHAPTER XV.

EDWARD CLARE DISCOVERS A LIKENESS.

'Hazlehurst Rectory, February 22nd.—Dear Ned,—Do you remember my saying, when Laura refused to have a proper wedding-gown, that her marriage was altogether an ill-omened business? I told her so, I told you so; in fact, I think I told everybody so; if it be not an unpardonable exaggeration to call the handful of wretched dowdies and frumps in such a place as Hazlehurst everybody. Well, I was right. The marriage has been a complete *fiasco*. What do you think of our poor Laura's coming home from her honeymoon *alone*? Without even so much as her husband's portmanteau! She has shut herself up in the Manor-house, where she lives the life of a female anchorite, and is so reserved in her manner towards me, her oldest friend, her all but sister, that even I do not know the cause of this extraordinary state of affairs.

'"My dear Celia, don't ask me anything about it," she said, when we had kissed each other, and cried a little, and I had looked at her collar and cuffs to see if she had brought a new style from Paris.

'"My dearest, I must ask you," I replied; "I don't pretend to be more than human, and I am burning with curiosity and suppressed indignation. What does it all mean? Why have you challenged public opinion by coming home alone? Have you and Mr. Treverton quarrelled?"

'"No," she said, decisively; "and that is the last question about my married life that I shall ever answer, Celia, so you need not ask me any more."

'"Where did you part with him?" I asked, determined not to give way. My unhappy friend was obstinately silent.

'"Come and see me as often as you like, so long as you do not talk to me of my husband," she said a little later. "But if you insist upon talking about him, I shall shut my door upon you."

'"I hear he has acted most generously with regard to the settlements, so he cannot be altogether bad," I said—for you know I am not easily put down—but Laura was adamant. I could not extort another word from her.

'Perhaps I ought not to tell you this, Ned, knowing what I do about your former affection for Laura; but I felt that I must open my heart to somebody. Parents are so stupid that it's impossible to tell them things.

'I can't conceive what this poor girl is going to do with her life. He has settled the whole estate upon her, papa says, and she is awfully rich. But she is living like a hermit, and not spending more than her own small income. She even talks of selling the carriage horses, Tommy and Harry, or sending them back to the plough, though I know she dotes upon them. If this is meanness, it is too awful. If she has conscientious scruples about spending John Treverton's money, it is simply idiotic. Of the two, I could rather think my friend a miser than an idiot.

'And now, my dear Ned, as there is nothing else to tell you about the dismalest place in the universe, I may as well say goodbye.—Your loving sister,

'CELIA.'

'P.S.—I hope you are writing a book of poems that will make the Laureate burst with envy. I have no personal animosity to him; but you are my brother, and, of course, your interest must be paramount.'

This letter reached Edward Clare in his dingy lodgings, in a narrow side street near the British Museum, lodgings so dingy that it would have grieved the heart of his country-born and country-bred mother to see her boy in such a den. But the apartments were quite dear enough for his slender means. The world had not yet awakened to the stupendous fact that a new poet had been born into it. Stupid reviewers went on prosing about Tennyson, Browning, and Swinburne, and the name of Clare was still unknown, even though it had appeared pretty often at the foot of a neat triplet of verses filling an odd page in a magazine.

'I shall never win a name in the magazines,' the young man told himself. 'It is worse than not writing at all. I shall rot unknown in my garret, or die of hunger and opium, like that poor boy who perished within a quarter of a mile of this dismal hole, unless I can get some rich publisher to launch me properly.'

But in the meantime a man must live, and Edward was very glad to get an occasional guinea or two from a magazine. The supplies from home fell considerably below his requirements, though to send them strained the father's resources. The embryo Laureate liked to take life pleasantly. He liked to dine at a popular restaurant, and to wash down his dinner with good Rhine wine, or sound claret. He liked good cigars. He could not wear cheap boots. He could do without gloves at a pinch, but those he wore must be the best. When he was in funds he preferred a hansom to pedestrianism. This, he told himself, was the poetical temperament. Alfred de Musset was, doubtless, just such a man. He could fancy Heine leading the same kind of life in Paris, before disease had chained him to his bed.

That letter from Celia was like vitriol dropped into an open wound. Edward had not forgiven Laura for accepting John Treverton, or the estate that went with him. He hated John Treverton with a vigorous hatred that would stand a great deal of wear and tear. He pondered long over Celia's letter, trying to discover the clue to the mystery. It seemed to him tolerably clear. Mr. and Mrs. Treverton had married with a deliberate understanding. Love between them there was none, and they had been too honest to pretend an affection which neither felt. They had agreed to marry and live apart, sharing the dead man's wealth, fulfilling the letter of the law, but not the spirit.

'I call it sheer dishonesty,' said Edward. 'I wonder that Laura can lend herself to such an underhand course.'

It was all very well to talk about John Treverton's liberality in settling the entire estate upon his wife. No doubt they had their private understanding duly set forth in black and white. The husband was to have his share of the fortune, and squander it how he pleased in London or Paris, or any part of the globe that seemed best to him.

'There never was such confounded luck,' exclaimed Edward, angry with Fate for having given this man so much and himself so little; 'a fellow who three months ago was a beggar.'

In his idle reverie he found himself thinking what he would have done in John Treverton's place, with, say, seven thousand a year at his disposal.

'I would have chambers in the Albany,' he thought, 'furnished on the purest æsthetic principles. I'd keep a yacht at Cowes, and three or four hunters at Melton Mowbray. I'd spend February and March in the South, and April and May in Paris, where I should have a *pied à terre* in the Champs Elysées. Yes, one could lead a very pleasant life, as a bachelor, on seven thousand a year.'

Thus it will be seen that, although Mr. Clare had been seriously in love with Miss Malcolm, it was the loss of Jasper Treverton's money which he felt most keenly, and it was the possession of that fortune for which he envied John Treverton.

One afternoon in February, one of those rare afternoons on which the winter sun glorifies the gloomy London streets, Mr. Clare called at the office of a comic periodical, the editor of which had accepted some of his lighter verses—society poems in the Praed and Locker manner. Two or three of his contributions had been published within the last month, and he came to the office with the pleasant consciousness that there was a cheque due to him.

'I shall treat myself to a careful little dinner at the *Restaurant du Pavillon*,' he told himself, 'and a stall at the Prince of Wales's to wind up the evening.'

He was not a man of vicious tastes. It was not the *aqua fortis* of vice, but the champagne of pleasure that he relished. He was too fond of himself, too careful of his own well-being, to fling away youth, health, and vigour in the sloughs and sewers of evil living. He had a refined selfishness that was calculated to keep him pure of low iniquities. He had no aspiration to scale mountain peaks, but he had sufficient regard for himself to eschew gutters.

The cheque was ready for him, but when he had signed the formal receipt the clerk told him the editor wanted to speak to him presently, if he would be kind enough to wait a few minutes.

'There's a gentleman with him, but I don't suppose he'll be long,' said the clerk, 'if you don't mind waiting.'

Mr. Clare did not mind, particularly. He sat down on an office stool, and made himself a cigarette, while he thoughtfully planned his dinner.

He was not going to be extravagant. A plate of bisque soup, a slice of salmon *en papilotte*, a wing of chicken with mushrooms, an omelette, half a bottle of St. Julien, and a glass of vermuth.

While he was musing pleasantly thus, the swinging inner door of the office was dashed open, and a gentleman walked quickly through to the open doorway that led into the street, with only a passing nod to the clerk. Edward Clare just caught a glimpse of his face as he turned to give that brief salutation.

'Who's that?' he asked, starting up from his stool, and dropping the half-made cigarette.

'Mr. Chicot, the artist.'

'Are you sure?'

The clerk grinned.

'Pretty positive,' he said. 'He comes here every week, sometimes twice a week. I ought to know him.'

Edward knew the name well. The slap-dash caricatures, more Parisian in style than English, which adorned the middle page of the weekly paper called 'FOLLY AS IT FLIES,' were all signed 'Chicot.' The dancer's admirers, for the most part, gave her the credit of those productions, an idea which Mr. Smolendo had taken care to encourage. It was an advantage that his dancer should be thought a woman of many accomplishments—a Sarah Bernhardt in a small way.

Edward Clare was mystified. The face which he had seen turned towards the clerk had presented a wondrous likeness of John Treverton. If this man who called himself Chicot had been John Treverton's twin brother, the two could not have been more alike. Edward was so impressed with this idea that, instead of waiting to see his editor, he hurried out into the street, bent upon following Mr. Chicot the artist. The office was in one of the narrow streets northward of the Strand. If Chicot had turned to the left, he must be by this time following the strong current of the Strand, which flows westward at this hour, with its tide of human life, as regularly as the river flows to the sea. If he had turned to the right, he was most likely lost in the labyrinth between Drury Lane and Holborn. In either case—three minutes having been wasted in surprise and interrogation—there seemed little chance of catching him.

Edward turned to the right, and went towards Holborn. Accident favoured him. At the corner of Long Acre he saw Chicot, the artist, button-holed by an older man, of somewhat raffish aspect. That Chicot was anxious to get away from the button-holer was obvious, and before Edward could reach the corner he had done so, and was off at a rapid pace westward. There would be no chance of overtaking him, except by running; and to run in Long Acre would be to make oneself unpleasantly conspicuous. There was no empty hansom within sight. Edward looked round despairingly. There stood the raffish man watching him, and looking as if he knew exactly what Mr. Clare wanted.

Edward crossed the street, looked at the raffish man, and lingered, half inclined to speak. The raffish man anticipated his desire.

'I think you wanted my friend Chicot,' he said, in a most insinuating tone.

He had the accent of a gentleman, and in some wise the look of a gentleman, though his degradation from that high estate was patent to every eye. His tall hat, sponged and coaxed to a factitious polish, was of an exploded shape; his coat was the coat of to-day; his stock was twenty years old in style, and so frayed and greasy that it might have been worn ever since it first came into fashion. The hawk's eye, the iron lines about the mouth and chin, were warnings to the man's fellow-creatures. Here was a man capable of anything—a being so obviously at war with society as to be bound by no law, daunted by no penalty.

Edward Clare dimly divined that the creature belonged to the dangerous classes, but in his excellent opinion of his own cleverness deemed himself strong enough to cope with half a dozen such seedy sinners.

'Well, yes, I did rather want to speak to him—er—about a literary matter. Does he live far from here?'

'Five minutes' walk. Cibber Street, Leicester Square. I'll take you there if you like. I live in the same house.'

'Ah, then you can tell me all about him. But it isn't the pleasantest thing to stand and talk in an east wind. Come in and take a glass of something,' suggested Edward, comprehending that this shabby-genteel stranger must be plied with drink.

'Ah,' thought Mr. Desrolles, 'he wants something of me. This liberality is not motiveless.'

Tavern doors opened for them close at hand. They entered the refined seclusion of a jug and bottle department, and each chose the liquor he preferred—Edward sherry and soda water, the stranger a glass of brandy, 'short.'

'Have you known Mr. Chicot long?' asked Edward. 'Don't suppose I'm actuated by impertinent curiosity. It's a matter of business.'

'Sir, I know when I am talking to a gentleman,' replied Desrolles, with a stately air. 'I was a gentleman myself once, but it's so long ago that the world and I have forgotten it.'

He had emptied his glass by this time, and was gazing thoughtfully, almost tearfully, at the bottom of it.

'Take another,' said Edward.

'I think I will. These east winds are trying to a man of my age. Have I known Jack Chicot long? Well, about a year and a half—a little less, perhaps—but the time is of no moment, I know him well.'

And then Mr. Desrolles proceeded to give his new acquaintance considerable information as to the outer life of Mr. and Mrs. Chicot. He did not enter into the secrets of their domesticity, save to admit that Madame was fonder of the brandy bottle—a lamentable propensity in so fair a being—than she ought to be, and that Mr. Chicot was not so fond of Madame as he might be.

'Tired of her, I suppose?' said Edward.

'Precisely. A woman who drinks like a fish and swears like a trooper is apt to pall upon a man, after some years of married life.'

'Has this Chicot no other income than what he earns by his pencil?' asked Edward.

'Not a sou.'

'He has not been flush of money lately—since the new year, for instance?'

'No.'

'There has been no change in his way of life since then?'

'Not the slightest—except, perhaps, that he has worked harder than ever. The man is a prodigious worker. When first he came to London he had an idea of succeeding as a painter. He used to be at his easel as soon as it was light. But since the comic journals have taken him up he has done nothing but draw on the wood. He is really a very good creature. I haven't a word to say against him.'

'He is remarkably like a man I know,' said Mr. Clare, musingly; 'but of course it can't be the same. The husband of a French dancer. No, that isn't possible. I wish it were,' he muttered to himself, with clenched teeth.

'Is he like some one you know?' interrogated Desrolles.

'Wonderfully like, so far as I could make out in the glimpse I got of his face.'

'Ah, those glimpses are sometimes deceptive. Is your friend residing in London?'

'I don't know where he is just at present. When last I saw him he was in the west of England.'

'Ah, nice country that,' said Desrolles, kindling with sudden eagerness. 'Somersetshire or Devonshire way, you mean, I suppose?'

'I mean Devonshire.'

'Charming county—delightful scenery!'

'Very, for your Londoner, who runs down by express train to spend a fortnight there. Not quite so lively for your son of the soil, who sees himself doomed to rot in a God-forsaken hole like Hazlehurst, the village I came from. What! you know the place!' exclaimed Edward, for the man had given a start that betokened surprised recognition of the name.

'I do know a village called Hazlehurst, but it's in Wilts,' the other answered, coolly. 'So the gentleman who resembles my friend Chicot is a native of Devonshire, and a neighbour of yours?'

'I didn't say he was either,' returned Edward, who did not want to be catechised by a disreputable-looking stranger. 'I said I had last seen him at Hazlehurst. That's all. And now, as I've an appointment at five o'clock, I must wish you good afternoon.'

They both left the bar together, and went out into Long Acre, whence the wintry sunshine had departed, giving place to that dull, thick greyness which envelopes London at eventide, like a curtain.

To those who love the city, as Charles Lamb loved it, for instance, there is something comfortable even in this all-enshrouding grey, through which the lamps shine cheerfully, like friendly eyes.

'I'm sorry I haven't got my card case with me,' said Desrolles, feeling in his breast pocket.

'It doesn't matter,' the other answered, curtly. 'Good-day to you.'

And so they parted, Edward Clare walking swiftly away towards the little French restaurant hard by St. Ann's Church, where he meant to solace himself with a comfortable dinner.

'A cad!' mused Desrolles, looking after him. 'Provincial, and a cad! Strange that he should come from Hazlehurst.'

Mr. Clare dined entirely to his own satisfaction, and with what he considered a severe economy; for he contented himself with half a bottle of claret, and took only one glass of green chartreuse after his small cup of black coffee. The coffee made him bright and wakeful, and he left the purlieus of St. Ann in excellent spirits. He had changed his mind about the Prince of Wales's. Instead of indulging himself with a stall at that luxurious theatre, he would rough it and go to the pit at the Prince Frederick, to see Mademoiselle Chicot. He had been haunted by her name on the walls of London, but he had never yet had the desire to see her. Now all at once his curiosity was aroused. He went, and admired the dancer, as all the world admired her. He was early enough to get a seat in the front row of the pit, and from this position could survey the stalls, which were filled with men, all declared worshippers of La Chicot. There was one squat figure—a stout dark man, with sleek black hair, and colourless Jewish face—which attracted Edward's particular attention. This man watched the dancer, from his seat at the end of a row, with an expression that differed markedly from the vacuous admiration of other countenances. In this man's face, dull and weary as it was, there was a look that told of passion held in reserve, of a purpose to be pursued to the very end. A dangerous admirer for any woman, most of all perilous for such a woman as La Chicot.

She saw him, and recognised him, as a familiar presence in an unknown crowd. One brilliant flash of her dark eyes told as much as this, and perhaps was a sufficient reward for Joseph Lemuel's devotion. A slow smile curled his thick lips, and lost itself in the folds of his fat chin. He flung no bouquet to the dancer. He had no desire to advertise his admiration. When the curtain fell upon the brilliant tableau which ended the burlesque—a picture made up of handsome women in dazzling dresses and eccentric attitudes, lighted by the broad glare of a magnesium lamp—Edward left the pit and went round to the narrow side street on which the stage-door opened. He had an idea that the dancer's husband would be waiting to escort her home.

He waited himself in the dark chilly street for about a quarter of an hour, and then, instead of Mr. Chicot, the artist, he saw his acquaintance of the tavern stroll slowly to the stage-door, wrapped in an ancient poncho, made of shaggy stuff, like the skin of a wild beast, and smoking a gigantic cigar. This gentleman took up his stand outside the stage-door, and waited patiently for about ten minutes, while Edward Clare walked slowly up and down on the opposite pavement, which was in profound shadow.

At last La Chicot came out, a tall, commanding figure in a black silk gown, which swept the pavement, a sealskin jacket, and a little round hat set jauntily on her dark hair.

She took Desrolles' arm as if it were an accustomed thing for him to escort her; and they went away together, she talking with considerable animation, and as loud as a lady of the highest rank.

'Curious,' thought Edward. 'Where is the husband all this time?'

The husband was spending his evening at a literary club, of somewhat Bohemian character, where there was wit to cheer the saddened soul, and where the nightly talk was of the wildest, breathing ridicule that spared nothing between heaven and earth, and a deep scorn of fools, and an honest contempt for formalism and veneer of all kinds—for the art that follows the fashion of a day, for the literature that is made to pattern. In such a circle Jack Chicot found temporary oblivion. These riotous assemblies, this strong rush of talk, were to him as the waters of Lethe.

CHAPTER XVI.

SHALL IT BE 'YES' OR 'NO'?

'This looks as if he were serious, doesn't it?' asked La Chicot.

The question was addressed to Mr. Desrolles. The two were standing side by side in the wintry dusk, in front of one of the windows that looked into Cibber Street, contemplating the contents of a jewel-case, which La Chicot held open.

Embedded in the white velvet lining there lay a collet necklace of diamonds, each stone as big as a prize pea; such a necklace as Desrolles could not remember to have seen, even in the jewellers' windows, before which he had sometimes paused out of sheer idleness, to contemplate such finery.

'Serious!' he echoed. 'I told you from the first that Joseph Lemuel was a prince.'

'You don't suppose I am going to keep it?' said La Chicot.

'I don't suppose you, or any other woman, would send it back, if it were a free gift,' answered Desrolles.

'It is not a free gift. It is to be mine if I consent to run away from my husband and live in Paris as Mr. Lemuel's mistress. I am to have a villa at Passy, and fifteen hundred a year.'

'Princely!' exclaimed Desrolles.

'And I am to leave Jack free to live his own life. Don't you think he would be glad?'

There was something almost tigerish in the look which emphasised this question.

'I think that it would not matter one jot to you whether he were glad or sorry. He would make a row, I suppose, but you would be safe on the other side of the Channel.'

'He would get a divorce,' said La Chicot. 'Your English law breaks a marriage as easily as it makes one. And then he would marry that other woman.'

'What other woman?'

'I don't know—but there is another. He owned as much the last time we quarrelled.'

'A divorce would make you a great lady. Joseph Lemuel would marry you. The man is your slave; you could twist him round your little finger. And then, instead of your little box at Passy, you might have a mansion in the Champs Elysées, among the ambassadors. You would go to the races in a four-in-hand. You might be the most fashionable woman in Paris.'

'And I began life washing dirty linen in the river at Auray, among a lot of termagants who hated me because I was young and handsome. I had not much pleasure in those days, my friend.'

'Your Parisian life would be a change. You must be very tired of London.'

'Tired! But I detest it prettily, your city of narrow streets and dismal Sundays.'

'And you must have had enough dancing.'

'I begin to be tired of it. Since my accident I have not the old spirit.'

She had the jewel-case in her hand still, and was turning it about, admiring the brightness of the stones, which sparkled in the dim light. Presently she went back to her low chair by the fire, and let the case lie open in her lap, with the fire-glow shining on the gems, until the pure white stones took all the colours of the rainbow.

'I can fancy myself in a box at the opera, in a tight-fitting ruby velvet dress, with no ornaments but this necklace and single diamonds for eardrops,' mused La Chicot. 'I do not think there are many women in Paris who would surpass me.'

'Not one.'

'And I should look on while other women danced for my amusement,' she pursued. 'After all, the life of a stage dancer is a poor thing at best. There are only so many rungs of the ladder between me and a dancing girl at a fair. I am getting tired of it.'

'You will be a good deal more tired when you are a few years older,' said Desrolles.

'At six-and-twenty one need not think of age.'

'No; but at six-and-thirty age will think of you.'

'I have asked for a week to consider his offer,' said La Chicot. 'This day week I am to give him an answer, yes or no. If I keep the diamonds, it will mean yes. If I send them back to him, it will mean no.'

'I can't imagine any woman saying no to such a necklace as that,' said Desrolles.

'What is it worth, after all? Fifteen years ago a string of glass beads bought in the market at Auray would have made me happier than those diamonds can make me now.'

'If you are going to moralise, I can't follow you. I should say, at a rough guess, those diamonds must be worth three thousand pounds.'

'They are to be taken or left,' said La Chicot, in French, with her careless shrug.

'Where do you mean to keep them!' inquired Desrolles. 'If your husband were to see them, there would be a row. You must not leave them in his way.'

'*Pas si bête*,' replied La Chicot. 'See here.'

She flung back the loose collar of her cashmere morning gown, and clasped the necklace round her throat. Then she drew the collar together again, and the diamonds were hidden.

'I shall wear the necklace night and day till I make up my mind whether to keep it or not,' she said. 'Where I go the diamonds will go—nobody will see them—nobody will rob me of them while I am alive. What is the matter?' she asked suddenly, startled by a passing distortion of Desrolles' face.

'Nothing. Only a spasm.'

'I thought you were going to have a fit.'

'I did feel queer for the moment. My old complaint.'

'Ah, I thought as much. Have some brandy.'

Though La Chicot made light of Mr. Lemuel's offering in her talk with Desrolles, she was not the less impressed by it. After she had come from the theatre that night she sat on the floor in her dingy bedroom with a looking-glass in her hand, gloating over her reflection with that string of jewels round her neck, turning her swan-like throat every way to catch the rays of the candle, thinking how glorious she would look with those shining stars upon her ivory neck, thinking what a new and delightful life Joseph Lemuel's wealth could give her; a life of riot and dissipation, fine clothes, epicurean dinners, late hours, and perfect idleness. She even thought of all the famous restaurants in Paris where she would like to dine; fairy palaces on the Boulevard, all lights, and gilding, and crimson velvet, which she knew only from the outside; houses where vice was more at home than virtue, and where a single cutlet in its paper frill cost more than a poor man's family dinner. She looked round the shabby room, with its blackened ceiling and discoloured paper, on which the damp had made ugly blotches; the tawdry curtains, the rickety deal dressing-table disguised in dirty muslin and ragged Nottingham lace—and the threadbare carpet. How miserable it all was! She and her husband had once gone with the crowd to see the house of a Parisian courtesan, who had died in the zenith of her days. She remembered with what almost reverential feeling the mob had gazed

148

at the delicate satin draperies of boudoir and salon, the porcelain, the tapestries, the antique lace, the tiny cabinet pictures which shone like jewels on the satin walls. Vice so exalted was almost virtue.

In the dining-room, paramount over all other objects, was enshrined the portrait of the departed goddess, a medallion in a frame of velvet and gold. La Chicot well remembered wondering to see so little beauty in that celebrated face—a small oval face, grey eyes, a nondescript nose, a wide mouth. Intelligence and a winning smile were the only charms of that renowned beauty. Cosmetiques and Wörth had done all the rest. But then the dead and gone courtesan had been one of the cleverest women in France. La Chicot made no allowance for that.

'I am ten times handsomer,' she told herself, 'and yet I shall never keep my own carriage.'

She had often brooded over the difference between her fate and that of the woman whose house, and horses, and carriages, and lap dogs, and jewels she had seen, the sale of which had made a nine days' wonder in Paris. She thought of that dead woman to-night as she sat with the mirror in her hand admiring the diamonds and her beauty, while Jack Chicot was doing his best to forget her in his Bohemian club near the Strand. She remembered all the stories she had heard of that extinguished luminary—her arrogance, her extravagance, the abject slavery of her adorers, her triumphal progress through life, scornful and admired.

It was not the virtuous who despised her, but she who despised the virtuous. Honest women were the chosen mark for her ridicule. People in Paris knew all the details of her brazen, infamous life. Very few knew the history of her death-bed. But the priest who shrived her and the nursing sister who watched her last hours could have told a story to make even Frivolity's hair stand on end.

'It was a short life, but a merry one,' thought La Chicot. 'How well I remember her the winter the lake in the Bois was frozen, and there was skating by torchlight! She used to drive a sledge covered all over with silver bells, and she used to skate dressed in dark red velvet and sable. The crowd stood on one side to let her pass, as if she had been an empress.'

Then her thoughts took another turn.

'If I left him, he would divorce me and marry that other woman,' she said to herself. 'Who is she, I wonder? Where did he see her? Not at the theatre. He cares for no one there. I have watched him too closely to be deceived in that.'

Then she half-filled a tumbler with brandy, and flavoured it with water, in order to delude herself with the idea that she was drinking brandy and water; and then, lapsing into a state of semi-intoxication—a dreamy, half-consciousness, in which life, seen hazily, took a brighter hue—she flung aside her mirror, and threw herself half-dressed upon the bed.

Jack Chicot, who had taken to coming home long after midnight, slept on the sofa in a little third room, where he worked. There was not much chance of his seeing the jewels. He and his wife were as nearly parted as two people could be, living in the same house.

La Chicot contemplated the diamonds, and abandoned herself to much the same train of thought, for several nights; and now came the last night of the week which Mr. Lemuel had allowed for reflection. To-morrow she was to give him his answer.

He was waiting for her at the stage-door when she came out. Desrolles, her usual escort, was not in attendance.

'Zaïre, I have been thinking of you every hour since last we spoke together,' Joseph Lemuel began, delighted at finding her alone. 'You are as difficult to approach as a princess of the blood royal.'

'Why should I hold myself cheaper than a princess?' she asked, insolently. 'I am an honest woman.'

'You are handsomer than any princess in Europe,' he said. 'But you ought to compassionate an adorer who has waited so long and so patiently. When am I to have your answer? Is it to be yes? You cannot be so cruel as to say no. My lawyer has drawn up the deed of settlement. I only wait your word to execute it.'

'You are very generous,' said La Chicot, scornfully, 'or very obstinate. If I run away with you and my husband gets a divorce, will you marry me?'

'Be faithful to me, and I will refuse you nothing.' He went with her to the door of her lodgings for the first time, pleading his cause all the way, with such eloquence as he could command, which was not much. He was a man who had found money all powerful to obtain everything he wanted, and had seldom felt the need of words.

'Send me a messenger you can trust at twelve o'clock to-morrow, and if I do not send you back your diamonds——'

'I shall know that your answer is yes. In that case you will find my brougham waiting at a quarter-past seven o'clock to-morrow evening, at the corner of this street, and I shall be in the brougham. We will drive straight to Charing Cross, and start for Paris by the mail. It will be too dark for any one to notice the carriage. What time do you generally go to the theatre?'

'At half-past seven.'

'Then you will not be missed till you are well out of the way. There will be no fuss, no scandal.'

'There will be a tremendous fuss at the theatre,' said La Chicot. 'Who is to take my place in the burlesque?'

'Any one. What need you care? You will have done with burlesque and the stage for ever.'

'True,' said La Chicot.

And then she remembered the Student's Theatre in Paris, and how her popularity had waned there. The same thing might happen here in London, perhaps, after a year or two. Her audience would grow tired of her. Already people in the theatre had begun to make disagreeable remarks about the empty champagne bottles which came out of her dressing-room. By-and-by, perhaps, they would be impudent enough to call her a drunkard. She would be glad to have done with them.

Yet, degraded as she was, there were depths of vice from which her better instincts plucked her back; as if it were her good angel clutching her garments to drag her from the edge of an abyss. She had once loved her husband; nay, after her own manner, she loved him still, and could not calmly contemplate leaving him. Her brain, muddled by champagne and brandy, shaped all thoughts confusedly; yet at her worst the idea of selling herself to this Jewish profligate shocked and disgusted her. Her soul was swayed to and fro, to this side and to that. She had no inclination to vice, but she would have liked the wages of sin; for in this lower world the wages of sin meant a villa at Passy, and a couple of carriages.

'Good night,' she said abruptly to her lover. 'I must not be seen talking to you. My husband may come home at any minute.'

'I hear that he generally comes home in the middle of the night,' said Mr. Lemuel.

'What business is it of yours if he does?' asked La Chicot, angrily.

'Everything that concerns you is my business. When I, who love the ground you walk upon, hear how you are neglected by your husband, do you suppose the knowledge does not make me so much the more determined to win you?'

'Send your messenger for my answer to-morrow,' said La Chicot, and then she shut the door in his face.

'I hate him,' she muttered, when she was alone in the passage, stamping her foot as if she had trodden upon a venomous insect.

She went upstairs, and again sat down, half undressed, upon the floor, to look at the diamond necklace. She had a childish love of the gems—a delight in looking at them—which differed very little from her feelings when she was fifteen years younger, and longed for a blue bead necklace exposed for sale in the quaint old market-place at Auray.

'I shall send them back to him to-morrow,' she said to herself. 'The diamonds are beautiful—and I am getting tired of my life here, and I know that Jack hates me—but that man is too horrible—and—I am an honest woman.'

She flung herself on her knees beside the bed, in the attitude of prayer, but not to pray. She had lost the habit of prayer soon after she left her native province. She was sobbing passionately for the loss of her husband's love, with a dim consciousness that it was by her own degradation she had forfeited his regard.

'I've been a good wife to him,' she murmured in broken syllables, 'better than ever I was——'

And then speech lost itself in convulsive sobs, and she cried herself to sleep.

CHAPTER XVII.

MURDER.

Murder! an awful word under the most ordinary circumstances of every-day life—an awful word even when spoken of an event that happened long ago, or afar off. But what a word shouted in the dead of night, through the close darkness of a sleeping house, thrilling the ear of slumber, freezing the blood in the half-awakened sleepers' veins.

Such a shout—repeated with passionate clamour—scared the inhabitants of the Cibber Street lodging-house at three o'clock in the winter morning, still dark as deepest night. Mrs. Rawber heard it in her back bedroom on the ground floor. It penetrated confusedly—not as a word, but as a sound of fear and dread—to the front kitchen, where Mrs. Evitt, the landlady, slept on an ancient press bedstead, which by day made believe to be a book-case. Lastly, Desrolles, who seemed to have slept more heavily than the other two on that particular night, came rushing out of his room to ask the meaning of that hideous summons.

They all met on the first-floor landing, where Jack Chicot stood on the threshold of his wife's bedroom, with a candle in his hand, the flickering flame making a patch of sickly yellow light amidst surrounding gloom—a faint light in which Jack Chicot's pallid countenance looked like the face of a ghost.

'What is the matter?' Desrolles asked the two women, simultaneously.

'My wife has been murdered. My God, it is too awful! See—see——'

Chicot pointed with a trembling hand to a thin thread of crimson that had crept along the dull grey carpet to the very threshold. Shudderingly the others looked inside, as he held the candle towards the bed, with white, averted face. There were hideous stains on the counterpane, an awful figure lying in a heap among the bed-clothes, a long loose coil of raven hair, curved like a snake round the rigid form—a spectacle which not one of those who gazed upon it, spellbound, fascinated by the horror of the sight, could ever hope to forget.

'Murdered, and in my house!' shrieked Mrs. Evitt, unconsciously echoing the words of Lady Macbeth, on a similar occasion. 'I shall never let my first floor again. I'm a ruined woman. Seize him, 'old 'im tight,' she cried, with sudden intensity. 'It must 'ave been her 'usband done it. You was often a-quarrelling, you know you was.'

This fierce attack startled Jack Chicot. He turned upon the woman with his ghastly face, a new horror in his eyes.

'I kill her!' he cried. 'I never raised my hand against her in my life, though she has tempted me many a time. I came into the house three minutes ago. I should not have known anything, for when I come in late I sleep in the little room, but I saw that——' (he pointed to the thin red streak which had crept across the threshold, and under the door, to the carpetless landing outside), 'and then I came in and found her lying here, as you see her.'

'Somebody ought to go for a policeman,' suggested Desrolles.

'I will,' said Chicot.

He was the only person present in a condition to leave the house and before any one could question his right to leave it he was gone.

They waited outside that awful chamber for a quarter of an hour, but no policeman came, nor did Jack Chicot return.

'I begin to think he has made a bolt of it,' said Desrolles. 'That looks rather bad.'

'Didn't I tell you he'd done it?' screamed the landlady. 'I know he'd got to hate her. I've seen it in his looks—and she has told me as much, and cried over it, poor thing, when she'd taken a glass or two more than was good for her. And you let him go, like a coward as you was.'

'My good Mrs. Evitt, you are getting abusive. I was not sent into the world to arrest possible criminals. I am not a detective.'

'But I'm a ruined woman!' cried the outraged householder. 'Who's to occupy my lodgings in future, I should like to know? The house'll get the name of being haunted. Here's Mrs. Rawber even, that has been with me close upon five year, will be wanting to go.'

'I've had a turn,' assented the tragic lady, 'and I don't feel that I can lie down in my bed again downstairs. I'm afraid I may have to look for other apartments.'

'There,' whimpered Mrs. Evitt, 'didn't I tell you I was a ruined woman?'

Desrolles had gone into the front room, and was standing at an open window watching for a policeman.

One of those guardians of the public peace came strolling along the pavement presently, with as placid an air as if he had been an inhabitant of Arcadia, to whom Desrolles shouted, 'Come up here, there's been murder.'

The public guardian wheeled himself stiffly round and approached the street door. He did not take the word murder in its positive sense, but in its local significance, which meant a row, culminating in a few bruises and a black eye or two. That actual murder had been done, and that a dead woman was lying in the house, never entered his mind. He opened the door and came upstairs with slow, creaking footsteps, as if he had been making a ceremonious visit.

'What's the row?' he asked curtly, when he came to the first floor landing, and saw the two women standing there, Mrs. Evitt wrapped in a waterproof, Mrs. Rawber in a yellow cotton dressing-gown of antiquated fashion, both with scared faces and sparse, dishevelled hair.

Mr. Desrolles was the coolest of the trio, but even his countenance had a ghastly look in the light of the guttering candle which Jack Chicot had set down on the little table outside the bedroom door.

They told him breathlessly what had happened.

'Is she dead?' he asked.

'Go in and look,' said Mrs. Evitt. 'I dared not go a-nigh her.'

The policeman went in, lantern in hand, a monument of stolid calm, amidst the terror of the scene. Little need to ask if she were dead. That awful face upon the pillow, those glazed eyes with their wide stare of horror, that gaping wound in the full white throat, from which the life-blood had poured in a crimson stream across the white counterpane, until it made a dark pool beside the bed, all told their own tale.

'She must have been dead for an hour or more,' said the policeman, touching the marble hand.

La Chicot's hand and arm were flung above her head, as if she had known what was coming, and had tried to clutch the bell-pull behind her. The other hand was tightly clenched as in the last convulsion.

'There'll have to be an inquest,' said the policeman, after he had examined the window, and looked out to see if the room was easily accessible from without. 'Somebody had better go for a doctor. I'll go myself. There's a surgeon at the corner of the next street. Who is she, and how did it happen?'

Mrs. Evitt, in a torrent of words, told him all she knew, and all she suspected. It was La Chicot's husband that had done it, she was sure.

'Why?' asked the policeman.

'Who else should it be? It couldn't be burglars. You saw yourself that the window was fastened inside. She'd no valuables to tempt any one. Light come light go was her motto, poor thing. Her money went as fast as it came, and if it wasn't him as did it, why haven't he come back?'

The policeman asked what she meant by this, whereupon Desrolles told him of Mr. Chicot's disappearance.

'I must say that it looks fishy,' concluded the second floor lodger. 'I don't want to breathe a word against a man I like, but it looks fishy. He went out twenty minutes ago to fetch a policeman, and he hasn't come back yet.'

'No, nor never will,' said Mrs. Rawber, who was sitting on the stairs shivering, afraid to go back to her bedroom.

That ground floor bedroom of hers was a dismal place at the best of times, overshadowed by the wall of the yard, and made dark and damp by a protruding cistern, but how would it seem to her now when the house was made horrible by murder?

'Do you know what time it was when the husband gave the alarm?' asked the policeman.

'Not more than twenty minutes ago.'

'Any of you got a watch?'

Desrolles shrugged his shoulders. Mrs. Evitt murmured something about her poor husband's watch which had been a good one in its time, till one of the hands broke short off and the works went wrong. Mrs. Rawber had a clock on her bedroom mantelpiece, and had noticed the time when that awful cry awoke her, scared as she was. It was ten minutes after three.

'And now it wants twenty to four,' said the sergeant, looking at his watch. 'If the husband did it, he must have done it a good hour before he gave the alarm; at least that's my opinion. We shall hear what the doctor says. I'll go and fetch him. Now, look here, my good people: if you value your own characters, you'll none of you attempt to leave this house to-night. Your evidence will be wanted at the inquest to-morrow, and the quieter and closer you keep yourselves meanwhile the safer for you.'

'I shall go back to bed,' said Desrolles, 'as I don't see my way to being of any use.'

'That's the best thing you can do,' said the sergeant, approvingly; 'and you, ma'am,' he added, turning to Mrs. Rawber, 'had better follow the gentleman's example.'

156

Mrs. Rawber felt as if her bedroom would be peopled with ghosts, but did not like to give utterance to her fears.

'I'll go down and set a light to my parlour fire, and mix myself a wine-glassful of something warm,' she said. 'I feel chilled to the marrow of my bones.'

'You, ma'am, had better wait up here till I come back with the doctor,' said the policeman.

Desrolles had returned to his room by this time. Mrs. Rawber went downstairs with the policeman, glad of his company so far. He waited politely while she struck a lucifer and lighted her candle, and then he hurried off to find the doctor.

'There's company in a fire,' mused Mrs. Rawber, as she groped for wood and paper in the bottom of a cupboard not wholly innocent of black beetles.

There was company in a glass of hot gin-and-water, too, by-and-by, when the tiny kettle had been coaxed into a boil. Mrs. Rawber was a temperate woman, but she liked what she called her 'little comforts,' and an occasional tumbler of gin-and-water was one of them.

'It's very hard upon me,' she said to herself, thinking of the dreadful deed that had been done upstairs; 'the rooms suit me, and I'm used to them; and yet I believe I shall have to go. I shall fancy the place is haunted.'

She glanced round over her shoulder, fearful lest she should see La Chicot in her awful beauty—a marble face, a blood-stained throat, and glassy eyes regarding her with sightless stare.

'I shall have to leave,' thought Mrs. Rawber.

Meanwhile Mrs. Evitt was alone upstairs. She was a ghoul-like woman, for whom horrors were not without a ghastly relish. She liked to visit in the house of death, to sit beside the winter fire with a batch of gossips, consuming tea and toast, dwelling on the details of a last illness, or discussing the order of a funeral. She had a dreadful courage that came of familiarity with death. She took up the candle, and went in alone and unappalled to look at La Chicot.

'How tight that hand is clenched!' she said to herself; 'I wonder whether there's anything in it?'

She forced back the stiffening fingers, and with the candle held close, bent down to peer into the marble palm. In the hollow of that dead hand she found a little tuft of iron-grey hair, which looked as if it had been torn from a man's head.

Mrs. Evitt drew the hairs from the dead hand, and with a careful precision laid them in an old letter which she took from her pocket, and folded up the letter into a neat little packet, which she returned to the same calico receptacle for heterogeneous articles.

'What a turn it has given me!' she said to herself, stealing back to the landing, her petticoats lifted, lest the hem of her garments should touch that dreadful pool beside the bed.

The expression of her face had altered since she entered the room. There was a new intelligence in her dull gray eyes. Her countenance and bearing were as of one whose mind is charged with the weight of an awful secret.

The surgeon came, an elderly man, who lived close at hand, and was experienced in the ways of that doubtful section of society which inhabited the neighborhood of Cibber Street. In his opinion La Chicot had been dead three hours. It was now on the stroke of four. One o'clock must, therefore, have been the time of the murder.

The police-sergeant came back in company with a man in plain clothes, and these two made a careful examination of the premises together, the result of which inspection went to show that it would have been extremely difficult for any one to enter the house from the back. The front door was left on the latch all night, and had been for the last eleven years, and no harm had ever come of it, Mrs. Evitt declared, plaintively. It was a Chubb lock, and she didn't believe there was another like it in all London.

The two men went into every room in the house, disturbed Mr. Desrolles in a comfortable slumber, and surveyed his bedchamber with eyes which took in every detail. There was very little for them to see: a tent bedstead draped with flabby faded chintz, a rickety washstand, a small chest of drawers with a looking-glass on the top, and three odd chairs, picked up at humble auctions.

After inspecting Mr. Desrolles' rooms and overhauling his limited wardrobe, they looked in upon Mrs. Rawber, and roused that talented woman's ire by opening all her drawers and cupboards, and peering curiously into the same, whereby they beheld more mysteries of theatrical attire than ought to be seen by the public eye.

'You don't suppose I did it, I hope?' protested Mrs. Rawber, in her grandest tragedy voice.

'No, ma'am, but we're obliged to do our duty,' answered the police officer. 'It's only a form.'

'It's a very disagreeable form,' said Mrs. Rawber, 'and if you tallow-grease my Lady Macbeth dresses, I shall expect you to make them good.'

The man in plain clothes committed himself to no opinion, nor did he enter upon any discussion as to the motive of a crime apparently so motiveless. He made his notes of the plain facts of the case, and went away with the sergeant.

'What am I to do about laying her out?' asked Mrs. Evitt of the doctor. 'I wouldn't lay a finger upon her for a hundred pounds.'

'I'll send round a nurse from the workhouse,' said the doctor, after a moment's thought. 'They're not easily scared.'

Half an hour later the workhouse nurse came, a tall, bony woman, who executed her horrible task in a business-like manner, which testified to the strength of her nerve and the variety of her experience.

By five o'clock in the morning all was done, and La Chicot lay with meekly folded hands under clean white linen—the heavy lids closed for ever on the once lovely eyes, the raven hair parted on the classic brow.

'She's the handsomest corpse I've laid out for the last ten years,' said the nurse, 'and I think she does me credit. If you've got a kettle on the bile, mum, and can give me a cup of tea, I shall be thankful for it; and I think a teaspoonful of sperrits in it would do me good. I've been up all night with a fractious pauper in the small-pox ward.'

'Oh, lor!' cried Mrs. Evitt, with an alarmed countenance.

'You've been vaccinated, of course, mum,' said the nurse cheerfully. 'You don't belong to none of them radical anti-vaccinationists, I'm sure. And as to catching complaints of that kind, mum, it's only your pore-spirited, nervous people as does it. I never have no pity for such weak mortals. I look down on 'em too much.'

CHAPTER XVIII.

WHAT THE DIAMONDS WERE WORTH.

The inquest was held at noon next day. The news of the murder had spread far and wide already, and there was a crowd gathered round the house in Cibber Street all the morning, much to Mrs. Evitt's aggravation. The newspaper reporters forced their way into her house in defiance of her protests, and finding her slow to answer their questions, got hold of Mr. Desrolles, who was very ready to talk and to drink with every comer.

George Gerard called at the house in Cibber Street between nine and ten o'clock. He had heard of the murder on his way from the Blackfriars Road, where he was now living as assistant to a general practitioner, to the hospital where he was still attending the clinical lectures. He had heard an exaggerated version of the event, and came expecting to find a case of murder and suicide, the husband stretched lifeless beside the wife he had sacrificed to his jealous fury.

It was not without some difficulty that he got permission to enter the room where the dead woman lay. The hospital nurse had been put in charge of that chamber by the police, and Gerard was obliged to enforce his arguments with a half-crown, which he could ill afford, before the lady's conscientious scruples were quieted, and she gave him the key of the room.

He went in with the nurse, and stayed for about a quarter of an hour, engaged in a careful and thoughtful examination of the wound. It was a curious wound. La Chicot's throat had not been cut, in the common acceptation of the phrase. The blow that had slain her was a deep stab; a violent thrust with some sharp, thin, and narrow instrument, which had pierced the hollow of her neck, and penetrated in a slanting direction to the lungs.

What had been the instrument? Was it a dagger? and, if so, what kind of dagger? George Gerard had never seen a dagger thin enough to inflict that fine, narrow slit through which the blood had oozed so slowly. The crimson stream that stained coverlet and floor had flowed from the livid lips of the corpse, betokening hæmorrhage of the lungs.

There had been a struggle before that fatal wound was given. On

160

the round, white wrist of the dead a purple bruise showed where a savage hand had gripped that lovely arm; on the right shoulder, from which the loose night-dress had fallen, appeared the marks of strong fingers that had fastened their clutch there. The nurse showed Gerard these bruises.

'They tell a tale, don't they?' she said.

'If we could only read it aright,' sighed Gerard.

'It looks as if she had fought for her life, poor soul,' suggested the nurse.

Gerard made no further remark, but stood beside the bed, looking round him with thoughtful, scrutinizing gaze, as if he would have asked the very walls to tell him the secret of the crime they had looked upon a few hours before.

'The police have been here and have discovered nothing?' he said, interrogatively.

'Whatever they've discovered they've kept to themselves,' answered the nurse, 'but I don't believe it's much.'

'Did they go in there?' asked Gerard, pointing to the open door of that small inner room, a mere den, where Jack Chicot had painted in the days when he cherished the hope of earning his living as a painter. Here of late he had drawn his wood-blocks, and here, on a wretched narrow couch, he had slept.

'Yes, they went in,' replied the nurse, 'but I'm sure they didn't find anything particular there.'

Gerard passed into the dusty little den. There was an old easel with an unfinished picture, half-covered with a ragged chintz curtain. Gerard plucked the curtain aside, and looked at the picture. It was crude, but full of a certain melodramatic power. The subject was from a poem of De Musset's, a Venetian noble, crouching in the shadow of a doorway, at dead of night, dagger in hand, waiting to slay his enemy. There was a deal table, ink-stained, decrepit, scattered with papers, pens, pencils, a battered pewter inkstand, an empty cigar-box, a file of 'Folly as it Flies,' and odd numbers of other comic journals. On the old-fashioned window-seat—for these houses in Cibber Street were two hundred years old—there was a large wooden paint-box, full of empty tubes, brushes, a couple of palettes, an old palette-knife, rags, sponges. At the bottom of the box, hidden under rags and rubbish, there lay a long thin dagger, of Italian workmanship, the handle of finely-wrought silver, oxidized with age—just such a dagger as an artist would fancy for his armoury. One glance at the canvas yonder told Gerard that this was the dagger in the picture.

George Gerard took up the dagger and looked at it curiously—a long thin blade, flexible, sharp, a deadly weapon in a strong hand, a weapon to inflict just such a wound as that deep stab which had slain La Chicot.

He examined the blade, the handle—looking at both through his pocket microscope. Both were darkly tarnished, possibly with the recent stain of blood; but the weapon had been carefully cleansed, and there was no actual speck of blood upon either handle or blade.

'Strange that the detectives should have overlooked this,' he said to himself, replacing the dagger in the box.

Mrs. Evitt had told him of Jack Chicot's unaccountable disappearance, how he had gone out to call the police, and had never come back. What could this mean, except guilt? And here in the husband's colour-box was just such a weapon as that with which the wife had been stabbed.

'And I know that he was weary of her, I know that he wanted her to die,' mused Gerard. 'I read that secret in his face six months ago.'

He left the room presently, without any expression of opinion to the hospital nurse, who was eager to discuss the deed that had been done, and had theories of her own about it. He left the house and walked the neighbouring streets for an hour, waiting for the inquest.

'Shall I volunteer my opinion before the Coroner?' he asked himself. 'To what end? It is but a theory, after all. And a Coroner is rarely a man inclined to give his ear to speculations of that kind. I'd better write to one of the newspapers. Would it do any good if I were to bring the crime home to the husband? Not much, perhaps. Wherever the wretch goes he carries with him a conscience that must be a worse punishment than the condemned cell. And to hang him would not bring her back to life. Poor foolish, lost creature, the only woman I ever loved.'

The Prince of Wales's Feathers—more popularly known as the Feathers—a public-house at the corner of Cibber Street and Woodpecker Court, was the scene of the inquiry. The witnesses were the doctor, the police-sergeant, the detective who had assisted in the examination of the premises, Desrolles, Mrs. Evitt, and Mrs. Rawber. Jack Chicot, the most important witness of all, had not been seen since he left the house under the pretence of summoning the police. This disappearance of the husband, after giving an alarm which roused the sleeping household—an altogether unnecessary and foolish act, supposing him to be the murderer—was the most remarkable feature in the case, and puzzled the Coroner.

He questioned Mrs. Evitt closely as to the habits of the dancer and her husband.

'You say they quarrelled frequently,' he said. 'Were their disputes of a violent character?'

'I have heard her violent, but never him. She was very fond of him, poor thing; though she wasn't a woman to give way or to be guided by a husband. She was fonder of drink than she ought to be, and he tried to keep her from it—leastways, when they first came to my house. Later he seemed to have give her up, as you may say, and let her go her own way.'

'Did he seem attached to her?'

'Not to my fancy. I thought the love was all on her side.'

'Was he a man of violent temper?'

'No; he was one that took things very quiet. I used to think there was something underhand in his character. I can call to mind her saying to me once, after they had been quarrelling, "Mrs. Evitt, that man hates me too much to strike me. If he was once to give way to his temper he'd be the death of me." Those words of hers made an impression upon me at the time——'

'Come, come,' interrupted the Coroner, 'we can't hear anything about your impressions. This isn't evidence!' but Mrs. Evitt's slow speech flowed onward like a tranquil stream meandering through a valley.

'"I'd rather have a low brute that beat me black and blue," she said to me another time, poor dear thing, "if he was sorry for it afterwards, than a cold-hearted gentleman that can sting me to death with a word."'

'I want to hear facts, not assertions,' said the Coroner, impatiently. 'Did you ever know the husband of the deceased to be guilty of any act of violence, either towards his wife or any one else?'

'Never.'

'Do you know if Madame Chicot had money or any other valuables in her possession?'

'I should say she had neither. She was a woman of extravagant habits. It wasn't in her to save money.'

Mrs. Rawber's evidence merely confirmed Mrs. Evitt as to the hour at which they had been aroused, and the conduct of Jack Chicot. The two women agreed as to the ghastly look of his face, and the sudden eagerness with which he had caught at the idea of going to fetch a policeman, an idea suggested by Desrolles.

Desrolles was the last witness examined. As he stood up to answer the Coroner, he caught sight of a familiar face in the crowd near the doorway. It was the countenance of Joseph Lemuel, the stockbroker, sorely changed since Desrolles had seen it last. Close by Mr. Lemuel's side appeared a well-known criminal lawyer. Desrolles' bistre complexion grew a shade grayer at sight of these two faces, both intently watchful.

The evidence of Desrolles threw no new light upon the mystery. He had known Mr. Chicot and his wife intimately—rarely had passed a day without seeing them. They were both excellent creatures, but not suited to each other. They did not live happily together. He had never seen Jack Chicot guilty of any act of absolute violence towards his wife, but he believed that there was a good deal of bitterness in his mind; in short that they could not have gone on living together peaceably much longer. Mr. Chicot had absented himself from home very much of late. He had kept late hours, and avoided his wife's company. In a word, it was an ill-assorted marriage, and they were a very unhappy couple—much to be pitied, both.

This was all. The coroner adjourned the inquiry for a week, in the hope that further evidence would be forthcoming. There was a feeling in the court that a very strong suspicion attached to the dead woman's husband, and that if he did not turn up speedily he would have to be looked for.

George Gerard watched the inquest from a crowded corner of the room, but he held his peace as to that discovery of the dagger in Jack Chicot's colour-box.

La Chicot was buried two days afterwards, and there was a tremendous crowd at Kensal Green to see the foreign dancing woman laid in her untimely grave. Mr. Smolendo, with his own hands, placed a wreath of white camellias on the coffin. Desrolles stood beside the grave, decently attired in a suit of black, hired for the occasion from a dealer in cast-off clothes, and 'looking quite the gentleman,' Mrs. Evitt said to her gossips afterwards. Mrs. Evitt and Mrs. Rawber were both at the funeral; indeed, it may be said that the whole of Cibber Street turned out for the occasion. There had not been such a crowd since the burial of Cardinal Wiseman. All the company from the Prince Frederick was there, besides much more of dramatic and equestrian London.

Poor Mr. Smolendo was in the depth of despair. He had found an all-accomplished lady to take La Chicot's place in the burlesque; but the public did not believe in the all-accomplished lady—who was old enough to have been La Chicot's mother,—and Mr. Smolendo saw his theatre a desert of empty benches. No matter that his scenery, his ballet, his orchestra, his lime-lights were the best and most costly in London. The public had run after La Chicot, and her unhappy fate cast a gloom over the house, not easily to be dispersed. The tide of fashion rolled away to other theatres; and the bark that carried Mr. Smolendo's fortunes was left stranded on the shore.

The press was very vehement upon the case of La Chicot. The more popular of the penny dailies went into convulsions of indignation against everybody concerned. They reviled the coroner; they denounced the surgeon as a simpleton; they insinuated dark things about the landlady; they branded the witnesses as perjurers; but they reserved their most scathing denunciations for the police.

Here was an atrocious murder committed in the very heart of civilized London; in the midst of a calmly slumbering household; in a house in which almost every room was occupied; and yet the murderer is suffered to escape, and yet no ray of light from the combined intelligence of Scotland Yard pierces the gloom of the mystery.

The husband of the victim, against whom there is the strongest presumptive evidence, whose own conduct is all-sufficient to condemn him, this wretch is suffered to roam at large over the earth, a modern Cain, without the brand upon his brow by which his fellow-men may know him. Perhaps at this very hour he is haunting our taverns, dining at our restaurants, polluting the innocent atmosphere of our theatres, a guilty creature sitting at a play—nay, even, with the hypocrite's visage, crossing the hallowed threshold of a church! Where are the police? What are they doing that this scoundrel has not been found? They should be able to recognise him at a glance, even without the brand of Cain. Are there no photographs of the monster, who has been described as good-looking, and who was doubtless vain! Letters pour in to the *Morning Shrieker* by the bushel, every correspondent suggesting his own particular and original method for catching a murderer.

Strange to say, Jack Chicot, although a fair subject for the camera, has had no passion for seeing what kind of picture the sun can make of him. At any rate, there is no portrait of him, large or small, good, bad, or indifferent, to be found in Cibber Street, where the police naturally came to look for one. Mr. Desrolles, who, throughout the case, shows himself accommodating without being officious, gives a graphic description of his late fellow-lodger; but no verbal picture ever yet conjured up the image of a man, and the detectives leave Cibber Street possessed of the idea of a personage no more like Jack Chicot than Jack Chicot was like the Emperor of China. This imaginary Chicot they hunt assiduously in all the worst parts of London, and often seem on the brink of catching him. They watch him dining at low eating-houses, they see him playing billiards in dubious taverns, they follow him on to penny steamers, and accompany him on railroad journeys, always to find that, although sufficiently disreputable, he is not Jack Chicot.

Working thus conscientiously, it was hard to be girded at by the *Morning Shrieker* and an army of letter-writers.

Assuredly the evidence against the missing husband was strong enough to weave the rope that should hang him.

A letter to the *Times* from George Gerard describing the dagger found in the colour-box had attracted the attention of the famous surgeon who set La Chicot's broken leg, and that gentleman had hurried at once to Cibber Street to examine the wound. He afterwards saw the dagger which, with the rest of the missing man's effects, was in the custody of the police. He wrote to the *Times* next day, confirming Gerard's statement. Such a wound could have been inflicted by just such a dagger, and hardly by any other form of knife or dagger known to civilization. The thin flexible blade was unlike the blade of any other dagger the surgeon had ever seen—the wound corresponded to the form of the blade.

The leader-writers on the popular journals took up the idea. They depicted the whole scene as vividly as if it had been shown to them in a charmed sleep. They gushed as they described the beauty of the wife; they wept as they told of her intemperate habits. The husband they painted in the darkest dyes of iniquity. A man who had battened on his wife's earnings—a poor creature—a led captain—idle, luxurious, intemperate, since it was doubtless his example which had taught that glorious creature to drink. They painted, in a blaze of lurid light, the scene of the murder. The husband's midnight return from haunts of vice—the wife's recriminations—her natural outbreak of jealousy—hot words on both sides. The husband brutalized by drink, stung to fury by the wife's well-merited reproaches, snatches the dagger from the table where he had lately flung it after a desultory half-hour of labour, and plunges the blade into his wife's bosom. The leader-writer saw the whole thing, as in a picture. The public read, and at street corners and on the roofs of omnibuses the public talk for the next three weeks was of Jack Chicot's crime, and the miserable stupidity of the police in not being able to find him.

* * * *

Between eight and nine o'clock on the night after La Chicot's funeral an elderly man called upon Mr. Mosheh, a diamond merchant in a small way, who lived in one of the streets near Brunswick Square. The gentleman was respectably clad in a long overcoat, and wore a grey beard which had been allowed to grow with a luxuriance that entirely concealed the lower part of his face. Under his soft felt hat he wore a black velvet skull-cap, below which there appeared no vestige of hair; whereby it might be inferred that the velvet cap was intended to hide the baldness of the skull it covered. Under the rim of the cap, which was drawn low upon the brow, appeared a pair of shaggy grey eyebrows, shadowing prominent eyes. Mr. Mosheh came out of his dining-room, whence the savoury odour of fish fried in purest olive oil followed him like a kind of incense, and found the stranger waiting for him in the front room, which was half parlour, half office.

The diamond merchant had a sharp eye for character, and he saw at a glance that his visitor belonged to the hawk rather than to the pigeon family.

'Wants to do me if he can,' he said to himself.

'What can I do for you?' he asked, with oily affability.

'You buy diamonds, I want to sell some; and as I sell them under the pressure of peculiar circumstances I am prepared to let you have them a bargain,' said the stranger, with a tone at once friendly and business-like.

'I don't believe in bargains. I'll give you a fair price for a good article, if you came by the things honestly,' replied Mr. Mosheh, with a suspicious look. 'I am not a receiver of stolen goods. You have come to the wrong shop for that.'

'If I'd thought you were I shouldn't have come here,' said the grey-bearded old man. 'I want to deal with a gentleman. I am a gentleman myself, though a decayed one. I have not come on my own business, but on that of a friend, a man you know by name and re-pute as well as you know the Prince of Wales—a man carrying on one of the most successful businesses in London. I'm not going to tell you his name. I only give you the facts. My friend has bills coming due to-morrow. If they are dishonoured he must be in the *Gazette* next week. In his difficulty he went to his wife, and made a clean breast of it. She behaved as a good woman ought, put her arms round his neck and told him not to be down-hearted, and then ran for her jewel-case, and gave him her diamonds.'

'Let us have a look at these said diamonds,' replied Mr. Mosheh, without vouchsafing any praise of the wife's devotion.

The man took out a small parcel, and unfolded it. There, on a sheet of cotton wool, reposed the gems, five-and-thirty large white stones, the smallest of them as big as a pea.

'Why, they're unset!' exclaimed the diamond merchant. 'How's that?'

'My friend is a proud man. He didn't want his wife's jewels to be recognised.'

'So he broke up the setting? Your friend was a fool, sir. What do these stones belong to?' speculated Mr. Mosheh, touching the gems lightly with the tip of his fleshy forefinger, and arranging them in a circle. 'A collet necklace, evidently, and a very fine collet necklace it must have been. Your friend was an idiot to destroy it.'

'I believe it was a necklace,' assented the visitor. 'My friend celebrated his silver wedding last year, and the diamonds were a gift to his wife on that occasion.'

The room was dimly lighted with a single candle, which the servant had set down upon the centre table when she admitted the stranger.

Mr. Mosheh drew down a moveable gutta-percha gas tube, and lighted an office lamp which stood beside his desk. By this light he examined the jewels. Not content with the closest inspection, he took a little file from his waistcoat pocket, and drew it across the face of one of the stones.

'Your friend is doubly a fool, if he isn't a knave,' said Mr. Mosheh. 'These stones are sham.'

There came a look so ghastly over the face of the grey-bearded man that the aspect of death itself could hardly have been more awful.

'It's a lie!' he gasped.

'You are an impudent rascal, sir, to bring me such trumpery, and a blatant ass for thinking you could palm your paste upon Benjamin Mosheh, a man who has dealt in diamonds, off and on, for nearly thirty years. The stones are imitation, very clever in their way, and a very good colour. Look here, sir; do you see the mark my file leaves on the surface? Father Abraham, how the man trembles! Do you mean to tell me that you've been fooled by these stones—that you've given money for them? I don't believe a word of your cock-and-a-bull story about your London tradesman and his silver wedding. But do you mean to say you didn't know these stones were duffers, and that I shouldn't be justified in giving you in charge for trying to obtain money upon false pretences?'

'As I am a living man, I thought them real,' gasped the grey-bearded man, who had been seized with a convulsive trembling awful to see.

'And you advanced money upon them?'

'Yes.'

'Much?'

'All I have in the world. All! all!' he repeated, passionately. 'I am a ruined man. For God's sake give me half a tumbler of brandy, if you don't want me to drop down dead in your house.'

The man's condition was so dejected that Mr. Mosheh, though inclined to believe him a swindler, took compassion upon him. He opened the door leading into his dining-room, and called to his wife.

'Rachel, bring me the brandy and a tumbler.'

Mrs. Mosheh obeyed. She was a large woman, magnificently attired in black satin and gold ornaments, like an ebony cabinet mounted in ormolu. Nobody could have believed that she had fried a large consignment of fish that very day before putting on her splendid raiment.

'Is the gentleman ill?' she asked, kindly.

'He feels a little faint. There, my dear, that will do. You can go back to the children.'

'They're uncommonly clever,' said Mr. Mosheh, fingering the stones, and testing them one by one, sometimes with his file, sometimes by the simpler process of wetting them with the tip of his tongue, and looking to see if they retained their fire and light while wet. 'But there's not a real diamond among them. If you've advanced money on 'em, you've been had. They're of French manufacture, I've no doubt. I'll tell you what I'll do for you. If you'll leave 'em with me, I'll try and find out where they were made, and all about them.'

'No, no,' answered the other, breathlessly, drawing the parcel out of Mr. Mosheh's reach, and rolling up the cotton wool, hurriedly. 'It's not worth while, it's no matter. I've been cheated, that's all. It can't help me to know who manufactured the stones, or where they were bought. They're false, you say, and if you are right I'm a ruined man. Good night.'

He had drunk half a tumbler of raw brandy, and the brandy had stopped that convulsive trembling which affected him a few minutes before. He put his parcel in his breast pocket, pulled himself together, and walked slowly and stiffly out of the room and out of the house, Mr. Mosheh accompanying him to the door.

'You can show those stones to as many dealers as you like,' said the Jew; 'you'll find I'm right about 'em. Good night.'

'Good night,' the other answered, faintly, and so disappeared in the wintry fog that wrapped the street round like a veil.

'Is the fellow a knave or a fool, I wonder?' questioned Mr. Mosheh.

CHAPTER XIX.

'TO A DEEP LAWNY DELL THEY CAME.'

It was summer-time again, the beginning of June, the time when summer is fairest and freshest, the young leaves in the woods tender and transparent enough to let the sunlight through, the ferns just unfurling their broad feathers, the roses just opening, the patches of common land and furzy corners of meadows ablaze with gold, the sky an Italian blue, the day so long that one almost forgets there is such a thing as night in the world.

It was a season that Laura had always loved; and even now, gloomy as was the outlook of her young life, she felt her spirits lightened with the brightness of the land. Her cheerfulness astonished Celia, who was in a state of chronic indignation against John Treverton, which was all the more intense because she was forbidden to talk of him.

'I never knew any one take things so lightly as you do, Laura,' she exclaimed one afternoon when she found Mrs. Treverton just returned from a long ramble in the little wood that adjoined the Manor House grounds.

'Why should I make the most of my troubles? Earth seems so full of gladness and hope at this season that one cannot help hoping.'

'You cannot, perhaps. Don't say one cannot,' Celia retorted, snappishly, 'if you mean to include me. I left off hoping before I was eighteen. What is there to hope for in a parish where there are only two eligible bachelors, one of the two as ugly as sin, and the other an incorrigible flirt, a man who seems always on the brink of proposing, yet never proposes?'

'You have not counted your devoted admirer, Mr. Sampson. He makes a third.'

'Sandy-haired, and village-solicitor. Thank you, Laura, I have not sunk so low as that. If I married him I should have to marry his sister Eliza, and that would be quite too dreadful. No, dear, I can manage to exist as I am, "in maiden meditation, fancy free." When I change my situation I shall expect to better myself. As for you, Laura, you are a perfect wonder. I never saw you looking so well. Yet in your position I am sure I should have cried my eyes out.'

'That wouldn't have made the position better. I have not left off hoping, Celia, and when I feel low-spirited I set myself to work to forget my own troubles. There is so much to be looked after on an estate like this—the house, the grounds, the poor people,—I can always find something to do.'

'You are a paragon of industry. I never saw the garden as pretty as it is this year.'

'I like everything to look its best,' said Laura, blushing at her own thoughts.

The one solace of her life of late had been to preserve and beautify the good old house and its surroundings. The secret hope that John Treverton would come back some day, and that life would be fair and sweet for her again, was the hidden spring of all her actions. Every morning she said to herself, 'He may come to-day;' every night she consoled herself with the fancy that he might come to-morrow.

'I may have to wait for years,' she said in her graver moments, 'but let him come when he will, he shall find that I have been a faithful steward.'

She had never left the Manor House since she came back from her lonely honeymoon. She had received various hospitable invitations from the county families, who were anxious to be civil to her now that she was firmly established among them as a landowner; but she refused all such invitations, excusing herself because of her husband's enforced absence. When he returned to England she would be delighted to visit with him, and so on; whereby the county people were given to understand that there was nothing extraordinary or unwarrantable in Mr. Treverton's non-appearance at the Manor House.

'His wife seems to approve of his conduct, so one can only suppose that it's all right,' said people; notwithstanding which the majority clung affectionately to the supposition that it was all wrong.

Despite Laura's hopefulness, and that sweetness of temper and gaiety of mind which preserved the youthful beauty of her face, there were hours—one hour, perhaps, in every day—when her spirits drooped, and hope seemed to sicken. She had pored over John Treverton's last letter until the paper upon which it was written had grown thin and worn with frequent handling; but at the best, dear as the letter was to her, she could not extract much hope from it. The tone of the writer was not utterly hopeless. Yet he spoke of a parting that might be for life; of a tie that might last for ever, a tie that bound him in honour, if not in fact, to some other woman.

He had wronged her deeply by that broken marriage—wronged

her by supposing that the possession of Jasper Treverton's estate could in any wise compensate her for the false position in which that marriage had placed her; and yet she could not find it in her heart to be angry with him. She loved him too well. And this letter, whatever guilt it vaguely confessed, overflowed with love for her. She forgave him all things for the sake of that love.

When had she begun to love him? she asked herself sometimes in a sad reverie. She had questioned him closely as to the growth of his love, but had been slow to make her own confession.

How well she remembered his pale, tired face that winter night, just a year and a half ago, when he came into the lamp-lit room and took his seat on the opposite side of the hearth, a stranger and half an enemy.

She had liked and admired him from the very first, knowing that he was prejudiced against her. The pale, clear-cut face, the grey eyes with their black lashes, which made them look black in some lights, hazel in others; the thoughtful mouth, and that all-pervading expression of melancholy which had at once enlisted her sympathy,—all these had pleased her.

'I must have been dreadfully weak-minded,' she said to herself, 'for I really think I fell in love with him at first sight.'

That little wood behind the Manor House grounds was Laura's favourite resort in this early summer-time. It was the most picturesque of woods, for the ground sloped steeply to a narrow river, on the further side of which there was a rugged bank, topped by a grove of fir trees. The stream ran brawling over a rocky bed; and the bold masses of rock, here shining purple or changeful grey, there green with moss; the fringe of ferns upon the river brink, the old half-ruined wooden bridge that spanned the torrent; the background of beech and oak, mingled with the darker foliage of old Scotch firs; and towering darkly above all, the lofty ridge of moorland, made a picture that Laura fondly loved. Here she came when the prim gardens of the Manor House seemed too small to hold her thoughts and cares. Here she seemed to breathe a freer air.

She came to this spot one evening in June, after a day of sunny weather which had seemed longer and wearier and altogether harder to bear than the generality of her days. Celia had been with her all day, and Celia's small-talk had been drearier than solitude. Laura was thankful to be alone in this quiet shelter, where the indefatigable labours of the woodpecker and the babble of the stream were the only sounds that stirred the summer silence.

All day long the heat had been hardly endurable; now there was a breath of coolness in the air, and nothing left of that fierce sun but a soft yellow light in the western sky.

Laura had a volume of Shelley in her pocket, taken up from among the books on the table in her favourite room. It was one of the books she loved best, and had been the companion of many a ramble. She seated herself on a fallen trunk of oak beside the river, and opened the volume haphazard at 'Rosalind and Helen,' and she read on till she came to those lovely lines which picture such a spot as that where she was sitting.

> 'To a deep lawny dell they came,
> To a stone seat beside a spring,
> O'er which the columned wood did frame
> A roofless temple, like the fane
> Where, ere new creeds could faith obtain,
> Man's early race once knelt beneath
> The overhanging Deity.'

She read on. The scene suited the poem, and its deep melancholy harmonized but too well with her own feelings. A story of love, the fondest, truest, most unworldly, ending in hopeless sorrow. Never had the gloom of that poem sunk so heavily upon her spirit.

She closed the book suddenly, with a half-stifled sob. The moon was rising, silver pale, above the dark ridge of moorland. The last streak of golden light had faded behind the red trunks of the firs. The low, melancholy cry of an owl sounded far off in the dark heart of the wood. It was indeed as if—

> 'The owls had all fled far away,
> In a merrier glen to hoot and play.'

In such a spot a mind attuned to melancholy might easily shape spectral forms out of the evening shadows, and call up the ghosts of the loved and lost. Laura looked up from her book with a strange uncanny feeling, as if, indeed, some ghostly presence were near. Her eyes wandered slowly across the rocky bed of the river, and there, on the opposite bank, half in shadow, half in the tender light of the big round moon, she saw a tall figure and a pale face looking at her. She rose with a half-stifled cry of fear. That face looked so spectral in the mystical light. And then she clasped her hands joyously and cried, 'I knew you would come back!'

This was the deserter's welcome. No frowns, no upbraidings—a sweet face beaming with delight, a happy voice full of fondest welcome.

'Humph!' cries the woman-hater, 'what fools these women are!'

John Treverton came stepping lightly across the rocks, at some risk of measuring his length in the stony bed of the river, and in less than a minute was by his wife's side.

Not a word did he say for the first moment or so. His greeting was dumb. He took her to his heart, and kissed her as he had never kissed her yet.

'My own one, my wife!' he cried. 'You are all mine now. Love, I have been patient. Don't be hard with me.'

This last remonstrance was because she had drawn herself away from his arms, and was looking at him with a smile which was no longer tender, but ironical.

'Have you come back to Hazlehurst to spend an evening?' she asked, 'or can you prolong your visit for a week?'

'I have come back to spend my life with you—I have come back to stay for ever! They may begin to build me a vault to-morrow in Hazlehurst churchyard. I shall be here to occupy it when my time comes—if you will have me. That is the question, Laura. It all depends on you. Oh, love, love, answer me quickly. If you but knew how I have longed for this moment! Tell me, sweet, have I quite worn out your love? Has my conduct forfeited your esteem for ever?'

'You have behaved very unkindly to me,' she answered, slowly, gravely, her voice trembling a little. 'You have used me in a manner which I think a woman with proper womanly pride could hardly forgive.'

'Laura!' he cried, piteously.

'But I fear I am not possessed of proper womanly pride; for I have forgiven you,' she said, innocently.

'My treasure! my delight!'

'But it would have been so much easier to forgive if you had trusted me, if you had told me all the truth. Oh, John, husband and yet no husband, you have treated me very cruelly.'

Here she forgot her unreasoning joy at seeing him again, and suddenly remembered herself and her wrongs.

'I know, love,' he said, on his knees beside her, 'I seem to have acted vilely, and yet, believe me, dearest, my sole motive was the desire to protect your interests.'

'Your conduct has put me to shame before all mankind,' urged Laura, meaning the village of Hazlehurst. 'You have no right to approach me, no right to look me in the face. Have you not confessed in that cruel letter that you were not free to marry me, that you belong in some way to another woman?'

'That other woman is dead. I am free as the air.'

'What was she? your wife?'

There was a look of infinite pain in John Treverton's face. His lips moved as if about to speak, but he was silent. There are some truths difficult of utterance; and it is not easy to all men to lie.

'It is too painful a story,' he began at last, speaking hurriedly, as if he wanted to make a speedy end of a hateful subject. 'A good many years ago, when I was very young, and a most consummate fool, I got myself entrapped into a Scotch marriage. You have heard of the peculiarities of the marriage law in Scotland.'

'Yes, I have heard and read about them.'

'Of course. Well, it was a marriage and no marriage—a reckless, half-jesting promise, tortured, by false witnesses, into a legal undertaking. I found myself, unawares, a married man—a millstone tied round my neck. I will tell you no more of that wretched entanglement, dearest. It would not be good for you to hear. I will only say that I bore my burthen more patiently than most men would have borne it, and now I thank God with all my heart and soul for my freedom. And I come to you, dear love, to implore your forgiveness, and to ask you to join me, three weeks hence, in some quiet place thirty or forty miles from here, where no one will know us, and where we may be married again some fine summer morning; so that, if that Scotch marriage of mine were really binding, and our former marriage illegal, we may tie the knot securely, and for ever.'

'You should have trusted me at first, John,' Laura said reproachfully.

'I ought to have done so, love, but I so feared to lose you. Oh, my darling, grant all I ask, and you shall never have cause to regret your goodness. Forgive me, and forget all that I have told you tonight. Let it be as if it had never been. The second marriage which I ask for is a precautionary act—needless, perhaps—but it will make me feel more secure in my happiness. My beloved, will you do what I ask?'

She had dried her tears. Her heart was welling over with gladness and love for this sinner, still kneeling by her side as she sat on the ferny river bank in the brightening moonlight, holding both her hands in his, looking up pleadingly as he made his prayer. There was no thought of denying him in her mind. She only wanted to yield with good grace, not to humiliate herself too deeply.

'It must be as you wish,' she said. 'When you have arranged this second marriage you can write to me and tell me where and when it is to be. I will come to the place you appoint with my maid. She is a good girl, and I can trust her. She can be one of the witnesses of our wedding.'

'Are you sure she will not talk about it afterwards?'

'I have proved her already, and I know she is trustworthy.'

'Be it so, love. See here.' He took a Cornish guide-book from his pocket, and opened it at the map of the county. 'I have been thinking that we might go farther west, to some remote parish. Here is Camelot, for instance. I never heard of any one living at Camelot, or going to Camelot, since the time of King Arthur. Surely there we should be safe from observation. The guide-book acknowledges that there is nothing particular to be seen at Camelot. It has not even a good word for the inns. The place is miles away from everything. It is an anomaly in towns, for though it has a town hall and a market-place, it has no church that it can call its own, but hooks itself on to a brace of outlying churches, each a mile and a half away. Let us be married at one of those out-of-the-way churches, Laura, and I shall love Camelot all the days of my life, as one loves the plain face of a friend who has done one a great service.'

Laura had nothing to say against Camelot; so it was finally resolved that John Treverton should get there as quickly as rail and coach would carry him, and that he should have the banns put up at one of the churches, and that he should meet Laura at Didford Junction three weeks from that day, and escort her by coach across the wild moors and under the shadow of giant brown tors, to the little town of Camelot, where a modest population of six or seven hundred souls seemed to have lost themselves among the hills, and got somehow left behind in the march of time and progress.

John Treverton and his wife lingered for a long time beside the brawling river, walking arm in arm along the narrow woodland path, half in moonshine, half in shadow, talking of the future; both supremely happy, and one of them, at least, tasting pure and perfect happiness for the first time in his life.

'Shall we go to Penzance after our wedding, love, and then cross to the Scilly Isles for our honeymoon? It will be so sweet to inhabit a little rock-bound world of our own, circled by the Atlantic.'

Laura assented that it would be sweet. Her world was henceforth to be small, John Treverton its sun and centre, and all things outside him and beyond him a mere elementary universe.

He looked at his watch presently when they came out of the

pinewood into the broad moonlight.

'By Jove, dearest, I shall have no more than time to see you as far as the orchard gate, and then run off to catch the last train for Didford. I shall sleep at the hotel there to-night. I don't want to be seen within twenty miles of Hazlehurst till you and I come back from the Scilly Isles, sunburnt and happy, to take up our abode at the dear old Manor House. Oh, Laura, how I shall love that good, honest, respectable old home! how earnestly I shall thank God night and morning for my blissful life! Ah, love, you can never fully understand what a kicked-about waif I have been for the last seven years of my worthless existence. You can never fully know how thrice blessed is a tranquil haven after stormy seas.'

They had opened their hearts and minds fully to each other in that long talk beside the river; she withholding nothing, he entering into no details of his life-history, but frankly admitting his unworthiness. She told him how she had borne her life at Hazlehurst after her solitary return from a supposed honeymoon; how she had hidden the truth from all her little world. It would seem the most natural thing for her to go away to meet her husband on his return from abroad, and then for them both to come home together.

They parted at the orchard gate hurriedly, for John had three miles to walk to the station, and only three-quarters of an hour for the walk. There was but one hasty kiss at parting, but oh, the blissfulness of such a kiss on the threshold of so fair a future! Laura threaded her way slowly through the moonlit orchard, where the old apple trees cast their crooked shadows on the soft deep turf, and happy tears poured down her flushed cheeks as she went.

'God is good to us, God is very good,' she kept repeating inwardly. 'Oh, how can we ever be grateful enough, how can we ever be earnest enough in doing our duty?'

In all her talk with John Treverton she had not said a word about the settlement. She had not praised him or thanked him for his generosity. All thought of Jasper Treverton's fortune was as remote from her mind as if the old man had died a pauper, and there had been not a shilling of loss or gain contingent upon her marriage with his kinsman.

CHAPTER XX.

THE CHURCH NEAR CAMELOT.

Celia opened her eyes to their widest extent a fortnight later, when Mrs. Treverton informed her that she was going to meet her husband, and that, after a few weeks' holiday, they were coming home together for good.

'For good,' repeated Celia, drily, after which her eyes slowly resumed their normal state, and her lips drew themselves tightly together. 'I am glad to hear that your existence as a married woman is about to assume a reasonable shape. Up to this time you have been as insoluble a mystery as that horrid creature, the Man in the Iron Mask; and, pray, may I be permitted to ask, without being considered offensive, where you are to meet the returning wanderer?'

'At Plymouth,' said Laura, who had received minute instructions from John as to what she was to say.

'Why blush at the mention of Plymouth?' asked Celia. 'There is nothing improper in the name of Plymouth; nothing unfit for publication. I presume that, as Mr. Treverton arrives at Plymouth, he comes from some distant portion of the globe?'

'He is coming from Buenos Ayres, where he had business that absolutely required his personal attention.'

'What an extraordinary girl you are, Laura!' ejaculated Celia, her eyes again widening.

'Why extraordinary?'

'Because you must have been perfectly aware that I, and I think I may go so far as to say all the inhabitants of Hazlehurst, have been bursting with curiosity about your husband for the last six months, and yet you could not have the good grace to enlighten us. If you had said he had gone to Buenos Ayres on business, we should have been satisfied.'

'I told you he had affairs that detained him abroad.'

'But why not have given his affairs a local habitation and a name?'

'My husband did not wish me to talk about him.'

'Well, you are altogether the oddest couple. However, I am very glad things are going to be different. Would it be too much to ask if

Mr. Treverton will remain at the Manor House, or if he is going to reappear only in his usual meteoric fashion?'

'I hope he will stay at Hazlehurst all his life.'

'Poor fellow!' sighed Celia. 'If he does I'm sure I shall pity him.'

'You need not be so absurdly literal. Of course we shall go far afield sometimes and see the world, and all that is interesting and beautiful in it.'

'How glibly you talk about what "we" are going to do. A week ago you could not be induced to mention your husband's name. And how happy you look; I never saw such a change.'

'It is all because I am going to see him again. I hope you do not begrudge me my happiness?'

'No, but I rather envy you. I only wish some benevolent old party would leave me a splendid estate on condition I married a handsome young man. You would see how willingly I would obey him. There should be no mystery about my conduct, I assure you. I should not make an iron mask of myself.'

Celia wrote next day to her brother to tell him how that most incomprehensible of husbands, John Treverton, was expected home from Buenos Ayres, and how his wife was going to Plymouth to meet him. 'And I never saw any human creature look so happy in my life,' wrote Celia. 'I have seen dogs look like it when one has given them biscuits, and cats when they sit blinking at the fire, and young pigs lying on a bank in the sunshine. Yes, I have seen those dumb things appear the image of perfect, unreasoning, unquestioning happiness, which looks neither behind nor before; but such an expression is rarely to be seen in humanity.'

A nice letter for Edward Clare to get—disappointed, more or less out at elbows, with a growing sense of failure upon him, sick to death of his London lodging, sick of the few literary men whose acquaintance he had contrived to make, and with whom he did not amalgamate as well as he had anticipated. He tore his sister's lively epistle into morsels and sent them flying over Waterloo Bridge, upon the light summer wind, and felt as if he would like to have gone over with them.

'Yet once I thought she loved me,' he said to himself, 'and so she did, before that plausible scoundrel came in her way. But I ought to remember how much she gains by loving him. If the old man had happened to leave me his estate, perhaps she might have looked unutterably happy at the idea of my return after a long absence. Only God, who made women, knows what hypocrites they are;' and then Mr. Clare went home to his shabby lodging, and sat down in bitterest mood, and dipped his pen in the ink, and wrung out of himself a passionate page of verse for one of the magazines—not without labour and the sweat of his brow—and then took his poem and sold it, and dined luxuriously on the proceeds, hugging his wrongs and nursing his wrath to keep it warm, as he sat in a corner of the bright little French restaurant he liked best, slowly sipping his modest half-bottle of Pomard.

That which Celia had told him was perfectly true. There never was a happier woman than Laura, after that interview by the river. During the last week before her departure she was full of business, preparing for her husband's return.

'Your master will be here in a few weeks,' she said to the old housekeeper, with infinite pride, 'and we must have everything ready for him.'

'So we will, ma'am, spick and span,' answered Mrs. Trimmer. 'It will be happiness to have him settle down among us. It must have been a sore trial to you both, to be parted so, just at the beginning of your married life, too. It would have come more nat'ral afterwards.'

'It was a sore trial, Trimmer,' Mrs. Treverton answered, full of confidential friendliness. 'But it's all over now. I could hardly have borne to speak about it before.'

'No, ma'am, I noticed as you was close and silent like, and I knew my place too well to say anything. Troubles take hold of people different. If there's anything on my mind I must out with it, if it was but to Ginger, the tortoiseshell cat; but some folks can keep their worrits screwed up inside 'em. It hurts 'em to speak.'

'That was my case, Trimmer. It hurt me to speak my husband's name, or to hear it spoken, while he was forced to be far away from me. But now it's all different. You cannot talk of him too much to please me. I hope you will be as fond of him as you were of the dear old man who is gone.'...

Mr. Treverton must have a sitting-room of his own, of course; a den where he might write his letters, and see his bailiff, where he could smoke and meditate at his leisure, study if he ever cared to study, read novels even, were he disposed to be lazy; and where his happy wife could only come on sufferance, deeming it a vast indulgence to be allowed to sit at his feet sometimes, or even to fill his pipe for him, or, in rough winter weather, to kneel down before the blazing fire and warm his slippers, when he had come in from a cold ride round his land, doing good wherever he went, like a benevolent fairy in the modern form of an enlightened landlord.

After much debate and perplexity, Laura decided upon giving

her husband, for his own particular sanctum, that very room in which they two had met for the first time, on the snowy winter night when John Treverton came to see his dying kinsman. It was a good old room, not large, but pleasant, oak-panelled, with a fireplace in the corner, which gave a quaintness to the room; an oak mantel-piece with half-a-dozen narrow shelves running in a pyramid above it, and on these shelves an arrangement of old blue Nankin cups and saucers, crowned at the apex with the most delightful thing in teapots. There was an old cabinet in the room, so full of secret draw-ers, and mysterious boxes and recesses at the back of the drawers, that it was in itself the study of a lifetime.

'Never hide anything in it, my dear,' Jasper Treverton had said to his adopted daughter, 'for be sure if you do you won't be able to find it.'

To this room Laura brought other treasures; the most comfort-able easy chairs in the house, the best of the small Dutch pictures, the softest of the Turkey carpets, the richest tapestry curtains, two or three fine bronzes, a lovely little Chippendale book-case. This last she filled with all her own favourite books, robbing the book-room below ruthlessly, in the delight of enriching her husband's study, as this room was henceforth to be called.

'He shall know and feel that he is welcome,' she said to herself, softly, as she lingered in the room, touching everything, re-arrang-ing, polishing, whisking away invisible grains of dust with a dainty feather brush, caressing the things that were so soon to belong to the man she loved.

The adjoining room—the room in which Jasper Treverton had died—was to be her own bedchamber. It was a spacious room with three long windows and deep window seats, a fireplace at which an ox, or at all events a baron of beef, might have been roasted—a tall four-post bed, with twisted columns richly carved; curtains of Utrecht velvet, crimson and amber, lined with white silk, all some-what faded, but splendid in decay—a noble room altogether, yet Laura had rather a horror of it, dearly as she had loved him whose generous spirit seemed to haunt the chamber.

But Mrs. Trimmer told her that, as the mistress of Hazlehurst Manor, she ought to occupy this room. It always had been the Squire's bedchamber, and it ought to be so still.

'Nothing like old ways,' said Mrs. Trimmer, decisively.

The room opened into John Treverton's study. That was a reason why Laura should like it.

If he were to sit up late at night reading or writing, she would be near him. She might see the face she loved, through the open door, bending over his papers in the lamplight.

'We are going to be a regular Darby and Joan, Mrs. Trimmer,' she said to the housekeeper, as she made all her small domestic arrangements.

In such trivial work she contrived to get rid of the third week, and then came the lovely summer noontide when she started on her journey, with the faithful Mary in attendance.

'Mary,' she had said, the night before, 'I am going to trust you with a great secret, because I believe you are staunch and true.'

'If you could find another young woman in my capacity, mum, that would be stauncherer or truerer, I'll undertake to eat her without a grain of salt,' protested Mary, sacrificing grammar to intensity.

The train from Beechampton took them across a stretch of wild moorland, where the granite cropped up in scattered boulders, as if Titans had been pelting one another, to Didford Junction. At Didford they found John Treverton waiting for them, and here they got on to another line of railway, and into a more pastoral landscape, and so on to Lyonstown—pronounced Linson—where they mounted the stage-coach which was to take them across the moor to Camelot. It was about four o'clock in the afternoon by this time, and it would be evening before they reached the little town among the Cornish hills. Oh, what a happy drive it was across the free open moorland, in the mild afternoon light, a thousand feet above the sea-level, above the smoke and turmoil of cities, far away from all mankind, in a lonely world of heather and granite. The dark brown hills, twin brothers, rose between them and the western sun, now blending into one dark mass of mountain, now standing far apart, as some new turn of the narrow moorland road seemed to alter their position in the landscape. It was like a new world even to Laura, though she came from the sister county, and had lived the best part of her life under the edge of Dartmoor.

'I really think I should like to spend my life on these hills,' said Laura, as she and John Treverton sat side by side behind the sturdy little coachman, whose quaintly comical face might have made the fortune of a low comedian. 'It seems such a beautiful world, even in its wildness and solitude, so pure and fair, and free from the taint of sin.'

The sunlight behind the big brown tors was fading, and the air growing crisp and cool, keenly biting even, at odd times, though it was midsummer. John drew a soft woollen shawl round his companion's shoulders, and even in this little action his heart thrilled at the thought that henceforward it was his duty to protect her from all the ills of life. And so through the deepening gloom they came to Camelot, a narrow street on the slant of a hill, folded in gray twilight as in a mantle.

The inn where Laura and her maid were to put up for the night was commonplace and commercial—a house that had evidently seen better days, but which had plucked up its spirits and furbished up its rickety old furniture since the establishment of the North Cornwall coach, a blessed institution, linking a wild and solitary district with railways and civilization.

Here Laura rested comfortably enough through the short summer night, while John Treverton endured the discomforts of a second-rate tavern over against the market-place. At eight o'clock next morning he presented himself at the hotel where Laura and her maid were waiting for him, and then the three went on foot to the outlying church where John Treverton was to take this woman, Laura, for his wife for the second time within six months.

'I could not have been happier in my choice of a locality than I was in fixing upon Camelot,' said John, as they walked side by side along the country lane, between tall banks of brier and fern, in the sweet morning air, with the faithful Mary strolling discreetly in the rear. 'I found the most accommodating old parson, who quite entered into my views when I told him that for certain reasons which I need not explain, I wished my marriage to be kept altogether quiet. "I shall not speak of it to a creature," replied the good old soul. "No man would come to Camelot to be married who did not wish to hide himself from the eye of the world. I shall respect your secret, and I'll take care that my clerk does the same."'

The old church smelt rather like a vault when they went in out of the breezy summer day, but it was a cleanly whitewashed vault, and the sun was shining full upon the faded crimson velvet of the communion table, above which appeared the ten commandments and the royal arms in the good old style. Steeped in that sunshine stood the bride and bridegroom, gravely, earnestly repeating the solemn words of the service; no witnesses of the act save the gray-headed clerk and the girl Mary, who seemed to think it incumbent upon somebody to be moved to tears, and who therefore gently sniffed and faintly sobbed in the background. Never had Laura looked lovelier than when she stood beside her husband in the little closet of a vestry, signing her name in the mouldy old register; never had she felt happier than when they walked away from the lonely old church, after a friendly leave-taking of the good vicar, who blessed them and gave

184

them God speed as heartily as if they had been born and bred in his parish. The coach was to pick them up at the cross-roads about half a mile from the church, having previously picked up their luggage in Camelot, and they were to go back across the moor to Lyonstown, and from Lyonstown by rail to the extreme west, and thence to the Scilly Isles.

'Can nothing happen now to part us, John?' Laura asked, while they were sitting on a ferny bank waiting for the coach. 'Are our lives secure from all evil in the future?'

'Who can be armed against all misfortune, love?' he asked. 'Of one thing I am certain. You are my wife. Against the validity of our marriage of to-day no living creature can say a word.'

'And the legality of our previous marriage might have been questioned?'

'Yes, dearest, there would have always been that hazard.'

CHAPTER XXI.

HALCYON DAYS.

There were no bonfires or floral arches, no rejoicings of tenantry or farm labourers, when John Treverton and his wife came home to Hazlehurst Manor. They came unannounced one fine July afternoon, arriving in a fly hired at Beechampton, much to the distress of Mrs. Trimmer, who declared that there was absolutely nothing in the house. Yet many an anxious city housekeeper would have considered the noble array of hams, pendant from the massive beams of the kitchen ceiling, the flitch of bacon, the basket of new-laid eggs, the homely saffron-hued plum cakes, the dainty sweet biscuits, the ox tongues and silver side of beef in pickle, the chickens waiting to be plucked—worthy to count as something.

'You might have sent me a telegram, mum, and then I might have done myself credit,' said Mrs. Trimmer, dolefully. 'I don't believe there's a bit of fish to be had in Hazlehurst. I was in the village at twelve o'clock this blessed day, and there was one sole frizzling on the slates at Trimpson's, and I'll warrant he's been sold by this time.'

'If he isn't sold he must be pretty well baked, so we won't have anything to say to him,' said John Treverton, laughing. 'Don't worry yourself about dinner, my good creature; we are too happy to care what we eat.'

And then he put his arm round his wife's waist and led her along the corridor that ended in the book-room, where she had left him in his despair seven little months ago. They went into this room together, and he shut the door behind them.

'Dear love, to think that I should enter this room the happiest of men. I, who sat by that table in such anguish as few men are ever called upon to suffer. Oh, Laura, that was the darkest day in my life.'

'Forget it,' she said earnestly; 'never let the past be named between us. There is so much of it that is still a mystery to me. You have told me so little of your early life, John, that if I were to think of the past I might begin to doubt you. Oh, love, I have trusted you blindly. Even when all things looked dark I went on trusting you; I clung to my belief in your goodness. I don't know whether it was my weakness or my strength which made me so confident.'

'It was your strength, dearest, the strength of innocence, the strength of that divine charity which "thinketh no evil." Dear love, it shall be the business of my life to prove you right, to show myself worthy of your trust.'

They roamed about the house together, looking at everything, as if each object were new to both, happy as children. They recalled their first meeting—their second—and confessed all they had felt on each occasion. It was delightful to them to travel backward through the history of their love, now that life was bright and the future seemed all secure.

So their life went on for many days, Laura initiating her husband in his position as Squire of Hazlehurst. She took him round to all the cottages and introduced him to their inmates, and together they planned improvements which were to make Hazlehurst Manor one of the most perfect estates in the country. Above all things was there to be happiness for every one. Drainage and sanitation were to be so improved that fever and infection would be almost an impossibility. Every farm labourer was to have a clean and comfortable shelter, and a patch of ground where he might grow his cabbages, and, if blessed with a love of the beautiful, rear roses and carnations that might vie with the flowers in a ducal garden. Here in this mild western world, where frost and snow were almost strangers, the labouring man might clothe his cottage wall with myrtle, and grow fuchsias as big as apple-trees.

To John Treverton, sick to the heart of cities, the novelty of this country life was full of delight. He was interested in the stables, the home farm, the gardens, even the poultry yard. He had a kindly word for the lowest hind upon his land. It seemed as if, in the great happiness of his married life, he had opened his heart to all mankind.

'And are you really happy, Laura?' he asked one day, when he and his wife were dawdling through the August afternoon beside the river where they had met in the June moonlight. 'Do you honestly believe that your adopted father made the best possible provision for your future when he gave you to me?'

He asked this question in a moment of delicious idleness, lying at his wife's feet, she sitting in a natural easy chair formed by two blocks of granite, moss-grown, ferny, luxurious, books and work half-forgotten by her side, and by his an idle fishing-rod. He had little doubt as to the answer to his question, or he would hardly have asked it.

'I think dear papa must have had a prophetic power to choose what was best for me,' she said, smiling down at her husband.

And then they went on in a strain which was very sweet to them both, travelling step by step over those early days when they were almost strangers, recalling with a studious minuteness what he had felt and thought, what she had dreamed and hoped. How he had begun with a fixed determination to detest her; and how that gloomy resolve had slipped out of his mind at their first interview, despite his endeavour to hold it fast.

'There is one question that I have wanted to ask you, Laura,' he said, presently, growing suddenly grave, with a look in which there was a shadow of trouble, 'but I have shrunk from asking it, somehow, and put it off indefinitely. And yet it is a very natural curiosity on my part, and can hardly offend you.'

Her face was even more serious than his by this time, and wore a look of fear. She answered not a word, but sat, with lips slightly parted, waiting for him to go on.

'You remember your interview with a gentleman whom you admitted to the garden after dark, and whom you described to me afterwards as a relation. How is it, love, that in all our confidential talk you have never told me anything about that man?'

'The answer is simple enough,' she said quietly, yet he could but wonder to see how pale she had grown. 'In all our talk together we have spoken of things that belong to our happiness. You have never touched upon the dark passages in your life, nor I on those in mine. You remember what Longfellow says:—

"Into each life some rain must fall,
Some days must be dark and dreary."

The relation of whom you speak is one who has not done well in this world. My dear adopted father was prejudiced against him, or at any rate he thought so. From time to time he has appealed to me secretly for aid, and I have helped him secretly. I am sorry for him, deeply sorry, and I am glad to help him, at a distance; but there are reasons why I have never sought, why I never should seek, to bring him nearer to me.'

'I feel sure that whatever you have done has been wise and right, dearest. There must be a black sheep in every family. I have played the part myself, and ought to sympathize with all such delinquents.'

Delicacy prevented his pursuing the subject further. Could he do less than trust her fully, who had shown such noble confidence in him?

A life so happy would have been bounded within a very narrow circle had John Treverton and his wife consulted only their own inclination; but society expects something from a well-born country gentleman with fourteen thousand a year. The Lady Parkers and Lady Barkers, of whom Celia had spoken somewhat disparagingly, came in state, swinging lightly on C springs in their old family carriages, to call upon the young couple.

Invitations to ceremonious dinners followed in due course, and were reluctantly accepted, since it would have seemed ungracious to refuse them: and by-and-by Mrs. Trimmer, the housekeeper, suggested that the Manor House ought to give a series of dinners, such as she remembered when she was a giddy-pated young kitchen-maid in the service of Jasper Treverton's father and mother.

'They used to send out invitations for two or three dinner parties when the pheasant shooting began, and get it over,' said Mrs. Trimmer, 'for they were homely people, and didn't care much for company. The old gentleman was wrapped up in his books, and the old lady was wrapped up in her garden; but when they gave a dinner there was no mistake about it.'

Laura submitted to inexorable custom.

'We have eaten people's dinners, and I suppose we must invite them here,' she said, with an air of serio-comic vexation, 'or they will consider us dishonest. Shall I make a list of the people to be asked, Jack, and shall we give Trimmer *carte blanche* about the dinner?'

'I suppose that will be best,' assented John, whose Christian name affection had corrupted to Jack. 'Trimmer is a capital cook of the substantial English school. Her *menu* may be wanting in originality, but it will be safe.'

'Well, I am glad you are awaking to the necessity of living like civilized Christians, instead of spooning all day in the seclusion of a house, compared with which Robinson Crusoe's island must have been a vortex of dissipation,' exclaimed Celia Clare, who was present at this discussion. 'I am glad that at last, if it were only for my sake, you are going to conform to the laws of society. How am I to get a husband, I should like to know, unless I meet people here? There is no other house worth visiting in the neighbourhood.'

'We'll take your necessities into consideration, my dear girl,' answered John, gaily, 'and if you can suggest any eligible bachelors, we'll ask them to dinner.'

'That's exactly what I cannot do,' said Celia, with a despairing shrug. 'There are no eligible bachelors indigenous to the soil. The only plan would be to put a *nota bene* to your cards of invitation, "If you have any nice young men about you, pray bring them.'''

'Laura might give a dance at Christmas, and then we might beat up for young men,' answered John. 'I'm afraid as long as we confine ourselves to dinner parties, we shall not be able to do much for you, my poor Celia.'

'But are you not going to have people to stay in the house when the pheasant shooting begins?' inquired Celia, with uplifted eyebrows. 'Are not your old friends going to rally round you? I thought they always did when a man came into a fortune.'

'I believe that is one of the characteristics of friendship,' said John. 'But I lost sight of my old friends—the friends of my soldiering days, that is to say—nearly seven years ago, and I don't care about digging them out.'

'I wonder they don't come to the surface of their own accord,' said Celia. 'And how about the friends you have made since you sold out? You can't have existed seven years without society.'

'I have existed quite as long as that without what you would call society.'

'Ah, I see,' assented Celia; 'the people you have known are not people you would care to bring here, or to introduce to your wife.'

'Precisely.'

'Poor Laura!' thought Celia, and then there followed a pause, brief but uncomfortable.

'Shall I write the list of invitations?' asked Laura, who was sitting at her davenport. They were in the book-room, the fresh autumnal air blowing in across beds and borders filled with September's gaudy flowers.

'Yes, dear, beginning, of course, with Sir Joshua and Lady Parker, and descending gradually in the social scale to——'

'My father and mother,' interrupted Celia, 'if you mean to ask them. I'm sure you can't go lower than the parson of the parish; for he's generally the poorest man in it.'

'And often the most beloved,' said John Treverton.

'Do you think I should give my first dinner party without inviting your father and mother, Celia?' asked Laura, reproachfully. 'They will be my most honoured guests.'

'Heaven knows how the mater is to get a new gown,' ejaculated Celia; 'but I'm sure she can't come in the old one. That gray satin of hers has been to so many dinner parties that I should think it could go by itself, and would know how to behave, without having poor mother inside it. How well all the servants hereabouts must know the back of that dress, and the dark patch on the shoulder, where La-

190

dy Barker's butler spilt some lobster sauce. It is like the blood-stain on Lady Macbeth's hand. All the benzine in the world won't take it out. Oh, by-the-bye,' pursued Celia, rattling on breathlessly, 'if you really don't mind being overrun with the Clare family, would you write a card for Ted?'

'With pleasure,' said Laura; 'but is he not in London?'

'At this present moment he is; but we are expecting him daily at the Vicarage. The fact is he has not made his mark, poor fellow, and he is rather tired of London. I suppose there are too many young men there, all wanting to make their mark.'

CHAPTER XXII.

A VILLAGE IAGO.

Edward Clare came back to his native village a few days later, looking somewhat dilapidated by his campaign in the great metropolis. He had found the gates of literature so beset with aspirants, many of them as richly endowed as himself, that the idea of pushing his way across the threshold seemed almost hopeless, indeed quite hopeless, for a young man who wanted to succeed in life without working very hard, or with at most a little spasmodic industry. His verses, when he was lucky, had earned him something like five pounds a month; when luck was against him he had earned nothing. A newspaper man, whose acquaintance he made at the Cheshire Cheese, had advised him to learn shorthand, and try his fortune as a reporter, working upwards from that platform to the editorial chair. This was an honest drudgery which might do very well for your dull plodders, but against which the fiery soul of Edward Clare revolted.

'I am a poet, or I am nothing,' he told his friend. '*Aut Cæsar aut nullus.*'

'That was a first-rate motto——for Cæsar,' said the journalist, 'but I think it's rather misleading for fellows of average talent. The result is so often *nullus.*'

Mr. Clare was on the point of asking his friend to take another brandy and soda, but at this remark he coiled up, as the Yankees say! Average talent, indeed. Imagine one of Mr. Swinburne's most facile plagiarists hearing himself called a fellow of average talent!

Edward Clare would not yoke his noble mind to the newspaper plough, nor would he stoop even so low as to write prose. A wretched publisher had told him that if he would write children's books there was a field open for him; but Edward left that publisher's office bursting with offended pride.

'Children's books, forsooth!' he muttered. 'I suppose if Catnach had been alive he would have asked me to write halfpenny ballads.'

So having failed to carve his way to fame, or to make a regular income, and having wasted the money he had earned on kid gloves and stalls at fashionable theatres, Mr. Clare conceived an intense disgust for the metropolis, which had treated him so scurvily, and turned his thoughts homewards to woodland and moor, to trout stream and meadow. He found that the poetic temperament required rural scenery, blue skies, and pure air. Heine had contrived to live and write in Paris, and so had De Musset: but Paris is not London. Edward made up his mind that the streets and squares of Blooms-bury were antagonistic to poetry. No bird could sing in such a cage. True that Milton had composed 'Paradise Lost' within close City lanes, under the Clamorous bells of St. Bride's, but then Milton was blind, and Edward Clare was like a popular lady novelist of the present day, who begged that she might not be compared with Dickens. He would have protested against being put on a level with such a passionless bard as Milton.

'I shall never achieve any great work in London,' he told himself. 'For my *magnum opus* I must have the tranquillity of wood and moor.'

He had quite made up his mind that he was to write a great poem, though he had settled neither the subject nor the form. He was waiting for the divine breath to inspire him. The poem was to be as popular as the 'Idylls of the King,' but as passionate as 'Chastelard.' He was not going to write in a goody-goody strain to please anybody.

Edward Clare felt himself a little like the prodigal son, when he came home to the Vicarage after this abortive campaign in the field of literature. If he had not wasted his substance, it was only because he had little substance to waste. He had spent all that his father had sent him, and had received small additions to this allowance out of his mother's scantily-supplied purse. He came home penniless and dispirited: and he felt rather offended that no fatted calf was slain to do him honour, and that his parents received him with an air of un-mistakable despondency.

'Really, my dear Edward, you ought to begin to think of some definite course,' said the father. 'It may be too late for a profession, but the Government offices——'

'Red tape and drudgery, with a salary that would scarcely afford dry bread and a garret,' interrupted Edward contemptuously. 'No, my dear father, as a poet I will stand or fall.'

'I'm sorry to hear it,' sighed the Vicar, 'for at present it looks like falling.'

What Edward really meant was that he would depend upon his father until the public and the critics, or the critics and the public, could be brought to acknowledge him as one of the new lights in the starry world of imagination. Mr. Clare understood this, and felt that it was rather hard upon him as a man of limited means.

Edward arrived at Hazlehurst only the night before Mrs. Treverton's dinner-party.

'Oh, yes, I'm going,' he told Celia, when she asked him if he had accepted Laura's invitation. 'I want to see how this Treverton fellow plays the country squire.'

'As if to the manner born,' answered Celia. 'The part suits him admirably. I don't want to wound your feelings, Ted, dear, but Mr. Treverton and Laura are the happiest couple I ever saw.'

> *'"These violent delights have violent ends,*
> *And in their triumph die,"'*

quoted Edward, with a diabolical sneer. 'I am not going to envy them their happiness, my dear. Whatever feeling I once entertained for Laura is dead and buried. A woman who could sell herself, as she has done—'

'Sell herself! Oh, Ted, how can you say anything so dreadful? I tell you she is devotedly attached to John Treverton.'

'And he rewards her devotion by running away from her before the end of their honeymoon; and when he turns up again, after an interval of six months or so, during which nobody knows what he has been doing, she receives him with open arms. A curious couple assuredly. But an estate worth fourteen thousand pounds a year excuses a good deal of eccentricity; and I can quite understand that Mr. and Mrs. Treverton are immensely popular in the neighbourhood.'

'They are,' said Celia, warmly; 'and they deserve to be. If you knew how good they are to their tenants, their servants, and the poor.'

'Goodness of that kind is a very sagacious investment, my unsophisticated child. It may cost a man five per cent. of his income, and it buys him respectability.'

'Don't be bitter, Edward.'

'I am a man of the world, Celia, and not to be hoodwinked by shams and appearances.'

'Then you'll never be a poet,' protested his sister. 'A man who doesn't believe that good deeds come from the hearts of men—a man who looks for an unworthy motive behind every generous action—such a man as that will never be a great poet. It is quite too dreadful to hear you talk, Edward. That odious London has corrupted you.'

Edward went to the dinner next day, but not with his family. He came alone, and rather late, in order to observe the effect of his entrance upon Laura Treverton. Alas, for his wounded vanity! She welcomed him with a frank smile and a friendly grasp of the hand.

'I am so glad you have come back in time to be with us to-night,' she said.

'I came back on purpose for to-night,' he answered, throwing as much tenderness as he could into a commonplace remark.

'I think you know every one here. I need not introduce you.'

'I know the local magnates, of course. But I dare say there are some of your husband's swell friends who are strangers to me.'

'There are none of my husband's friends,' answered Laura, 'we are strictly local.'

'Then I'm afraid you'll find the evening rather uphill work.'

'I expect you to help me through it by the brilliancy of your conversation,' Laura answered lightly, as Edward moved aside to make way for a new arrival.

He had contrived to make her uncomfortable for a minute or so, for that speech of his had set her wondering why her husband had no friends worth summoning to his side now that fortune smiled upon him.

The dinner-party was not a very joyous festivity, but everybody felt, nevertheless, that it was a great social success. Lady Parker, in ruby velvet and diamonds, and Lady Barker in black satin and rubies, made two central lights round which the lesser planets revolved. There was the usual county and local talk; reprobation against the farming parson of a neighbouring parish for having treacherously trapped and slain four cub foxes since last season; cordial approval of a magistrate who had sent a lad of nine to jail for stealing three turnips, and who had been maligned and held up to ridicule by the radical newspapers for that necessary assertion of the rights of property; a good deal of discussion as to the prospects of the hunting season; a good deal of talk about horses and dogs, and a little about the outside world, and its chances of peace or war, famine or plenty. The party was too large for general conversation, but now and then the subdued Babel of tongues became concentrated here and there into a focus, and a gentle hush descended on a select few listening eagerly to a single talker. This happened oftenest at that part of the table near which Edward Clare was sitting, next but one to John Treverton. Mr. and Mrs. Treverton were seated opposite each other in the middle of the long table, with all the more important guests clustered about them in a constellation of local splendour, leaving the two ends of the table for youth and obscurity. Edward Clare had got himself into the constellation by a fluke; a portly justice of the peace having suddenly succumbed to gout, and sent an apology at the last moment; whereupon Laura had despatched Celia with a message to the butler, and had contrived that there should be a shuffling of cards, and that Edward Clare should be put into this place of honour.

She did this from a benevolent desire to soothe his wounded feeling, suspecting that there might be some soreness in his mind at this first meeting with her in her new character, and knowing that vanity made the larger half of this young man's sensibility.

Edward had rewarded her by talking remarkably well. He was fresh from London, and well posted in all that is most interesting in the butterfly life of a London season. He told them all about the pictures of the year, let fly some sharp arrows of ridicule against the new school of painting, described the belle of the season, and let his hearers into the secret of her popularity.

'The curious part of the story' he said, in conclusion, 'is that nobody ever considered the lady pretty till she burst all at once upon society as the one perfect creature that the world had seen since the Venus was dug up at Milo. She never was thought so in her own world. No one was more surprised than her own family when she was elected queen of beauty, unless it was herself. Her mother never suspected it. At school she was considered rather plain than otherwise. They say she was married off early because she was the dowdy of the family, and now she cannot take her drive in the park without all London craning its neck and straining its eyes to get a look at her. When she goes into society the women stand upon chairs to stare at her over other people's shoulders. I suppose they want to find out how it's done. This kind of popularity may seem very pleasant in the abstract, but I think it's rather hard upon the lady.'

'Why hard upon her?' inquired John Treverton.

'Because there's no salary goes with the situation. The belle of the season ought to get something to lighten the expenses of her year of office like the Lord Mayor. See what is expected of her! Every eye is upon her. Every woman in London looks to her as a model of taste and elegance, and eagerly strives to dress after her. How is she to put a limit upon her milliner's bill, when she knows that all the society journals are lying in wait to describe her last gown, to eulogise her newest bonnet, to write an epigram upon her parasol, to be ecstatic about her boots. Can she ride in a hired carriage? No. Can she be absent from Goodwood, or missing at Cowes? No. She must die standing. I say that since she furnishes the public with interest and amusement—much better than the Lord Mayor does, by the way—she ought to get a handsome allowance out of the public purse.'

When he had exhausted pictures, and reigning beauties, and the winner of the Leger, Edward began to talk about crime.

'People in London have a knack of wearing a subject to tatters,' he said. 'I thought neither the newspapers nor the public would ever get tired of talking about the Chicot murder.'

'The Chicot murder. Ah, that was the ballet dancer, was it not?' inquired Lady Barker, who was so interested in this vivacious young man on her right hand, that she had hardly given due attention to Mr. Treverton, who was on her left. 'I remember feeling rather interested in that mystery. A diabolical murder, certainly. And how stupid the police must have been not to find the murderer.'

'Or how clever the murderer to sink his identity so completely as to give the police the slip,' suggested Edward.

'Oh, but he must have got away to the Colonies, or somewhere, surely,' cried Lady Barker. 'There are so many vessels leaving England now-a-days. You don't imagine for a moment that the murderer of that wretched woman remained in England?'

'I think it highly probable that he did, discreetly hidden under some outer shell of intense respectability.'

'I suppose you think it was the husband?' put in Sir Joshua Parker, from his place at Laura's right hand.

'I don't see any ground for doubt,' replied Edward. 'If the husband was not guilty, why should he disappear the moment the crime was discovered?'

'He may have had reasons of his own for wishing to get away, reasons unconnected with the mode and manner of his wife's death,' hazarded John Treverton.

'What reasons could he have had strong enough to induce him to run the risk of being thought a murderer?' asked Edward, incredulously. 'No innocent man would place himself in such a position as that.'

'Not knowingly,' said John, 'but this man may have acted on impulse, without reckoning the consequences of his act.'

'To admit that would be to consider him a fool,' retorted Edward; 'and from all I have heard of the fellow, he belonged to the other half of humanity.'

'You mean that he was a knave?'

'I mean that he was a fellow who knew the ropes. He was not the sort of man to find his wife's throat cut, and to make a bolt, leaving every newspaper in London free to brand him as a coward and a murderer,' said Edward, decisively.

John Treverton pursued the subject no further. Lady Parker, who sat at his left, had just begun to question him about a late importation of Jersey cows, in which she was deeply interested; whereupon he favoured her with a detailed account of their graces and merits. Laura happened to look up at Edward Clare as he finished speaking, and the expression of his countenance startled and shocked her. Never had she seen so keen a look of malice in any living face. Only in the face of Judas in an old Italian picture had she ever beheld such craft and such venom. And that malignant look—brief as a flash of lightning—glanced at her unconscious husband, whose face was gravely courteous as he bent his handsome head a little to tell Lady Parker about the Jersey cows.

'Good heavens!' thought Laura, with a sense of absolute fear. 'Is it possible that this young man can be so bitter against my husband because I loved him best? What could the love be like that could engender such malice?'

Later in the evening when Edward came and hung over the ottoman where Laura was sitting, she turned from him with an involuntary movement of disgust.

'Have I offended you?' he asked, in a low voice.

'Yes. I saw a look in your face at dinner that told me you dislike my husband.'

'Do you expect me to love him—very dearly—at first? You must at least give me time to get accustomed to the idea that he is your husband. Time cures most wounds. Give me time, Laura, and do not judge me too hardly. I possess the poet's curse, a mind more sensitive than the minds of ordinary men—dowered with the love of love, the hate of hate, the scorn of scorn.'

'I hope you will leave your dowry outside when you come across this threshold,' said Laura, with a smile that was more contemptuous than relenting. 'I can accept friendship from no one who does not like my husband.'

'Then I will struggle with the original man within me, and try to like John Treverton. Believe me, Laura, I want to be your friend—in honest and unequivocal friendship.'

'That is the kind of friendship I expect from your father's son,' said Laura, in a gentler tone.

She was too happy, too secure in her own happiness to be unforgiving. She reasoned with herself—arguing against instinct and conviction—and told herself that Edward Clare's malevolent look had meant less than it seemed to mean.

Edward looked on, and saw John Treverton play his part as host and master in a manner that he was compelled to admit was irreproachable. The new squire showed none of the pride in himself and his surroundings which might have been anticipated in a man unexpectedly raised to the possession of a large fortune. He did not brag of his wine, or his horses, his pictures, or his farm. He accepted his position as quietly, and filled it as naturally, as if he had been born heir to an entailed, unalienable estate.

'Upon my word, they are a charming couple,' said Sir Joshua Parker, in his fat voice, 'and an acquisition to our county families.'

Sir Joshua was very fond of talking about our county families, although his own establishment in that galaxy had been but recent, his father and grandfather having made their fortunes in the soap-boiling business, amidst the slums of Lambeth. Lady Barker, the dowager, was of the *vieille roche*, having been a Trefusis and an heiress when she married the late General Sir Rodney Barker, K.C.B.

After that one little flash of anger on the night of the dinner-party, Edward Clare was all friendliness. Celia spent a large portion of her life at the Manor House, where she was always welcome; and it seemed only natural that her brother Edward should drop in frequently, almost as he had done in the old days when Jasper Treverton was alive. There were so many reasons for his coming. The library at the Manor House was much larger and better than the vicar's modest collection of old-fashioned books. The gardens were a delight to the young man's poetic soul. John Treverton showed no dislike to him. He appeared to consider the poet a poor creature, whose going or coming could make no difference.

'I confess that I have a contempt for that kind of man,' he told his wife, candidly. 'An effeminate, white-handed mortal, who sets up as a wit and a poet on the most limited stock-in-trade—all his best goods in his windows, and nothing but empty shelves inside the shop. But, of course, as long as you like him, Laura, he will be welcome here.'

'I like him for the sake of his father and mother, who are my oldest and best friends,' answered Laura.

'Which means in plain English that you only tolerate him?' said John, carelessly. 'Well, he is harmless, and sometimes amusing. Let him come.'

Edward came, and seemed at home and happy in the small family circle. He lounged beside the fire in the snug book-room, and joined in the easy familiar talk, when the autumn dusk was deepening, and Laura made tea at her pretty little table, with her husband by her side, while Celia, who had a fancy for eccentric positions and attitudes, sat on the hearthrug.

One November evening, about a month after the dinner party, the conversation happened to light upon the county magnates who had adorned that banquet.

'Did anybody ever see such a funny little figure as Lady Barker, surmounted by that wig!' cried Celia. 'I really think her dressmaker must be very clever to make any kind of gown that will hold together upon her. I don't complain of her being fat. A woman may weigh sixteen stone and carry herself like a duchess. But Lady Barker is such an undecided figure. There's no consistency in her. When she sinks on a sofa one expects to see her collapse, like a mould of jelly that hasn't cooled properly. Oh, Edward, you should see Mr. Treverton's portrait of her—the most delicious caricature.'

'Caricature!' echoed Edward. 'Why, that is another new talent. If Treverton goes on in this way we shall have to call him the admirable Crichton. It was only last week that I found out he could paint; and now you say he is a caricaturist. What next?'

'I believe you have come to the end of my small stock of accomplishments,' said John Treverton, laughing. 'I used once to amuse myself by an attempt to illustrate the absurdities of human nature in pen and ink. It pleased my brother officers, and helped to keep us alive sometimes in the dulness of country quarters.'

'Talking of caricature, by the way,' said Edward, lazily, as he slowly stirred his cup of tea, 'did you ever see "Folly as it Flies?"'

'The comic newspaper? Yes, often.'

'Ah, then you must have noticed the things done by that fellow Chicot—the man who murdered his wife. They were extraordinarily clever—out and away the best things I have ever seen since the days of Gavarni; rather too French, perhaps, but remarkably good.'

'It was natural the style should be French, since the man was French.'

'I beg your pardon,' said Edward, 'he was as English as you or I.'

Celia had risen from the floor and lighted a pair of candles on Laura's open davenport, near which Edward was sitting. She selected a sheet of paper from a heap of loose sheets lying there and showed it to her brother, candle in hand.

'Isn't that too lovely?' she asked.

Edward examined the sketch with a critical air.

'I don't want you to suppose I'm trying to flatter you,' he said at

200

last, 'but, upon my word, this little sketch is as good as anything of Chicot's, and very much in his style.'

'It is the only accomplishment of my husband's that I cannot praise,' said Laura, with gentlest reproof, 'for it cannot be exercised without unkindness to the subject of the caricature.'

'"He that is robbed not wanting what is stolen, let him not know it, and he is not robbed,"' quoted Celia, who had resumed her lowly place at Laura's feet. 'Shakespeare's ineffable wisdom found that out; and may not the same thing be said of caricature? If Lady Barker never knows what a lifelike portrait you have drawn of her, with half-a-dozen scratches of a Hindoo pen, the faithfulness of the picture can't hurt her.'

'But isn't it the usual course to show that kind of thing to all the lady's particular friends, till the knowledge of it percolates to the lady herself?' inquired Edward with his lazy sneer.

'I had rather cut off my right hand than make a harmless good-natured old lady unhappy,' said Laura, warmly.

'Turn up your cuff, Mr. Treverton, and prepare your wrist for the chopper,' cried Celia. 'But really now, if Lady Barker's figure is like a dilapidated mould of jelly, she ought to know it. Did not one of those seven old plagues of Greece, whose names nobody ever could remember, resolve all the wisdom of his life into that one precept, "Know thyself"?'

Celia rattled on gaily; Laura and Edward both joined in her careless talk; but John Treverton sat grave and silent, looking at the fire.

CHAPTER XXIII.

'IN THE MEANWHILE THE SKIES 'GAN RUMBLE SORE.'

After that portrait of Lady Barker, John Treverton drew no more caricatures. It seemed as if he had laid aside the pen of the caricaturist in deference to his wife's dislike of that somewhat ill-natured art. But he had not abandoned the higher walks of art, for he had made himself a studio out of one of the spare bedrooms that looked northward, and was engaged on a portrait of his wife, an altogether fanciful and ideal picture, which he worked at for an hour or two daily with infinite delight. He had many pleasant labours and occupations at this period of his life. The farm, the hunting field, the business details of a large property, which he wished to conduct in an orderly manner, not hiding his talents in a napkin, but improving the estate, which Jasper Treverton had considerably increased during his long life, but upon which the old man had been somewhat loth to spend money. It was altogether a full and happy life which John Treverton led with his wife in this first year of their union, and it seemed to both that nothing was wanting to perfect their happiness. And yet, by-and-by, when there came the prospect of a child being born in the grave old house which had so long been undisturbed by the patter of childish feet, the fulfilment of this sweet hope seemed the one thing needed to fill their cup of joy.

While at the Manor House all was bliss, life dawdled on comfortably enough at the Vicarage, where the good, easy-tempered, hard-working Vicar had begun to be reconciled to the idea that his only son was to be an idler all his life; until perchance this seemingly barren plant should some day put forth the glorious flower of genius. And then the father's patience, the mother's love, would be rewarded all at once for weary days of waiting and despondency.

Edward had contrived to make himself particularly agreeable since his return to the family roof tree. He was less cynical than of old; less apt to rail against fate for not having set his lines in pleasanter places.

Even Celia was beguiled into the belief that her brother was completely cured of his attachment to Laura.

'I suppose his passion was like that poor sentimental old Petrarch's,' mused Celia, who had read about half-a-dozen sonnets of the illustrious Italian's in the whole course of her life, 'and he will go on spinning verses about the lady of his love for the next twenty years, without feeling any the worse for his platonic affection. He seems to enjoy being at the Manor House; and he and John Treverton get on very well together, considering how different they are in character.'

Edward made himself very comfortable in his rural home. He had tried London life, and had grown heartily sick of it; and he was now less disposed than of old to grumble at the dulness of a Devonshire village. What though he saw the same stolid bovine faces every day? Were they not better and fairer to look at than the herd of strange faces—keen and sharpened as if the desire for gain was an absolute physical hunger—that had passed him by in the smoke-tainted streets of London? These faces knew him. Here hats were touched as he passed by. People noticed whether he looked well or ill. Here, at least, he was somebody, an important figure in the sum of village life. His death would cause a sensation, his absence would make a blank. Edward did not care a straw about these simple villagers; but it pleased him that they should care for him. He settled himself down in his old home—the good substantial old Vicarage, a roomy house with stone walls, high gables, and heavy chimney stacks, shut in from the road by a holly hedge of a century's growth, sheltered at the back by the steep slope of the moor, while its front windows faced undulating pastures and distant woods.

Here Edward made himself a study, or den, where he could work at his *magnum opus*, and where his solitude was undisturbed by intrusion. It was understood that his labours in this sanctuary of genius were of the hardest. Here he gave up his soul to convulsive throes and struggles, as of Pythoness on her tripod. The chamber was at the end of a long passage, and had a lattice overlooking the moor. Here tobacco was not forbidden, although the Vicar was no smoker, and had an old-fashioned detestation of cigars. Edward found a good deal of smoke necessary to relax the tension of his nerves, during the manufacture of his poem. If the door was suddenly opened by Celia or Mrs. Clare, the poet was apt to be discovered reclining in his rocking chair, with a cigar between his lips, and his eyes fixed dreamily upon the topmost ridge of moorland. At such times he told his mother and sister he was doing his thinking. The scored and blotted manuscript on his writing-table testified to the severity of his labours; but the sharp-eyed Celia perceived that the work progressed but slowly. There was a good deal of meditation and cigar smoke necessary to its elaboration. Once or twice Edward had been discovered reading a French novel.

'One so soon forgets a language if one doesn't read a thoroughly idiomatic work now and then,' he said, explaining this seeming frivolity.

He kept up his connection with the popular magazines, sending them as many trifles in the drawing-room style as they could expect from him; and by this means he contrived to be well dressed and provided with pocket-money, without sponging on his father.

'All I want is the run of my teeth for the next year or so, till I have made a name,' he told his mother; 'that is not much for an only son to ask of his father.'

The Vicar agreed that the demand was modest. He would have preferred a son of a more active and eager temperament—a son who would have taken to the church, or law, or medicine, or even soldiering. But it was not for him to complain if Heaven had given him a genius, instead of a commonplace plodder. It was the old story of the ugly duck, no doubt. By-and-by, the snow-white wings would unfold themselves for a noble flight, and the admiring world would acknowledge the beauty of the swan. Mrs. Clare, who adored her only son, after the manner of weak-minded mothers, was delighted to have him at home, for good, as she said, delightedly. She made his den as luxurious as her small means would allow; put up bookshelves wherever he wanted them, covered his mantleboard with velvet, and draped it with point lace of her own working, bought him cigar stands and ash trays, tobacco jars and fusee boxes, blotting books, slippers, down pillows for his hours of lassitude, soft fluffy rugs to cover his feet when he sank on his snug little couch, prostrate after lengthened wrestling with an unpropitious muse. All that a doting mother can do to spoil a young man, Mrs. Clare did for her son; and it happened, unfortunately, that he was not made of that strong stuff which the sweet flatteries of love cannot corrupt.

There were certain hours when the poet was approachable. At five o'clock on those evenings when the brother and sister were not at the Manor House, Celia used to bring him a cup of coffee, and the small stock of gossip which she had been able to collect in the course of her frivolous day. She would seat herself on a hassock beside the fire, or even on the edge of the fender, and chatter gaily, while Edward lay back in his easy chair, sipping his coffee, and listening with an air of condescending indulgence.

A good deal of Celia's talk was naturally about her friends at the

Manor House. She had got over her prejudice against John Treverton, and was even enthusiastic in her praise of him. He was 'quite too lovely.' As a husband she declared him 'perfect.' She wished that Heaven had made her such a man.

'I really think Laura is the luckiest girl in creation!' she exclaimed. 'Such a husband, such a house, such a stable, such gardens, such a rent-roll! It is almost provoking to see her take everything so quietly. I believe she is grateful to Providence, because she is dreadfully religious, you know. But her placidity almost enrages me. If I had half such good fortune I should want to jump over the moon!'

'Laura is thoroughly good style, my dear. Well-bred people never want to jump over the moon,' Edward remarked, languidly.

'Strictly fraternal,' ejaculated Celia, with a shrug.

'I am very glad to hear she is so happy,' pursued Edward, with an air of ineffable good nature. 'Thank heaven, I have quite got over my old weakness about her, and can contemplate her happiness without a twinge of jealousy. But at the same time I do rather wonder that she can be thoroughly happy with a man of whose antecedents she knows nothing.'

'How can you say that, Ted? She knows who he is, and what he is. She knows that he was a lieutenant in a crack regiment, and sold out because he had run through his money——'

'Sold out just seven years ago,' interrupted Edward. 'What has he been doing with himself in the meantime?'

'Knocking about London.'

'That is a very vague phrase. Seven years! He must have earned his living somehow during the greater part of that time. The money he got for his commission would not last him long. He must have had his own particular circle of acquaintances during that interval. Why are none of them forthcoming? Why is he so silent about the experiences of those seven years? Man is an egotistical animal, my dear Celia. Be sure that there is always something to be ashamed of when a man keeps silence about himself.'

'There is something rather odd about that, certainly,' assented Celia, in a musing tone. 'John Treverton never talks of his past life, or, at any rate, of the time that has gone by since he left the army. I suppose he has been in London all the time, for he talks as if he were awfully disgusted with London life. If I were Laura I should insist upon knowing all about it.'

'There can be no happiness between man and wife without perfect confidence,' said Edward. 'No enduring happiness, at least.'

'Poor, dear Laura,' sighed Celia. 'I always said it was an ill-omened marriage; but lately I have thought that I was going to turn out a false prophet.'

'Has she ever told you what took her husband away after their marriage?'

'No, on that point she has been as silent as the grave. She told me once that he had been to Buenos Ayres, called away on business. I have never been able to extort anything more out of her.'

'It must have been a curious kind of business which called a man away from his newly-wedded wife,' said Edward.

Celia nodded significantly, and looked at the fire. She loved Laura well, but she loved scandal better.

Edward gave a short, impatient sigh, and turned his head fretfully upon the cushion which maternal hands had worked in softest wool. That movement, expressive of disgust with life in general, did not escape the sharp eyes of his sister.

'Ted, dear, I'm afraid you have not left off being unhappy about Laura,' she murmured, sympathetically.

'I am only unhappy about her when I think she is married to a scoundrel.'

'Oh, Ted, how can you say such a thing?'

'Celia, a man who can give no account of seven years of his life must be a scoundrel,' Edward Clare said decisively. 'Say nothing to alarm Laura, I beg you. I am talking to you to-day as if you were a man, and to be trusted. Wait and watch. Wait and watch, as I shall.'

'Edward, how you frighten me! You make me feel as if we were living in one of those villages at the foot of Vesuvius, with a fiery mountain getting itself ready to explode and destroy us.'

'There will be an explosion some day, Celia, depend upon it; an explosion that will blow up the Manor House as surely as Kirk o' Field was blown up the night Darnley was slain.'

He said no more, though Celia did not willingly let the subject drop. Indeed, he was inclined to be angry with himself for having said so much, though he had not given his sister his confidence without a motive. He wanted to know all that could be known about John Treverton, and Celia was in a position to learn much that he could not discover for himself.

'I really thought you were beginning to like Mr. Treverton,' the girl said, presently. 'You and he seem to get on so well together.'

'I am civil to him for Laura's sake. I would be guilty of a worse hypocrisy if I thought it would serve her interests.'

Edward sighed, and gave his head another angry jerk upon the cushion. He wanted to do John Treverton deadly harm; and yet he knew that the worst he could do to his rival would bring about no good result to himself. There was nothing to be gained by it. The injury would be irrevocable, deadly; a blight upon name and fortune—perchance the gallows—a shame so deep that a loving wife would scarcely survive the blow. All this was in Edward Clare's mind as a not impossible revenge. And unhappily there was no smaller revenge possible. He felt himself possessed of a deadly power; but of no power to wound without slaying. He was like the cobra, whose poisonous fangs are provided with an ingenious mechanism which keeps them in reserve until the creature wants to use them. Two hinged teeth lie back against the roof of the snake's mouth. When he attacks his victim the hinge moves, the fangs descend, the poison gland is pressed, and the deadly poison runs down a groove in the tooth, and drops into the puncture prepared to receive it. Lop off the wounded limb ere the shadow on the dial has marked the passage of twenty seconds, or the venom will have done its work. Medicine has yet to discover the antidote that can save the life of the victim.

CHAPTER XXIV.

'AND PURPLE LIGHT SHONE OVER ALL.'

Christmas was at hand, the first Christmas in Laura's married life, and to her happy fancy it seemed the most wonderful season that had ever been marked on the calendar of the ages. How could she and John Treverton be thankful enough for the blessings Providence had given them? How could they do enough to make other people happy? About a fortnight before the sacred festival she carried Celia off to Beechampton in the pony carriage, to buy a tremendous stock of blankets and flannel petticoats for the old women, and comfortable homespun coats for the rheumatic old men.

'Have you any idea as to the amount you are spending, Laura?' asked the practical Celia.

'No, dear; but I have one fixed idea, and that is that no one near Hazlehurst shall be cold and wretched this Christmas, if I can help it.'

'I'm afraid you are encouraging pauperism,' said Celia.

'No, Celia; I am waging war against rheumatism.'

'I hope you don't expect gratitude.'

'I only expect the blankets to keep out Jack Frost. And now for the grocer's.'

She shook the reins gaily, and drove on to the chief grocer of Beechampton, in whose plate-glass windows a pair of tall Japanese jars announced the superior character of the trade transacted inside. Here Mrs. Treverton ordered a hundred parcels of plums, currants, sugar, spice, and candied peel, each parcel containing an ample supply for a family Christmas pudding. The shopman rejoiced as he booked the order, and was eloquent in his praise of 'our new fruit.'

From the grocer's they drove to the confectioner's, and there Laura ordered such a supply of plum cake and buns, muffins and tea cakes, all to be delivered at the Manor House on Christmas Eve, that Celia began to be seriously alarmed for her friend's sanity.

'What can you want with all that indigestible rubbish?' she exclaimed. 'Are you going to open a pastrycook's shop?'

'No, dear. These things are for my juvenile party.'

'A juvenile party—already! I can't understand your motive, unless it is to get your hand in for the future. Who are you going to have? All Lady Parker's nursery, of course—and Lady Barker's grandchildren, and Mrs. Pendarvis's seven boys, the Briggses, and the Dropmores, and the Seymours. You'll want dissolving views, and a conjuror; and you might have *tableaux vivants*, as you don't seem to care how much money you waste. People expect so much at juvenile parties now-a-days.'

'I think my guests will be quite happy without *tableaux vivants*, or even a conjuror.'

'I doubt it. Those little Barkers are intensely old for their age.'

'The little Barkers are not coming to my party.'

'And the Pendarvis boys give themselves as many airs as undergraduates after their first term.'

'But I have not invited the Pendarvis boys.'

'Then what children, in goodness' name, are to eat all those cakes?' cried Celia.

'My party is for the children of the cottagers. All your father's infant school will be there.'

'Then all I can say is, I hope you have arranged for the ventilation of your rooms; for if you expect me to spend Christmas Eve in an atmosphere at all resembling that of our infant schoolroom you are reckoning without your host.'

'I am not reckoning without a knowledge of Celia Clare's good nature. I shall expect you to help me with all your heart and soul. Even your brother might do something for us. He could give us a comic reading—"Mrs. Brown at the play," or something of that kind.'

'Picture to yourself Algernon Swinburne reading "Mrs. Brown" to a herd of charity children,' exclaimed Celia, laughingly. 'I assure you my brother Edward thinks himself quite as important a person as Mr. Swinburne. Would you have him lay aside his *magnum opus* to study "Mrs. Brown at the play"?'

'I am sure he won't mind helping us,' said Laura. 'I shall have a Christmas tree loaded with gifts, a good many of them useful ones. I shall hire a magic lantern from London; and for the rest we can have all the old-fashioned games—Blind Man's Buff, Oranges and Lemons, Thread my Needle—all the noisiest, wildest romps we can think of. I am going to have the servants' hall cleared out and decorated for the occasion; so there will be no fear of any of the dear old furniture coming to grief.'

'If poor old Mr. Treverton could come to life again, and see such goings on!' ejaculated Celia.

'I am sure he would be glad to know that his wealth was employed in making other people happy. Think of all those poor little children, Celia, who hardly know the meaning of the word pleasure, as rich people understand it.'

'All the happier for them,' said Celia, philosophically. 'The pleasures of the rich are dreadfully hollow; as sickly-sweet and crumbly as a meringue from an inferior pastry-cook, with the cream gone sour inside. Well, Laura, you are a good soul, and I will do my very best to help you through your juvenile muddle. I wonder if fourteen thousand a year would make me benevolent. I'm afraid my expenses would increase at such a rate that I should have no margin for charity.'

Before Christmas Eve came a shadow had fallen upon Laura's life, which made complete happiness impossible, even for one who was bent upon giving joy to others. John Treverton fell ill of a low fever. He was not dangerously ill. Mr. Morton, the local doctor, who had attended Jasper Treverton for twenty years, and who was a general practitioner of skill and experience, made very light of the malady. The patient had got a chill riding a tired horse a long way home through the rain, after his last hunt, and the chill had resulted in slightly feverish symptoms, and Mr. Treverton was a little below par. That was all. The only remedies wanted were rest and good nursing, and for a man in John Treverton's position both were easy.

'Ought I to put off my children's party?' Laura asked, anxiously, the day before Christmas Eve. 'I should be very sorry to disappoint the poor little things, but,' here her voice faltered, 'if I thought John was going to be worse——'

'My dear Mrs. Treverton, he is not going to be worse; in fact, he is rapidly mending. Didn't I tell you the pulse was stronger this morning? He will be well in a few days, I hope; but I shall keep him in his room to the end of the week, and I shall not allow him to take part in any Christmas festivities. As for your children's party, if you can prevent the noise of it reaching him, there is no reason in the world why it should be postponed.'

'The servants' hall is quite on the other side of the house,' said Laura. 'I don't think the noise can possibly reach the next room.'

This conversation between Mrs. Treverton and the doctor had taken place in John Treverton's study—the panelled room adjoining his bedroom—the room in which he and Laura had first met.

'Then that's all you need care about,' replied Mr. Morton.

Laura had been her husband's only nurse throughout his illness. She had sat with him all day, and watched him through the night,

210

taking snatches of slumber at intervals on the comfortable old sofa at the foot of the big old-fashioned four-post bed. In vain had John Treverton urged the danger of injury to her own health from the fatigue involved in this tender care of him. She told him she had never felt better or stronger, and never enjoyed more refreshing sleep than on the roomy old sofa.

They had been happy together, even in this time of anxiety. It was Laura's delight to read aloud to the invalid, to write his letters, to pour out his medicine, to minister to all the trivial wants of an illness that caused at its most only a sense of languor and helplessness. Her only regret with regard to the children's party was that for this one evening she must be for the most part absent from the sick room. Instead of reading aloud to her husband, she must give her mind to 'Blind Man's Buff,' and all her energies to 'Thread my Needle.'

The winter twilight came gently down, bringing a light snow shower with it, and at four o'clock Laura was seated at the little Chippendale table by her husband's bed, drinking tea with him for the first time since the beginning of his illness. He had been sitting up for a few hours in the middle of the day, and was now lying outside the bed, wrapped warmly in his long fur-bordered dressing-gown.

He was intensely interested in the children's party, and asked Laura all about her arrangements for entertaining her guests.

'I should think the great point was to give them enough to eat,' he said, meditatively. 'The nearest approach to perfect happiness I ever beheld is a child eating something it considers nice. For the moment the mind of that infant is in a state of complete beatitude. It lives in the present, and the present only. Its little life is rounded into the narrow circle of NOW. Slowly, thoughtfully, it smacks its lips, and gloats upon the savour it loves. Hardly an earthquake would disturb it from that deep and tranquil delight. With the last mouthful, its gladness departs, and the child learns that earthly pleasure is fleeting. Let your children stuff themselves all the evening and stuff their pockets before they go home, Laura, and they will realise the perfection of bliss.'

'And to-morrow the poor little creatures would be ill and miserable. No, Jack, they shall enjoy themselves a little more rationally than you propose; and every one of them shall have something to take back to the person they love best at home, so that even a child's idea of enjoyment shall not be utterly selfish. But I shall be so sorry to be away from you all the evening Jack.'

'And I shall be still more sorry to lose you, love. I shall try to sleep away the hours of your absence. Could you not give me a good dose of chloral now, Laura?'

'Not for the world, dear. I have a horror of opiates, except in extreme cases. I shall contrive to be with you for an odd half hour or two in the course of the evening. Celia is to be my lieutenant.'

'Then I hope you will let her do a good deal of your work, and that I shall see the sweet face I love, very often. Who is coming, besides the children?'

'Only Mr. Sampson and his sister, and Edward Clare. Edward is going to read an Ingoldsby legend. I suggested "Mrs. Brown at the play;" but he would not hear of her. I am afraid the children won't understand Ingoldsby.'

'You and Celia must start all the laughter.'

'I don't think I could laugh while you are a prisoner here.'

'It has been a very short imprisonment and your sweet society has made it very happy.'

CHAPTER XXV.

THE CHILDREN'S PARTY.

The servants' hall was one of the finest rooms in the Manor House. It was at the back of the house, remote from all the reception rooms, and had been part of a much older building than the Carolian mansion to which it now belonged. It was lighted by two square latticed windows with stone mullions, looking into the stable yard. There was also a door opening directly into the same stable yard, and offering a convenient approach for the wandering tribes of tramps, hawkers, and gipsies, who boldly defied the canine guardians of the yard, knowing that the stoutest mastiff that ever thundered forth his abhorrence of rags and beggary is only formidable within the circle described by the length of his chain.

On this Christmas Eve the servants' hall looked as cheerful a room as one could choose for a night's revelry. Huge logs flamed and crackled in the wide old fireplace, and shone and sparkled on the whitewashed wall, which was glorified with garlands of holly and ivy, and lighted with numerous candles in tin sconces made for the occasion by the village blacksmith. Two long tables on trestles were spread with such a meal as a rustic child might see in some happy dream, but could scarcely hope to behold in sober reality. Such mountains of plum cake, such mighty piles of buns, such stacks of buttered toast, such crystal jars of ruby jam and amber marmalade! The guests had been invited for the hour of six, and, as the clock struck, they all came trooping in, with shining faces, and cheeks and noses cherry red, after their run through the lightly falling snow. It was not often that snow fell in this western world, and a snowstorm at Christmas was considered altogether pleasant and seasonable, an event for the children to rejoice at.

Laura was ready to receive her young visitors, supported by Mr. Sampson and his sister, Celia Clare, and all the servants. Edward had promised to drop in later. He had no objection to distinguish himself by a comic reading, but he had no idea of sharing all the fatigue of the entertainment. Mr. and Mrs. Clare were to come in the course of the evening to see their small parishioners enjoying themselves.

The tea party was a great success. Celia worked nobly. While

Mrs. Treverton and Miss Sampson poured out the tea, this vivacious damsel flew hither and thither with plates of cake, spread innumerable slices of bread and jam, tied the strings of a score of pinafores, filled every plate the instant it was empty, and provided at every turn for the pleasure of the revellers, who sat in a happy silence—stolid, emotionless, stuffing automatically.

'You'd hardly think they were enjoying themselves intensely, would you?' whispered Celia, coming to Laura for a fresh supply of tea, 'but I know they are, because they all breathe so hard. If this was a gathering of the county families, you might think it a failure; but silence in this case means ecstasy.'

At the stroke of seven the tables were being cleared, while Celia, in wild spirits, ran about after the smiling housemaids, crying, 'more light, ye knaves, and turn the tables up.' Then came a merry hour at 'Blind Man's Buff' and 'Thread my Needle,' and the silent tea party grew clamorous as a flight of rooks at sunset. At eight Mr. and Mrs. Clare arrived, followed a little later by Edward, who sauntered in with a somewhat languid air, as if he had not quite made up his mind that he ought to be there.

He came straight to Laura, who had just returned from a stolen half-hour by her husband's bedside.

'What an uproar!' he said. 'I've come to keep my promise; but do you really think these little animals will care for the "Jackdaw of Rheims"?'

'I think they will be glad to sit still for a little while after their romp, and I've no doubt they'll laugh at the "Jackdaw." It's very good of you to come.'

'Is it? If you knew how I detest infant school children you might say so, but if you knew how I——' He left the sentence unfinished. 'How is Treverton?' he asked.

'Much better. Mr. Morton says he will be well in a day or two.'

'I passed a curious-looking fellow in the road just outside your gates, a regular London Bohemian; a man whose very walk recalled the most disreputable quarters of that extraordinary city. I have no idea who the fellow is; but I'll swear he's a Londoner, a swindler, and an adventurer; and I have a lurking idea that I have seen him before.'

'Indeed! Was it that which attracted your notice?'

'No, it was the man's style and manner altogether. He was loitering near the gate, as if with some intention; possibly not the most honourable. You've heard perhaps of a kind of robbery known as the portico dodge?'

214

'No. I am not learned in such distinctions.'

'It is a common crime now-a-days. A country house with a portico is a fine field for the display of genius in burglary. One of the gang scales the portico after dusk, most likely at the family dinner-hour, gets from the roof of the portico through a convenient window, and then quietly admits his accomplices. In all such robberies there is generally one member of the gang, the cleverest and best educated, who has no active part in the crime. He does all the intellectual work, schemes and directs the whole business; but though the police know him and would give their eyes to catch him tripping, he never tumbles into their trap. The fellow I saw at your gates to-night seemed to me just this sort of man.'

Laura looked very serious, as if she were alarmed at the idea of robbery.

'Was this man young or old?' she asked thoughtfully.

'Neither. He is middle-aged, perhaps even elderly, but certainly not old. He is as straight as a dart, spare but broad-shouldered, and with something of a military air.'

'What made you fancy he had some evil design upon this house?' asked Laura, her face clouded with anxious thought.

'I did not like the way in which he loitered by the gate. He seemed to be looking for some one or something, watching his opportunity. I don't want to scare you, Laura. I only want to put you on your guard, so that you may have all the doors and shutters looked after with extra care to-night. After all, the man may be perfectly harmless—some seedy acquaintance of your husband, perhaps. A man cannot live in the world of London without that kind of burr sticking to his coat.'

'You do not flatter my husband by such a supposition,' said Laura, with an offended look.

'My dear Laura, do you think a man can live his life without making acquaintance he would not care to exhibit in the glare of noonday? You know the old adage about poverty and strange bedfellows. I hope there is no treason in reminding you that Mr. Treverton was not always rich.'

'No. I am not ashamed of his having been poor; but it would shame me if I thought he had any acquaintance in his poverty whom he would blush to own now he is rich. Will you begin your reading? The children are ready.'

The infants, flushed and towzled by their sports, had been ranged on benches by the joint efforts of Tom Sampson, his sister, and Celia Clare, and were now being regaled with cake and negus. Celia had placed a small table, with a pair of candles and a glass of water, at the end of the room, for the accommodation of the reader.

'Silence!' commanded Mr. Sampson, as Edward walked to his place, gave a little preparatory cough, and opened his book. 'Silence for "The Jackdaw of Rheims."'

> *'The Jackdaw sat on the Cardinal's chair!*
> *Bishop, and abbot, and prior were there;*
> *Many a monk and many a friar,*
> *Many a knight and many a squire,'*

began Edward.

A loud peal of the front-door bell startled him. He stopped for a moment, and looked at Laura, who was sitting with the Vicar and his wife in a little group near the fireplace at the other end of the room. At the sound of the bell she looked up quickly, and, with an agitated air, kept her eyes fixed on the door, as if she expected some one to enter.

He had no excuse for leaving off reading, curious as he felt about that bell, and Laura's evident concern. He went on mechanically, full of wondering speculations as to what was going on in the entrance hall, hating the open-mouthed and open-eyed infants who were hanging on his words; while Celia, seated at the end of the front row, started all the laughter and applause.

'Where did I meet that man?' he asked himself over and over again while he read on.

The answer flashed upon him in the middle of a sentence.

'It is the man I saw with Chicot in Drury Lane; the man I talked to in the public-house.'

The door opened, and the slow and portly Trimmer came in, and softly made his way to the place where his mistress was seated. He whispered to her, and then she whispered to Mrs. Clare—doubtless an apology for leaving her—and anon followed Trimmer out of the room.

'What can that man—if it is that man who rang the bell—want with *her*?' wondered Edward, so deeply moved that he could scarcely go on reading. 'Is the secret going to be told to-night? Are the cards going to be taken out of my hands?'

CHAPTER XXVI.

A DISINTERESTED PARENT.

'A person has called to see you, ma'am. He begs to apologise for coming so late, but he has travelled a long way, and will be very thankful if you can see him.'

This is what the butler had whispered in Mrs. Treverton's ear, handing her at the same time a card on which there was a name written—

'Colonel Mansfield.'

At sight of this name Laura rose, whispered her excuse to Mrs. Clare, and glided quietly from the room.

'Where have you left this gentleman?' she asked the butler.

'I left him in the hall, ma'am. I did not feel sure you would see him.'

'He is related to my family,' said Laura, faltering a little; 'I cannot refuse to see him.'

This brief conversation occurred in the corridor leading from the servants' hall to the front of the house. A tall man, wrapped in a loose, rough great-coat, was standing just inside the hall door, while Trimmer's subordinate, a rustic youth in a dark-brown livery, stood at ease near the fireplace, evidently placed there to protect the mansion from any evil designs on the part of the unknown intruder.

Laura went to the stranger and gave him her hand, without a word. She was very pale, and it was evident the visitor was as unwelcome as he was unexpected.

'You had better come to my study,' she said. 'There is a good fire there. Trimmer, take candles to the study and some wine.'

'I'd rather have brandy,' said the stranger. 'I am chilled to the bone. An eight hours' journey in a cattle truck is enough to freeze the youngest blood. For a man of my age, and with chronic neuralgia, it means martyrdom.'

'I am very sorry,' murmured Laura, with a look in which compassion struggled against disgust. 'Come this way. We can talk quietly in my room.'

She went upstairs, the stranger following close at her heels, to the gallery out of which John Treverton's study, which was also her own favourite sitting-room, opened. It was the room where she and her husband had met for the first time, two years ago, on just such a night as this. It adjoined the bedroom where John Treverton was now lying. She had no desire that he should be a witness to her interview with this visitor of to-night; but she had a sense of protection in the knowledge that her husband would be within call. Hitherto, on the rare occasions when she had been constrained to meet this man, she had confronted him alone, defenceless; and she had never felt her loneliness so keenly as at those times.

'I ought to have told John the whole truth,' she said to herself; 'but how could I—how could I bear to acknowledge——'

She glanced backward, with a suppressed shudder, at the man following her. They were at the door of the study by this time. She opened it, and he went in after her and shut the door behind him.

A fire was burning cheerily on the pretty, bright-looking hearth, antique in its quaint ornamentation, modern in the artistic beauty of its painted tiles and low brass fender. There were candles on the mantelpiece and on the table, where an old-fashioned spirit bottle on a silver tray cheered the soul of the wayfarer. He filled a glass of brandy and drained it without a word.

He gave a deep sigh of contentment or relief as he set down the glass.

'That's a little bit better,' he said, and then he threw off his overcoat and scarf, and planted himself with his back to the fire, and the face which he turned to the light was the face of Mr. Desrolles.

The man had aged within the last six months. Every line in his face had deepened. His cheeks were hollow, his eyes haggard and bloodshot. The sands of life run fast for a man whose chief nourishment is brandy.

'Well,' he exclaimed, in a hard, husky voice. 'You do not welcome me very warmly, my child.'

'I did not expect you.'

'The surprise should be all the pleasanter. Picture to yourself, now, our meeting as it would be represented in a novel or a stage play. You would throw your arms wide apart, shriek, and rush to my breast. Do you remember Julia in the "Hunchback"? With what a yell of rapture she flings herself into Master Walter's arms!'

'Do you remember what Master Walter had been to Julia?' asked Laura, looking steadily into the haggard eyes, which shifted their gaze as she looked.

218

'Real life is flat and tame compared with a stage play,' said Desrolles. 'For my part I am heartily sick of it.'

'I am sorry to see you looking so ill.'

'I am a perambulating bundle of aches. There is not a muscle in my body that has not its particular pain.'

'Can you find no relief for this complaint? Are there not baths in Germany that might cure you?'

'I understand,' interrupted Desrolles. 'You would be glad to get me out of the way.'

'I should be glad to lessen your suffering. When I last wrote to you I sent you a much larger remittance than I had ever done before, and I told you that I should allow you six hundred a year, to be paid quarterly. I thought that would be enough for all your requirements. I am grieved to hear that you have been obliged to ride in a third-class carriage in cold weather.'

'I have been unlucky,' answered Desrolles. 'I have been at Boulogne; a pleasant place, but peopled with knaves. I fell among thieves, and got cleaned out. You must give me fifty or a hundred to-night, and you must not deduct it from your next quarterly payment. You are now a lady of fortune, and could afford to do three times as much as you are doing for me. Why did you not tell me you were married? Pretty treatment that from a daughter!'

'Father,' exclaimed Laura, looking at him with the same calm gaze which his shifting eyes had refused to meet just now, 'do you want me to tell you the truth?'

'Of course. Whatever else do you suppose I want?'

'Even if it seems hard and cruel, as the truth often is?'

'Speak away, girl. My poor old bones have been too long battered about in this world for hard words to break them.'

'How can you ask me for a daughter's dutiful love?' asked Laura, in low, earnest tones. 'How can you expect it from me? What of a father's affection or a father's care have you ever given to me? What do I know of your life except fraud and mystery? Have you ever approached me except in secret, and as an applicant for money?'

'It's a true bill,' ejaculated Desrolles, with a laugh that ended in a groan.

'When I was a little motherless child you gave me to the one true friend of your youth. He took me as his adopted daughter, leaving you dying, as he supposed. Years passed, and you let him believe you dead. For ten years you made no sign. Your daughter, your only child, was being reared in a stranger's house, and you did not trouble yourself to make one inquiry about her welfare.'

219

'Not directly. How do you know what measures I may have taken to get information indirectly, without compromising your future? It was for your advantage that I kept myself dark, Laura; it was for your sake that I let my old friend believe me dead. As his adopted daughter your prosperity was assured. What would your life have been with me? To save you I lent myself to a lie.'

'I am sorry for it,' said Laura coldly. 'In my mind all lies are hateful. I cannot conceive that good can ever come of them.'

'In this case good has come of my innocent deception. You are mistress of a fine estate, wife of a husband whom, as I hear, you love.'

'With all my heart and soul.'

'Is it too much to ask for a ray of your sunshine—a little benefit from your large wealth?'

'I will do anything in reason,' answered Laura, 'but not even for my own father—had you been all that a father should be to his child—would I suffer Jasper Treverton's wealth to be turned to evil uses. You told me that you stood alone in the world, with no one dependent on you. Surely six hundred a year is an income that should enable you to live in comfort and respectability?'

'It will, when I have got myself clear of past liabilities. Remember that until six months ago the help you gave me amounted only to a hundred a year, except when I appealed to you, under the pressure of circumstances, for an extra trifle. A hundred a year in London, to a man in bad health, hardly served to keep the wolf from the door. I had debts to pay. I have been unfortunate in a speculation that promised well.'

'In future you will have no occasion to speculate.'

'True,' said Desrolles, with a sigh, as he filled himself another glass of brandy.

Laura watched him with a face full of pain. Was this a father she could acknowledge to the husband she loved? Only with deepest shame could she confess her close kindred with a creature so sunk in degradation.

Desrolles drank the brandy at a gulp, and then flung himself into the chair by the hearth.

'And pray how long have you been married?' he asked.

Laura's face crimsoned at the question. It was just the one inquiry calculated to give her acutest pain; for it recalled all that was painful in the circumstances of her marriage.

'We were married on the last day of last year,' she said.

'You have been a year married, and I only learn the fact to-night

220

from the village gossips at the inn where I stopped to eat a crust of bread and cheese on my way here!'

'You might have seen the announcement in the *Times*.'

'I might, but did not. Well, I suppose I surrendered a father's rights when I gave my child to another man's keeping; but it seems hard.'

'Why pain yourself and me with useless reproaches? I am prepared to do all that duty can dictate. I am deeply anxious that your future life should be comfortable and respected. Tell me where you intend to live, and how I can best assure your happiness.'

'Happiness!' cried Desrolles, with a derisive shrug. 'I have never known that since I was five-and-twenty. Where am I going to live, do you ask? Who knows? Not I, you may be sure. I am a wanderer by habit and inclination. Do you think I am going to shut myself in a speculative builder's brick and mortar box—a semi-detached villa in Camden Town or Islington—and live the monotonous life of a respectable annuitant? That kind of vegetation may suit a retired tradesman, who has spent three-fourths of his life behind the same counter. It would be living death to a man with a mind—a man who has travelled and lived among his fellow-men. No, my dear; you must not attempt to limit my movements by the inch-measure of middle-class respectability. Give me my pittance unfettered by conditions of any kind. Let me receive it quarterly from your London agent, and, since you repudiate my claim to your affection, I pledge myself never again to trouble you with my presence after to-night.'

'I do not ask that,' said Laura thoughtfully. 'It is only right that we should see each other sometimes. By the deception which you practised upon my benefactor, you have made it impossible that I should ever own you as my father before the world. Everybody in Hazlehurst believes that my father died when Jasper Treverton adopted me. But to my husband, at least, I can own the truth: I have shrunk from doing so hitherto, but to-night, while we have been sitting here, I have been thinking that I have acted weakly and foolishly. John Treverton will respect your secret for my sake, and he ought to know it.'

'Stop,' cried Desrolles, starting to his feet, and speaking in a louder tone than he had used hitherto. 'I forbid you to breathe a word of me or my business to your husband. When I revealed myself to you I pledged you to secrecy. I insist——'

He stopped and stood facing the doorway between the two rooms, staring aghast, horror-stricken, as if he had seen a ghost.

'Great heaven!' he exclaimed, 'what brings you here?'

John Treverton stood in the open doorway, a tall, dark figure, in a long velvet dressing-gown. Laura flew to his side.

'Dearest, why did you get up?' she cried. 'How imprudent of you!'

'I heard a voice raised as if threateningly. What has brought this man here—with you?'

'He is the relation about whom you once questioned me, John,' Laura answered, falteringly. 'You have not forgotten?'

'This man related to you?' cried Treverton. 'This man?'

'Yes. You know each other?'

'We have met before,' answered Treverton, who had never taken his eyes from the other man's face. 'We last met under very painful circumstances. It is a surprise to find a relation of yours in Mr.——'

'Mansfield,' interrupted Desrolles. 'I have changed the name of Malcolm for Mansfield—a name in my mother's family—for Laura's sake. It might be disadvantageous for her to own kindred with a man whom the world has played football with for the last ten years.'

Desrolles had grown ashy pale since the entrance of Laura's husband, and the hand with which he poured out his third glass of brandy shook like a leaf.

'Highly considerate on your part, Mr. Mansfield,' replied John Treverton. 'May I ask for what reason you have favoured my wife with this late visit?'

'The usual motive that brings a poor relation to a rich man's house. I want money, and Laura can afford to give it. Why beat about the bush?'

'Why indeed! Plain dealing will be best in this case. I think, as it is a simple matter of business, you had better let me arrange it with you. Laura, will you leave your kinsman's claims for me to settle? You may trust me to take a liberal view of his position.'

'I will trust you, dearest, now and always,' answered his wife, giving him her hand, and then she went to Desrolles, and offered him the same frank hand, looking at him with tender earnestness. 'Good night,' she said, 'and good-bye. I beg you to trust my husband, as I trust him. Believe me, it will be the best for all of us. He will be as ready to recognise your claim as I am, if you will only confide in him. If I have trusted him with my life, cannot you trust him with your secret?'

'Good night,' said Desrolles curtly. 'I haven't got over my astonishment yet.'

'At what?'

'At finding you married.'

'Good night,' she said again, on the threshold of the door, and then she came back to tell her husband not to fatigue or excite himself. 'I can only give you a quarter of an hour,' she said to Desrolles. 'Pray remember that my husband is an invalid, and ought to be in bed.'

'Go to your school children, dearest,' said Treverton, smiling at her anxiety. 'I shall be careful.'

The door closed behind Laura, and the two men—fellow-lodgers a year ago in Cibber Street—stood face to face with each other.

'So you are John Treverton?' said Desrolles, wiping his lips with that tremulous hand of his, and looking with a hungry eye at the half-empty decanter, looking anywhere rather than straight into the eyes of his fellow-man.

'And you claim relationship with my wife?'

'Nearer, perhaps, than you would care to hear; so near that I have some right to know how you, Jack Chicot, came to be her husband—how it was that you married her a year ago, at which period the lovely and accomplished Madame Chicot, whom I had the honour to know, was still living? Either that charming woman was not your wife, or your marriage with Laura Malcolm is invalid.'

'Laura is my wife, and her marriage as valid as law can make it,' answered John Treverton. 'That is enough for you to know. And now be good enough to explain your degree of kindred with Mrs. Treverton. You say your real name is Malcolm. What was your relationship with Laura's father?'

'Laura urged me to trust you with my secret,' muttered Desrolles, throwing himself into his former seat by the fire, and speaking like a man who is calculating the chances of a certain line of policy. 'Why should I not be frank with you, Jack—Treverton? How much handier the old name comes! Had you been the punctilious piece of respectability I expected to meet in the heir of my old friend Jasper Treverton, I might have shrank from telling you a secret that hardly redounds to my credit, from the churchgoer and ratepayer's point of view. But to you—Jack—the artist and Bohemian, the man who has tumbled on every platform and acted in every show at the world's fair—to you I may confide my secret without a blush. Come, fill me another glass, like a good fellow; my hand shakes as if I had the scrivener's palsy. You know the history of Jasper Treverton's adopted daughter?'

'I have heard it, naturally.'

'You have heard how Treverton, who had quarrelled with his friend Stephen Malcolm about a foolish love affair, was summoned many years after to that friend's sick bed—found him dying, as every one supposed—then and there adopted Malcolm's only child, and carried her off with him, leaving a fifty-pound note to comfort his old friend's last moments and pay the undertaker?'

'Yes, I have heard all this.'

'But not what follows. When a doctor gives a patient up for dead, he is sometimes on the high road to recovery. Stephen Malcolm contrived to cheat the doctor. Perhaps it was the comfort provided by that fifty-pound note, perhaps it was the knowledge that his only child's future was provided for,—anyhow, it seemed as if a burden had been lifted from the sick man's shoulders, for from the time Jasper Treverton left him he mended, got a new lease of life, and went out into the world again—a lonely wayfarer, happy in the knowledge that his daughter's fate was no longer allied with his, that whatever evil might befall him her lines were set in pleasant places.'

'Do you mean to tell me that Stephen Malcolm recovered—lived for years—and allowed his daughter to suppose herself an orphan, and his friend to believe him dead?'

'To tell the truth would have been to hazard his daughter's good fortune. As an orphan, and the adopted child of a rich bachelor, her lot was secure. What would it have been if she had been flung back upon her actual father, to share his precarious existence? I considered this, and took the unselfish view of the question. I might have claimed my daughter back; I might have sponged on Jasper. I did neither—I went my solitary way, along the stony highway of life, uncheered, unloved.'

'You!' cried John Treverton. 'You!'

'Yes. In me you behold the wreck of Stephen Malcolm.'

'You Laura's father! Great heaven! Why, you have not a feature, not a look in common with her! Her father! This is indeed a revelation.'

'Your astonishment is not flattering to me. My child resembles her mother, who was one of the loveliest women I ever saw. Yet I can assure you, Mr. Treverton, that at your age, Stephen Malcolm had some pretension to good looks.'

'I am not disputing that, man. You may have been as handsome as Adonis; but my Laura's father should have at least something of her look and air; a smile, a glance, a turn of the head, a something that would reveal the mystic link between parent and child. Does she know this? Does she recognise you as her father?'

'She does, poor child. It is at her wish I have revealed myself to you.'

224

'How long has she known?'

'It is a little more than five years since I told her. I had just re-turned from the Continent, where I had spent seven years of my life in self-imposed exile. Suddenly I was seized with the outcast's yearning to tread his native soil again, and look upon the scenes of youth once more before death closes his eyes for ever. I came back—could not resist the impulse that drew me to my daughter—put myself one day in her pathway, and told her my story. From that time I have seen her at intervals.'

'And have received money from her,' put in John Treverton.

'She is rich and I am poor. She has helped me to live.'

'You might have lived upon the money she gave you a little more reputably than you were living in Cibber Street, when we were fellow-lodgers.'

'What were my vices in Cibber Street? My life was inoffensive.'

'Late hours and the brandy bottle—the ruin of body and soul.'

'I have a chronic malady which makes brandy a necessity for me.'

'Would it not be more exact to say that brandy is your chronic malady? Well, Mr. Mansfield, I shall make a proposition to you in the character of your son-in-law.'

'I have a few words to say to you before you make it. I have told you my secret, which all the world may know, and welcome. I have committed no crime in allowing my old friend to suppose me dead. I have only sacrificed my own interests to the advantage of my daughter; but you, Mr. Treverton, have your secret, and one which I think you would hardly like to lay bare to the world in which you are now such an important personage. The master of Hazlehurst Manor would scarcely care to be identified with Jack Chicot, the caricaturist, and husband—at least by common repute—of the dancer whose name used to adorn all the walls of London.'

'No,' said Treverton, 'that is a dark page in my life which I would willingly tear out of the book; but I have always known the probability of my finding myself identified with the past, sooner or later. This world of ours is monstrous big when a man tries to make a figure in it; but it's very small when he wants to hide himself from his fellow-men. I have told my wife all I can tell her without stripping the veil from that past life of mine. To reveal more would be to make her unhappy. You can have no motive for telling her more than I have told her. I can rely on your honour in this matter?'

'You can,' answered Desrolles, looking at him curiously; 'but I shall expect you to treat me handsomely—as a son-in-law, whose wealth has come to him through his marriage, should treat his wife's father.'

'What would you call handsome treatment?' asked Treverton.

'I'll tell you. My daughter, who has a woman's petty notions about money, has offered me six hundred a year. I want a thousand.'

'Do you?' asked Treverton, with half-concealed contempt. 'Well, live a respectable life, and neither your daughter nor I will grudge you a thousand a year.'

'I shall live the life of a gentleman. Not in England. My daughter wants to get me out of the country. She said as much just now; or, at any rate, what she did say implied as much. A continental life would suit my humour, and perhaps mend my health. Annuitants are long-lived.'

'Not when they drink a bottle of brandy a day.'

'In a milder climate I may diminish the quantity. Give me a hundred in ready money to begin with, and I'll go back to London by the first train to-morrow morning, and start for Paris at night. I ask for no father's place at your Christmas table. I don't want you to kill the fatted calf for me.'

'I understand,' said Treverton, with an involuntary sneer, 'you only want money. You shall have it.'

He took a bunch of keys from his pocket, and unlocked a despatch box, in which he was in the habit of keeping money received from his steward before he sent it off to the bank. There was a little over a hundred pounds in the box, in notes and gold. John Treverton counted a hundred; the crisp notes, the bright gold, lay in a tempting heap on the table before him, but he kept his hand upon the money for a minute or two, while he sat looking at it with a meditative countenance.

'By the way, Mr. —— Mansfield,' he began after that thoughtful silence, 'when, after a lapse of so many years, you presented yourself to your daughter, what credentials did you bring with you?'

'Credentials?'

'Yes. In other words, how did you prove your identity? You had parted with her when she was a child of six years old. Did her memory recall your features when she met you as a girl of seventeen, or did she take your word for the fact that you were the father she had believed to be in his grave?'

'She remembered me when I recalled myself to her. At first her memory was naturally vague. She had a dim recollection of my face, but no certainty as to when and where she had last seen it, until I recalled to her the circumstances of her childhood, the last days we

226

spent together before my serious illness, her mother, the baby brother that died when she was three years old. John Treverton, you libel nature if you suppose that a daughter's instinct can fail her when a father appeals to it. Had material proofs been wanted to convince my child that her father stood before her, I had those proofs, and I showed them to her—old letters, the certificate of her birth, her mother's picture. The portrait I gave to Laura. I have the documents about me to-night. I have never parted with them.'

He produced a bloated pocket-book, the leather worn greasy with long usage, the silk lining frayed and ragged, and from this receptacle brought forth half-a-dozen papers, yellow with age.

One was the certificate of Laura Malcolm's birth. The other five were letters addressed to Stephen Malcolm, Esq., Ivy Cottage, Chiswick. One of these, the latest in date, was from Jasper Treverton.

'I am deeply grieved to hear of your serious illness, my poor friend,' he wrote; 'your letter followed me to Germany, where I have been spending the autumn at one of the famous mineral baths. I started for England immediately, and landed here half-an-hour ago. I shall come on as fast as rail and cabs can bring me, and indeed hope to be with you before you get this letter.

'Yours in all friendship,
'JASPER TREVERTON.

'The Ship Hotel, Dover,
'October 15th, 185—.'

The other letters were from friends of the past, like Jasper. One had enclosed aid in the shape of a post-office order. The rest were sympathetic and regretful refusals to assist a broken-down acquaintance. The writers offered their impecunious friend every good wish, and benevolently commended him to Providence. In every case the respectability and the respectful tone of Stephen Malcolm's correspondents went far to testify to the fact that he had once been a gentleman. There was a deep descent from the position of the man to whom these letters were written to the status of Mr. Desrolles, the second-floor lodger in Cibber Street.

So far as they went his credentials were undeniable. Laura had recognised him as her father. What justification could John Treverton find for repudiating his claim? For the money the man demanded he cared not a jot; but it pained him unspeakably to accept this dissipated waif, soaked in alcohol, as the father of the woman he loved.

'There is your hundred pounds, Mr. Mansfield,' he said, 'and since you have taught the little world of Hazlehurst to consider my wife an orphan, the less you show yourself here the better for all of us. Villages are given to scandal. If you were to be seen at this house, people would want to know who you are and all about you.'

'I told you I should start for Paris to-morrow night,' answered Desrolles, strapping his pocket-book, which was now distended to its uttermost with notes and gold. 'I shan't change my mind. I'm fond of Paris and Parisian ways, and know my way about that glorious city almost as well as you, though I never married a French wife.'

John Treverton sat silent, with his thoughtful gaze bent on the fire, apparently unconscious of the other man's sneer.

'Ta ta, Jack. Any message for your old friends in the Quartier Latin? No? Ah, I suppose the Squire of Hazlehurst has turned his back on the companions of Jack Chicot; just as King Harry the Fifth threw off the joyous comrades of the Prince of Wales. The desertion broke poor old Falstaff's heart; but that's a detail. Good night, Jack.'

Laura re-entered the room at this moment, and drew back startled at hearing her father address her husband with such friendly familiarity.

'I have told Mr. Treverton everything, my dear,' said Desrolles.

'I am so glad of that,' answered Laura, and then she laid her hand upon the old man's shoulder, with more affection than she had ever yet shown him, and said, with grave gentleness, 'Try to lead a good life, my dear father, and let us hear from you sometimes, and let us think of each other kindly, though Fate has separated us.'

'A good life,' he muttered, turning his bloodshot eyes upon her for a moment with a look that thrilled her with a sudden horror. 'The money should have come sooner, my girl. I've travelled too far on the wrong road. There, good-bye, my dear. Don't trouble yourself about an old scapegrace like me. Jack, send me my money quarterly to that address,'—he threw down a dingy-looking card—'and I'll never worry you again. You can blot me out of your mind, if you like; and you need never fear that my tongue will say an evil word of you, go where I may.'

'I will trust you for that,' answered John Treverton, holding out his hand.

Desrolles either did not see the gesture, or did not care to take the hand. He snatched up his greasy-looking hat and hurried from the room.

'Dearest, do you think any worse of me now you know that man is my father?' asked Laura, when the door had closed upon Desrolles, and the bell had been rung to warn Trimmer of the guest's departure.

'Do I think any worse of a pearl because it comes out of an oyster?' said her husband, smiling at her. 'Dear love, if the parish workhouse were peopled with your relations, not one of them more reputable than Mr. Mansfield, my love and reverence for you would not be lessened by a tittle.'

'You don't believe in hereditary genius, then. You don't think that we derive our characters mainly from our fathers and mothers?'

'If I did I should believe that your mother was an angel, and that you inherited her disposition.'

'My poor father,' said Laura, with something between a sigh and a shudder. 'He was once a gentleman.'

'No doubt, love. There is no saying how low a man may descend when he once takes to travelling down-hill.'

'If he had not been a gentleman my adopted father could never have been his friend,' mused Laura. 'It would not have been possible for Jasper Treverton to associate with anything base.'

'No, love. And now tell me, when first your father presented himself to you, was not his revelation a great surprise, a shock to your feelings?'

'It was indeed.'

'Tell me, dear, how it happened. Tell me all the circumstances, if it does not pain you.'

'No, dear. It pained me for you to know that my father had fallen so low, but now that you know the worst, I feel easier in my mind. It is a relief to me to be able to speak of him freely. Remember, Jack, he had bound me solemnly to secrecy. I would not break my promise, even to you.'

'I understand all, dear.'

'The first time I saw my father,' Laura began falteringly, as if even to speak of him by that sacred name were painful to her, 'it was summer time, a lovely August evening, and I had strolled out after dinner into the orchard. You know the gate that opens from the orchard into the field. I saw a man standing outside it smoking, with his arms resting on the top of the gate. Seeing a stranger there, I turned away to avoid him, but before I had gone three steps he stopped me. "Miss Malcolm, for God's sake let me speak to you," he said. "I am an old friend whom you must remember." I went up to him and looked him full in the face; for there was such earnestness in his manner that it never occurred to me that he might be an impostor. "Indeed, I do not remember you," I said. "When have I ever seen you?" Then he called me by my Christian name. "Laura," he said, "you were six years old when Mr. Treverton brought you here. Have you quite forgotten the life that went before that time?"'

She paused, and her husband drew her to the low chair by the fire, and seated himself beside her, letting her head rest on his shoulder.

'Go on, love,' he said gently, 'but not if these memories agitate you.'

'No, dear. It is a relief to confide in you. I told him that I did remember the time before I came to the Manor House. Some events I could remember distinctly, others faintly, like the shadows in a dream. I remembered being in France, by the sea, in a place where the fisherwomen wore bright-coloured petticoats and high caps, where I had children of my own age to play with, and where the sun seemed always shining. And then that life had changed to dull gray days in a place near a river, a place where there were narrow lanes, and country roads and fields; and yet there was a town close by with tall chimneys and busy streets. I remembered that here my mother was ill, lying in a darkened room for many weeks; and then one day my father took me to London in the omnibus, and left me in a large, cold-looking house in a great square—a house where all the rooms were big and lofty, and had an awful look after our little parlour at home, and where I used to sit in a drawing-room all day with an old lady in black satin, who let me amuse myself as best I could. My father had told me that the old lady was his aunt, and that I was to call her aunt, but I was too much afraid of her to call her anything. I think I must have stayed there about a week, but it seemed ages, for I was very unhappy, and used to cry myself to sleep every night, when the maid had put me to bed in a large, bleak room at the top of the house; and then my father came and took me home again in the red omnibus. I could see that he was very unhappy, and while we were walking in the lane that led to our house he told me that my dear mamma had gone away, and that I should never see her again in this world. I had loved her passionately, Jack, and the loss almost broke my heart. I am telling you much more than I told the stranger. I only said enough to him to prove that I remembered my old life.'

'And how did he reply?'

'He took a morocco case from his pocket and gave it into my hand, telling me to look at the portrait inside it. Oh, how well I remembered that sweet face! The memory of it flashed upon me like a dream one has forgotten and tried vainly to recall, till it comes back suddenly in a breath. Yes, it was my mother's face. I could remember her looking just like that as she sat at work on the rocks by the sands where I played with the other children, at that happy place in France. I remembered her sitting by my cot every night before I fell asleep. I asked the stranger how he came to possess this picture. "I would give all the money I have in the world for it," I said. "You shall do nothing of the kind," he answered. "I give it you as a free gift, but I should not have done that if you had not remembered your mother's face. And now, Laura, look at me and tell me if you have ever seen me before?"'

'You looked and could not remember him,' said John Treverton.

'No. Yet there was something in the face that seemed familiar to me. When he spoke I knew that I had heard the voice before. It seemed kind and friendly, like the voice of some one I had known long ago. He told me to try and realize what change ten years of evil fortune would make in a man's looks. It was not time only which had altered him, he told me, but the world's ill-usage, bad health, hard work, corroding sorrow. "Make allowance for all this," he said, "and look at me with indulgent eyes, and then try to send your thoughts back to that old life at Chiswick, and say what part I had in it." I did look at him very earnestly, and the more I looked the more familiar the face grew. "I think you must be a friend of my father's," I said at last. "Poverty has no friends," he answered; "at the time you re-member your father was friendless. Oh, child, child, can ten years blot out a father's image? I am your father."'

Laura paused, with quickened breathing, recalling the agitation of that moment.

'I cannot tell you how I felt when he said this,' she continued, presently. 'I thought I was going to fall fainting at his feet. My brain clouded over; I could understand nothing; and then, when my senses came slowly back, I asked him how this could be true? Did not my father die a few hours after I was taken away by Jasper Treverton? My benefactor had told me that it was so. Then he—my father—said that he had allowed Jasper Treverton to suppose him dead, for my sake; in order that I might be the adopted child of a rich man, and well placed in life, while he—my real father—was a waif and stray, and a pauper. Mr. Treverton had received a letter announcing his old friend's death—a letter written in a feigned hand by my father him-self and had never taken the trouble to inquire into the particulars of the death and burial. He felt that he had done enough in leaving money for the sick man's use, and in relieving him of all care about his daughter. This is what my father told me. How could I reproach him, Jack, or despise him for this deception, for a falsehood which so degraded him? It was for my sake he had sinned.'

'And you had no doubt as to his identity? You were fully assured that he was that very father whom you had supposed dead and buried ten years before?'

'How could I doubt? He showed me papers—letters—that could have belonged to no one but my father. He gave me my mother's portrait; and then, through the mist of years, his face came back to me as a face that had been very familiar; his voice had the sound of long ago.'

'Did you give him money on this first meeting?'

'He told me that he was poor, a broken-down gentleman, without a profession, with bad health, and no means of earning his living. Could I, his daughter, living in luxury, refrain from offering him all the help in my power? I begged him to reveal himself to Mr. Treverton—papa, as you know I always called him—but he shrank, not unnaturally, from acknowledging a deception that placed him in such a false position. "No," he said, "I told a lie for your sake, I must stick to it for my own." I could not urge him to alter his resolution upon this point, for I felt how hard it would be for him to stand face to face with his old friend under such degrading circumstances. I promised to keep his secret, and I told him that I would send him all the money I could possibly spare out of my income, if he would give me an address to which I might send it.'

'How often did you see him after this?' asked John Treverton.

'Before to-night, only three times. One of those occasions was the night on which you saw me admit him at the garden-door.'

'True,' said Treverton, blushing as he remembered the cruel suspicions that had been awakened in his mind by that secret interview. 'And you never told my cousin anything about your father?'

'Never. He made me promise to keep his existence a secret from all the world; and even if I had not been so bound I should have shrunk from telling Mr. Treverton the cheat that had been practised upon him; for I felt that it was a cheat, however disinterested and generous the motive.'

'A purposeless cheat, I should imagine,' said John musingly, 'for once having promised to take care of you, I should hardly think that my cousin Jasper would have flung you back upon poverty and gloomy days. No, love, once knowing your sweetness, your truthful, loving nature, it would not have been human to give you up.'

'My poor father thought otherwise, unhappily.'

'Dearest love, do not let this error of your father's cast a shadow upon your life. I, who have known the shifts and straits to which poverty may bring a man, can pity and in some measure understand him. We will do all that liberality can do to make the remnant of his days respectable and happy.'

CHAPTER XXVII.

DESROLLES IS NOT COMMUNICATIVE.

Mr. Desrolles left the Manor House a new man. He held his head erect, and bore himself with a lofty air even before the butler who showed him out. He was respectabilised by a full purse. There was nothing left in him of the shabby, downcast stranger who had approached the house with an air of mingled mystery and apprehension. Trimmer hardly knew him. The man's seedy overcoat hung with the reckless grace of artistic indifference to attire, and not with the forlorn droop of beggary. His hat was set on with a debonair slant. He looked a Bohemian, a painter, an actor, a popular parson gone to the bad: anything rather than an undistinguished pauper. He flung Trimmer half-a-crown with the lofty elegance of a Lauzun or a Richelieu, nodded a condescending good-night, and walked slowly along the gravel drive, humming *La Donna e mobile*, with not an unskilful mimicry of him who, of all men that ever walked the boards of Covent Garden, looked and moved like a prince of the blood royal, and the thinnest thread of whose fading voice sent a thrill through every heart in the vast opera-house.

The snow was no longer falling. It lay in patches here and there upon the grass, and whitened the topmost edge of the moor, but there was an end of the brief snowstorm. The stars were shining in a deep blue sky, calm and clear as at midsummer. The moon was rising behind the dark ridge of moor. It was a scene that might have stirred the heart of a man fresh from the life of cities; but the thoughts of Desrolles were occupied in considering the new aspect given to affairs by his discovery of Jack Chicot in the young squire of Hazlehurst, and in calculating how he might best turn the occasion to his own peculiar profit.

'A good, easy-going fellow,' he reflected, 'and he seems inclined to be open-handed. But if the dancer was his legal wife, and if he married Laura a year ago, that poor girl is no more his wife than I am. Awkward for me to wink at such a position as that, in my paternal character; yet it might be dangerous for me to interfere.'

'Good evening, Mr. Desrolles,' said a voice close behind him.

He had been so deeply absorbed in self-interested speculations that he had not heard footsteps on the gravel. He turned sharply round, surprised at the familiar mention of his name, and encountered Edward Clare.

In that dim light he failed to recognise the man whom he had met in Long Acre, and talked with for about ten minutes, nearly a year ago.

'You seem to have forgotten me,' said Clare pleasantly; 'yet we have met before. Do you remember meeting me in Long Acre one afternoon and our talking together of your fellow-lodger, Mr. Chicot?'

'Your face and voice are both familiar to me,' said Desrolles thoughtfully. 'Yes, you are the gentleman with whom I conversed for some minutes in the bar of the Rose Tavern. I remember your speaking of Hazlehurst. You belong to this part of the world, I presume?'

'I do; but I am rather surprised to see you in such an out-of-the-way nook and corner of the universe—on Christmas Eve, too——'

'When I ought to be hanging up holly in my ancestral mansion, and kissing my grandchildren under the mistletoe,' interjected Desrolles, with a harsh laugh. 'Sir, I am a floating weed upon the river of life, and you need never be surprised to see me anywhere. I have no cable to moor me to any harbour, no dock but the hospital, no haven but the grave.'

Desrolles uttered this dismal speech with positive relish. He had a hundred pounds in his pocket, and the world before him where to choose. What did he want with dock or haven? He was by nature a rover.

'I am very glad we have met,' said Edward gravely; 'I have something serious to say to you—so serious that I would rather say it within four walls. Can you come with me to my house for half-an-hour, and let me talk to you over a tumbler of toddy?'

Toddy had but little temptation for the brandy drinker; it was almost as if some one had offered him milk and water.

'I want to get away by the mail,' said Desrolles doubtfully; 'and what the deuce can you have to say to me?'

'Something of the utmost importance. Something that may put money in your purse.'

'The suggestion provokes my curiosity. Suppose I forego the idea of the mail? It's a cold night, and I've had a good deal of travelling since morning. Does your village boast an inn where a man can get a decent bed?'

'Yes, they will make you comfortable at the George. You had better come home with me, and hear what I have to say. It's a quarter past nine, and the mail goes at ten thirty. You could hardly do it, if you tried.'

'Well, let the mail go without this Cæsar and his fortunes; I'll hear what you have to say.'

They walked together to the Vicarage. Mr. and Mrs. Clare and Celia were still at the Manor House, where the Christmas-tree was being stripped by the tumultuous infants, with shouts of rapture and shrill screams of delight. Edward had slipped out directly he had finished the 'Jackdaw,' under the pretence of smoking a cigar, and had gone round to the front of the house to watch for the unknown visitor's departure.

The Vicarage was wrapped in darkness, save in the servants' quarters, where some mild rejoicings were in progress. Edward let himself in at the hall door, and went up to his den, followed by Mr. Desrolles. The fire had burnt low, but there was a basket of wood by the hearth. Edward flung on a log, and lighted the candles on the table. Then he opened a cosy little corner cupboard in the panelling, and took out a black bottle, a couple of tumblers, and a sugar basin.

'If your whisky's good, don't trouble to mix it,' said Desrolles; 'I'd rather taste it neat.'

He settled himself comfortably in the chair beside the hearth, the poet's own particular rocking-chair, in which he was wont to cradle his fine fancies, and sometimes hush his genius to placid slumber.

'A tidy little crib,' said Desrolles, looking curiously round the room, with all its masculine luxuries and feminine frivolities. 'I wonder you should speak so disparagingly of a village in which you've such snug quarters.'

'The grub is snug in his cocoon,' retorted Edward, 'but that isn't life.'

'No. Life is to be a butterfly, at the mercy of every wind that blows. I think on the whole the grub has the best of it.'

'Help yourself,' said Edward, pushing the whisky bottle across the table to his visitor.

Desrolles filled a glass and emptied it at a draught. 'New and raw,' he said, disapprovingly. 'Well, Mr. ——. By the way, you did not favour me with your card when last we met.'

'My name is Clare.'

'Well, Mr. Clare, here I am. I have gone out of my own way to put myself at your disposal. What is this wondrous communication you have to make to me?'

'First, let us discuss your own position.'

'I beg your pardon,' exclaimed Desrolles, rising and taking up

236

his hat. 'I did not come here to talk about that. If you've set a trap for me you'll find you've got the wrong customer. I belong to the ferret tribe.'

'My dear fellow, don't be in such a hurry,' said Edward, putting up his white, womanish hand in languid entreaty; 'as a prelude to what I have got to say I am obliged to speak of your own position with reference to Laura Treverton and her husband, John Treverton, otherwise Jack Chicot.'

'What do you mean?'

'Simply what I say. John Treverton, squire of Hazlehurst, and Jack Chicot—Bohemian, adventurer, artist in black and white, unsuccessful painter in oils, what you will—are one and the same. It may suit Mr. Treverton to forget that he was ever Jack Chicot; but the story of his past life is not blotted out because he is ashamed of it. You know, and I know, that the present lord of Hazlehurst Manor is Mrs. Evitt's old lodger.'

'You must be crazy to suggest such a thing,' said Desrolles, looking at the other with an air of half stupefied inquiry, as a man in whom he did verily perceive indications of insanity. 'The two men have not one attribute in common.'

'If the man I saw talking to you in Long Acre was Chicot, the caricaturist, then Chicot and Treverton are one.'

'My dear fellow, your eyes played you false. Possibly there may be a kind of likeness, as far as height, figure, complexion, go.'

'I saw the man's face at the magazine office, and I'll swear it was Treverton's face.'

Desrolles shrugged his shoulders, as much as to say, 'Here is a poor half-cracked fellow labouring under a harmless delusion. I must indulge him.'

'Well, my dear sir,' he said presently, stretching his well-worn boots before the hearth, and luxuriating in the warmth of the blazing wood, 'if this is all you have to say, you might as well have let me get away by the mail.'

'You deny the identity of John Treverton and Chicot, the caricaturist?'

'Most emphatically. I have the honour to know both men, and am in a position to state that they are totally distinct individuals—bearing a kind of resemblance to each other in certain broad characteristics—height, figure, complexion—a resemblance that might mislead a man seeing one of the two for a few moments, as you saw Chicot——'

'How do you know how often I saw Chicot?'

'I draw my inference from your own conduct. If you had seen him often—if you had seen him more than once—you could not possibly mistake him for Mr. Treverton, or Mr. Treverton for him.'

Edward Clare shrugged his shoulders, and sat looking frowningly at the fire for some moments. Whatever this man Desrolles knew, or whatever he thought, it was evident that there was very little to be got out of him.

'You are very positive,' Edward said presently, 'so I suppose you are right. After all, I can have no desire to identify the husband of a woman I highly esteem with such a fellow as this Chicot. I want only to protect her interests. Married to a scoundrel, what might not be her fate? Perhaps as terrible as that of the dancer.'

Desrolles answered nothing. He was lying back in the rocking chair, resting, his eyes half closed.

'Have you seen Chicot since his wife was murdered?' asked Edward, after a pause.

'No one has seen him. It is my belief that he made straight for one of the bridges, and drowned himself.'

'In that case his body would have been found, and his death made known to the police.'

'You would not say that if you were a Londoner. How many nameless corpses do you think are fished out of the Thames every week—how many unrecognised corpses lie in the East-end deadhouses waiting for some one to claim them, and are never claimed or identified, and go to the paupers' burial-ground without a name? The police did not know Chicot. They had only his description to guide them in their search for him. I am very clear in my mind that the poor devil put himself out of their way in the most effectual manner.'

'You think he murdered his wife?'

Desrolles shrugged his shoulders dubiously.

'I think nothing,' he answered. 'Why should I think the very worst of a man who was my friend? But I know he bolted. The inference is against his innocence.'

'If he is alive it shall be my business to find him,' said Edward savagely. 'The crime was brutal—unprovoked—inexcusable—and if it is in my power to bring it home to him he shall suffer for it.'

'You speak as if you had a personal animosity,' said Desrolles. 'I could understand the detectives being savage with him, for he has led them a pretty dance, and they have been held up to ridicule for their failure in catching him. But why you—a gentleman living at ease here—should feel thus strongly——'

'I have my reasons,' said Edward.

'Well, I'll wish you good night. It's getting late, and I suppose the George is an early house. *Au revoir*, Mr. Clare. By the way, when you told me your name just now I forgot to ask you how you came to be so familiar with mine.'

'I saw it in the newspapers, in the report of the inquest on Madame Chicot.'

'True. I had told you that I was Jack Chicot's fellow-lodger. I had forgotten that. Good night.'

'You are still living in Cibber Street, I suppose?'

'No, the house became hateful to me after that terrible event. Mrs. Evitt lost both her lodgers. Mrs. Rawber, the tragédienne, moved two doors off. My address is at the Poste Restante all over Europe. But for the next week or so I may be found at Paris.'

'Good night,' said Edward. 'I must come downstairs and let you out. My people ought to be home by this time, and perhaps you may not care to meet them.'

'It is indifferent to me,' Desrolles answered loftily.

They did not encounter the Vicar or his wife on the stairs. The children's party had been kept up till the desperate hour of half-past ten, and Mr. and Mrs. Clare were now on their road home, leaving Celia behind them to spend Christmas Day with the Trevertons.

CHAPTER XXVIII.

EDWARD CLARE GOES ON A VOYAGE OF DISCOVERY.

To sit beside a man's hearth, drink his wine, shoot his pheasants and ride his horses, would in a savage community be incompatible with the endurance of a deadly hatred against that man. The thoroughbred savage hates only his enemy and the intruding stranger. Mr. Stanley tells us that if he could once get close enough to a tribe to hold a parley with them, he and his followers were safe. The difficulty was that they had to encounter a shower of arrows before they could get within range for conversation. When the noble African found that the explorer meant kindly, he no longer thirsted for the white man's blood. His savagery for the most part meant self-defence.

The ways of civilization are not as the ways of the desert. There are men and women whose animosity is not to be appeased by kindness—who will take all they can get from a man, and go on detesting him cordially to the end. Edward Clare, the sleek, white-handed poet, possessed this constancy in hatred. John Treverton had done him no direct injury; for the poet's love for Laura had never been strong enough to outweigh prudence. He had wanted Laura and Hazlehurst Manor: not Laura with her modest income of two hundred and fifty pounds a year. He was angry with fate and Jasper Treverton for the will which had made Laura's wealth dependent on her marriage with the heir; he hated John Treverton for the good fortune which had fallen into his lap. And this hatred wore such a noble aspect in the man's own mind. It was no base envy of another's prosperity; it was not even jealous anger against a rival, Edward told himself. No, it was a chivalrous ardour in the defence of the woman he had loved; it was a generous desire to serve her which urged him to pluck the mask from this smooth hypocrite's face. If this man was indeed, as Edward believed, the husband of Zaïre Chicot, the dancer, then his marriage with Laura was no marriage, and the conditions of the will had not been fulfilled. The estate, the possession of which could only be secured by a legal marriage within the year following Jasper Treverton's death, had been obtained by an audacious fraud.

Was this great wrong to pass undetected and unpunished? Was Laura, whose love had been so easily won by this scoundrel, to go on blindly trusting him, until some day an accident should reveal his infamy and her dishonour? No, Edward believed that it was his duty to let in the light upon this iniquitous secret; and he determined to leave no stone unturned in the fulfilment of his mission.

This fellow Desrolles was evidently a creature of John Treverton's. His denial of the identity between the two men went for nothing in Edward's mind. There must be plenty of people in the neighbourhood of Cibber Street able to identify the missing Chicot, if they could only be brought face to face with him.

'I wonder you and Mrs. Treverton have not been photographed since your marriage,' Edward said one afternoon in the Christmas week, when John Treverton was well enough to join the kettledrum party in the book-room, and they four, Mr. and Mrs. Treverton, Celia, and Edward, were sitting round a glorious fire.

He had been looking over a volume of photographs by the light of the blazing wood, so the question seemed natural enough.

'Ah, by-the-by, Jack, I really must have you photographed,' said Laura gaily. 'Lady Barker was very particular in her request for our photographs the other day. She has a very fine collection, she tells me.'

'About a hundred and fifty of her bosom friends, I suppose,' retorted John Treverton, 'all simpering in the highest style of art, and trying to look unconscious of the photographer's iron collar gripping them by the scruff of the neck. No, Laura, I am not going to let the sun make a correct map of my wrinkles in order that I may join the simperers in Lady Barker's photograph album, that fashionable refuge for the destitute in brains, after a dull dinner.'

'Do you mean to say that you have never been photographed?' asked Edward.

'No, I do not. I had my photograph taken by Nadar a good many years ago, when I was young and frivolous.'

'Oh, Jack, how I should like to have a picture of what you were years ago!' exclaimed Laura. 'What has become of all the photographs?'

'Heaven knows,' answered John carelessly; 'given to Tom, Dick, and Harry—scattered to the four winds. I have not kept one of them.'

'Nadar,' repeated Edward musingly; 'you are talking of the man in Paris, I suppose?'

'Yes.'

'You know Paris well?'

'Every Englishman who has spent a fortnight there would say as much as that,' answered John Treverton carelessly. 'I know my way from the Louvre to the Palais Royal, and I know two or three famous restaurants, where a man may get an excellent dinner if he likes to pay for it with its weight in gold.'

Nothing more was said upon the subject of photographs. Edward Clare left Hazlehurst next day for London. He was not going to be long away, he told his father and mother, but he wanted to see a manager who had made overtures to him for a legitimate historical drama, in blank verse.

'He was struck by a dramatic fragment I wrote for one of the magazines,' said Edward, 'and he has taken it into his head that I could write as good a play as the "Hunchback" or the "Lady of Lyons."'

'Oh, do go and see him, Ted,' cried Celia, with enthusiasm. 'It would be awfully jolly if you were to write a play. We should all have to go up to town to see the first performance.'

'Should we?' interrupted the Vicar, without looking up from his *John Bull*, 'and pray who would find the money for our railway fare, and our hotel bill?'

'Why, you, of course,' cried Celia. 'That would be a mere bagatelle. If Edward were to burst upon the world as a successful dramatic author he would be on the high road to fortune, and we could all afford a little extravagance. But who is your manager, Ted, and who are the actors who are to act in your play?' inquired Celia, anxious for details.

'I shall say nothing about that till my play is written and accepted,' answered Edward. 'The whole affair is in the clouds at present.'

Celia gave a short impatient sigh. So many of her brother's literary schemes had begun and ended in the clouds.

'I suppose I am to take care of your den while you are away,' she said, presently, 'and dust your books and papers?'

'I shall be glad if you will preserve them from the profane hand of my mother's last domestic treasure in the shape of a new housemaid,' answered Edward.

Before any one could ask him any more questions the 'bus from the 'George' was at the Vicarage gate, waiting to take him to the station at Beechampton, in company with two obese farmers, and a rosy-cheeked girl going out to service, and carrying a nosegay of winter flowers, a bandbox, and an umbrella.

How sweet and fresh the air was in the clear December morning, almost the last of the year! How picturesque the winding lane, the wide sweep of cultivated valley and distant belt of hill and moor.

Edward Clare's eyes roamed across the familiar scene, and saw nothing of its tranquil beauty. His mind was absorbed in the business that lay before him. His heart was full of rancour. He was tormented by that worst of all foes to a man's peace—an envious mind. The image of John Treverton's good fortune haunted him like a wicked conscience. He could not go his own way, and forget that his neighbour was luckier than himself. Had Fate smiled upon his poetic efforts, had some sudden and startling success whisked him up into the seventh heaven of literary fame, at the same time filling his pockets, he might possibly have forgiven John Treverton; but with the sense of failure goading him, his angry feelings were perpetually intensifying.

He was in the London streets just as dusk was falling, after a cold, uncomfortable journey. He took his travelling bag in his hand, and set out on foot to find a lodging, for his funds were scanty, as he had not ventured to ask his father for money since his return to the Vicarage. It was an understood thing that he was to have the run of his teeth at Hazlehurst, and that his muse was to supply all other wants.

He did not go to the street where he had lodged before—a narrow, dismal street, between Holborn and the British Museum. He went to the more crowded quarter, bounded on one side by Leicester Square, on the other by St. Martin's Lane, and betook himself straight to Cibber Street. He had made up his mind to get a room in that uninviting spot, if any decent shelter were available there.

Before seeking for this accommodation elsewhere, he went to look at the house to which La Chicot's murder had given such an awful notoriety. He found it more reputable of aspect than when he had last seen it, a few days after the murder. A new wire blind shaded the lower part of the parlour window; new red curtains drooped gracefully over the upper panes. The window itself looked cleaner and brighter than it had ever looked during the stately Mrs. Rawber's occupation of the ground floor. A new brass plate on the door bore the inscription, 'Mr. Gerard, surgeon.'

Edward Clare contemplated this shining brass plate with the blank gaze of disappointment. He concluded, not unnaturally, that the whole house had passed into the possession of Mr. Gerard, surgeon, and that Mrs. Evitt had gone forth into the wilderness of London, where she would be more difficult to find than poor Hagar and her son in the sandy wastes of the great desert. While he stood ruminating upon this apparent change in the aspect of affairs, his eye wandered to a window looking upon the area beneath the parlour, from which there came a comfortable glow of light. The occupant of the basement had not drawn down the illuminated blind which generally shaded her domesticity from the vulgar eye; and, seated by her kitchen fire, indulging in the inexpensive luxury of slumber, Edward beheld that very Mrs. Evitt whom he had supposed lost in the metropolitan labyrinth. He had no doubt as to those corkscrew curls, that vinegar visage. This was the woman with whom he had talked for half-an-hour one bleak March morning, when he had inspected the scene of the murder, under the pretence of looking for lodgings.

He went up the steps to the door. There were two bells, one labelled 'SURGERY,' the other 'HOUSE.' Edward rang the latter, which was answered after an interval by the landlady, looking cross and sleepy.

At the sight of Mr. Clare, with his travelling bag in his hand, she scented a lodger, and brightened.

'Have you a decent bedroom to let, on your second floor?' he asked, for although he was no believer in the influences of the spirit world, he would have preferred spending the December night upon the bleakest and windiest of the bridges to lying down to rest in the room where La Chicot had been slain.

'I've got my first floor empty,' said Mrs. Evitt, 'beautiful rooms, all new papered and painted.'

'I'd rather go higher up,' answered Edward. 'You had a lodger named Desrolles. What has become of him?'

'Gone to travel in foreign parts,' replied the landlady. 'I believe he had money left him. He was quite a gentleman when he started—everything new, from his portmanchew to his railway rug.'

'Can I have his rooms for a few nights? I am only in town as a bird of passage, but I don't want to go to an hotel.'

'Their charges are so 'igh, and there's no privacy in 'em,' said Mrs. Evitt, with a sympathetic air, as if she divined his inmost feelings. 'You can have Mr. Desrolles' rooms, sir, and we shan't quarrel about the rent.'

'The rooms are clean, I suppose?' Edward hazarded.

'Clean!' exclaimed Mrs. Evitt, lifting up her eyebrows with the indignation of outraged innocence. 'Nobody that has ever lodged with me would ask that question. Clean! No house of mine ever 'arboured dirt.'

'I should like to see the bedroom,' said Edward. 'The sitting-room matters very little. I shall be out all the day.'

'If you'll wait while I fetch a candle, I'll show you both rooms,'

244

replied the landlady. 'I suppose you want to come in at once?'

'Yes. I have just come from the country, and have no more luggage than this bag. I can pay you for the rooms in advance, if you like.'

'Money comes uncommonly handy now that provisions have rose to such a heighth,' returned Mrs. Evitt, with an insinuating air. 'Not that I could ever feel an instant's doubt respecting a young gent of your appearance.'

'Money down is the best reference,' said Edward. 'I'm a stranger in London. Here's a sovereign. I suppose that'll square us if I only keep the rooms a week?'

'There'll be a trifle for boot-cleaning,' insinuated Mrs. Evitt.

'Oh, very well.'

'And half-a-crown for kitching fire.'

'Oh, come now, I won't stand kitchen fire. You don't suppose I'm going to dine here. If you bring me up a cup of tea of a morning it is all I shall want, and the fire that boils your kettle will boil mine.'

'A trifle for attendance, then.'

'I'll promise nothing. If you make me comfortable, I shall not forget you at parting.'

'Very well, sir,' sighed the landlady. 'I suppose it will come to the same in the end, but I always think it best for all parties to put things clear.'

She retired into the darkness at the end of the narrow passage, the dark brown wainscot of which was dimly lighted by an old-fashioned oil lamp, and returned in a minute or two with a tallow candle in a capacious tin candlestick. With this light she preceded Mr. Clare up the staircase, whose shallow, uneven steps and heavy balustrade gave evidence of its age.

On the first-floor landing Mrs. Evitt paused to recover her breath, and Edward felt an icy thrill of horror as he found himself opposite the bedroom door.

'Is that the room where that poor woman was murdered?' he asked.

'Yes, sir,' replied Mrs. Evitt, with a deprecating sigh, 'it is the room, and I won't deceive you. But it has been done up so nice that nobody as ever knew it before would be able to recognise it. My landlord acted very liberal; "anything that paint and paper can do to set you right with your lodgers, Mrs. Evitt, shall be done," says he. "You've been a good tenant," says he, "always punctual to the minute with your rent," he says, "and I should take it to heart if you was to suffer." Come in and look at the room, sir, and you'll see that there isn't a more cheerful bedroom in this part of London.'

Mrs. Evitt flung open the door with a flourish of pride, and led the way into the room with uplifted candlestick.

'That's a brand new bedstead,' she said, 'which cost me two pound ten without the curtains. And there ain't a inch of carpet or a bit of bedding that was in the room when—when—what you mentioned took place.'

Mrs. Evitt had pinned her faith upon vivid colour as a charm to exorcise poor Zaïre's ghost. A sixpenny chintz of all the colours in the rainbow draped window and bed. A painted drugget of corresponding violence hid the worm-eaten old boards, upon which soap, sand, and soda had been vainly expended in the endeavour to remove the dark traces of that awful stream which had travelled from the bed to the threshold. The dressing-table was draped with white muslin and rose-coloured calico. The chimney-piece was resplendent with a pair of Bohemian glass vases, and a gilded clock. Coloured lithographs in the vilest German art brightened the walls.

'Don't it look cheerful?' asked Mrs. Evitt.

'Is that the little room where the husband used to work?' inquired Edward, pointing to the door.

'Yea, but that doesn't go with the drawing-room floor. I've let it to Mr. Gerard for a room to put his books in. He's such a man for books. They overrun the place.'

'Who is Mr. Gerard? Oh, by the way, that is the surgeon downstairs. How long has he been lodging with you?'

'It was about a month after poor Madame Chicot's death when he come. "I'm going to set up in business for myself, Mrs. Evitt," he says. "I ain't rich enough to buy a practice," says he, "so I must try and make one for myself, somehow," he says. "Now yours is a crowded neighbourhood, and I think I might do pretty well here, if you let me your ground floor cheap. It would be for a permanency," says he, "so that ought to make a difference." "I'll do my best to meet you," says I, "but my rent is high, and I never was a hour behind with it yet, and I never will be." Well, sir, I let him have the rooms very low, considering their value, for I was that depressed in my sperrits it wasn't in me to 'aggle. That ungrateful viper, Mrs. Rawber—a woman I'd waited on hand and foot, and fried onions for her until I've many a time turned faint over the frying pan—and she's gone and turned her back upon me in my trouble, and took a first floor over a bootmaker's, where the smell of the leather must be enough to poison a female of any refinement!'

'Has Mr. Gerard succeeded in getting a practice?' asked Edward.

'Well, he do have patients,' answered the landlady, dubiously; 'gratis ones a many, between the hours of eight and nine every morning. He's very steady and quiet in his 'abits, and that moderate that he could live where another would starve. He's a wonderful clever young man, too; it was him—much more than the grand doctor—that pulled Madame Chicot through, after her accident.'

'Indeed!' said Edward, becoming suddenly interested; 'then Mr. Gerard knew the Chicots?'

'Knew 'em! I should think he did, indeed, poor young man! He attended Madame Chicot night and day for months, and if it hadn't been for him I believe she'd have died. There never was a doctor so devoted, and all for love. He didn't take a penny for his attendance.'

'A most extraordinary young man,' said Edward.

They went up to the second-floor, and Mr. Clare was introduced to the apartments upon which Desrolles had turned his back for ever. The furniture was of the shabbiest, but the rooms looked tolerably clean, much cleaner than they had appeared during the occupation of Mr. Desrolles. Edward flung down his travelling bag, and expressed himself contented with the accommodation.

'Don't put me into damp sheets,' he said, whereupon Mrs. Evitt threw up her hands in horror, and almost wept as she protested against so heartless an imputation.

'There isn't a carefuller woman than me about airing linen in all London,' she exclaimed. 'I'm over-particular. I've scorched many a good piller-case in my carefulness; but I'm the only loser by that, and I don't mind.'

'I must go and get some dinner,' said Edward. 'And then I think I'll drop in at a theatre. I suppose you can give me a latch-key?'

'You can have the very key that Mr. Desrolles had,' replied Mrs. Evitt graciously, as if according a peculiar privilege.

'I don't care whose key it is as long as it will open the door,' answered the unappreciative poet; and then he put the key in his pocket, and went out to regale himself cheaply at a French restaurant, and then to the pit of a popular theatre. He had come to London on a particular errand, but he meant to get as much pleasure out of his visit as he could.

From the moment that Edward Clare heard of George Gerard's attendance upon Madame Chicot he became desirous of making Mr. Gerard's acquaintance. Here was a man who could help him in the business he had to carry through. Here was a man who must know the dancer's husband intimately—a man who could identify Jack Chicot in the present Squire of Hazlehurst. This was the man of men

247

whom it was valuable for Edward Clare to know. Having once made up his mind upon this point, Mr. Clare did not lose any time in making use of his opportunities. He called upon Mr. Gerard on the morning after his arrival in town. It was only half-past eight when he presented himself at the surgeon's door, so anxious was he to secure an interview before Mr. Gerard left home.

He found George Gerard sitting at his modest breakfast of bread and butter and coffee, an open book beside him as he ate. Edward's eyes marked the neatness of the surgeon's attire, marked also that his coat had been worn to the last stage of shabbiness at all compatible with respectability. A month's wear more and the wearer would be out at elbows. He observed also the thick slices of bread and butter—the doubtful-looking coffee, with an odour suggestive of horse-beans. Here, evidently, was a man for whom the struggle of life was hard. Such a man would naturally be easy to deal with.

George Gerard rose to receive his guest with a pleasant smile.

'Mrs. Evitt told me that you wanted to see me,' he said, waving his hand to a chair beside his somewhat pinched fire.

A scientific arrangement of firebrick had been adapted to the roomy old grate since Mrs. Rawber's tenancy, and it now held a minimum of fuel.

'Yes, Mr. Gerard, I very much want half-an-hour's talk with you.'

'I can give you just half-an-hour before I start for my day's work,' answered Gerard, with a business-like air and a glance at the neat little clock on the chimney-piece.

The room was curiously changed since Mrs. Rawber's occupation. It had then appeared the model of the vulgar lodging-house parlour. It now looked the room of a student. George Gerard had been able to spend very little money on the decoration of his apartments, but he had lined the walls with deal shelves, and the shelves were filled with books; such volumes as your genuine book-hunter collects with loving toil in the lanes and by-ways of London. He had put a substantial, old-fashioned writing table in the window, a pair of comfortable arm-chairs by the hearth, a skeleton clock, and a couple of bronze figures—picked up in one of the back slums of Covent Garden for a song—on the mantelpiece. The general effect was of a room which a gentleman might occupy without a blush.

Edward Clare saw all this, not without a sharp pang of envy. He recognised, in the capacity to endure such an existence, the power to climb the rugged hill of fame.

'This is the kind of fellow to succeed in life,' he thought. 'But one can't expect this dogged endurance in a man of poetic temperament.'

'Do you wish to consult me professionally?' asked Gerard.

'No. What I have to say relates to a very serious matter, but it is neither a professional question for you, nor a personal affair of mine. You knew the Chicots.'

It was Gerard's turn to be interested. He looked at the speaker with sudden intensity, which brightened every feature in his face.

'Yes. What of them? Did you know them? I never saw you here when she was ill. You knew them in Paris, perhaps?'

'No; I never saw Madame Chicot off the stage. But I am deeply interested in the discovery of her murderer: not for my own sake, but for the protection of some one I esteem. Have you seen John Chicot since the murder?'

'No. If I had——'

George Gerard stopped suddenly, and left his sentence unfinished.

'If you had you would have given him up to the police, as his wife's murderer. Is that what you were going to say?'

'Something very near it. I have strong reason to believe that he killed her; and yet there is ground for doubt. If he were the murderer, why should he alarm the house? He might have gone quietly away, and the crime would not have been discovered for hours afterwards.'

'An excess of caution, no doubt. Murderers often over-act their parts. Yet, if you look at the thing, you will see he was obliged to give the alarm. Had he not done so, had he gone away and left his wife lying dead, it would have been obvious that he, and he alone, was her assassin. By rousing the household he put on at least the semblance of innocence, however his flight might belie it afterwards.'

'It is a profound mystery,' said Gerard.

'A mystery only to those who refuse to accept the natural solution of the enigma. Here was a man with a drunken wife. It is an acknowledged fact, I believe, that Madame Chicot was a drunkard?'

'Yes, poor soul. He might have let her kill herself with a brandy bottle. He would not have had long to wait.'

'A man so fettered may get desperate. Suppose that I could prove to you that this Chicot had the strongest possible temptation to rid himself of his wife by any means, fair or foul. Suppose I could tell you that his inheritance of a large estate was contingent upon his marriage with another woman, that he had already, in order to secure that estate, contracted a bigamous marriage with that other woman—she innocent as an angel, poor girl, throughout the plot. Suppose I could prove all this, what would you say of Jack Chicot then?'

'Most assuredly I would say that he did the deed. Only show me that he had a motive strong enough to urge him to crime—I know of my own experience that he was tired of his wife—and I will accept the evidence that points to him as the murderer.'

'Do you think that evidence strong enough to convict him?'

'On that point I am doubtful. His flight is damning evidence against him; and then there is the fact that at the bottom of his colour-box there lay a dagger which corresponded in form to the gash upon that poor creature's throat. I found that dagger, and it is now in the possession of the police. It bears the dark tarnished stain that blood leaves upon steel, and I have no doubt in my own mind that it was with that dagger La Chicot was killed. But these two points comprise the whole evidence against the husband. They are strong enough to afford a presumption against his innocence; but I doubt if they are strong enough to hang him.'

'Let it be so. I don't want to hang him. But I do want to rescue the woman I once fondly loved—for whom I still care more than for any other woman on earth—from a marriage that may end in her misery and untimely death. What must be the fate of such a man as this Chicot, if he is, as you believe, and as I believe, guilty? Either remorse will drive him mad, or he will go on from crime to crime, sinking lower in the scale of humanity. Let me but strip the mask from his face, separate him for ever from his innocent wife, and I am content. To do this I want your aid. Jack Chicot has disappeared from the ken of all who knew him. The man who bore that name is now a gentleman of landed estate, respected and respectable. Will you be disinterested enough to waste a couple of days, and travel over three hundred miles, in order to help me to identify the late adventurer in the present lord of the manor? Your journey shall not cost you sixpence.'

'If I go at all, I shall go at my own expense,' answered Gerard curtly; 'but you must first show me an adequate reason for doing what you ask.'

'To do that I must tell you a long story,' answered Edward.

And then, without mentioning the names of people or of places, he told the story of Jasper Treverton's will, and of Laura Malcolm's marriage. The facts, as he stated them, went far to show John Treverton a scheming scoundrel, capable of committing a crime of the darkest kind to further his own interest.

'The case against him looks black, I admit,' said Gerard, when Clare had finished. 'But there is one difficult point in the story. You say that in order to secure the fortune Chicot married the young lady in the January before Madame Chicot's death. Now if he had made up his mind to get rid of his lawful wife by foul means, why did he not do it before he contracted that marriage instead of afterwards? The crime would have been the same, the danger of detection no greater. The murder committed after the second marriage was an anachronism.'

'Who can fathom his motives? He may have had no design against his wife's life when he married the lady I know. He may have believed it possible to so arrange his life that no one would ever recognise Jack Chicot in the country squire. He may have thought that he could buy his freedom from Madame Chicot. Perhaps it was only when he found that her love, or her jealousy, was not to be hoodwinked that he conceived the idea of murder! No man—assuredly no man of decent antecedents—reaches the lowest depth of iniquity all at once.'

'Well,' sighed Gerard, after a pause, 'I will go with you and see this man. I had a curious interest in that poor creature's career. I would have done much to save her from the consequence of her own folly, had it been possible. Yes, I will go with you; I should like to know the end of the story.'

It was agreed between the two young men that they were to go to Devonshire together in the first week of the new year, Edward Clare remaining only a week in London. Gerard was to accompany Clare as his friend, and to stay at the Vicarage as his guest.

CHAPTER XXIX.

GEORGE GERARD.

John Treverton was out of the doctor's hands before Christmas was over, and able to appear on his mare, Black Bess, with his wife, mounted on the gentlest of gray Arabs, at the lawn meet which was held at the Manor House on New Year's Day. It was the first time the hounds had met there since the death of old John Treverton, Jasper's father, who had been a hunting man. Jasper had never cared for field sports, and had subscribed to the hounds as a duty. But now, John Treverton, the younger, who loved horses and hounds, as it is natural to an Englishman to love them, meant that things should be as they had been in the days of his great-uncle, generally known among the elder section of the community as 'the old Squire.' He had bought a couple of hunters and a first-rate hack for himself, an Arabian and a smart cob for his wife; and Laura and he had ridden for many a mile over the moor in the mild afternoons of early autumn, getting into good form for the work they were to do in the winter.

Laura took kindly to the cob, and petted the Arab to a distracting degree. After a month's experience on the moors, and a good many standing jumps over furze and water, she began to ride really well, and her husband looked forward to the delight of piloting her across the country in pursuit of the red deer before the hunting season was over. But he meant, if he erred at all, to err on the side of caution, and on this New Year's Day he had declared that he should only take Laura quietly through the lanes, and let her have a peep at the hounds from a distance. Celia, in the shortest of habits, a mere petticoat, and the most coquettish of hats, was mounted on her father's steady-going roadster, a stalwart animal of prodigious girth, which contemplated the hounds with unvarying equanimity.

'What has become of your brother?' Laura asked, as she and Celia waited about, side by side, watching the assembling of the field. 'I haven't seen him since my children's party.'

'Oh, didn't I tell you? He is in London, making arrangements about a play that he is to write for one of the big theatres. Mother had a letter from him this morning. He is coming home the day after to-morrow, and he is going to bring a London acquaintance to stay

252

two or three days at the Vicarage. A young doctor, good-looking, clever, a bachelor. Now, Laura, don't you really think the world must be coming to an end very soon?'

'No, dear; but I congratulate you on the bachelor. He will be an acquisition. You must bring him to us.'

'Oh, but Edward says he can only stay two or three days. He has his practice to attend to. He is only coming for a breath of country air.'

'Poor fellow! What is his name?'

'Edward did not tell us that. Something horrid, I dare say. Smith, or Jones, or Johnson—a name to dispel all pleasant illusions.'

'Here comes Mr. Sampson.'

'Yes, on the horse he drives in his dogcart. Could you believe, Laura, that a horse could support existence with so much bone and so little flesh?'

This was all Laura heard about the expected guest at the Vicarage, but poor Celia was in a flutter of wondering anticipation for the next two days. She took particular pains to make her brother's den attractive, yet sighed as she reflected how much of the stranger's brief visit would be spent within the closed doors of that masculine snuggery.

'I wonder whether he is fond of tea?' she mused, when she had given the last heightening touch to the multifarious frivolities of the poet's study; 'and whether I shall be allowed to join them at kettle-drum. Very likely he is one of those dreadfully mannish men who hate to talk to girls, and look glum whenever they're forced to endure women's society. A doctor? scientific, perhaps, and devoted to dry bones. Edward calls him handsome; but I dare say that was only said in order to prepossess us in his favour, and secure a civil reception for him.'

Thus, in maiden meditation, mused the damsel on that January evening when her brother and her brother's friend were expected. The omnibus from the 'George' was to bring them from the station, and that omnibus would be due at a quarter past seven. It was now striking seven by the deep-toned church clock; a solemn chime that had counted out Celia's hours ever since she could remember. She hardly knew time or herself out of earshot of that grave old clock.

'Seven,' she exclaimed, 'and my hair anyhow.'

She slipped off to her room, lighted her dressing-table candles, and took up her hand mirror, the better to survey the edifice of frizzy little curls which crowned her small, neatly-shaped head.

'Shine out, little head, sunning over with curls,' she sang gaily, smiling at herself in the glass, as she put her pet ringlets in their proper places, and smoothed the corner of an eyebrow with her little finger.

'What a blessing not to be obliged to powder, and to have lips that are naturally red!' she said to herself. 'It might almost reconcile one to be buried alive in a village.'

She put on her prettiest gown in honour of the visitor. It was by no means an elaborate costume. There were no intricacies of style, no artistic combinations of material. Celia's best indoor gown was only a dark-green French merino, brightened by a good deal of ribbon, artfully disposed in unexpected bows and knots, and floating sash-ends. Happily, the colour suited Celia's complexion, and the soft fabric fell in graceful folds upon her slender figure. Altogether Celia felt herself looking nice when she put out her candles and ran downstairs.

A substantial tea-dinner was waiting for the travellers in the dining-room, to the sore discomfort of the Vicar, who hated a tea-dinner, and was accustomed to dine at a punctual half-past six.

'Why must we have a makeshift meal of this kind?' he asked fretfully. 'Why couldn't these young men be here in time for our regular dinner?'

'Why, because there was no train to bring them, you dear, stupid old pater,' retorted the flippant Celia. 'I'm sure the table looks quite too lovely.'

A fine piece of cold roast beef at the end opposite the urn and tea-tray, a pigeon pie, a salad, an apple pasty, a home-made cake or two, diamond-cut jars of marmalade and jam, and a noble glass bowl of junket, did not promise badly for two hungry young men; but the Vicar looked across the board, from Dan even to Beer-sheba, and found it all barren.

'I suppose nobody has thought of ordering anything hot for me?' he remarked with an injured air.

It was a tradition in the family that the Vicar could not eat a cold dinner. It was not that he would not, but that he could not. The consequences were too awful. No one but himself knew the agonies which he suffered if he was forced to dine on cold beef or mutton. His system could accommodate lobster, he could even reconcile nature to cold chicken, but his internal economy would have nothing to do with cold mutton or beef.

'Dearest creature,' said Celia, raising herself on tiptoe in order to caress her father's iron-gray beard, 'there is a particular dish of cutlets for you, with the mushroom sauce your soul loveth.'

The Vicar gave a sigh of satisfaction, and just at that moment the wheels of the omnibus sounded on the road outside, the Vicarage gate fell back with a clang, and Mr. Clare and his daughter went out to receive the travellers, while Mrs. Clare, who had been indulging herself with a nap by the drawing-room fire, opened her eyes, and began to wonder vaguely whether it was night or morning.

What sort of man did Celia behold when she went into the lamp-lit hall, sheltering herself shyly under her father's wing, to welcome her brother and his guest? Not at all the kind of young man she expected to see, yet his appearance impressed her favourably, notwithstanding. He was strikingly original, she told Laura afterwards, and that in an age of humdrum was much. She saw a tall, broad-shouldered man, with marked features, well shaped yet somewhat rugged, a pale complexion slightly pitted with small-pox, black hair and beard, dark gray eyes, with a wonderful power and light in them, under thick black brows.

'The idea of calling this stern-looking creature handsome!' thought Celia, while her father and Mr. Gerard were shaking hands, and then in the next instant the stern-looking creature smiled, and Celia admitted to herself that his smile was nice.

'You must be desperately hungry,' said the Vicar, 'unless you've dined on the way.'

'Dined on the way!' echoed Edward peevishly. 'We've travelled third-class, and we've had nothing but a split soda and a couple of Abernethy biscuits since nine this morning.'

'Poor dear things!' cried Celia, with intense pity; 'but I can't help being rather glad, for you will so enjoy your tea.'

Edward had introduced his friend to his father and sister, and now presented him to Mrs. Clare, who came out of the drawing-room smiling blandly, and trying not to look sleepy.

They all went into the dining-room, where the table which the Vicar had despised seemed to the two young men a land of promise. The urn hissed, and Celia made the tea, while Mrs. Clare sat at the other end of the board and carved the beef with a liberal, motherly hand. It was quite a merry party, for George Gerard had plenty to say for himself, and the Vicar was pleased to get hold of an intelligent young man, fresh from London, and steeped to the lips in the knowledge of metropolitan politics, which are about a month ahead of rural politics. They sat at table for an hour and a half, and the three-quarters of an hour during which Gerard leaned back in his chair, talking to Celia on one side and the Vicar on the other, and consuming numerous cups of tea, was in that young man's estimation the pleasantest part of the time.

It was long, very long, since Gerard had found himself in so bright a room, or in such agreeable company. The homelike air of his surroundings warmed his heart, which had been chilled by long homelessness. The family history that lay behind his hard career was not a happy one. A profligate father wasting his opportunities and squandering his resources, a mother struggling nobly against adversity, trying against all disadvantages to maintain, by her own efforts in art and literature, a home for her unworthy husband and her idolised son. A boyhood at a cheap Scotch university, and, just on the threshold of manhood, the loss of this patient, dearly loved mother, some years a widow. And then the young man had found himself face to face with stern necessity, and in a hard, indifferent world, that knew nothing of him and cared nothing for him.

He had begun the battle of life with a determination to place himself amongst those who conquer. His ambition was hard and bitter. He had none of those incentives to effort that sweeten toil, where a man knows that he is working for mother, or wife, or children. There was no creature of his own race to rejoice in his success, or to compassionate his ill-fortune. If nature had not made him of strong stuff he would most likely have drifted to the gutter. For a weaker soul the unaided struggle would have been too dreary.

Happily for George Gerard he loved his profession for its own sake. That love stood him in the stead of human sympathy and human affection. A word of commendation from one of the famous men at the hospital, a word of gratitude from one of his own patients, the knowledge that he had managed a case well, these things cheered and sustained him, and he tramped along the difficult road with a bold front and a lofty heart, sure of success at the end of it, if he but lived to reach the end.

To-night he abandoned himself to the new delight of pleasant society. A bright room, furnished with that heterogeneous comfort which marks the gradual growth of a family dwelling; dark crimson curtains drawn across the broad bay window; family portraits on the walls; lamps on the table, candles on the mantelpiece and sideboard; a fire heaped high with wood and coal; the Vicar's favourite collie stretched luxuriously on the hearthrug.

'I don't think I will go into the drawing-room to-night, said the Vicar, wheeling his chair round to the fire when the table had been cleared. 'I'm sure you haven't so good a fire as this in there.'

Mrs. Clare admitted that the drawing-room fire was not so good as it might be.

'Very well, then, we'll finish the evening here. If these two young men want to smoke, they can go to Ted's room.'

Mr. Gerard declared that he did not want to smoke. He was much too comfortable where he was. And then the Vicar began to question him about his profession, what such and such men were doing, and what these new men were like who had won reputation lately. Gerard talked best when he talked of his own calling, and Celia, working point lace in a corner by the fire, thought that he looked really handsome when he was animated. It was a face so different from all those prosperous, fresh-coloured, country-bred faces that her daily life had shown her; a face marked with the strongest determination, vivified by a powerful intellect. The girl's observant eye noted every characteristic in that interesting countenance. She saw, too, that the young man's black frock coat had undergone harder wear than any garment she had ever seen worn by her brother; that his boots were of a thick and useful kind, and lacked the style of a fashionable maker; that he wore a silver watch-chain, and exhibited none of the trinkets affected by prosperous youth.

Now Celia Clare was not fond of poverty. She considered it a necessary evil, but liked to give it as wide a berth as possible. Any visiting she did amongst her father's poor went sorely against the grain; and she always wondered how it was that Laura got on so well with the distressed classes. Yet she felt warmly interested in this young doctor, who was evidently most uninterestingly poor.

CHAPTER XXX.

THOU ART THE MAN.

The next day was Sunday. George Gerard was up as soon as it was light, and off for a ramble on the moor before the nine o'clock breakfast. This glimpse of the country was sweet to him, even in the bleak January weather, and he wanted to make the most of his brief opportunity. When he came back to the Vicarage after his walk, he found Edward Clare smoking a cigar in the shrubbery.

'What a fellow you are to be rambling about in such wintry weather!' cried Edward, by way of salutation. 'I want a few minutes' talk before we go in to breakfast. We may not get a chance of being alone afterwards. Celia is so fussy on Sunday mornings. I should like you to go to church with us, if you don't object?'

'I had made up my mind to go. I hope you don't suppose I have an antipathy to churches?'

'One never knows how that may be. I don't imagine there's much church-going among young professional men in London.'

'I used to escort my mother to church every Sunday morning when I was a little boy, and those were my happiest days. If I didn't like the Sunday morning service for its own sake, I should like it because it puts me in mind of her.'

'Ah,' sighed Edward, 'I dare say when a fellow loses his mother early in life he feels sentimental about her ever afterwards. But when a mother gets to the elderly and twaddly age, one may be fond of her, but one can't feel poetical about her. I'll tell you why I want you to go to church with us, Gerard. John Treverton is sure to be there. It will be a capital opportunity for you to take stock of him. Our pew is just opposite the Manor House pew. You'll have him in full view all through the service.'

'Very good,' assented Gerard. 'If this Mr. Treverton and Jack Chicot are the same, I shall know him wherever I see him.'

Celia was in excellent spirits all breakfast-time, and poured out tea and coffee with a vivacity and a grace worthy of French comedy. The presence of a strange young man had a wonderfully brightening influence. Celia felt grateful to her brother for having afforded this unaccustomed variety in the monotonous course of rural life.

She took more pains than usual in putting on her bonnet for church, though that was an operation which she always performed carefully; and she happened somehow to be walking by Mr. Gerard's side for the few hundred yards between the Vicarage and the lych-gate.

The Vicarage party were amongst the first arrivals. There were only the charity children in the gallery, and a few gaffers and goodies in the free seats. The gentry dropped in slowly. Here was Mr. Sampson, the lawyer, looking his sandiest, accompanied by Miss Sampson, in a distinctly new bonnet. Here was Lady Barker, short and fat and puffy, in an ancient velvet mantle, bordered with brown fur, like a common councillor's cloak on Lord Mayor's Day, and with a bonnet that reached the climax of dowdiness—but when one is Lady Barker, and has lived in the same house for five-and-thirty years, it matters very little what one wears.

Here came the Pugsleys, the retired ironmonger and his wife, from Beechampton, Mrs. Pugsley positively gorgeous in velvet and sable, and with a bird of many colours in her bonnet. Next arrived Mrs. Daracott, the rich widow, whose husband was the largest tenant farmer in the district, and who looked as if all Hazlehurst belonged to her; and here, after a sprinkling of nobodies, came John Treverton and his wife.

The Vicar gave out a New Year's hymn two minutes after this last arrival, and the congregation rose.

'The man is marvellously changed,' George Gerard said to himself as he stood face to face with John Treverton, 'but he is the man I knew in Cibber Street, and no other.'

Yes, it was Jack Chicot. Happiness had given new life and colour to the face, prosperity had softened the harshness of its outline. The hollow cheeks had filled, the haggard eyes had recovered the glory and gladness of youth. But the man was there—the same man in whose face Gerard had looked a year and a half ago, reading the secret of his loveless marriage.

Did he look like an undetected murderer? Did he look like a man tormented by remorse, weighed down with the burden of a guilty secret? Assuredly not. He had the straight outlook of one whose conscience is clear, whose heart is free from guile. If he were verily guilty, he must be the prince of hypocrites.

His wife was at his side, and George Gerard looked at her with painful interest. What a lovely, trustful face, radiant with innocence and contentment! And was this guileless creature to be made wretched by the knowledge of her husband's deceit? Was her heart to be broken in order that John Treverton should be punished?

Edward Clare had said that it was for her sake he wanted to know the truth about her husband, it was that she might be rescued from a degrading alliance, protected from a man who was at heart a villain.

George Gerard watched the husband and wife at intervals during the service. He could see nothing but placid content, a mind at ease, in the face of John Treverton. The idea of this freedom from care on the part of him who had been La Chicot's husband embittered Gerard.

'Had that woman been my wife I should have been sorry for her cruel fate; I should have mourned for her honestly, in spite of her degradation. But had she been my wife, she would never have sunk so low. I would have made it the business of my life to have saved her.'

Thus argued the man who had passionately loved the beautiful, soulless woman, and who had never comprehended the emptiness of her mind and heart.

Once in the progress of the service John Treverton looked across the aisle, and saw the stern gray eyes watching him. In that one glance Gerard saw that he was recognised.

'What will he do if we meet presently?' Gerard asked himself. 'He'll cut me dead, no doubt.'

They did meet, for in leaving the church porch Laura stopped to talk to Mrs. Clare and Celia. Edward and his friend were close behind.

'Is it the man?' Edward asked, in a whisper.

'Yes,' answered Gerard.

They went along the churchyard path together, and at the gates there was a pause. Laura wanted the Vicarage party to go to luncheon at the Manor House, but Mrs. Clare declined. Of course the children could do what they liked, she said; as if her children had ever done anything else since they had emerged from the helplessness of infancy. Even in their cradles they had had wills of their own.

Celia looked at her brother, and saw by a warning twitch of his eyebrows that she was to say no.

'I think we had better go home to luncheon,' she said meekly. 'Papa likes us to be at home on Sundays.'

Then she gave her brother's sleeve a little tug.

'You haven't introduced Mr. Gerard,' she whispered.

'Ah, to be sure. Mr. Gerard, Mrs. Treverton, Mr. Treverton.'

'Mr. Gerard and I have met before, under circumstances that made me deeply indebted to him,' said John Treverton, holding out his hand.

Gerard lifted his hat, but appeared not to see the offered hand. This unexpected frankness took him by surprise. He had been prepared for anything rather than for John Treverton's acknowledgment of their past acquaintance.

It was a bold stroke if the man were guilty; but Gerard's experience had taught him that guilt is generally bold.

'I should be glad of ten minutes' talk with you, Mr. Gerard,' said Treverton. 'Will you walk my way?'

'We'll all walk as far as the Manor House,' said Celia. 'We need not be home till two, need we, mother?'

'No, dear, but be sure you are punctual,' answered the good-natured mother. 'I shall say good-bye, Laura, my dear.'

While Laura lingered a little to take leave of Mrs. Clare, Treverton and Gerard walked on in front of Celia and her brother, along the frost-bound road, under the leafless elms.

'The world is much smaller than I took it to be,' John Treverton began, after a pause, 'or you and I would hardly meet in such an out-of-the-way corner of it as this.'

Gerard said nothing.

'Were you not surprised to see me in so altered a position?' the other asked, after an uncomfortable pause.

'Yes, I was certainly surprised.'

'I am going to appeal to your kind feeling—nay, to your honour. My wife knows nothing of my past life, save that it was wild and foolish. You know too well what degradation there was for me in my first marriage. I am not going to speak ill of the dead——'

'Pray do not,' interposed Gerard, very pale.

'But I must speak plainly. When you knew me I was a most miserable man. I have stood upon one of the bridges many a night, and thought that the best thing I could do with myself was to drop quietly over. Well, Providence cut the knot for me—in a terrible manner—but still the knot was cut. I have profited by my release. Fate has been very kind to me. My wife is the dearest and noblest of women. To pluck the veil from my past history would be to give her infinite pain. I ask you, then, as a gentleman, as a man of honour, to keep my secret and to spare her and me.'

'And you,' said Gerard bitterly. 'Yes, it is doubtless of yourself you think when you ask me to be silent. To spare you? Did you pity or spare the wretched creature who loved you fondly even in her degradation? As for your secret, as you call it, it is no secret. Mr. Clare, the Vicar's son, knows as well as I do that John Chicot and John Treverton are one and the same.'

'He knows it? Edward Clare?'

'Yes.'

'Since when?'

'Positively, since this morning in church. He had his suspicions before. This morning I was able to confirm them.'

'I am sorry for it,' said John Treverton, after they had walked a few paces in silence. 'I am sorry for it. I had hoped that part of my life was dead and buried—that no phantom from that hateful past would ever arise to haunt my innocent young wife. It is very hard upon me; it is harder upon her.'

'There are some ghosts not easily laid,' returned Gerard. 'I should think the ghost of a murdered wife was one of them.'

'Edward Clare is no friend to me,' pursued Treverton, hardly hearing Gerard's remark. 'He will make the most malicious use of this knowledge that he can. He will tell my wife.'

'Might he not do something worse than that?'

'What?'

'What if he were to tell the police where Chicot, the wife-murderer, is to be found?'

'My God!' cried Treverton, turning upon the speaker with a look of horror. 'You do not think me that?'

'Unhappily, I do.'

'On what grounds?'

'First, on the strength of your cowardly conduct that night. Why should you shirk the responsibility of your position if you were not guilty? Your flight was damning evidence against you. Surely you must have known that when you fled?'

'I ought to have known it, perhaps; but I thought of nothing except how best and quickest to escape from the entanglement which had been the bane and blight of my manhood. My wife was dead. Those glassy eyes, with their awful look of horror—that marble hand—told me that life had been gone for hours. What good could I do by remaining? Attend an inquest at which the story of my life would be ripped up for the delight of every gossip-monger in the kingdom; until I, John Treverton, *alias* Chicot, stood face to face with the world, so tainted and infected that no innocent woman could own me as her husband? What good to me, to that poor dead woman, or to society at large, could have come of my cross-examination at the inquest?'

'This much good, at least: your innocence—if you are innocent—might have been made manifest. As it is, the inferences are all in favour of your guilt.'

262

'How could I have proved my innocence? I could have offered no stronger proof at the inquest than I offer you now—my own word, the word of a man who at his worst never stooped to dishonour. I tell you face to face, as man to man, that I never lifted my hand against my wife: never, even when words were bitter between us, and of late we had many bitter words. I tried, honestly, to save her from her own weakness. The day had been when I was fond of her, in a reckless way, never looking forward to the future, or thinking what kind of a couple she and I would be when age had sobered us, and life had grown real and serious. No, Mr. Gerard, I am not a cruel man; and though the fetters hung heavily upon me I should never have striven to set myself free. When I saw those people—Desrolles and the two women—standing round me that night, it flashed upon me all at once that in their eyes I might look like a murderer. And then I foresaw suspicion, difficulties of all kinds, and above all that which I most dreaded, a hideous notoriety. If I stayed all this was inevitable. I might escape everything if I could get away. At that moment I considered only my own interest. I saw as it were a gate standing open leading into a new world. Was I very much to blame if I took advantage of my chance, and left my old life behind me?'

'No man can leave his past life behind him,' answered Gerard. 'If you are innocent I am sorry for you; as I should be sorry for any innocent man who had acted so as to seem guilty. I am still more sorry for your wife.'

'Yes, you have need to be sorry for her,' said Treverton, with a quiet anguish that touched even the man who thought him guilty. 'God help her, poor girl! We have been very happy together: but if Edward Clare holds our happiness in his hand our peaceful days are at an end.'

They were at the Manor House gate by this time, and here they stopped and waited in silence for the others to join them. Celia and Laura had been talking together merrily, while Edward walked beside them, silent and thoughtful.

John Treverton shook hands with Celia, but he only gave Edward a curt nod of adieu.

'Good morning, Mr. Gerard,' he said, with cold courtesy. 'Come, Laura, if Celia has made up her mind to go home to luncheon we mustn't detain her.'

'Duty prevails over inclination,' said Celia laughingly. 'If I were to come to the Manor House I should forget my Sunday school work. From three to four o'clock I have to give my mind to Scripture history. How dreadfully absorbed you look, Mr. Gerard!' she exclaimed, struck by the surgeon's thoughtful aspect. 'Have you any serious case in London that is preying upon your mind?'

'I have plenty of serious cases, Miss Clare, but I was not thinking of them just then,' he answered, smiling at her piquant little face, turned to him interrogatively. 'My patients are mostly sufferers from an incurable malady.'

'Good gracious, poor things! Is it an epidemic?'

'No, a chronic disorder—poverty.'

'Oh, poor souls, then I'm sure I pity them. I've been subject to occasional attacks towards the end of the quarter ever since I've been an independent being with a fixed allowance.'

They were walking homewards by this time, Edward in the rear.

'Now, do you seriously think, Miss Clare, that a young lady, living in her father's house, with every want provided for, can know the meaning of the word poverty?'

'Certainly I do, Mr. Gerard. But I must tell you that you start upon false premises. Young ladies living in their fathers' houses have not always every want provided for. I have known what it is to be desperately in want of six-button gloves, and not to be able to get them.'

'You have never known what it is to want bread.'

'I'm not particularly fond of bread,' said Celia, 'but I have often had to complain of the disgusting staleness of the loaf they give us at luncheon.'

'Ah, Miss Clare, when I was a student at Marischal College, Aberdeen, I have seen many a young fellow walking the street in his scarlet gown, gaunt and hungry-eyed, to whom a hunch of your stale loaf would have been a luxury. When a Scotch parson sends his son to the University he is not always able to give him the price of a daily dinner. Well for the lad if he can be sure of a bowl of porridge for his breakfast and supper.'

'Poor dear creatures!' cried Celia. 'I'm afraid Edward spends as much money on gloves and cigars as would keep an economical young man at a Scotch University—but then he is a poet.'

'Is a poet necessarily a spendthrift?'

'Upon my word I don't know, but poets seem generally given that way, don't they? One can hardly expect them to be very careful about pounds, shillings, and pence. Their heads are in the clouds, and they have no eyes for the small transactions of daily life.'

After this they walked on for a little while in silence, George Gerard thoughtfully contemplative of the fair young face, with its mignon prettiness and frivolous expression.

'It would be a misfortune, as well as a folly, for a man of my stamp to admire such a girl as that,' he told himself; 'but I may allow myself to be amused by her.'

A minute afterwards Edward Clare came up to him, and took him by the arm.

'Well,' he said, 'what passed between you and Treverton?'

'A good deal, yet it amounts to very little. I am sorry for him.'

'Then you do not believe that he killed his wife?'

'I don't know. It is a profound mystery. I should advise you to let things take their own course. What good will it do for you to make that poor wife of his miserable? If he is guilty, punishment will come sooner or later. If he is innocent, it would be a hard thing for you to persecute him.'

'What, do you suppose I am such a milksop as to let him go on his way unquestioned? I, who have loved Laura, and lost her? Suppose him even innocent of the murder—which is more than I am ready to believe,—he is guilty of a cruel fraud upon his present wife, of an impudent fraud upon the trustees to Jasper Treverton's estate, of whom my father is one. He has no more right to yonder Manor House than I have. His marriage with Laura Malcolm is no marriage. Am I to hold my peace, knowing all this?'

'To reveal what you know will be to break Mrs. Treverton's heart, and to reduce her to beggary. Hardly the act of a friend.'

'I may give her pain, but I shall not reduce her to beggary. She has a small income of her own.'

'And the Manor House estate will be devoted to the creation of an hospital.'

'Those are the conditions of Jasper Treverton's will.'

'As a professional man I am bound to rejoice; but as a mere human being I can't help feeling sorry, for Mrs. Treverton. She seems devoted to her husband.'

'Yes,' answered Edward, 'he has contrived to hoodwink her; but perhaps when she knows that John Treverton is Jack Chicot, the ballet-dancer's husband, she will be disenchanted.'

Gerard made no reply. He began to understand that personal malignity was the mainspring of Edward's anxiety to let in the light upon John Treverton's secret. He was almost sorry that he had lent his aid to the discovery; yet he had ardently desired that justice should be done upon La Chicot's murderer. It was only since his recent conversation with John Treverton that his opinion as to the husband's guilt had begun to waver.

He was haunted all the rest of the day by uncomfortable thoughts about the master of Hazlehurst Manor and his fair young wife; thoughts so uncomfortable as to prevent his enjoyment of Celia's lively company, which had all the charm of novelty to a man whose youth had not been brightened by girlish society, and whose way of life had been dull, and hard, and laborious. He was to go back to London next morning by the first train, and although the Vicar pressed him to remain, and even Celia put in a kindly word, he stuck to his intention.

'My practice is not of a kind that will bear being trifled with,' he said when he had thanked Mr. Clare for his proffered hospitality. 'The few remunerative patients I have would be quick to take offence if they fancied I neglected them.'

'But you give yourself a holiday sometimes, I suppose?' said Mrs. Clare, whose large maternal heart had a kindly feeling for all young men, simply because her son belonged to that section of society. 'You go to stay with your relations now and then, don't you?'

'No, my dear Mrs. Clare, I do not; and for the best of all reasons—I have no relations. I am the last twig of a withered tree.'

'How sad!' replied the Vicar's wife.

Celia echoed the sigh, and looked compassionately at the surgeon, and compassion in Celia's blue eyes was a sentiment no man could afford to despise.

'If you will let me come again some day, when I have made a little progress in my profession, you will be giving me something pleasant to look forward to,' said Gerard.

'My dear fellow, we shall always be glad to see you,' the Vicar answered heartily. 'It strikes me you are the kind of friend my son wants.'

CHAPTER XXXI.

WHY DON'T YOU TRUST ME?

That winter Sabbath was a dreary day for John Treverton. He walked home almost in silence, Laura wondering at his thoughtfulness, and speculating anxiously upon the possible reasons for this sudden change in his mood. Had this friend of the Clares brought him bad news? Yet how could that be? Must it not rather be that this meeting with an old acquaintance had recalled some painful period in that past life of which she knew so little?

'That is my misfortune,' she thought. 'I am only half a wife while I am ignorant of all his old sorrows.'

She did not disturb her husband by questions of any kind, but walked quietly by his side through the wintry shrubberies, where the holly berries were gleaming in the mid-day sun, and the fearless robins fluttered from hawthorn to laurel.

'I won't come in to luncheon, dear,' said John when they came to the hall door. 'I feel a little dull and headachy, and I think it might do me good to lie down for an hour or two.'

'Shall I come and read you to sleep, Jack?'

'No, dear, I shall be better alone.'

'Oh, Jack, why are you not frank with me?' exclaimed his wife piteously. 'I know there is something on your mind. Why don't you trust me?'

'Not yet, dear. You will know everything that can be known about me very soon, I dare say. But we need not anticipate the revelation. It will not be too pleasant for either of us.'

'Do you think that anything I can ever learn about you will change me?' she asked, with her hand upon his arm, looking up at him intently. 'Have I not trusted you, and loved you, blindly?'

'Yes, dearest, blindly. But how can I tell how you may feel when your eyes are opened?'

She looked at him for some moments in silence, trying to read his face; and then, with most pathetic earnestness, she said:—

'John, if there is anything to be told to your discredit, if there is any act of your past life that you are ashamed to remember—ashamed to acknowledge—an act known to others, for pity's

267

sake let me hear it from you, and not from the lips of an enemy. Am I so severe a judge that you should fear to stand before me? Have I not been weakly fond, blindly trustful? Can you doubt my power to excuse and to pardon, where all the rest of mankind might be inexorable?'

'No,' he answered quickly, 'I will not doubt you. No, dear love, it is not because I feared to trust you that I have tried to keep my secret. I wished to spare you pain; for I knew that it would pain you to know how low I had sunk before your influence, your love, came to lift me out of the slough into which I had fallen. But it seems the pain must come. Good and pure as you are, there are those who will not spare you that bitter knowledge. Yes, dear, it is best that you should learn the truth first from my lips. Whatever garbled version of this story may be told you afterwards, you shall have the truth from me.'

He put his arm round her, and they went up the broad old staircase side by side to the room that had been Jasper Treverton's study, and which Laura had beautified for her husband. Here they were secure from intrusion. John Treverton drew his wife's favourite chair to the fire, and sat down by her side, as they had sat on the night when Laura told her husband the story of Mr. Desrolles.

They sat for some minutes in silence, John Treverton looking at the fire, meditating how best to begin his confession.

'Oh, Laura, I wonder whether you will hate me when you have heard what my past life was like?' he said at last. 'I will not spare myself; but even at this last moment I shrink from uttering the words that may destroy our happiness, and part us for ever. You shall be free to decide our fate. If, when you have heard all, you should say to yourself, "This man is unworthy of my love," and if you should recoil from me—as you may—with disgust and abhorrence, I will bow my head to your decree, and disappear out of your life for ever.'

His wife turned her stricken face to him, pale as death.

'What crime have you committed, that you can think it possible that I should withdraw my love from you?' she asked, with tremulous lips.

'I have committed no crime, Laura, but I have been suspected of the worst of crimes. Do you remember the story of a man whose name was bandied about in the newspapers nearly a year ago; a man whose wife was murdered, and whom some of the London papers plainly denounced as the murderer; the man called Chicot, whose disappearance was one of the social mysteries of the year?'

'Yes,' she answered, looking at him wonderingly. 'What can you have to do with that man?'

'I am that man!'

'You? You, John Treverton?'

'I, John Treverton, *alias* Chicot.'

'The husband of a stage dancer?'

'Yes, Laura. There have been two loves in my life. First, my love for a woman who had nothing but her beauty to make her dear to the hearts of men. Secondly, my love for you, whose beauty is the lightest part in your power to win and keep my affection. My history may be briefly told. I began life in a cavalry regiment, with a small fortune in shares and stocks. These were so handy to get rid of, that before I had been five years in the army I had contrived to make away with my last sixpence. I had not been particularly dissipated or extravagant; I had not vied with my captain, who was the son of a West-end confectioner, and spent money like water; or with my colonel, who was a man of rank, and £30,000 in debt; but I had kept good horses, and mixed in the best society, and the day I got my company saw me a beggar. There was nothing for it but to sell out, and I sold out; and being of a happy-go-lucky temperament, and tired of the confinement of country quarters, I crossed the Channel, and wandered over the loveliest half of Europe with a knapsack and a sketch-book. When I had spent the price of my commission I found myself in Paris, out at elbows, penniless, with a taste for literature and a facile pencil. I lived in a garret in the Quartier Latin, found friends in a thoroughly Bohemian set, and contrived to earn just enough to keep body and soul together. I began this life with the idea that I might one day win distinction in art. I had the will to work, and a good deal of ambition. But the young men among whom I lived, small journalists and hangers-on at the minor theatres, soon taught me a different story. I learned to live as they lived, from hand to mouth. All higher aspirations died out of my mind. I became a hanger-on at stage doors, a scribbler of newspaper paragraphs—a collaborateur in Palais Royal farces—happy when I had the price of a dinner in my waistcoat pocket and a decent coat on my back. It was at this stage of my career that I fell in love with Zaïre Chicot, a popular dancer at the theatre most affected by students in law and medicine. She was the handsomest woman I had ever seen. No one had a word to say against her character. She was not a lady; I knew that, even when I was most in love with her. But the vulgarities and ignorances that would have revolted me in an Englishwoman amused and even pleased me in this daughter of the people. She was fond of me, and I of her. We married without a thought of the future: with very little care even for the present. My wife—the popular dancer at a popular theatre—was so much the more important person of the two, that from the hour of my marriage I was known by her name—first, as La Chicot's husband; then as Jack Chicot, *tout court*. We were reasonably happy together, till my wife began to fall into those wretched habits of intemperance which finally blighted both our lives. God knows I did my best to cure her. I tried my uttermost to hold her back from the dreary gulf into which she was descending. But I was powerless. No words of mine could ever tell you the misery—the degradation—of my life. I endured it. Perhaps I hardly knew the full measure of my wretchedness till the day on which I heard my cousin Jasper's will read, and knew the happiness which might have been mine had I been free from that hateful bondage.'

Laura sat by his side in silence, her face hidden in her hands, her head bowed down upon the cushion of the chair, crushed by the deep shame involved in her husband's confession.

'There is little more to tell. When I first saw and loved you I was La Chicot's husband—a man bound hand and foot. I had no right to come near you, yet I came. I had a vague, wicked hope that Fate would set me free somehow. Yet I tried, honestly, to do my duty to that unhappy woman. When her life was in peril, I helped to nurse her. I bore patiently with her violent temper after she recovered. When the year was nearly gone it came into my mind that my cousin's estate might be secured to you by a marriage which should fulfil the terms of his will without making me your husband save in name. And then, if in some happier day I should be released from my bonds, we could be married again—as we were.'

He paused, but there was no answer from Laura except a half-stifled sob.

'Laura, can you pity and pardon me? For God's sake say that I am not utterly despicable in your eyes!'

'Despicable? no!' she said, lifting up her tear-stained face, ashy pale, and drawn with pain, 'not despicable, John. You could never be that, in my eyes. But wrong, oh, so deeply wrong! See what shame and anguish you have brought upon both of us! What was Jasper Treverton's fortune worth to either of us, that you should be guilty of a fraud in your endeavour to gain it for me?'

'A fraud?'

'Yes. Do you not see that our first marriage, being really no marriage, was an imposition and a sham—that neither you nor I have a right to a sixpence of Jasper Treverton's money, or an acre of his land. All is forfeited to the hospital trusts. We have no right to live in this house. We possess nothing but my income. We can live upon that, Jack. I am not afraid to face poverty with you; but I will not live an hour under the weight of this shameful secret. Mr. Clare and Mr. Sampson must know the truth at once.'

Her husband was kneeling at her feet, looking up at her with a radiant face.

'My love, my dearest, you have made me too happy. You do not shrink from me—you do not abandon me. Poverty! No, Laura, I am not afraid of that. I have feared only the loss of your love. That has been my ever-present fear. That one great dread has sealed my lips.'

'You can never lose my love, dear. It was given to you without the power of recall. But if you want to regain my esteem, you must act bravely and honourably. You must undo the wrong you have done.'

'We will hold a council to-night, Laura. We will take Edward Clare's cards out of his hands.'

'What? Does Edward know?'

'He knows that I and Chicot are one.'

'Ah, then I can understand the look he gave you on the night of our first dinner-party—a look full of malignity. He had just been talking of Chicot.'

She shuddered as she pronounced a name associated with such unspeakable horror. And that name was her husband's; the man branded with the suspicion of a hideous crime was her husband.

'I am afraid Edward is your secret enemy,' she said, after a pause.

'I am sure he is—and I believe he is on the eve of becoming my open enemy. It will be a triumph in a small way for me to take the initiative, and resign the estate.'

CHAPTER XXXII.

ON HIS DEFENCE.

A letter was brought to the Vicar just as he was sitting down to his five o'clock dinner that Sunday evening in the bosom of his family. The Vicar dined at five on Sundays, giving himself an hour for his dinner, and fifty minutes for repose after it, before he left home for the seven o'clock service. There were those among his congregation who affirmed that the tone of the Vicar's evening sermon depended very much upon his satisfaction with his dinner. If he dined well he took a pleasant view of human nature and human frailty, and was milder than Jeremy Taylor. If his dinner had been a failure the bitterest Calvinism was not severe enough for him.

'From the Manor House, sir,' said the parlour-maid. 'An answer waited for.'

'Why do people bring me letters just as I am sitting down to my dinner?' ejaculated the Vicar pettishly. 'From Treverton, too. What can he have to write about?'

Edward Clare looked up, with an eager face.

'Wants to see me after church this evening—particular business,' said the Vicar. 'Tell Mr. Treverton's man, yes, Susan. My compliments, and I'll be at the Manor House before nine.'

Edward was mystified. Was John Treverton going to throw himself upon the Vicar's mercy—to win that good, easy man, over to his cause—and persuade him to wink at the fraud upon the trusts under Jasper's will? Edward had no opinion of his father's wisdom, or his father's strength of mind. The Vicar was so weakly fond of Laura.

'I hate going out of an evening in such weather,' said Mr. Clare, 'but I suppose Treverton has something important to say, or he would hardly ask me to risk a bronchial attack.'

Tom Sampson, sitting by his comfortable fireside, solacing himself for the Sabbath dulness with a cup of strong tea and a dish of buttered toast, was also surprised by a letter from the Manor House, asking him to go there between eight and nine that evening.

'I am sorry to trouble you about business on Sunday, but this is a matter which will not keep,' wrote John Treverton.

'I never did!' exclaimed Eliza Sampson, when her brother had read the brief letter aloud.

Eliza was always protesting that she never did. This fragmentary phrase was her favourite expression of astonishment.

And then Miss Sampson began to speculate upon the probable nature of the business which required her brother's presence at the Manor House. People who live in such a secluded village as Hazle-hurst are very glad of anything to wonder about on a Sunday evening in winter.

At half-past eight precisely, Mr. Sampson presented himself at the Manor House, and was shown into the library. This room was rarely used, as Mr. and Mrs. Treverton kept all their favourite books elsewhere. Here, on these massive oaken shelves, there was no lit-erature that was not at least a century old. It was a repository for the genius of the dead. Travels, from Marco Polo to Captain Cook; histories, from Herodotus to Mrs. Catherine Macaulay; poetry, from Chaucer to Milton; all bound in soberest brown calf, all with the dust of years thick upon their upper edges. It was a long, narrow room, with three tall windows, curtained with faded crimson cloth. It had an awful and almost judicial look on this Sunday evening, dimly lighted by a pair of moderator lamps on the centre table, making a focus of light in the middle of the room, and leaving the corners in darkness. There was a good fire in the wide old basket-shaped grate, and Tom Sampson sat beside it, waiting for his host to appear. Trim-mer had told him that Mr. Treverton would be with him presently.

Presently seemed to mean half an hour, for the clock struck nine while Mr. Sampson still waited. Not having any inclination to dip into the literature of the past, he had allowed the fire to draw him to sleep, and was slumbering placidly when the door opened and Trim-mer announced Mr. Clare.

Tom Sampson started up, and rubbed his eyes, thinking for the moment that he had fallen asleep by the fire in his snuggery, and that Eliza had come to call him to supper—supper being another of those solaces which Mr. Sampson required to beguile the dulness of Sun-day leisure.

The Vicar was surprised to see Mr. Sampson, and Mr. Sampson was equally surprised to see the Vicar. They told each other how they had been summoned.

'It must be something rather important,' said Mr. Clare.

'It must be something connected with the estate, or he would scarcely want you and me,' said Sampson.

John Treverton and his wife entered the room together. Both were very pale, but Laura's countenance wore a look of keen distress, which had no part in the expression of her husband's face. Secure of his wife's allegiance, he was ready to meet calamity, whatever shape it might assume.

'Mr. Clare, Mr. Sampson, I have sent for you as the trustees under my cousin Jasper's will,' he began, when he had apologized to the lawyer for letting him wait so long, and had placed Laura in a chair near the fire.

'That's a misnomer,' said Sampson. 'Our trusts under Jasper Treverton's will determined on your wedding day. We are only trustees to the settlement made for Miss Malcolm's benefit, sixteen years ago, and to your wife's marriage settlement.'

'I have sent for you to tell you that I have been guilty of a fraud upon you, and upon this lady,' answered John Treverton, in a steady voice.

He was going on with his self-denunciation, when the door opened, and Trimmer announced Mr. Edward Clare.

The young man came into the room quickly, looking round him with a swift, viperish glance. He was surprised to see Laura, still more surprised at the presence of Tom Sampson. He had expected to find his father and Treverton alone.

John Treverton looked at the intruder with undisguised irritation.

'This is an unexpected pleasure,' he said; 'but perhaps when I tell you that your father and Mr. Sampson are here to discuss a business of some importance to me—and to them as my wife's trustees—you'll be kind enough to amuse yourself in the drawing-room until we've finished our conversation.'

'I have come to speak to Mrs. Treverton. I have something to say to her which she ought to hear—which she must hear—and that without an hour's delay,' said Edward. 'Accident has made me acquainted with a secret which concerns her and her welfare—and I am here to communicate it to her, and—in the first instance—to her alone. It will be for her to act upon that knowledge—for me to defer to her.'

'If your secret concerns me, it must concern my husband also,' said Laura, rising and taking her stand beside John Treverton. 'Whatever touches my happiness must involve his. You can speak out, Edward. Possibly your fancied secret is no secret.'

'What do you mean?' stammered Edward, startled by her calm look and resolute tone.

'Have you come to tell me that my husband, John Treverton, was for a short period of his life known by the name of Chicot?'

'Yes, that, and much else,' answered Edward, deeply mortified

274

at finding himself forestalled.

'You wish to tell me, perhaps, that he has been suspected of murder.'

'So strongly suspected, and upon such evidence, that it will need all your wifely trustfulness to believe him innocent,' retorted Edward, with a malignant sneer.

'Yet I do believe in his innocence—I am as certain of it as I am that I myself am no murderess—and if the evidence against him were doubly strong, my trust in him would not fail,' said Laura, facing the accuser proudly.

'And now, Mr. Clare, since you find that your secret is everybody's secret, and that my wife knows all you can tell her about me——'

'Your wife,' sneered Edward. 'Yes, it is as well to call her by that name.'

'She is my wife—bound to me as securely as the law and the church can bind her.'

'You had another wife living when you married her—unless you have been remarried since your first wife's death——'

'We have been so married. My wife was never mine, save in name, until I was a free man,—free to claim her before God and the world.'

'Then your first marriage was a deliberate felony, and a deliberate fraud,' cried Edward: 'a felony because it was a bigamous marriage, for which the law of the land could punish you, even now; a fraud because by it you pretended to fulfil the conditions of your cousin's will, when you were not in a position to comply with them.'

'Stop, Mr. Edward Clare,' exclaimed Tom Sampson, whose quick perception had by this time made him master of the case; 'you are assuming a great deal more than you can sustain. You are going very much too fast. What evidence have you that my client's first marriage was a legal one? What evidence have you that he was ever married to Mademoiselle Chicot? We know how very loosely tied such alliances are apt to be in that class of life.'

'How do I know that he was married to her?' echoed Edward. 'Why, by his own admission.'

'My client admits nothing,' said Sampson with dignity.

'He admits everything when he tells you that he was remarried to Miss Malcolm after Madame Chicot's death. Had he known his first marriage with Miss Malcolm to be valid there would have been no occasion for a repetition of the ceremony.'

'He may have erred from excess of caution,' said Sampson.

'John Treverton,' said the Vicar, who had been looking from one speaker to the other, the facts of the case slowly dawning upon him, 'this is very dreadful. Why is my son here as your accuser? What does it all mean?'

'It means that I have been guilty of a great wrong,' answered Treverton quietly, 'and that I am ready to undo that wrong, so far as it lies in my power. But I cannot discuss this question in your son's presence. He has entered this room to-night as my avowed enemy. To you—to Sampson—as the trustees under my cousin's will, I am prepared to speak with fullest confidence—as I have already spoken to my wife—but I have no confession to make to your son. I recognise no right of his to interfere in my affairs.'

'No, Edward, really, this is no concern of yours,' said the Vicar.

'Is it not?' cried his son, bitterly. 'But for my discovery, but for the presence of George Gerard in the church to-day, do you suppose this virtuous gentleman would have made his confession to his wife or his wife's trustees? He saw himself identified to-day by the doctor who attended his first wife, who knows the story of his late career under the *alias* of Chicot. Finding himself face to face with an inevitable discovery, Mr. Treverton very cleverly yields to the pressure of circumstances, and makes a clean breast of it. Had Gerard never appeared in Hazlehurst, this honourable gentleman would have gone on till doomsday, untroubled by any scruples of conscience.'

The Vicar looked at his son wonderingly. Was this a loyal regard for truth and justice, or was it the spirit of hatred and envy which moved the youth so strongly? The good, easy-going Vicar, full of charity for all the world, except a bad cook, could not bring himself all in a moment to think evil of his son. Nor was he ready to believe John Treverton the vilest of sinners. Yet here was John Treverton accused by the Vicar's own son of an unpardonable fraud, and suspected of the darkest crime.

'If you will tell your son to retire, we may discuss this business without prejudice or passion,' said John. 'But as long as he is present my lips are sealed.'

'I have no wish to remain a moment longer,' answered Edward. 'I hope Mrs. Treverton knows that I am ready to serve her with zeal and devotion, should she deign to demand my aid.'

'I know that you are my husband's enemy,' answered Laura, with freezing contempt, 'and that is all I know or care to know about you.'

'That's hard upon an old friend, Laura,' remonstrated the Vicar, as Edward left the room.

'Has he not dealt hardly by my husband?' answered Laura, with a stifled sob.

'Now, let us try and look this business in the face,' said Mr. Sampson, seating himself quietly at the table and taking out his note-book. 'According to your confession, Mr. Treverton, you had a wife living at the date of your first marriage with Miss Malcolm, December the thirty-first of the year before last. We have nothing to do with your second marriage—except so far, of course, as the lady's honour is concerned. That second marriage can't touch the property. Now I am sorry to tell you that if your marriage with the French dancer was a good marriage, you have no more right to be in this house, or to hold an acre of Jasper Treverton's land, than the meanest hind in Hazlehurst.'

'I am ready to deliver up all I hold to-morrow. Let the hospital be founded. I acknowledge myself an impostor. Shameful as the act appears now that I contemplate it coldly, it seemed hardly a fraud when it first suggested itself to my mind. I saw a way of securing the estate to my cousin's adopted daughter. I knew it had been his dearest wish that she should possess it. When I went through the ceremony of marriage with Laura Malcolm in Hazlehurst Church, I had but the faintest hope of ever being really her husband. When I made the post-nuptial settlement which was to secure to her the full enjoyment of the estate, I had no hope of ever sharing that estate with her. On my honour, as a man and a gentleman, it was for this dear girl's sake I did these acts, and with no view to my own happiness or aggrandisement.'

Laura's hand had been in his all the time he was speaking. Its warm grasp at the close of this speech told him that he was believed.

'If you make these facts public, you beggar yourself and your wife,' said Sampson.

'No, we shall not be penniless,' exclaimed Laura. 'There will be my income left. It is not quite three hundred a year, but we can manage to live upon that, can't we, John?'

'I could live contentedly on a crust a day in the dingiest garret in Seven Dials if you were with me,' answered her husband, in a low voice.

Mr. Clare was walking up and down the room in a state of suppressed excitement. The whole business was too dreadful; he was hardly able to realize the enormity of the thing. This John Treverton was a scoundrel, and the estate must all go to found a hospital. Poor Laura must leave her luxurious home. The parish would be a heavy loser. It was sad, and troublesome, and altogether fraught with perplexity. And the Vicar had a cordial liking for this John Treverton.

'What have you to say about the murder of that poor creature—your first wife?' he exclaimed presently, walking up to the hearth by which Treverton and Laura were standing.

'Only that I know no more who killed her than you do,' answered John Treverton. 'I did a foolish thing, perhaps a cowardly thing, when I left the house that night, with the determination never to return to it; but if you could know how intolerable my old life had become to me, you would hardly wonder that I took the first opportunity of getting away from it.'

'We had better look at things from a business point of view,' said Mr. Sampson. 'We are not going to do anything in a hurry. There will always be time enough for you to surrender the estate, Mr. Treverton, and to acknowledge yourself guilty of bigamy. But before you take such a step we may as well make ourselves sure of our facts. You married Mademoiselle Chicot in Paris.'

'Yes, on the eighteenth of May, sixty-eight. We were married at the Mairie. There was no other ceremony.'

'Under what name were you married?'

'My own, naturally. It was only afterwards that I got to be known by my wife's name.'

'Were you known to many people in Paris by your own name?'

'To very few. I had written in the newspapers under a *nom de plume*,—my sketches at that time were all signed "Jack." I was generally known as Jack, and after my marriage I became Jack Chicot.'

'How much did you know of your wife's antecedents?'

'Very little, except that she had come to Paris from Auray, in Brittany, about five years before I married her; that she lived reputably, although surrounded by much that was disreputable.'

'But of her life in Brittany you knew nothing?'

'I only knew what she told me. She was a fisherman's daughter, born and reared in extreme poverty. She had grown weary of the hard monotony of her life, and had come to Paris alone, and for the most part of the way on foot, to make her fortune. Auray is a long day's journey from Paris by rail. It took her nearly a month to travel the distance.'

'That is all you know?'

'Positively all.'

'Then you cannot know that she was free to contract a marriage—and you cannot know that you were legally married to her!' said Tom Sampson triumphantly.

His interests as well as his client's were at stake, and he was determined to make a hard fight for them. His stewardship was worth a good five hundred a year. If the estate came to be handed over for the establishment and maintenance of a hospital, he would in all probability lose his position of land steward and collector of rents. Some officious committee would oust him from his post. His trusteeship would bring him nothing but trouble.

'That is a curious way of looking at the question,' said Treverton thoughtfully.

'It is the only right way. Why should any man be in a hurry to prove himself guilty of felony? How do you know that Mademoiselle Chicot did not leave a husband behind her at Auray? It may have been to escape from his ill-treatment that she came to Paris. That was a desperate step for a young woman to take—a month's journey through a strange country, alone, and on foot.'

'She was so young,' said Treverton.

'Not too young to have married foolishly.'

'What would you advise me to do?'

'I'll tell you to-morrow, when I've had time to think the matter over. I can tell you in the meantime what I would advise you not to do.'

'What is that?'

'Don't surrender your estate till you—and we, as your wife's trustees—are thoroughly convinced that you have no right to hold it. Mr. Clare, I must ask you, as my co-trustee to Mrs. Treverton's marriage settlement, to be silent as to the whole of the facts that have become known to us to-night, and to request your son also to keep his knowledge to himself.'

'My son can have no motive for injuring Mr. and Mrs. Treverton,' said the Vicar.

'Of course not,' replied Sampson; 'yet I thought his manner this evening was somewhat vindictive.'

'I believe he was only moved by his regard for Laura,' answered the Vicar. 'He took up the matter warmly because he considered that she had been deeply injured. I can but think so too, and I do not wonder that my son should feel indignant. As to the legal bearing of the case, Mr. Sampson, I leave you to judge that, and to deal with that as you best may for the interests of your client. But as to its moral aspect, I should do less than my duty as a minister of the Gospel if I were not to declare that Mr. Treverton has been guilty of a sin which can only be atoned for by deep and honest repentance. I will say no more than that now. Good-night, Treverton. Good-night, Laura.'

He took her in his arms and kissed her with fatherly affection.

'Keep up your courage, my poor girl,' he said in a low voice. 'I wish your husband well out of his difficulties, for your sake. Will you come home to the Vicarage with me, and talk over your troubles with Celia? It might be a relief to you.'

'Leave my husband!' exclaimed Laura. 'Leave him in grief and trouble! How could you think me capable of such a thing?' And then she drew the Vicar aside, and in a tremulous voice, which was little more than a whisper, said to him, 'Dear Mr. Clare, try not to think evil of my husband, for my sake. I know that he has sinned; but he has been sorely tempted. He could not judge the extent of the wrong he was doing. Tell me that you do not suspect him as he has been suspected; that you are not influenced by Edward's cruel words. You do not believe that he killed his wife?'

'No, my dear,' answered the Vicar decidedly. 'First and foremost he is a Treverton, and comes of a stock I love and honour; and, secondly, I have lived in friendship with him for the last six months; and I don't think I'm such a fool that I could live so long upon intimate terms with a murderer and not find him out. No, my dear, I believe your husband has been weak and guilty; but I do not believe—I never will believe—that he has been a cold-blooded-assassin.'

'God bless you for those words,' said Laura as the Vicar left her.

'If Mrs. Treverton will go to bed and get a little rest after all this agitation, I shall be glad of some further conversation with you before I go home,' said Sampson, when the door had closed upon Mr. Clare.

Laura assented, turning her white, weary face to her husband, with a look full of trust and love, as he went with her to the bottom of the staircase.

'God bless and keep you, love,' he whispered. 'You have shown me the way out of all my difficulties. I can afford to lose everything except your affection.'

He went back to Tom Sampson, who was scribbling in his note-book, in a brown study.

'Now, Sampson, we are alone. What have you to say to me?'

'A great deal. You've got yourself into a pretty fix. Why didn't you trust me from the beginning? What's the use of a man having a lawyer if he keeps his affairs dark?'

'We won't go into that question now,' said John Treverton. 'I want your advice about the future, not your lamentations over the past. What do you recommend me to do?'

'Get away from this place to-night, on the best horse in your stable. Take the first train at the furthest station you can reach by daybreak to-morrow. Let me see. It's not much over thirty miles to Exeter. You might get to Exeter on a good horse.'

'No doubt. But what would be gained by such a course?'

'You would get out of the way before you could be arrested on suspicion of being concerned in your first wife's murder.'

'Who is going to arrest me?'

'Edward Clare means mischief. I am sure of that. If he has not already given information to the police, depend upon it he will do so without delay.'

'Let him,' answered Treverton. 'If he does, I must stand my ground. I got out of the way once; and I feel now that in so doing I committed the greatest mistake of my life. I am not going to fall into the same blunder again. If I am to be arrested—if I am to be tried for murder, I will face my position. Perhaps it would be the best thing that could happen to me, for a trial might elicit the truth.'

'Well, perhaps you are right. Anything like running away would tell against you. But I recommend you to get to the other side of the Channel without an hour's loss of time. It is of vital importance for you to find out your first wife's antecedents. If you could be fortunate enough to discover that she was a married woman when she left Auray, that she had a husband living at the time of your marriage——'

'Why do you harp so upon that string?' asked Treverton impatiently.

'Because it is the only string that can save your estate.'

'I have no hope of such a thing.'

'Will you go to Auray and hunt up your wife's history? Will you let me go with you?'

'I have no objection. A drowning man will cling to a straw I may as well cling to that straw as to any other.'

'Then we'll start by the first train to-morrow. We'll leave the place in the openest manner. You can tell people you are going to Paris on business; but if young Clare does set the police on your track, I think they'll find it hardish work to catch us.'

'Yes, I'll go to Auray,' said John Treverton, frowning meditatively at the fire. 'In my wife's antecedents there may lie the clue to the secret of her miserable death. Revenge must have been the motive of that murder. Who was it whom she had so deeply injured, that nothing but her life could appease his wrath?'

'Who, except a deserted husband or lover?' urged Sampson.

'Yet we lived together for two years in Paris, and no one ever assailed us.'

'The husband, or lover, may have been out of the way—beyond seas, perhaps—a sailor, very likely. Auray is a seaport, isn't it?'

'Yes.'

It was agreed that they should start for Exeter by the seven o'clock train from Beechampton, catch the Exeter express for Southampton, and cross from Southampton to St. Malo by the steamer which sailed on Monday evening. From St. Malo to Auray would be only a few hours' journey. They might reach Auray almost as soon as they could have reached Paris.

CHAPTER XXXIII.

AT THE MORGUE.

It was midnight when John Treverton went upstairs to his study, where there were lighted candles, and a newly replenished fire; for it was one of his habits to read or write late at night. This evening he was in no mood for sleep. He lifted the curtain that hung between the two rooms, and looked into the bedroom. Laura had sobbed herself to sleep. The disordered hair, the hand convulsively clasped upon the pillow, told how far from peace her thoughts had been when she sank into the slumber of mental exhaustion. John Treverton bent down and then turned from the bed with a sigh.

'My sins have fallen heavily upon you, my poor girl,' he said to himself as he went back to his study and sat down by the fire to think over his position, with all its perplexities and entanglements.

Sleep was out of the question. He could only sit and stare at the fire, and review his past life and its manifold follies.

How lightly had he flung away the treasure of liberty! Without a thought of the future he had bound himself to a woman for whom he had but the transient liking born of a young man's fancy—of whom he knew so little, that looking back now, he was unable to recall anything beyond the barest outline of her history. Well, he was paying dearly for that brief infatuation—he was paying a heavy forfeit for those careless days in which he had lived among men without principle, and had sunk almost to as low a level as his companions. He tried to remember anything that his wife had ever told him of her childhood and youth; but he could only remember that she had been very silent as to the past. Once, and once only, on a summer Sabbath night, when they two had been driving home alone together from a dinner in the Bois, and when Zaïre's tongue had been loosened by champagne and curaçao, she had talked of her journey to Paris; that long, lonely journey, during which she had so little money in her pocket that she could not even afford to give herself an occasional stage in a *diligence*, but had been content to get a gratuitous lift now and then in an empty wagon, or on the top of a load of buckwheat. She told him how she had entered Paris faint and thirsty, white with dust from head to foot, as if she had come out of a flour-mill; and how the great city—with its myriad lamps and voices, and the thunder of its wheels—had made her dazed and giddy as she stood at the junction of two great boulevards, looking down the endless vista, where the lights dwindled to a point on the edge of the dark sky. She told him of her career in Paris—how she had begun as a laundress on the quay, and how one Sunday night at the Chateau des Fleurs a man had come up to her after one of the quadrilles—a fat man with a gray moustache and a large white waistcoat—and had asked her where she had learned to dance; and how she had told him, laughingly, that she had never learned at all—that it came naturally to her, like eating and drinking and sleeping; and then he had asked her whether she would like to be a dancer at one of the theatres, and wear a petticoat of golden tissue and white satin boots embroidered with gold—such as she might have seen in the last great spectacle of the Hind in the Wood; and she had told him yes, such a life would suit her exactly; whereupon the gentleman in the white waistcoat told her to present herself at eleven o'clock next morning at a certain big theatre on the Boulevard. She obeyed, saw the gentleman in his private room at the theatre, was engaged as one of a hundred and fifty figurantes, at a salary of twenty francs a week. 'And from that to the time when I was the rage at the Students' Theatre, it was easy,' said La Chicot, with an insolent smile upon her full, red lips. 'If I had any other man for my husband I should be the rage at one of the Boulevard Theatres, and the *Figaro* would have an article about me every other week.'

'You have never had any fancy for going back to Auray, to see your old friends?' asked the husband once, wondering at the cold egotism of the creature.

'I never had a friend in Brittany for whom I cared that,' answered Zaïre, snapping her fingers. 'Every one ill-treated me. My father was a perambulating cider-vat—my poor mother—well, I can pity her, because she was so miserable—whined and whimpered. It was a mercy to all of us when the good God took her.'

'And you never had any one else to care for?' asked Jack, in a speculative mood. 'No lover, for instance?'

'Lover!' cried La Chicot, her great eyes flashing upon him angrily. 'What had I to do with a lover? I was but nineteen when I left that hole.'

'Lovers have been heard of even at that early age,' suggested Jack, in his quietest tone; and after that his wife said no more about her past history.

To-night, sitting in idle despondency, looking into the fire, John

Treverton, master of Hazlehurst Manor, husband of a wife he adored, utterly dissociated from that reckless, happy-go-lucky Jack Chicot of Bohemian surroundings, for whom the good and evil of each day had been all-sufficient, and who had never dared to look forward to the inevitable to-morrow, let his thoughts slip back to the bygone days, and saw, as in a picture, those scenes of the past which had impressed themselves most vividly upon his mind when they happened.

There was one incident in his married life which had made him wonder, for his wife had not been a woman of a sensitive temper, or easily moved to strong emotion, save when her own pleasure or her own interest was at stake. Yet in this particular instance she had shown herself as susceptible to pity and terror as a girl of seventeen, fresh from a convent school.

They two, husband and wife, had been strolling one summer afternoon upon the quays and bridges, loitering to look at the traffic on the river, sitting to rest under the trees, or turning over the leaves of the old books upon the stalls, and so sauntering carelessly on till they came to the Pont Neuf.

'Let us go across and look at Notre Dame,' said the husband, for whom the old church had an inexhaustible charm.

'Bah!' cried the wife. 'What a fancy you have for staring at old stones!'

They crossed the bridge, and sauntered to the front of the noble old cathedral, where already the hand of improvement was beginning to clear away the houses that surrounded and overshadowed its beauty. Jack Chicot was looking up at the glorious western door, built by Philip Augustus, thickly wrought with *fleurs-de-lys*, where in days of old had appeared the sculptured images of all the kings of Judah, shrined in niches of stonework, as delicate as lace or spring foliage. His wife's eyes roved right and left, and all around, seeking some diversion for a mind prone to weariness when not stimulated by amusement or dissipation.

'See, my friend,' she cried suddenly, clutching her husband's arm. 'There is something! Look, what a crowd of people. Is it a procession or an accident?'

'An accident, I think,' answered Chicot, looking down the street facing them, along which a closely-packed crowd was hastening, rolling towards them like a mighty wave of black water. 'We had better get out of the way.'

'But, no,' cried the wife eagerly. 'If there is something to see, let us see it. Life is not too full of distractions.'

'It may be something unpleasant,' suggested Jack. 'I am afraid they are carrying some poor creature to the Morgue.'

'That matters nothing. We may as well see.'

So they waited, and fell in among the hurrying crowd, and heard many voices discussing the thing that had happened, every voice offering a different version of the same ghastly story.

A man had been run over on the Boulevard—a seafaring man from the provinces—knocked down by the horses of a huge wagon. The horses had kicked him, the wheels had gone over his body. 'He was dead when they picked him up,' said one. 'No, he spoke, and hardly seemed conscious he was hurt,' said another. 'He died while they were waiting for the *brancard* on which to carry him to the hospital,' said a third.

And now they were taking him to the Morgue, the famous deadhouse of the city, down by the river yonder. He was being carried in the midst of that dense crowd, which had been gathering ever since the bearers started with their ghastly burden, from the Porte St. Denis, where the accident happened. He was there in the centre of that mass of human life, an awful figure, covered from head to foot, and hidden from all those curious eyes.

Jack and his wife were borne along with the rest, past the great cathedral, down by the river, to the doors of the dead-house.

Here they all came to a stop: no one was allowed to enter save the dead man and his bearers, and three or four *sergents de ville*.

'We must wait till they have made his toilet,' said La Chicot to her husband, 'and then we can go in and see him.'

'What!' cried Jack, 'surely you would not wish to look at a piece of shattered humanity? He must be a dreadful sight, poor creature.'

'On the contrary, monsieur,' said some one near them in the crowd. 'The poor man's face was not injured. He is a handsome fellow, tanned by the sun; a seafaring man, a fine fellow.'

'Let's go in and see him,' urged La Chicot, and when La Chicot wanted to do a thing she always did it.

So they waited amongst the crowd, close-packed still, though about two-thirds of the people had dropped off and gone back to their business or their pleasure; not because they shrank from looking upon death in its most awful aspect, but because the toilet might be long, and the spectacle was not worth the trouble of waiting a weary half-hour in the summer sun.

La Chicot waited with a dogged patience which was a part of her character when she had made up her mind about anything. Jack waited patiently too; for he was watching the faces in the crowd, and had an artistic delight in studying these various specimens of a somewhat debased humanity. Thus the half-hour wore itself out, the doors were opened, and the crowd poured into the dead-house, just as it would have poured into a theatre or a circus.

There he lay, the new-comer, with the summer light shining on him—a calm figure behind a sheet of glass, a brave, bronzed face, bearded, with strongly-marked brows and close-cropped black hair, gold rings in the ears, and on one bare arm, the arm which had escaped the wagon wheel, an inscription tattooed in purple and red.

Jack Chicot, after contemplating the dead man's face with curious interest, fixing the well-marked features in his mind, bent down to look at the tattooed device and inscription.

There was a ship, a rose, and these words, 'Dedicated to Saint Anne of Auray.'

The man was doubtless a native of Auray, La Chicot's birthplace.

Jack turned to remark this to his wife. She was standing close at his elbow, livid as the corpse behind the glass, her face convulsed, big tears rolling down her cheeks.

'Do you know him?' asked Jack. 'Is it any one you remember?'

'No, no!' she sobbed; 'but it is too dreadful. Take me away—take me out of this place, or I shall drop down in a fit.'

He hurried her out through the crowd, pushing his way into the open air.

'You overrated your strength of nerve,' he said, vexed at the folly which had exposed her to such a shock. 'You should not have a fancy for such horrid sights.'

'I shall be better presently,' answered La Chicot. 'It is nothing.'

She was not better presently. She was hysterical all the rest of the day, and at night had no sooner closed her eyes than she started up from her pillow, sobbing violently, and holding her hands before her face.

'Don't let me see him!' she cried passionately. 'Jack, why are you so cruel as to make me see him? You are holding me against the glass—you are forcing me to look at him. Take me away.'

Pondering to-night upon this strange scene of five years ago, John Treverton asked himself if there might not have been some kind of link between this man and Zaïre Chicot.

CHAPTER XXXIV.

GEORGE GERARD IN DANGER.

Although George Gerard had made up his mind to leave Beechampton by the first train on Monday morning, and although he began to feel doubtful as to the purity of Edward Clare's intentions, and altogether uncomfortable in the society of that young man, when Monday came and showed him a dark sky, and a world almost blotted out by rain, he yielded, more weakly than it was his nature to yield, to the friendly persuasion of Mrs. Clare and her daughter, who had come down to the breakfast room at an early hour to pour out the departing guest's tea.

'You really must not travel on such a wretched morning,' said the Vicar's wife, with maternal kindness. 'I wouldn't let Edward start on a long journey in such weather.'

George Gerard thought of the discomforts of a third-class carriage, the currents of icy air creeping in at every crack, the incursion of damp passengers at every station, breathing frostily, and flapping their muddy garments against his knees, the streaming umbrellas in the corners, the all-pervading wretchedness: and then his thoughtful eyes roamed round the pretty little breakfast room, where the furniture would hardly have fetched twenty pounds at an auction, but where the snugness and cosiness and homelike air were above price; and from the room he glanced at its occupants, Celia in her dark winter gown, of coarse blue serge, fitting to perfection, and set off by the last fashion in collar and cuffs.

'Why do you worry Mr. Gerard, mother?' asked Celia, looking up from her tea-making. 'Don't you see that we are so horribly dull here, and he is so anxious to get away from us, that he would go through a much worse ordeal than a wet journey in order to make his escape?'

'I almost wish you knew what a cruel speech that is, Miss Clare,' said Gerard, looking down at her with a grave smile from his station in front of the fire.

'Why cruel?'

'Because you unconsciously taunt me with my poverty. The eight or ten patients I ought to see to-morrow morning are worth a

288

hundred pounds a year to me at most, and yet I can hardly venture to jeopardise that insignificant income.'

'How you will look back and laugh at these days years hence when you are being driven in your brougham from Savile-row to the railway station, to start for Windsor Castle, at the command of a telegram from royalty.'

'Leaving royal telegrams and Windsor Castle out of the question, there is such a distance between my present abode and Savile-row that I doubt my ever being able to traverse it,' said Gerard; 'but in the meantime my few paying patients are of vital importance to me, and I have some rather critical cases among my poor people.'

'Poor dear things, I am sure they can all wait,' said Celia. 'Perhaps it will do them good to suspend their treatment for a day or two. Physic seems at best such a doubtful advantage.'

'I have a friend who looks after anything serious,' said Gerard dubiously. 'If I were to follow my own inclination I should most assuredly stay.'

'Then follow it,' cried Celia. 'I always do. Mamma, give Mr. Gerard some bacon and potatoes, while I run and tell Peter to go to the George, and let them know that the omnibus need not call here.'

'I am afraid I am imposing upon your kind hospitality, and giving you a great deal of trouble,' said Gerard, when Celia had slipped out of the room to give her orders.

'You are giving us no trouble; and you must know that I should be happy to receive any friend of my son's.'

Gerard's sallow cheek flushed faintly at this speech. He felt that there was a kind of imposture in his position at the Vicarage. Every one insisted upon regarding him as an intimate friend of Edward Clare; and already it had been made clear to him that Edward was a man whom he could never make his friend. But for Edward Clare's mother and sister he had a much more cordial feeling.

He sat down to breakfast with the two ladies. The Vicar would breakfast later, and one of Edward's privileges as a poet of the future was to lie in bed until ten o'clock every morning in the present. Never, perhaps, was a merrier breakfast eaten. Gerard, having made up his mind to stay, abandoned himself unreservedly to the pleasure of the moment. Celia questioned him about his life, and drew from him a lively description of some of the more curious incidents in his career. He had but rarely joined in the wilder amusements of his fellow students, but he had joined them often enough to see all that was strange and interesting in London life. Celia listened open-eyed, with rosy lips apart in wonder.

'Ah, that is what I call living,' she exclaimed. 'How different from our system of vegetation here. I'm sure if Harvey had lived all his life at Hazlehurst he would never have found out anything about the circulation of the blood. I don't believe ours does circulate.'

'If you could only know how sweet your rural stagnation seems to a dweller in cities,' said Gerard.

'Let the dweller in cities try it for a month or six weeks,' said Celia. 'He will be weary enough by the end of that time; unless he is one of those sporting creatures who are always happy as long as they can go about with a gun or a fishing rod murdering something.'

'I should want neither gun nor rod,' said Gerard. 'I think I could find complete happiness among these hills.'

'What, away from all your hospitals?'

'I am speaking of my holiday life. I could not afford to live always away from the hospitals. I have to learn my profession.'

'I thought you had done with all that when you passed your examination.'

'A medical man has never done learning. Medical science is progressive. The tyro of to-day knows more than the adept of a century ago.'

As Mr. Gerard had only one day to spend at the Vicarage, Celia gave herself up to the task of making that one day agreeable to him, with the utmost benevolence and amiability. Her brother seemed dull and morose, and shut himself in his den all day, upon the pretence of polishing a lyric he had flung off, in a moment of inspiration, for one of the magazines; so Celia had the visitor thrown altogether on her hands, as she complained afterwards rather plaintively, though she bore the infliction pretty cheerfully at the time.

The two young people spent the morning in conversation beside the breakfast-room fire, Celia pretending to work very hard at an antimacassar in crewels; while Gerard paced the room, and stared out of the window, and fidgeted on his chair, after the manner of a young man, not belonging to the tame cat species, when he finds himself shut up in a country house with a young woman. In spite of this restlessness, however, the surgeon seemed particularly well pleased with his idle morning. He found a great deal to talk about—people—places—books—life in the abstract—and, finally, his own youth and boyhood in particular. He told Celia much more than it was his habit to tell an acquaintance. Those blue eyes of hers expressed such gentle sympathy; the pretty, pouting, under lip had a tender look that tempted him to trust her. As a physiognomist he was inclined to think well of Celia, despite her frivolity. As a young man he was inclined to admire her.

'You must have had a very hard youth,' she said compassionately, when he had given her a sketch, half sad, half humorous, of his life at the Marischal College, Aberdeen.

'Yes, and I am likely to have a hard manhood,' he answered gravely. 'How can I ever dare ask a woman to share a life which has at present so little promise of sunshine?'

'But do not all your great men begin in that kind of way?' interrogated Celia; 'Sir Astley Cooper, for instance, and that poor dear who found out the separate functions of the nerves that direct our thoughts and movements—though goodness knows what actual use that discovery could have been to anybody——'

'I think you must mean Sir Charles Bell,' suggested Gerard, rather disgusted at this flippant mention of genius.

'I suppose I do,' said Celia. 'He wrote a book about hands, I believe. I only wish he had written a book about gloves; for your glove-maker's idea of anatomy is simply absurd. I never yet could find a maker who understands my thumb.'

'What an advantage my sex has over yours in that respect!' remarked Gerard.

'How so?'

'We never need wear gloves, except when we dance or when we drive.'

'Ah!' sighed Celia, with her wondering look. 'I suppose there are sane men in big places like London and Manchester, who walk about without gloves. They wouldn't do it here, where everybody knows everybody else.'

'I think I have bought about two pairs of gloves since I attained to man's estate,' said Gerard.

'But your dances? How do you manage for those?'

'Easily. I never dance.'

'What, are you never tired of playing the wallflower? Do not German waltzes inspire you?'

'I never go in the way of being inspired. I have never been to a party since I came to London.'

'Good gracious! Why don't you go to parties?'

'I could give you fifty reasons, but perhaps one will do as well. Nobody ever asks me.'

'Poor fellow!' cried Celia, with intense compassion. Nothing he had told her of his early struggles had touched her like this. Here was the acme of desolation. 'What, you live in London all the season, and nobody asks you to dances and things?'

'In that part of London I inhabit there is no season. Life there runs on the same monotonous wheels all the year round—poverty all the year round—hard work all the year round—debt, and difficulty, and sickness, and sorrow all the year round.'

'You are making my heart bleed,' said Celia; 'at least I suppose that's anatomically impossible, and I ought not to mention such an absurdity to a doctor; but you are making me feel quite too unhappy.'

'I should be sorry to do that,' returned Gerard gently, 'and it would be a very bad return for your kindness to me. Do not imagine that the kind of life I lead is a silent martyrdom. I am happy in my profession. I am getting on quite as fast as I ever expected to get on. I believe—yes, I do honestly believe, that I shall make name and fortune sooner or later, if I live long enough. It is only when I reflect how long it must be before I can conquer a position good enough for a wife to share, that I am inclined to feel impatient.'

Celia became suddenly interested in the shading of a vine leaf, and bent her face so low over her work, that a flood of crimson rushed into her cheeks, and she felt disinclined to look up again.

She gave a little, nervous cough presently, and, as Gerard was pacing the room in silence, felt herself constrained to say something.

'I dare say the young lady to whom you are engaged will not mind how long she has to wait,' Celia suggested; 'or, if she is very brave, she will not shrink from sharing your early struggles.'

'There is no such young lady in question,' answered Gerard. 'I am not engaged.'

'I beg your pardon. Ah, I forgot you had said you didn't go to parties.'

'Do you think a man should choose a wife at a dance?'

'I don't know. Such things do happen at dances, don't they?'

'Possibly. For my own part, I would rather see my future wife at home, by her father's fireside.'

'Darning stockings,' suggested Celia. 'I believe that is the real test of feminine virtue. A woman may be allowed to play and sing; she may even speak a couple of modern languages; but her chief merit is supposed to lie in her ability to darn stockings and make a pudding. Now, Mr. Gerard, is not that the old-established idea of perfection in womankind?'

'I believe that the darning and pudding-making are vaguely supposed to include all the domestic virtues. It may seem sordid in a lover to consider such details, but the happiness of a husband depends somewhat upon his wife's housekeeping. Could any home be

Eden in which the cook gave warning once a month, and the police-man ate up all the cold meat?'

Celia laughed, but the laugh ended with a sigh. She had made up her mind that if ever she married, her husband must be rich enough to be above the petty struggles of household economy, the cheese-parings of a limited income. He must be able to keep at least a pony carriage, and the pony carriage must be perfect in all its appoint-ments. A footman Celia might forego, but she must have the neatest of parlour-maids. She did not aspire to get her gowns from Wörth: but she must not be circumscribed as to collars and cuffs, and must be able to employ the best dressmaker in Exeter or Plymouth.

But here was a young man who must wait for years before he could marry; or must drag some poor young woman down into the dismal swamp of genteel poverty. Celia felt honestly sorry for him. Of all the men she had ever met he seemed to her the most manly, the brightest, the bravest—perhaps altogether the best. If not exactly handsome, there was that in his marked features and vivid expres-sion which Celia thought more attractive than absolute regularity of line, or splendour of colour.

Mrs. Clare had been absent all the morning, engaged in small do-mestic duties which she considered important, but which Celia de-scribed sweepingly as 'muddling.' She appeared by-and-by at lun-cheon—a meal which the Vicar never ate—and entertained her guest with a dissertation on the tiresomeness of servants, and the various difficulties of housekeeping, until Edward—who honoured the fami-ly circle with his society while he refreshed his exhausted muse with cold roast beef and pickles—ruthlessly cut short his mother's ser-monising, and entered upon a critical discussion with George Gerard as to the relative merits of Browning and Swinburne.

Celia was surprised to discover how widely the young surgeon had read. She had expected to find him ignorant of almost every-thing outside his own particular domain.

'How can you find time for light literature?' she asked.

'Light literature is my only relaxation.'

'You go to the theatres now and then, I suppose?'

'I like to go when there is something good to be seen,' answered Gerard, flushing at the recollection of the time when he had gone three nights a week to feast his eyes upon La Chicot's florid loveli-ness.

He felt ashamed of an infatuation which at the time had seemed to him as noble as the Greek's worship of abstract beauty.

By the time luncheon was finished the rain had ceased, and the gray, wintry sky, though sunless, looked no longer threatening.

'Not a bad afternoon for a ramble on yonder moor,' said Gerard, standing in the bay window, looking out at the landscape. 'Would you have the courage to be my pioneer, Miss Clare?'

Celia looked at her brother interrogatively.

'I'm not in the humour for any more scribbling to-day,' said Edward, 'so perhaps a good long walk would be the easiest way of getting rid of the afternoon. Put on your waterproof and clump soles, Celia, and show us the way.'

Celia ran off, delighted at the opportunity. A moorland ramble with a conversable young man was at least a novelty.

In the hall the damsel met her mother, and, in a sudden overflow of spirits, stopped to give her a filial hug.

'Let us have something nice for dinner, mother dear,' she pleaded. 'It's his last evening.'

The tone of the request inspired Mrs. Clare with vague fears. A girl could hardly have said more had the visitor been her plighted lover.

'What an idea!' she exclaimed good-humouredly. 'Of course I shall do the best I can, but Monday is such an awkward day.'

'Of course, dear. We all know that, but don't let it be quite a Monday dinner,' urged Celia.

'As for that young man, I don't believe he knows what he is eating.'

'Heaven forbid that he should be like my father, and his dinner the most important event in his day!' retorted Celia, whereat Mrs. Clare murmured mildly,—

'My love, your father has a very peculiar constitution. There are things which he can eat, and things which he cannot eat.'

'Of course, you dear deluded *mater*. Cold mutton is poisonous to his constitution; but I never heard of his being the worse for truffled turkey.'

And then Celia skipped off to attire herself, not unbecomingly, in a dark gray ulster, and the most impertinent of billycock hats.

The ramble on the moor was a success. Edward held himself aloof, and smoked his cigar in gloomy silence, but the two others were as merry as a brace of schoolboys taking a stolen holiday. They clambered the steepest paths, crossed the wildest bits of hill and hollow, narrowly escaped coming to grief in boggy ground, and laughed and talked with inexhaustible spirits all the time. George Gerard hardly knew himself, and was struck with wonder at finding that life could be so pleasant. The wintry air was fresh and clear, the wind

294

whistled gaily over the vast sweep of undulating turf and heather. Just at sunset there came a flood of yellow light over the low western sky; a farewell smile from a sun that had hidden himself all day.

'Good gracious!' cried Celia, 'we shall barely have time to scamper home to dinner; and if there is one thing that irritates papa more than another, it is to wait five minutes for his dinner. He never waits more than five minutes. If he did, I believe lunacy would ensue before the tenth. You ought not to have led me astray so far, Mr. Gerard.'

'I think it is you who have been leading me astray,' said Gerard, half grave, half gay. 'I never felt so far from my work-a-day self in my life. You have a great deal to answer for, Miss Clare.'

Celia blushed at the charge, but did not reply to it. She turned and surveyed the ground over which they had travelled.

'I can't see Edward anywhere,' she exclaimed.

'Do you know, I have an idea that he left us about an hour ago,' said Gerard.

'What a ridiculous young man! And now he will be home ever so long before us, and will make capital out of his punctuality with my father.'

'Could you imagine him capable of such meanness?'

'He is a brother,' answered Celia, 'and in that capacity capable of anything. Come along, pray, Mr. Gerard. We must scamper home awfully fast.'

'Won't you take my arm?' asked Gerard.

'Walk arm in arm over the moor! That would be too ridiculous,' exclaimed Celia, tripping on lightly over hillock and hollow. 'Do make haste, Mr. Gerard, or we shall be lost in the darkness.'

George Gerard thought it would be rather nice to be benighted on the moor with Celia, or at any rate to go astray for an hour or so and lengthen their ramble. Happily, however, the lights of the village, glimmering in the valley below, were a safe guide to their footsteps, and Celia knew the pathway that descended the moor as well as she knew her father's garden. The only peril was the risk of getting into some boggy patch of the common at the bottom of the moor, and even here Celia's knowledge availed to keep them out of mischief. They arrived at the Vicarage breathless, with glowing cheeks, just in time to make a hurried toilet for dinner.

Oh, how much too short that winter evening, though one of the longest in the year, seemed to George Gerard! And yet its pleasures were of the simplest. Three of Celia's particular friends—the one eligible youth of Hazlehurst and his two sisters—dropped in to spend the evening, and the Vicarage drawing-room resounded with youth-ful voices and youthful laughter. Celia and the two young ladies played and sang; and though neither playing nor singing was above the average young lady power, the voices were tuneful and fresh, and the fingers were equal to doing justice to a German waltz. The eligible young man was capable of joining in a glee, and George Gerard consented to try the bass part, and proved himself the pos-sessor of a fine bass voice and a correct ear, so they asked each oth-er, 'Who would o'er the downs so free?' and they requested every one to 'See our oars with feathered spray,' and they made valor-ous attempts at Bishop's famous 'Stay, pr'ythee, stay,' in which they did not break down more than fifteen times, and they altogether en-joyed themselves immensely, while the Vicar read *John Bull* and the *Guardian* from end to end, and good Mrs. Clare nodded comfortably over a crochet comforter, giving her ivory hook a vague dig into the woolly mass every now and then with an idea that she was working diligently.

Edward sat aloof reading Browning's "Paracelsus," and hardly understanding a word he read. His mind was full of perplexity and darkest thoughts were brooding there.

Thus the evening ran its course, till the appearance of a tray of sandwiches and a tankard of claret negus warned the revellers that it was time to disperse. The church clock chimed the half-hour after eleven as George Gerard went up to his room.

'And to-morrow night I shall be alone in my Cibber Street par-lour,' he said to himself, 'and I may never see Celia Clare again. Better so, perhaps. What should a piece of pretty frivolity like that have to do in so hard a life as mine?'

CHAPTER XXXV.

ON A VOYAGE OF DISCOVERY.

After pitching and tossing all night in a manner painfully suggestive of shipwreck, John Treverton and his faithful solicitor arrived at St. Malo early in the afternoon, where the comforts and luxuries of that most comfortable hotel, the 'Franklin,' were peculiarly grateful after their cold and dreary passage.

There was no train to carry them to Auray that afternoon, so they dined snugly by a glorious wood fire in a private sitting-room, and discussed the difficulties and dangers of John Treverton's position over a bottle of Chambertin with the true violet bouquet.

Throughout this long conversation, Tom Sampson showed himself as shrewd as he was devoted. He seized the salient points of the case; fully measured all its difficulties; saw that sooner or later John Treverton might be arrested on suspicion of his wife's murder, and would have to prove himself innocent. Sampson, as well as Treverton, had seen how much malice there was in Edward Clare's mind, and both foresaw the probability of that malice being pushed still further.

'If we could only prove that your first marriage was invalid, we should get rid at once of any motive on your part for the murder,' said Sampson.

'You could not prove that I knew my first marriage to be invalid,' answered Treverton, 'unless you are going to try to prove a lie.'

'I don't know what I might not try to do, if your neck were in danger,' retorted Sampson. 'I shouldn't stick at trifles, you may depend upon it. The grand thing will be to find out if there was a previous marriage. After your story about the sailor at the Morgue, I am inclined to hope for success.'

'Are you? Poor Sampson! I strongly suspect we are going in search of a mare's nest.'

They left St. Malo next morning, and arrived at Auray early in the afternoon. They were jolted down a long boulevard from the station to the town in an omnibus, which finally deposited them at the Pavillon d'en haut, a very comfortable hotel, where they were received by a smiling landlady, and a pretty chambermaid in a neat black gown, trimmed with velvet, a cambric cap as quaint as a nun's headgear, and apron, collar, and cuffs of the same spotless fabric.

As Tom Sampson's knowledge of the French language was that of the average British schoolboy, he naturally found himself unable to understand the natives of an obscure port in Brittany. He was with his client in the capacity of adviser; but it behoved his client to do all the work.

'Well, my dear fellow,' said Treverton, when they had deposited their travelling bags at the hotel, and were standing in the empty market-place, looking round them somewhat vaguely, 'here we are, and what is to be our first move now we are here?'

'I should think about the best plan would be to go to the churches and examine the registers,' suggested Sampson. 'I suppose you know your first wife's real name?'

'Not unless it was Chicot—I married her under that name.'

'Chicot,' repeated Sampson dubiously. 'It sounds rather barbarous, but it's nothing to the names over the shops here. I never saw such crack-jaw cognomens. Well, we'd better go and look up all the registers for the name of Chicot.'

'That would be slow work,' said Treverton, thinking of the sweet young wife at home, full of fear and trouble, left to brood upon her sorrows at that very time when life ought to have been made bright and happy for her, a time when her mind might be most prone to despondency.

He had written Laura a consoling letter from St. Malo, affecting hopefulness he did not feel; but he knew how poor a consolation any letter must be, and he was longing to finish his business and turn his face homewards.

'Can you suggest a quicker way?' asked Sampson.

'I think it might be a better plan to find out the oldest priest in the parish, and question him. A priest in such a place as this ought to be a living chronicle of the lives of its inhabitants.'

'Not half a bad idea,' said Sampson approvingly. 'The sooner you find your priest the better, say I.'

'Come along, then,' said Treverton, and they went up the steps of a church near at hand, and into the dusky aisle, where a few scattered old women were kneeling in the winter gloom, and where the sanctuary lamp shone like a red star in the distance.

'What would they say at Hazlehurst if they could see me in a Roman Catholic church?' thought Sampson. 'They'd give me over for lost.'

John Treverton walked softly round the church, till he met with a priest who was just shutting up his confessional, preparatory to departure. He was a youngish man, with a good-natured countenance, and acknowledged the stranger's salutation with a friendly smile. John Treverton followed him out of the church before he ventured to ask for the information he wanted, and then he explained himself as briefly as possible.

'I have come from England to obtain information about a native of this town,' he said. 'Do you think that among the priests connected with your church there is any gentleman who can remember the events of the last twenty years, and who would be obliging enough to answer my questions?'

'Most certainly, monsieur, since I apprehend your inquiries are to a good end.'

'I can give you my own word for that. This gentleman is my solicitor, and if he could speak French, or if you could speak English, he would be able to vouch for my respectability. Unhappily he cannot put half-a-dozen words together in your charming language. At least I'm afraid he can't. Do you think you could tell this gentleman who I am, Sampson?' John Treverton asked, turning to his ally.

Mr. Sampson became furiously red in the face, and blew out his cheeks like a turkey-cock.

'*Mon ami, monsieur,*' he began with a desperate plunge. '*Er, mon ami est bien riche homme, bien à faire, le plus fort riche homme dans notre part de la campagne. Il a un grand état, très grand. Je suis son lawyer—comprenney, monsieur?—son avocat.*'

The priest expressed himself deeply convinced of the honourable position of both travellers, though he was inwardly at a loss to understand why a man should go wandering about the country with his advocate.

He then went on to tell John Treverton that his superior, Father le Mescam, the curé of the parish, had been attached to that church for the last thirty years, and could doubtless recall every event of importance that had happened in the town during that period. He was likely to know much of the private history of his congregation; and as he was the most amiable of men, he would doubtless be willing to communicate anything which a stranger could have the right to know.

'Sir, you are most obliging,' said John Treverton. 'Extend your courtesy still further, and bring Father le Mescam to dine with me and my friend at six o'clock this evening, and you will weigh me down with obligations.'

'You are very kind, sir,' murmured the priest. 'We have vespers at five—yes, at six we shall be free. I shall feel much pleasure in persuading Father le Mescam to accept your very gracious invitation.'

'A thousand thanks. I consider it settled. We are staying at the Pavillon d'en haut, where I suppose that if a man cannot *dine*, he can at least eat.'

'Sir, I take it upon myself to answer for the hotel. As a type of the provincial cuisine the Pavillon d'en haut will prove itself worthy of your praise. You shall not be discontented with your dinner. I pledge myself to that. Till six o'clock, sir.'

The *Vicaire* lifted his biretta, and left them.

'It will go hard if I cannot find out something about my wife's antecedents from a man who has lived thirty years in Auray,' said John Treverton, as he and his companion walked down the narrow stony street leading to the river. 'So beautiful a woman must have been remarkable in a place like this.'

'Judging from the specimens of female loveliness I have met with so far, I should say very remarkable,' retorted Sampson; 'for, with the exception of that pretty chambermaid at the Pavillong dong Haw, I haven't seen a decent-looking woman since we left St. Mallow.'

They went down to the bridge, Sampson hobbling over the stony pathway, and vehemently abusing the vestry and local board of Auray, which settlement he appeared to think was governed exactly after the manner of our English country towns.

They crossed the bridge and went to look at an old church on the other side of the river, where the fisher folk had hung models of three-masters and screw steamers as votary offerings to their guardian saints; then they re-crossed the bridge and went up to an observatory on a hill above the little town, and surveyed as much as they could see of the landscape in the gathering winter gloom; and then Mr. Sampson, who might possibly have been impressed by Vesuvius in a state of eruption, but who had not a keen eye for the quaint and picturesque on a small scale, proposed that they should go back to their hotel and make themselves comfortable for dinner.

'I should like a wash if there's such a thing as a cake of soap in the place,' said the lawyer, 'but from the appearance of the inhabitants I should rather suspect there wasn't. Soap would be a mockery for some of them. Nothing less than scraping would be any real benefit.'

They found their sitting-room at the hotel bright with wax candles and a wood fire. Mr. Sampson nearly came to grief upon the beeswaxed floor, and protested against polished floors as a remnant of barbarism. Otherwise he found things more civilized than he had expected, never before having trusted himself across the Channel, and being strictly insular in his conception of foreign manners and customs.

'I should hope the old gentleman who is to dine with us can speak English,' he said; 'he ought at his time of life.'

'But if he has lived all his life at Auray?'

'Well, no doubt this is a sink of ignorance,' asserted Sampson. 'I dare say the stupid old man won't be able to understand a word I say.'

The two priests were announced as the great clock in the market-place struck six, town time, while the clock on the mantelpiece followed with its shriller chime. 'Father le Mescam, Father Gedain,' said the pretty chambermaid in most respectful tones, and thereupon the two gentlemen entered, neatly dressed, clean shaven, smiling, and having nothing of that dark and sinister air which Tom Sampson expected to discover in every Popish priest.

Father le Mescam was a little old man, with a quaint, comical face, which would have done admirably for the first gravedigger in 'Hamlet'; small, twinkling eyes, full of sly humour; a mobile mouth, and a pert little nose, cocked up in the air, as if in good-humoured contempt at the folly of human nature in general.

'I am extremely obliged to you for the kindness of this visit, Father le Mescam,' said John Treverton, when the *Vicaire* had presented him to his superior.

'My dear sir, when a pleasant-mannered traveller asks me to dinner, I am only too glad to accept the invitation,' answered the priest heartily. 'A whiff of air from the outside world gives an agreeable flavour to life in this quiet little corner of the universe.'

'Lord have mercy on us, how fast the old chap talks!' exclaimed Sampson inwardly. 'Thank goodness, we Englishmen never gabble like that.'

And then, determined not to be left altogether out of the conversation, Mr. Sampson pulled himself together for a bold attempt. He gazed benignantly at Father le Mescam, and shouted at the top of his voice,—

'*Fraw, Mossoo, horriblemong fraw.*'

The little priest smiled blandly, but shrugged his shoulders with serio-comic helplessness.

'*Non moing c'est saisonable temps pour le temp de l'ong,*' pursued Sampson, waxing bolder, and feeling as if all the French he had acquired in his school days was pouring in upon him like a flood of light.

Father le Mescam still looked dubious.

'Well,' exclaimed Sampson, turning to John Treverton, 'I've always heard that Frenchmen were slow at learning foreign languages; but I could not have believed they'd be so disgustingly stupid as not to understand their own. Upon my word, Treverton, I don't see any reason why you should explode in that fashion,' he remonstrated, as Treverton fell back in his chair in a fit of irrepressible laughter. '*Allong*,' cried Sampson. '*Voyci le pottage*; and I'm blessed if they haven't emptied the bread basket into it!' he exclaimed, contemplating with ineffable disgust the contents of the soup tureen, in which he beheld lumps of bread floating on the surface of a thin broth. '*Venez dong*, Treverton, *si vous avez finni de faire un sot de voter même, nous pouvons aussi bien commencer.*'

'*Mais, oui, monsieur,*' cried the curé, enchanted at understanding about two words of this last speech, and beaming at the Englishman in a paroxysm of good nature. '*Oui, oui, oui, monsieur, commençons, commençons. C'est tres-bien dit.*'

'Ah,' grunted Sampson, 'the old idiot is inspired when one talks about his dinner. If that bread-and-waterish broth is a specimen of the kewsine of this hotel, I don't think much of it,' he added.

Poor as the soup was in appearance, Mr. Sampson found it was not amiss in flavour, and when a savoury preparation of some unknown fish had followed the soup tureen, and a fricassee of fowl and mushroom had replaced the fish, he began to feel at peace with the Pavillon d'en haut. A leg of mutton from the salt marshes completed his reconciliation to provincial cookery, and a dish of vanilla cream *à la Chateaubriand* raised his spirits to enthusiasm. The two priests enjoyed their dinner thoroughly, and chatted gaily as they ate, but it was not till the dessert had been handed round by the brisk serving maid, and a bottle of Pomard had been placed on the table, that John Treverton approached the serious business of the evening. He waited till the chambermaid had left the room, and then, wheeling his chair round to the fire, piled with chestnut logs, invited Father le Mescam to do the same. Mr. Sampson and Father Gedain followed their example, and the four made a cosy circle round the hearth, each nursing his glass of red wine.

'I am going to ask you a good many questions, Father le Mescam,' began John Treverton. 'I hope you won't think me troublesome or impertinently inquisitive. However trivial my inquiries may seem, the result is a matter of life and death to me.'

'Ask what you will, sir,' answered the curé. 'So long as you ask no question which a priest ought not to answer, you may command me.'

CHAPTER XXXVI.

KERGARIOU'S WIFE.

'Father le Mescam,' said John Treverton, 'do you ever remember hearing of a girl who left this town a laundress to become afterwards a celebrity in Paris, as a stage dancer?'

'I ought to remember her,' answered the curé, looking somewhat astonished at the question, 'for I baptized her; I prepared her for her first communion, poor soul; and I married her.'

John Treverton started from his chair, and then sat down again profoundly agitated. Sampson was right. Yes; there had been a previous marriage. Yet it might be too soon for exultation. The first husband might have died before La Chicot came to Paris.

'Are we talking of the same woman?' he asked; 'a girl who was known as Mademoiselle Chicot?'

'Yes,' answered Father le Mescam, 'that was the only woman who ever left Auray to blossom into a stage dancer. Ours is not a soil which freely produces that kind of flower. I have good reason to remember that girl, for I was interested by her singular beauty, and I felt anxious for the safety of her soul amidst the snares and temptations to which such remarkable beauty is subject. I did my best to teach her—to fortify her against all future dangers; but she was as empty within as was lovely without. I hardly know whether one ought to consider such a creature responsible for all her errors. Hers was a case of invincible ignorance. The Church has to deal with many such characters—the heart hard as stone, the intellect a blank.'

'What's he jabbering about?' said Tom Sampson to his client. 'You look as if you had found out something.'

'Wait, my dear fellow. I am on the point of making a discovery. You were right in your guess, Sampson; there was a previous husband.'

'Of course,' cried Sampson triumphantly. 'My surprise in the case of a woman of that kind would be to discover only one previous husband; I should sooner expect to hear of six.'

'Hold your tongue,' said John Treverton authoritatively, and then he refilled Father le Mescam's glass before he proceeded with his inquiry. 'You say you married La Chicot?'

'She was not La Chicot when I married her, but plain Marie Pomellec, the eldest daughter of a drunken old fisherman down by the quay. Drink was hereditary in her family. Grandfather and great-grandfather, they had all been drunkards from generation to generation. The children had to shift for themselves from the time they could run. I think that may have helped to make them hard and cruel, though some sweet souls educate themselves for heaven in just as hard a life. As Marie grew up to a fine tall slip of a girl her handsome face attracted notice. She got to know that she was the prettiest woman in Auray, and the knowledge soon spoiled whatever good there was in her. I saw all the perils of her position—dissolute parents—utter want of guidance from without—a mind too frivolous to be a guide to itself. In my idea her only chance of salvation lay in an early marriage, and although she was but seventeen when Jean Kergariou asked her to be his wife, I did not hesitate in advising her to marry him.'

'Who was Kergariou?'

'A sailor, and as good a fellow as ever went to sea. He and Marie had been playfellows. They had attended the same class for instruction. Jean was intelligent, Marie was dull. Jean was frank and good-humoured, Marie was reserved and self-willed. But the poor fellow was dazzled by the girl's beauty, and she was endeared to him by old associations. He told me that she was the only woman he ever had cared for, the only woman he ever should care for. He had saved a little money, and could afford to furnish one of the cottages in the street by the quay. He would have to go to sea, of course, and Marie would stop at home and keep house, and perhaps earn a little money by washing linen, having the river so convenient. I would rather have had a home-staying husband for her, but Jean was a thoroughly good fellow, and I thought such a husband must keep her out of harm's way. He was not the kind of man that any woman could attempt to trifle with.'

'And he married her?'

'Yes, they were married in the church yonder, one Easter Monday.'

'Can you tell me the date?'

'I can find it for you in the book where such events are registered. I could not say at this moment how many years ago it may have been. I could tell you the year of poor Kergariou's death.'

'Oh, he is dead, then?' asked Treverton, with a dreadful sinking of the heart.

'Yes, poor fellow. Let me see; it must have been three years ago last summer that Kergariou met with his melancholy death.'

'His melancholy death,' repeated Treverton. 'Why melancholy?'

'He was killed—run over by a waggon, on the Boulevard St. Denis, in Paris.'

'Run over by a waggon, three summers ago, on the Boulevard,' echoed John Treverton. 'Yes, I recollect.'

'What—you knew him?'

'No, but I was in Paris at the time of the accident.'

John Treverton recalled that scene at the Morgue, and his wife's ghastly face when she entreated him to take her away. Yes, that one page which had stood boldly out from the book of memory, with a lurid light upon it, was indeed a page of momentous meaning.

'Tell me all about Jean Kergariou and his wife,' he said to the curé. 'It is a matter of vital importance for me to know. You are doing me a service which will make me grateful to you for the rest of my life.'

'Not quite so long, I hope,' retorted the priest, with a sly smile. 'A man would be but short-lived if his life were to be measured by the endurance of his gratitude. That is a delightful virtue, but not a lasting one.'

'Try me,' exclaimed John Treverton. 'Give me legal proof that Marie Pomellec and the dancer called Chicot were one, and that the man killed on the Boulevard three summers ago was Marie Pomellec's husband, and you may put me to the hardest proof you choose, but you shall never find me ungrateful.'

'There are noble exceptions, doubtless,' said the priest, shrugging his shoulders, 'just as there is now and then a baby born with two heads. As for the story of Marie Pomellec and her marriage, it is simple enough, and common enough, and the proof of it is to be found in the registers at the Mairie, while the fact is known to all the inhabitants of the quay, where Jean's wife lived. That the man killed in Paris was Jean Kergariou is also certain; he was recognised by a fellow-sailor while he was lying in the Morgue, and the account appeared in several of the Paris newspapers under the heading of *Faits divers*. The only point open to question might be the identity of the dancer, Mademoiselle Chicot, with Kergariou's wife, but even that was pretty well known to several people in Auray, who saw the woman dance in Paris, and brought back the news of her success—to say nothing of her photographs, which are unmistakable.'

'How did Marie Kergariou come to leave Auray?'

'Who knows? Not I. What man can explain a woman's caprice? She lived steadily enough for the first year after her marriage. Kergariou was away the greater part of the time, on board a whaler in Greenland. When he came home he and his pretty wife seemed monstrously fond of each other. But in the second year things were not so pleasant. Kergariou complained to me of his wife's temper. Marie avoided the confessional, and grew lax in her attendance at the services of the church. The neighbours told me there were quarrels—neighbours will talk of each other, you see, sir, and a priest must not always shut his ears, for the more he knows of his parishioners the better he can help them. I had some serious talk with Marie, but found her sadly impenetrable. She complained of her hard life. She had to work as hard as the ugliest woman in Auray. I reminded her that the blessed Virgin, who was portrayed in all our churches as the highest type of human loveliness, had led a humble and toilsome life on earth, before she ascended to be the queen of heaven. Was beauty to give exception from toil and hardship? If she had been feeble and deformed, I told her, she might plead her infirmity as an excuse for idleness; but God had given her health and strength, and she ought to be proud to think that her labour could help to keep a decent home for her husband, whose career was one of continual peril. I might as well have talked to a stone. Marie told me she was very sorry she had married a sailor. If she had waited a little she had no doubt she might have had a rich young farmer for her husband—a man who could have stayed at home and kept her company, and given her fine clothes to wear. When that year was half gone I heard that there had been a desperate quarrel between Kergariou and his wife the night before he left home for his Greenland voyage; and before he had been gone a week Marie disappeared. At first there was an idea that she had made away with herself; and some of the good-natured fisher folk, who had known her from childhood, set to work to drag the river. But when the neighbours came to examine her cottage they found that she had taken all her clothes, and the few trinkets that Jean had given her in his courting days, and soon after that a waggoner told how he had met her on the road to Rennes; and then every one knew that Kergariou's wife had run away because she was tired of her toilsome, honest life at Auray. She had let drop many a hint, it seemed, when she was washing linen among her companions down by the river; and it was pretty clear to them all that she had gone to Paris to make her fortune, and that if she could not make it in a good way she would make it in a bad one. She was only nineteen years of age, but as old in perversity as if she had been fifty.'

'When did her husband come back?'

'Not till late in the following year. He had been through all kinds of misfortune in the North Seas, and came back looking like the ghost of the fine, handsome young fellow I had married two years before. When he found out what had happened he wanted to set out for Paris in search of his wife; but he fell ill of fever and ague, and lay for months at a friend's house, between life and death. As soon as he was able to move about he went to Paris, and spent the remnant of his savings in hunting for his wife without success. She had not yet made herself notorious as a dancer, you must understand, and there were no photographs of her to be seen in the shops. She was only one among many foolish creatures painting their faces, and dancing before the foolish crowd. Kergariou came back to Auray in despair, and then went off to the North Seas again, caring very little whether he ever returned to his native place any more. He did come back, however, after an absence of more than three years. By that time Marie Pomellec had become notorious in Paris, under the name of Zaïre Chicot, and a Parisian photographer travelling through Brittany had left half-a-dozen of her photographs in Auray. They were to be seen at the bookseller's shop when Jean Kergariou came home from his last voyage, and no sooner did he comprehend what had happened than he started off again for Paris on foot this time, for the poor fellow had spent all his money during his former search for his wife. He left Auray about the middle of June, and in the second week of July I read of his death in the *Moniteur Universel*, which a friend sends me every week from Orleans. Whether he had found his wife or not, I never knew. No one ever heard any more about his fate than that he had reached Paris, and met his death there.'

'A melancholy end,' said John Treverton.

'Not more melancholy than that of his wife,' replied Father le Mescam, 'if there was any truth in a story I read last year, copied from an English newspaper. The poor creature seems to have been murdered by the man with whom she was living—possibly her husband.'

John Treverton's heart sank. Every one, even this unworldly old priest, looked upon the husband's guilt as a matter of course. And, if his innocence should ever be put to the proof, how was he to prove it? It was much to have made this discovery about his first wife, and to know that his second marriage had been valid. He stood possessed of Jasper Treverton's estate without a shadow of fraud. Although guilty in intention, he had been innocent in fact. But beyond this there remained that still darker peril, the possibility that he might have to stand in the dock, charged with La Chicot's murder.

The two priests helped to discuss a second bottle of Pomard, and then took their departure, after Father le Mescam had promised to introduce Mr. Treverton to a respectable notary, who would procure for him the legal evidence of Marie Pomellec's marriage. While this was being done at Auray, John Treverton and his companion would travel without loss of time to Paris, and there search out the details of Jean Kergariou's death and burial.

The appointment with the notary was made for nine o'clock next morning, so eager was John Treverton to push on the business.

'Well,' gasped Sampson, when the two priests had gone, 'if ever a man played patience on a monument for a long winter evening, I think I am that individual. Now they've gone, perhaps you'll tell me what that ridiculous old Jack-in-the-box, Father le Whatshisname, has been saying to you. I never saw an old fellow gesticulate in such a frantic way. If I hadn't been bursting with curiosity, I should have rather enjoyed the performance, as a piece of dumb show.'

John Treverton told his legal adviser the gist of all he had heard from the priest.

'Didn't I say so?' exclaimed Sampson. 'Didn't I say that it was more than likely there was a former husband in the background? It was a desperate guess, of course, and I don't know that I quite thought it when I made the suggestion. But anything was better than relinquishing the estate, as you would have been fool enough to do, if you hadn't had a shrewdish young man for your legal adviser. One of those tip-top firms in the City would have gone straight off to take counsel's opinion; and, before you knew where you were, you'd have been counselled and opinioned out of your property.'

Sampson was in a state of intense exultation at a result which he considered entirely due to his own acumen. He walked up and down the room, chuckling inwardly, in a burst of self-approval. His over-strung feelings at last sought relief in some kind of refreshment. He asked John Treverton to order him a glass of hot gin and water, and he was quite indignant when he was informed that the Pavillon d'en haut could not furnish that truly British luxury.

'I dare say if I order you "a grog" you will get something in the shape of hot brandy and water,' said Treverton.

'Oh, pray don't do anything of the kind. Ask that black-eyed girl to bring a jug—oh! here she is.'

And thereupon Mr. Sampson turned himself to the pretty waiting maid, gave a loud preliminary 'hem,' and thus addressed her:—

'*Mada-moyselle, voulez vous avez le bonty de—bringez—ong joug—ong too petty joug—O boyllong, prenez vous garde que c'est*

309

too boyllong, avec une demi pint de O di vi, et ong bassing de sooker, et, pardonnez, aussi ong quiller, n'oubliez pas le quiller.' Here the girl's vacant stare arrested him, and he saw that no ray of British light could pierce an intellect of such Gallic density. 'Here Treverton,' he cried, impatiently. 'You tell her. The girl's a fool.'

John Treverton gave the order, and Mr. Sampson had the pleasure of mixing for himself a strong jorum of thoroughly English brandy and water, and went to bed happy after drinking it.

As soon as the office was open next morning, John Treverton despatched the following telegram to his wife:—

'Good news for you. All particulars to follow in to-day's letter.'

At eleven, railroad time, Mr. Treverton and his lawyer were on their way to Rennes, *en route* for Paris.

CHAPTER XXXVII.

THE TENANT FROM BEECHAMPTON.

While John Treverton was in Paris, waiting to obtain proof of Jean Kergariou's identity with the sailor whose corpse he had seen carried to the Morgue, Laura was sitting alone in her husband's study, full of anxious thoughts. The telegram from Auray had been delivered at the Manor House early in the afternoon, and had given comfort to the weary heart of John Treverton's wife; but even this assurance of good news could not silence her fears. One horrible idea pursued her wherever she turned her thoughts, an ever-present source of terror. Her husband, the man for whom she would have given her life, had been suspected—even broadly accused—of murder. Let him go where he would, change his name and surroundings as often as he would, that hideous suspicion would follow him like his shadow. She recalled much that she had read about La Chicot's murder in the daily papers. She remembered how even she herself had been impressed with an idea of the husband's guilt. Every circumstance had seemed to point at him. And who else was there to be suspected?

Strong in her faith in the man she loved, Laura Treverton was as fully convinced of her husband's innocence as if she had been by his side when he came home on the night of the murder, and stood aghast on the threshold of his wife's chamber, gazing at the horrid crimson stream that had slowly oozed from under the door, dreadful evidence of the deed that had been done. There was no doubt in her mind, no uncertainty in her thoughts: but she knew that as she had thought in the past, when she had read of the man called Chicot, so others would think in the future, if John Treverton, *alias* Chicot, were to stand at the bar accused of his wife's murder.

An awful possibility to face, alone, with the husband she loved far away, perhaps secretly watched and followed by the police, who might distort his most innocent acts into new evidence of guilt.

'If he were at home, here at my side, I should not suffer this agony,' she thought. 'It is here that he ought to be.'

Celia had been at the Manor House twice since Mr. Treverton's departure, but on both occasions Laura had refused to see her, excusing herself on the ground that she was too ill to see any one. Edward Clare's conduct had filled her mind with loathing, and with fear. She had felt the hidden tooth of the cobra, and she knew that here was a foe whose hatred was fierce enough to mean death. She could not clasp hands with this man's sister, kiss as they two had been wont to kiss. She could not confide in Celia's sisterly love. Brother and sister were of the same blood. Could she be true when he was so profoundly false?

'From this day forth I shall feel afraid of Celia,' she told herself.

When the good-natured Vicar himself came on the day after the arrival of the telegram, anxious to comfort and cheer her in this period of distress, Laura was not able to harden her heart against him, even though he was of the traitor's blood. She could not think evil of him, upon whose knees she had often sat in the early years of her happy life at Hazlehurst Manor; she could not believe that he was her husband's enemy. He had behaved with exemplary gentleness when John Treverton stood before him accused of falsehood and fraud. Even his rebuke had been full of mercy. He was not perhaps a high-minded man, nor even a large-minded man. There was very little of the Apostle about him, though he honestly tried to do his duty according to his lights. But he was a thoroughly good-hearted man, who would have gone a long way out of his straight path to avoid treading on those human worms over whose vile bodies a loftier type of Christian will sometimes tramp rather ruthlessly.

Laura feared no reproaches from this old friend in her hour of misery. He might be prosy, perhaps, and show himself incapable of grappling a difficulty; but he would shoot no barbed arrow of scorn or contumely against that wounded heart. She felt secure in the assurance of his compassion.

'My dear, this is a very sad case,' he said, after he had seated himself by her side, and patted her hand, and hummed and hawed gently for a minute or so. 'You mustn't be down-hearted, my dear Laura; you mustn't give way; but it really is a very sad affair; such complications—such difficulties on every side—one scarcely knows how to contemplate such a position. Imagine such a gentlemanly young fellow as John Treverton married to a French ballet-dancer—a—French—dancer!' repeated the Vicar, dwelling on the lady's nationality, as if that deepened the degradation. 'If my poor old friend could have known I am sure he would have made a very different will. He would have left everything to you, no doubt.'

'Indeed, he would not!' cried Laura, almost indignantly. 'You forget that he had made a vow against that.'

312

'My dear, a vow of that kind could have been evaded without being broken. My dear old friend would never have bequeathed his fortune to a young man capable of marrying a French opera dancer.'

'Why should we dwell upon that hateful marriage?' said Laura. 'If—if—my husband was not free to marry me at the time of our first marriage—in Hazlehurst Church—we must surrender the estate. That is only common honesty. We are both quite willing to do it. You and Mr. Sampson have only to take up your trusts for the hospital.'

'My dear, you talk as lightly of surrendering fourteen thousand a year as if it were nothing. You have no power to realize your loss. You have lived in this house ever since you can remember—mistress of all its comforts and luxuries. You have no idea what life is like on the outside of it.'

'I know that I could live with my husband happily in any house, so long as we had clear consciences.'

'My love, have you considered what a pittance your poor little income would be? Two hundred and sixty pounds a year for two people, at the present price of provisions; and one of the two an extravagant young man.'

'My husband is not extravagant. He has known poverty, and can live on very little. Besides, he has talents, and will earn money. He is not going to fold his hands, and bewail his loss of fortune.'

'My dearest Laura, I shudder at the thought of your facing life upon a pittance, you who have never known the want of money.'

'Dear Mr. Clare, you must think me very weak—cowardly, even—if you suppose that I can fear to face a little poverty with the husband I love. I can bear anything except his disgrace.'

'My poor child, God grant you may be spared that bitter trial. If your husband is innocent of all part in his first wife's death, as you and I believe, let us hope that the world will never know him as the man who has been suspected of such an awful crime.'

'Your son knows,' said Laura.

'My son knows. Yes, Laura, but you cannot for a moment suppose that Edward would make any use of his knowledge against your interest. It was his regard for you that prompted him to the course he took last Sunday night.'

'Is it regard for me that makes him hate my husband? Forgive me for speaking plainly, dear Mr. Clare. You have been all goodness to me—always—ever since I can remember. My heart is full of affection for you and your kind wife; but I know that your son is my husband's enemy, and I tremble at the thought of his power to do us harm.'

The Vicar heard her with some apprehension. He, too, had perceived the malignity of Edward's feelings towards John Treverton. He ascribed the young man's malice to the jealousy of a rejected suitor; and he knew that from jealousy to hatred was but a step. But he could not believe that his son—his own flesh and blood—could be capable of doing a great wrong to a man who had never consciously injured him. That Edward should make any evil use of his knowledge of John Treverton's identity with the suspected Chicot was to the Vicar's mind incredible—nay, impossible.

'You have nothing to fear from Edward, my dear,' he said, gently patting the young wife's hand as it lay despondingly in his; 'make your mind easy on that score.'

'There is Mr. Gerard. He, too, knows my husband's secret.'

'He, too, will respect it. No one can look in John Treverton's face and believe him a murderer.'

'No,' cried Laura, naïvely; 'those cruel people who wrote in the newspapers had never seen him.'

'My dear Laura, you must not distress yourself about newspaper people. They are obliged to write about something. They could put themselves in a passion about the man in the moon if there were nobody else for them to abuse.'

Laura told the Vicar about the telegram received from Auray, with its promise of good news.

'What can be better than that? my dear,' he cried, delightedly. 'And now I want you to come to the Vicarage with me. Celia is most anxious to have you there, as she says you won't have her here.'

'Does Celia know!' Laura began to ask faltering.

'Not a syllable. Neither Celia nor her mother has any idea of what has happened. They know that Treverton is away on business. That is all.'

'Do you think Edward has said nothing?'

'I am perfectly sure that Edward has been as silent as the Sphinx. My wife would not have held her tongue about this sad business for five minutes, if she had had an inkling of it, or Celia either. They would have been exploding in notes of admiration, and would have pestered me to death with questions. No, my dear Laura, you may feel quite comfortable in coming to the Vicarage. Your husband's secret is only known to Edward and me.'

'You are very good,' said Laura gently, 'I know how kindly your invitation is meant. But I cannot leave home. John may come back at any hour. I am continually expecting him.'

314

'My poor child, is that reasonable? Think how far it is from here to Auray.'

'Think how fast he will travel, when once he is free to return.'

'Very well, Laura, you must have your own way. I'll send Celia to keep you company.'

'Please don't,' said Laura, quickly. 'You know how fond I have always been of Celia—but just now I had rather be quite alone. She is so gay and light-hearted. I could hardly bear it. Don't think me ungrateful, dear Mr. Clare; but I would rather face my trouble alone.'

'I shall never think you anything but the most admirable of women,' answered the Vicar; 'and now put on your hat and walk as far as the gate with me. You are looking wretchedly pale.'

Laura obeyed, and walked through the grounds with her old friend. She had not been outside the house since her husband's departure, and the keen wintry air revived her jaded spirits. It was along this chestnut avenue that she and John Treverton had walked on that summer evening when he for the first time avowed his love. There was the good old tree beneath whose shaded branches they had sealed the bond of an undying affection. How much of uncertainty, how much of sorrow, she had suffered since that thrilling moment, which had seemed the assurance of enduring happiness! She walked by the Vicar's side in silence, thinking of that curious leave-taking with her lover a year and a half ago.

'If he had only trusted me,' she thought, with the deepest regret. 'If he had only been frank and straightforward, how much misery might have been saved to both of us! But he was sorely tempted. Can I blame him if he yielded too weakly to the temptation?'

She could not find it in her heart to blame him—though her nobler nature was full of scorn for falsehood—for it had been his love for her that made him weak, his desire to secure to her the possession of the house she loved that had made him false.

Half-way between the house and the road they met a stranger—a middle-aged man, of respectable appearance—a man who might be a clerk, or a builder's foreman, a railway official in plain clothes, anything practical and business-like. He looked scrutinisingly at Laura as he approached, and then stopped short and addressed her, touching his hat:—

'I beg your pardon, madam, but may I ask if Mr. Treverton is at home?'

'No; he is away from home.'

'I'm sorry for that, as I've particular business with him. Will he be long away, do you think, madam?'

'I expect him home daily,' answered Laura. 'Are you one of his tenants? I don't remember to have seen you before.'

'No, madam. But I am a tenant for all that. Mr. Treverton is ground landlord of a block of houses I own in Beechampton, and there is a question about drainage, and I can't move a step without reference to him. I shall be very glad to have a few words with him as soon as possible. Drainage is a business that won't wait, you see, sir,' the man added, turning to the Vicar.

He was a man of peculiarly polite address, with something of old-fashioned ceremoniousness which rather pleased Mr. Clare.

'I'm afraid you'll have to wait till the end of the week,' said the Vicar. 'Mr. Treverton has left home upon important business, and I don't think he can be back sooner than that.'

The stranger was too polite to press the matter further.

'I thank you very much, sir,' he said; 'I must make it convenient to call again.'

'You had better leave your name,' said Laura, 'and I will tell my husband of your visit directly he comes home.'

'I thank you, madam, there is no occasion to trouble you with any message. I am staying with a friend in the village, and shall call directly I hear Mr. Treverton has returned.'

'A very superior man,' remarked the Vicar, when the stranger had raised his hat and walked on briskly enough to be speedily out of earshot. 'The owner of some of those smart new shops in Beechampton High Street, no doubt. Odd that I should never have seen him before. I thought I knew every one in the town.'

It was a small thing, proving the nervous state into which Laura had been thrown by the troubles of the last few days—even the appearance of this courteous stranger discomposed her, and seemed a presage of evil.

CHAPTER XXXVIII.

CELIA'S LOVERS.

The day after Mr. Clare's visit brought Laura the expected letter from her husband, a long letter telling her his adventures at Auray.

'So you see, dearest,' he wrote, after he had related all that Father le Mescam had told him, 'come what may, our position as regards my cousin Jasper's estate is secure. Malice cannot touch us there. From the hour I knelt beside you before the altar in Hazlehurst Church, I have been your husband. That unhappy Frenchwoman was never legally my wife. Whether she wilfully deceived me, or whether she had reasons of her own for supposing Jean Kergariou to be dead, I know not. It is quite possible that she honestly believed herself to be a widow. She might have heard that Kergariou had been lost at sea. Shipwreck and death are too common among those Breton sailors who go to the North Seas. The little seaports in Brittany are populated with widows and orphans. I am quite willing to believe that poor Zaïre thought herself free to marry. This would account for her terrible agitation when she recognised her husband's body in the Morgue. And now, dear love, I shall but stay in Paris long enough to procure all documents necessary to prove Jean Kergariou's death; and then I shall hasten home to comfort my sweet wife, and to face any new trouble that may arise from Edward Clare's enmity. I feel that it is he only whom we have to fear in the future; and it will go hard if I am not equal to the struggle with so despicable a foe. The omnibus is waiting to take us to the station. God bless you, love, and reward you for your generous devotion to your unworthy husband,—JOHN TREVERTON.'

This letter brought unspeakable comfort to Laura's mind. The knowledge that her first marriage was valid was much. It was still more to know that her husband was exempted from the charge of having possessed himself of his cousin's estate by treachery and fraud. The moral wrong in his conduct was not lessened; but he had no longer to fear the disgrace which must have attached to his resignation of the estate.

'Dear old house, dear old home, thank God we shall never be driven from you!' said Laura, looking round the study in which so many eventful scenes of her life had been passed, the room where she and John Treverton had first met.

While Laura was sitting by the fire with her husband's letter in her hand, musing upon its contents, the door was suddenly flung open, and Celia rushed into the room and dropped on her knees by her friend's chair.

'Laura, what has come between us?' she exclaimed. 'Why do you shut me out of your heart? I know there is something wrong. I can see it in papa's manner. Have I been so false a friend that you are afraid to trust me?'

The brightly earnest face was so full of warm and truthful feeling that Laura had not the heart to resent this impetuous intrusion. She had told Trimmer that she would see no one, but Celia had set Trimmer at defiance, and had insisted on coming unannounced to the study.

'You are not false, Celia,' Laura answered gravely, 'but I have good reason to know that your brother is my husband's enemy.'

'Poor Edward,' sighed Celia. 'It's very cruel of you to say such a thing, Laura. You know how devotedly he loved you, and what a blow your marriage was to him.'

'Was it really, Celia? He did not take much trouble to avert the blow.'

'You mean that he never proposed,' said Celia. 'My dear Laura, what would have been the use of his asking you to marry him when he was without the means of keeping a wife? It is quite as much as he can do to clothe himself decently by the uttermost exertion of his genius, though he is really second only to Swinburne, as you know. He has too much of the poetic temperament to face the horrors of poverty,' concluded Celia, quoting her brother's own account of himself.

'I think a few poets—and some of the first quality—have faced those horrors, Celia.'

'Because they were obliged, dear. They were in the quagmire, and couldn't get out; like Chatterton and Burns, and ever so many poor dears. But surely those were not of the highest order. Great poets are like Byron and Shelley. They require yachts and Italian villas, and thoroughbred horses, and Newfoundland dogs, and things,' said Celia with conviction.

'Well, dearest, I bear Edward no ill-will for not having proposed to me, because if he had I could have only refused him; but don't you think there is an extremity of folly and weakness in his affecting to feel injured by my marrying some one else?'

'It isn't affectation,' protested Celia. 'It's reality. He does feel deeply, cruelly injured by your marriage with Mr. Treverton. You can't be angry with him, Laura, for a prejudice that results from his affection for you.'

'I am very angry with him for his unjust and unreasonable hatred of my husband. I believe, Celia, if you knew the extent of his enmity, you too would feel indignant at such injustice.'

'I don't know anything, Laura, except that poor Edward is very unhappy. He mopes in his den all day, pretending to be hard at work; but I believe he sits brooding over the fire half the time—and he smokes like——I really can't find a comparison. Locomotives are nothing to him.'

'I am glad he is not without a conscience,' said Laura, gloomily.

'That means you are glad he is unhappy,' retorted Celia, 'for it seems to me that the chief function of conscience is to make people miserable. Conscience never stops us when we are going to do anything wrong. It only torments us afterwards. But now don't let's talk any more about disagreeable things. Mother told me I was to do all I could to cheer and enliven you. She is quite anxious about you, thinking you will get low-spirited while your husband is away.'

'Life is not very bright for me without him, Celia; but I have had a cheering letter this morning, and I expect him home very soon, so I will be as hopeful as you like. Take off your hat and jacket, dear, and make up your mind to stay with me. I have been very bearish and ungrateful in shutting the door against my faithful little friend. I shall write your mother a few lines to say I am going to keep you till Saturday.'

'You may, if you like,' said Celia. 'It won't break my heart to be away from home for a day or two; though of course I fully concur with that drowsy old song about pleasures and palaces, and little dicky-birds, and all that kind of thing.'

Celia threw off her hat, and slipped herself out of her sealskin jacket as gracefully as Lamia, the serpent woman, escaped from her scaly covering. Laura rang the bell for afternoon tea. The sky was darkening outside the window, the rooks were sailing westwards with a mighty clamour, and the shadows were gathering in the corners of the room. It was that hour in a winter afternoon when the firelight is pleasantest, the hearth cosiest, and when one thinks half regretfully that the days are lengthening, and that this friendly fireside season is passing away.

The tea-table was drawn up to the hearth, and Celia poured out the tea. Laura had eaten nothing with any appetite since that fatal Sunday, but her heart was lighter this evening, and she sat back in her chair, restful and placid, sipping her tea, and enjoying the delicate home-made bread and butter. Celia was unusually quiet during the next ten minutes.

'You say your mother gave you particular instructions about being cheerful, Celia,' said Laura presently; 'you are certainly not obeying her. I don't think I ever knew you hold your tongue for ten consecutive minutes before this evening.'

'Let's talk,' exclaimed Celia, jerking herself out of a reverie. 'I'm ready.'

'What shall we talk about?'

'Well, if you wouldn't object, I think I should like to talk about a young man.'

'Celia!'

'It sounds rather dreadful, doesn't it?' asked Celia naïvely; 'but, to tell you the truth, there's nothing else that particularly interests me just now. I've had a young man on my mind for the last three days.'

Laura's face grew graver. She sat looking at the fire for a minute or so in gloomy silence.

'Mr. Gerard, I suppose?' she said at last.

'How did you guess?'

'Very easily. There are only two eligible young men in Hazlehurst, and you have told me a hundred times that you don't care about either of them. Mr. Gerard is the only stranger who has appeared at the Vicarage. You might easily arrange that as a syllogism.'

'Laura, do you think I am the kind of girl to marry a poor man?' asked Celia, with sudden intensity.

'I think it is a thing you are very likely to do; because you have always protested most vehemently that nothing could induce you to do it,' answered Laura, smiling at her friend's earnestness.

'Nothing could induce me,' said Celia.

'Really.'

'Except being desperately in love with a pauper.'

'What, Celia, has it gone so far already?'

'It has gone very far, as far as my heart. Oh, Laura, if you only knew how good he is, how bravely he has struggled, his cleverness and enthusiasm, his ardent love of his profession, you could not help admiring him. Upon my word, I think there is more genius in such a career as his than in all Edward's poetic efforts. I feel quite sure that he will be a great man by-and-by, and that he will live in a beautiful house at the West-end, and keep a carriage and pair.'

'Are you going to marry him on the strength of that conviction?'

'He has not even asked me yet; though I must say he was on the brink of a declaration ever so many times when we were on the moor. We had a long walk on the moor, you know, on Monday afternoon. Edward was supposed to be with us, but somehow we were alone most of the time. He is so modest, poor fellow, and he feels his poverty so keenly. He lives in a dingy street, in a dingy part of London. He is earning about a hundred and fifty pounds a year. His lodgings cost him thirty. Quite too dreadful to contemplate, isn't it, Laura, for a girl who is as particular as I am about collars and cuffs?'

'Very dreadful, my pet, if one considers elegance in dress and luxurious living as the chief good in life,' answered Laura.

'I don't consider them the chief good, dear, but I think the want of them must be a great evil. And yet, I assure you, when that poor young fellow and I were rambling on the moor, I felt as if money were hardly worth consideration, and that I could endure the sharpest poverty with him. I felt lifted above the pettiness of life. I suppose it was the altitude we were at, and the purity of the air. But of course that was only a moment of enthusiasm.'

'I would not marry upon the strength of an enthusiastic moment, Celia, lest a lifelong repentance should follow. You can know so little of this Mr. Gerard. It is hardly possible you can care for him.'

'"Who ever loved that loved not at first sight?"' quoted Celia, laughing. 'I am not quite so foolish as to love at first sight; but in three days I seemed to know Mr. Gerard as well as if we had been friends as many years.'

'Your brother and he are intimate friends, are they not?'

'I cannot make out the history of their friendship. Edward is disgustingly reserved about Mr. Gerard, and I don't like to seem curious, for fear he should suppose I take too much interest in the young man.'

'Mr. Gerard has gone back to London, has he not?'

'Yes,' sighed Celia. 'He went early on Tuesday morning, by the parliamentary train. Fancy the Sir William Jenner of the future travelling by a horrid slow train, in a carriage like a cattle truck.'

'He will be amply rewarded by-and-by, if he is really the Jenner of the future.'

'Yes, but it's a long time to wait,' said Celia dolefully.

'No doubt,' assented Laura, 'and the time would seem longer to the wife sitting at home by a shabby fireside.'

'Sitting,' echoed Celia; 'she would never be able to sit. She would have no time for moping over the fire. She would always be dusting or sweeping, or making a pudding, or sewing on buttons.'

'I think you had better abandon the idea,' said Laura. 'You could never bear a life of deprivation. Your home-nest has been too soft and comfortable. You had much better think of Mr. Sampson, who admires you very sincerely, and who has a nice house, and a good income.'

'A nice house!' exclaimed Celia, with unqualified contempt. 'The quintessence of middle-class commonness. I would rather endure George Gerard's shabby lodgings. A nice house! Oh, Laura, how can you, living in these fine old rooms, call that stucco abomination of a modern villa, those dreadful walnut-wood chairs and sofas and chiffonnier, all decorated with horrid wriggling scroll-work, badly glued on; that sticky-looking mahogany sideboard, those all-pervading crochet antimacassars——'

'My dearest, the antimacassars are not fixtures. You could do away with them. Indeed, I dare say if Mr. Sampson thought his furniture was the only obstacle to his happiness, he would not mind refurnishing his house altogether.'

'His furniture the only obstacle!' echoed Celia indignantly. 'What have you ever seen in my conduct or character, Laura, that can justify you in supposing I could marry a stumpy little man with sandy hair?'

'In that case we will waive the marriage question altogether. You say you won't marry Mr. Sampson, and I am sure you ought not to marry Mr. Gerard.'

'There is no fear of my doing anything so foolish,' Celia replied, with a resigned air. 'He has gone back to London, and heaven knows if I shall ever see him again. But I am certain if you saw more of him, you would like him very much.'

Laura shuddered, remembering that it was by means of George Gerard that her husband had been identified with the missing Chicot. She could not have a very friendly feeling towards Mr. Gerard, knowing this, but she listened with admirable patience while Celia descanted upon the young man's noble qualities, and repeated all he had said upon the moor, where he really seemed to have recited his entire biography for Celia's edification.

Comforted by her husband's letter, Laura was able to support Celia's liveliness, and so the long winter evening wore itself away pleasantly enough. The next day was Saturday. Laura had calculated that, if things went easily with him in Paris, it would be just possible for John Treverton to be home on Saturday night. This possibility kept her in a flutter all day. It was in vain that Celia proposed a drive to Beechampton, or a walk on the moor. Laura would not go a step

322

beyond the gardens of the Manor House. She could not be persuaded even to go as far as the orchard, for there she could not have seen the fly that brought her husband to the door, and she had an ever-present expectation of his return.

'Don't you know that vulgar old proverb which says that "a watched pot never boils," Laura?' remonstrated Miss Clare. 'Depend upon it, your husband will never come while you are worrying yourself about him. You should try to get him out of your thoughts.'

'I can't,' answered Laura. 'All my thoughts are of him. He is a part of my mind.'

Celia sighed, and felt more sympathetic than usual. She had been thinking about George Gerard for the last four days more than seemed at all reasonable; and it occurred to her that if she were ever to be seriously in love, she might be quite as foolish as her friend.

The day wore on very slowly for both women. Laura watched the clock, and gave herself up to the study of railway time-tables, in order to calculate the probabilities as to John Treverton's return. She sent the carriage to meet an afternoon train, and the carriage came back empty. This was a disappointment, though she argued with herself afterwards that she had not been justified in expecting her husband by that train.

An especially excellent dinner had been ordered, in the hope that the master of the house would be at home to eat it. Seven o'clock came, but no John Treverton, and so the dinner was deferred till eight; and at eight Laura would have had it kept back till nine if Celia had not protested against such cruelty.

'I don't suppose you asked me to stay here with the deliberate intention of starving me,' she said, 'but that is exactly what you are doing. I feel as if it were weeks since I had eaten anything. There is no possibility—at least so far as the railway goes—of Mr. Treverton's being here before half-past ten; so you really may as well let me have a little food, even if you are too much in the clouds to eat your dinner.'

'I am not in the clouds, dear, I am only anxious.'

They went into the dining-room and sat down to the table, which seemed so empty and dismal without the master of the house. The carriage was ordered to meet the last train. Celia ate an excellent dinner, talking more or less all the time. Laura was too agitated to eat anything. She was glad to get back to the drawing-room, where she could walk up and down, and lift the curtain from one of the windows every now and then to look out and listen for wheels that were not likely to be heard within an hour.

323

'Laura, you are making me positively miserable,' Celia cried at last. 'You are as monotonous in your movements as a squirrel in his cage, and don't seem half so happy as a squirrel. It's a fine, dry night. We had better wrap ourselves up and walk to the gate to meet the carriage. Anything will be better than this.'

'I should enjoy it above all things,' said Laura.

Five minutes later they were both clad in fur jackets and hats, and were walking briskly towards the avenue.

The night was fine, and lit with wintry stars. There was no moon, but that clear sky, with its pale radiance of stars, gave quite enough light to direct the footsteps of the two girls, who knew every inch of the way.

They had not gone far before Celia, whose tongue ran on gaily, and whose eyes roamed in every direction, espied a man walking a little way in front of them.

'A strange man,' she cried. 'Look, Laura! I hope he's not a burglar!'

'Why should he be a burglar? No doubt he is some tradesman who has been delivering goods at the kitchen door.'

'At ten o'clock?' cried Celia. 'Most irregular. Why, every respectable tradesman in the village is in bed and asleep by this time.'

Laura made no further suggestion. The subject had no interest for her. She was straining her ears to catch the first sound of wheels on the frost-bound high-road. Celia quickened her pace.

'Let's try and overtake him,' she said; 'I think it's our duty. You ought not to allow suspicious-looking strangers to hang about your grounds without at least trying to find out who they are. He may have a revolver, but I'll risk it.'

With this heroic determination Celia went off at a run, and presently came up with the man, who was walking steadily on in front of her. At the sound of her footsteps he stopped and looked round.

'I beg your pardon,' gasped Celia, in a breathless condition, and looking anxiously for the expected revolver. 'Have you been leaving anything at the Manor House?'

'No, madam. I've only been making an inquiry,' the man replied quietly.

'It is one of John's tenants, Celia,' said Laura overtaking them. 'You have been to inquire about Mr. Treverton's return, I suppose,' she added, to the stranger.

'Yes, madam. My visit is to come to an end on Monday morning, and I am getting anxious. I want to see Mr. Treverton before I go

324

back. It will save me a journey to and fro, you see, madam, and time is money to a man in my position.'

'I expect him home this evening,' Laura answered kindly; 'and if he does come to-night, as I hope he will, I have no doubt he will see you as early as you like on Monday morning. At nine, if that will not be too early for you.'

'I thank you, madam. That will suit me admirably.'

'Good evening,' said Laura.

The man lifted his hat and walked away.

'A very decent person,' remarked Celia; 'not a bit like the popular notion of a burglar, but perhaps not altogether unlike the real thing. A respectable appearance must be a great advantage to a criminal.'

'There it is,' cried Laura joyfully.

'What?'

'The carriage. Yes, I am sure. Yes—he is coming. Let's run on to the gate, Celia.'

They ran as fast as a brace of school-girls, and arrived at the gate in a flutter of excitement, just in time to see the neat little brougham turn into the avenue.

'Jack,' cried Laura.

'Stop,' cried Jack, with his head out of the window, and the coachman pulled up his horses, as his master jumped out of the carriage.

'Come out, Sampson,' said Mr. Treverton. 'We'll walk to the house with the ladies.'

He put his wife's hand through his arm and walked on, leaving Celia to Mr. Sampson's escort.

They had much to say to each other, husband and wife, in this happy meeting. John Treverton was in high spirits, full of delight at returning to his wife, full of triumph in the thought that no one could oust him from the home they both loved.

Tom Sampson walked in the rear with Miss Clare. She was dying to question him as to where he and his client had been, and what they had been doing, but felt that to do so would be bad manners, and knew that it would be useless. So she confined herself to general remarks of a polite nature.

'I hope you have had what the Yankees call a good time, Mr. Sampson,' she said.

'Very much so, thanks, Miss Clare,' answered Sampson, recalling a dinner eaten at Véfour's just before leaving Paris on the previous evening. 'The kewsine is really first-class.'

If there was one word Celia hated more than another it was this last odious adjective.

'You came by the four o'clock express from Waterloo, I suppose,' hazarded Celia.

'Yes, and a capital train it is!'

'Ah!' sighed Celia, 'I wish I had a little more experience of trains. I stick in my native soil till I feel myself fast becoming a vegetable.'

'No fear of that,' exclaimed Mr. Sampson. 'Such a girl as you—all life and spirit and cleverness—no fear of your ever assimilating to the vegetable tribe. There's my poor sister Eliza, now, there's a good deal of the vegetable about her. Her ideas run in such a narrow groove. I know before I go down to breakfast of a morning exactly what she'll say to me, and I get to answer her mechanically. And at dinner again we sit opposite each other like a couple of talking automatons. It's a dismal life, Miss Clare, for a man with any pretence to mind. If you only knew how I sometimes sigh for a more congenial companion!'

'But I don't know anything about it, Mr. Sampson,' answered Celia tartly. 'How should I?'

'You might,' murmured Sampson tenderly, 'if you had as much sympathy with my ideas as I have with yours.'

'Nonsense!' cried Celia. 'What sympathy can there be between you and me? We haven't an idea in common. A business man like you, with his mind wholly occupied by leases and draft agreements and wills and writs and things, and a girl who doesn't know an iota of law.'

'That's just it!' exclaimed Sampson. 'A man in my position wants a green spot in his life—a haven from the ocean of business—an o—what's its name—in the barren desert of legal transactions. I want a home, Miss Clare—a home!'

'How can you say so, Mr. Sampson? I am sure you have a very comfortable house, and a model housekeeper in your sister.'

'A young woman may be too good a housekeeper, Miss Clare,' answered Sampson seriously. 'My sister is a little over-conscientious in her housekeeping. In her desire to keep down expenses she sometimes cuts things a little too fine. I don't hold with waste or extravagance—I shudder at the thought of it—but I don't like to be asked to eat rank salt butter on a Saturday morning because the regulation amount of fresh has run out, and Eliza won't allow another half-pound to be had in till Saturday afternoon. That's letting a virtue merge into a vice, Miss Clare.'

'Poor Miss Sampson. It is quite too good of her to study your purse so carefully.'

'So it is, Miss Clare,' answered the solicitor doubtfully, 'but I see ribbons round Eliza's neck, and bonnets upon Eliza's head, that I can't always account for satisfactorily to myself. She has a little income of her own, as you no doubt know, since everybody knows everything at Hazlehurst, and she has made her little investments in cottage property out of her little income, which, as you may also know, is derived from cottage property, and she has added a cottage here and a cottage there, till she is swelling out into a little town, as you may say—well, I should think she must have five-and-twenty tenements in all—and I sometimes ask myself how she manages to invest so much of her little income, and yet to dress so smart. There isn't a better-dressed young lady in Hazlehurst—present company, of course, excepted—than my sister. You may have noticed the fact.'

'I have,' replied Celia, convulsed with inward laughter. 'Her bonnets have been my admiration and my envy.'

'No, Miss Clare, not your envy,' protested Sampson, with exceeding tenderness. 'You can envy no one. Perfection has no need to envy. It must feel its own superiority. But I was about to observe, in confidence, that I would rather the housekeeping money was spent on butter than on bonnets; and that when I feel myself deprived of any little luxury, it is a poor consolation to know that my self-denial will provide Eliza with a neck ribbon. No, my dear Miss Clare, the hour must come when my sister will have to give up the keys of her cupboards at The Laurels, and retire to a home of her own. She is amply provided for. There will be no unkindness in such a severance. You know the old proverb, "Two is company, three is none." It doesn't sound grammatical, but it's very true. When I marry, Eliza will have to go.'

'But you are not thinking of matrimony yet awhile, I hope, Mr. Sampson?'

'Yet awhile,' echoed Sampson; 'I'm three-and-thirty. If I don't take the business in hand now, Miss Clare, it will be too late. I am thinking of matrimony, and have been thinking of it very constantly for the last six months. But there is only one girl in the world that I would care to marry, and if she won't have me I shall go down to my grave a bachelor.'

'Don't say that,' cried Celia. 'That is deciding things much too hastily. You haven't seen all the girls in the world. How can you know anything about it? Hazlehurst is such a narrow sphere. A man might as well live in a nutshell, and call that life. You ought to travel.

You ought to see the world of fashion. There are charming boarding-houses at Brighton, now, where you would meet very stylish girls. Why don't you try Brighton?'

'I don't want to try Brighton, or anywhere else,' exclaimed Mr. Sampson, with a wounded air. 'I tell you I am fixed, fixed as fate. There is only one girl in this magnificent universe I want for my wife. Celia, you must feel it, you must know it—you are that girl.'

'Oh, I am so sorry,' cried Celia. 'This is quite too dreadful.'

'It is not dreadful at all. Don't be carried away by the first shock of the thing. I may have been too sudden, perhaps. Oh, Celia, I have worshipped too long in silence, and I may, perchance'—Mr. Sampson rather dwelt on the perchance, which seemed to him a word of peculiar appropriateness, almost a lapse into poetry—'I may, perchance, have been too sudden in my avowal. But when a man is as much in earnest as I am, he does not study details. Celia, you must not say no.'

'But I do say no,' protested Celia.

'Not an irrevocable no?'

'Yes, a most irrevocable no. I am very much flattered, of course, and I really like you very much—as we all do—because you are good and true and honest. But I never, never, never could think of you in any other character than that of a trustworthy friend.'

'Do you really mean it?' asked poor Sampson, aghast.

He was altogether crushed by this unexpected blow. That any young lady in Hazlehurst could refuse the honour of an alliance with him had never occurred to him as within the range of possibility. He had taken plenty of time in making up his mind upon the matrimonial question. He had been careful and deliberate, and had waited till he was thoroughly convinced that Celia Clare was precisely the kind of wife he wanted, before committing himself by a serious declaration. He had been careful that his polite attentions should not be too significant, until the final die was cast. His journey to Brittany had given him ample leisure for reflection. Prostrate in his comfortable berth on board the St. Malo steamer, in the dim light of the cabin lamp, lulled by the monotonous oscillation of the steamer, he had been able to contemplate the question of marriage from every standpoint, and this offer of to-night was the result of those meditations.

Celia told him, with all due courtesy, that she really did mean to refuse him.

'You might do worse,' he said, dolefully.

'No doubt I might. Some rather vulgar person has compared matrimony to a bag of snakes, in which there is only one eel. Perhaps you are the one eel. But then you see I am not obliged to marry any-body. I can go on like Queen Elizabeth,

'"In maiden meditation, fancy free."'

'That's not likely,' said Mr. Sampson moodily. 'A young lady of your stamp won't remain single. You're too attractive and too live-ly. No, you'll marry some scamp for the sake of his good looks; and perhaps the day will come when you'll remember this evening, and feel sorry that you rejected an honest man's offer.'

They were at the house by this time, much to Celia's relief, as she felt that the conversation could hardly be carried on further with-out unpleasantness.

She stopped in the hall, and offered her hand to her dejected ad-mirer.

'Shake hands, Mr. Sampson, to show that you bear no malice,' she said. 'Be assured I shall always like and respect you as a friend of our family.'

She did not wait for his answer, but tripped lightly upstairs, de-termined not to make her appearance again that evening.

Tom Sampson was inclined to return to his own house, without waiting to say good night to his client, but while he stood in the hall making up his mind on this point, John Treverton came out of the dining-room to look for him.

'Why, Sampson, what are you doing out there?' he cried. 'Come in and have some supper. You haven't eaten much since we left Paris.'

'Much,' echoed Sampson dismally. 'A segment of hard biscuit on board the boat, and a cup of weak tea at Dover, have been my only sustenance. But I don't feel that I care about supper,' he added, surveying the table with a melancholy eye. 'I ought to be hungry, but I'm not.'

'Why, you seem quite low-spirited, Mr. Sampson,' said Laura, kindly.

'I am feeling a little low to-night, Mrs. Treverton.'

'Nonsense, man! Low-spirited on such a night as this, after the triumph you achieved at Auray! Wasn't it wonderful, Laura, that Sampson's acumen should have hit upon the idea of my first mar-riage being invalid? It was the only chance we had—the only thing that could have saved the estate.'

'Of course it was,' replied Sampson, 'and that was why I thought of it. A lawyer is bound to see every chance, however remote. I don't know that in my own mind I thought it really likely that your first wife had been encumbered with a living husband when you married her; but I saw that it was just the one loophole for your escape from a most confounded fix.'

Cheered by the idea that he had saved his client's fortune, and comforted by a tumbler or two of irreproachable champagne, Mr. Sampson managed to eat a very good supper, and he trudged briskly homewards on the stroke of midnight, tolerably content with himself and life in general.

'Perhaps after all I may be better off as a bachelor than with the most fascinating of wives,' he reflected. 'But I must come to an understanding with Eliza. Cheeseparing is all very well as long as *my* cheese is not pared. I must let Eliza know that I'm master, and that my tastes are to be consulted in every particular. When I think of the melted butter they gave me last night at Veefoor's, and the sauce with that *sole normong*, I shudder at the recollection of the bill-sticker's paste I've been asked to eat at my own table. If Eliza is to go on keeping house for me, there must be a revolution in the cookery.'

John Treverton and his wife spent a Sabbath of exceeding peacefulness. They appeared at church together morning and evening, much to the discomfiture of Edward Clare, who was surprised to see them looking so happy.

'Does he think the storm has blown over?' Edward said to himself. 'Poor wretch. He will discover his mistake before long.'

The Vicar went to the Manor House after the evening service, and he and John Treverton were closeted together in the library for an hour or more, during which time John told his wife's trustee all that had happened at Auray, and showed him documents which proved Marie Pomellec's marriage with Jean Kergariou, and Kergariou's death two years after her second marriage.

'Providence has been very good to you, John Treverton,' said the Vicar when he had heard everything. 'You cannot be too grateful for your escape from disgrace and difficulty. But I hope you will always remember that your own sin is not lessened by this discovery. I hope that you honestly and truly repent that sin.'

'Can I do otherwise?' asked John Treverton sadly. 'Has it not brought fear and sorrow upon one I love better than myself? The thing was done to benefit her, but I feel now that it was not the less dishonourable.'

'Well, we will try to forget all about it,' said the good-natured Vicar, who, in exhorting a sinner to repentance, never wished to make the burden of remorse too heavy. 'I only desired that you should see your conduct in a proper light, as a Christian and a gentleman. God knows how grateful I am to Him for His mercy to you and my dear Laura. It would have almost broken my heart to see you turned out of this house.'

'Like Adam and Eve out of Paradise,' said Treverton, smiling, 'and my poor Eve a sinless sufferer.'

After this serious talk the Vicar and his host went back to the drawing-room, where Laura and Celia were sitting by a glorious wood fire reading Robertson's sermons.

'What a darling he was!' cried Celia, with a gush. 'And how desperately in love with him I should have been if I had lived at Brighton in his time and heard him preach! His are the only sermons I can read without feeling bored. If that dear prosy old father of mine would only take a lesson——'

Her father's entrance silenced her just as she was about to criticise his capabilities as a preacher. The Vicar went straight to Laura, and took both her hands in his hearty grasp.

'My dear, dear girl,' he said, 'Providence has ordered all things well for you. You have no more trouble to fear!'

It was not till the next morning that Laura remembered her husband's anxious tenant from Beechampton. Husband and wife were breakfasting together *tête-à-tête* in the book-room at half-past seven, John Treverton dressed in his hunting gear, ready to start for a six-mile ride to the meet of staghounds among the pasture-clad hills. Celia, who did not consider that her obligations as a guest included early rising, was still luxuriating in morning dreams.

'Oh, by-the-bye,' exclaimed Laura, when she and her husband had talked about many things, 'I quite forgot to tell you about your tenant at Beechampton. He is coming to see you at nine o'clock this morning. It is a rather important matter he wants to see you about, he says. He has been extremely anxious for your return.'

'My tenant at Beechampton, dear?' said John Treverton, with a puzzled air. 'Who can that be? I have no property at Beechampton except ground rents, and Sampson collects those. I have nothing to do with the tenants.'

'Yes, but this is something about drainage, and your tenant wants to see you. He said you were the ground landlord of some houses which he holds.'

John Treverton shrugged his shoulders resignedly.

'Rather a bore,' he said, 'But if he is here at nine o'clock I don't mind seeing him—I shan't wait for him. I've ordered my horse at nine sharp. And I've ordered the pony carriage for you and Celia to drive to the meet. It's a fine morning, and the fresh air will do you good.'

'Then I'd better send a message to Celia,' said Laura. 'She is given to late hours in wintry weather.'

She rang the bell and told Trimmer to send one of the maids to Miss Clare to say that she was to be ready for a drive at nine o'clock; and then John and his wife dawdled over their talk and breakfast till half-past eight, by which time the January sun was bright enough to invite them into the garden.

'Run and put on your sealskin, Laura, and come for a turn in the grounds,' said Mr. Treverton.

The obedient wife departed, and came back in five minutes, in a brown cloth dress, with jacket, hat, and muff of darkest sealskin.

'What a delightful study in brown!' said John.

They went out into the Dutch garden—that garden where John Treverton had walked alone on the morning after his first arrival at Hazlehurst—the garden where he had seen Laura standing under the yew-tree arch, in the glad April sunshine. They passed under the arch to-day, and made the circuit of the orchard, and speculated as to how long it would be before the primroses would brighten the grassy banks, and the wild purple crocuses break through the sod, like imprisoned souls rising from a wintry grave. Never had they been happier together—perhaps never so happy, for John Treverton's mind was no longer burdened with the secret of an unhappy past. To-day it seemed to both as if there was not a cloud on their horizon. They strolled about orchard and garden until the church clock struck nine, and then John went straight to the hall door, where his handsome bay stood waiting for him, and where Laura's ponies were rattling their bits, and shaking their pretty little thoroughbred heads, in a general impatience to be doing something, were it only running away with the light basket carriage to which they were harnessed.

'Oh, there is your tenant,' said Laura, as she and her husband came round the gravel drive from the adjacent garden, 'standing at the hall door waiting for you.'

'Is that he?' exclaimed Treverton. 'He looks uncommonly like a Londoner.—Well, my good fellow,' he began, going up to the man, hunting-crop in hand, ready to mount his horse, 'what is your business with me? Please make it as short as you can, for I've six miles to ride before I begin my day's work.'

'I shall be very brief, Mr. Treverton,' answered the stranger, coming close up to the master of Hazlehurst Manor, and speaking in a low and serious tone, 'for I want to catch the up train at 11.30, and I must take you with me. I'm a police officer from Scotland Yard, and I am here to arrest you on suspicion of having murdered your wife, known as Mademoiselle Chicot, at Cibber Street, Leicester Square, on the 19th of February, 187—.'

John Treverton turned deadly pale, but he faced the man without flinching.

'I'll come with you immediately,' he said; 'but you can do me one favour. Don't let my wife know the nature of the business that takes me to London. I can get it broken to her gently after I am gone.'

'Don't you think you'd better tell her yourself?' suggested the detective, in a friendly tone. 'She'll take it better from you than from any one else. I've always found it so. Tell her the truth, and let her come to London with us, if she likes.'

'You are right,' said Treverton; 'she'll be happier near me than eating her heart out down here. You've got some one with you, I suppose. You didn't reckon upon taking me single-handed?'

'I didn't reckon upon your making any resistance. You're too much a gentleman and a man of the world. I've no doubt you can clear yourself when you come before a magistrate, and that the business will go no further. It was your being absent from the inquest, you know, that made things look bad against you.'

'Yes, that was a mistake,' answered Treverton.

'I've got a man inside,' said the detective. 'If you'll step into the parlour, and have it out with your wife, he can wait in the hall. Perhaps you wouldn't mind ordering a trap of some kind to take us to the station. It might look better for you to go in your own trap.'

'Yes, I'll see to it,' assented John Treverton absently. 'Answer me one question, there's a good fellow. Who set Scotland Yard on my heels? Who put you up to the fact that I am the man who called himself Chicot?'

'Never you mind how we got at that, sir,' replied the detective sagely. 'That's a kind of thing we never tell. We got the straight tip; that's all you need know. It don't make no difference to you how we got it, does it, now?'

'Yes,' said John Treverton, 'it makes a great difference. But I dare say I shall know all about it before long.'

CHAPTER XXXIX.

ON SUSPICION.

Mr. Treverton's hunter was taken back to his loose-box, where he executed an energetic *pas seul* with his hind legs, in the exuberance of his feelings at being let off his day's work. Mr. Treverton himself was closeted with his wife in the book-room, but not alone. The man from Scotland Yard was present throughout the interview, while his subordinate, a respectable-looking young man in plain clothes, paced quietly up and down the corridor outside.

Laura bore this last crushing blow as she had borne the first—with a noble heroism. She neither wept nor trembled, but stood by her husband's side, pale and steadfast, ready to sustain and comfort him, rather than to add to his burden with the weight of her own grief.

'I am not afraid, John,' she said. 'I am almost glad that you should face this hideous charge. Better to be put upon your trial, and prove yourself innocent, as I know you can, than to live all your life under the shadow of a groundless suspicion.'

She spoke boldly, yet her heart sickened at the thought that it might not be easy, perhaps not even possible, for her husband to prove himself guiltless. She remembered what had been said at the time of the murder, and how every circumstance had seemed to point at him as the murderer.

'My dearest, I shall be able to confront this charge,' answered John Treverton. 'I have no fear of that. I made a miserable mistake in not facing the difficulty at the time. The business may be a little more troublesome now than it would have been then, but I am not afraid. I would not ask you to go to London with me, darling, if I feared the result of my journey.'

'Do you think I would let you go alone in any case?' asked Laura.

She was thinking that even if this trouble were to end in the scaffold, she would be with him to the last, clinging to him and holding by him as other brave women had held by their loved ones, face to face with death. But no, it would not come to that. She was so convinced, in her own mind, of his innocence, that she could not suppose there would be much difficulty in proving the fact in a court of law.

'You will take your maid with you, of course?' said Treverton.

'Yes, I should like to take Mary.'

'Where am I to be during this inquiry?' asked Treverton, turning to the detective.

'At the House of Detention, Clerkenwell.'

'Not the most desirable neighbourhood, but it might be worse,' said Treverton.

'They are surely not going to put you in prison, John, before they have proved anything against you?' cried his wife, with a look of horror.

'It's only a form, dear. We needn't call it prison; but I shan't be exactly at large. I think, perhaps, the best plan would be for you to take quiet lodgings at Islington, say in Colebrook Row, for instance. That's a decent place. You'd prefer that to an hotel, wouldn't you?'

'Infinitely.'

'Very well. You had better put up at the Midland Hotel to-night, and to-morrow morning you and Mary can drive about in a cab till you find a nice lodging. I shall write a line to Sampson, asking him to follow us as soon as he can. He may be of use to us in London.'

Everything was settled as quietly as if they had been starting on a pleasure trip. The brougham was at the door in time to take them to the station. Celia, who was ready dressed to drive to the meet, was the only person who appeared excited or bewildered.

'What does it all mean, Laura?' she asked. 'Have you and Mr. Treverton gone suddenly mad? At eight o'clock you send up to tell me you are going to take me to the meet; and at nine I find you are starting for London, with two strange men. What can you mean by it?'

'It means very serious business, Celia,' Laura answered quietly. 'Do not worry yourself about it. You will know everything by-and-by.'

'By-and-by,' echoed Celia scornfully. 'I suppose you mean when I go to heaven, and look down upon you with a new pair of eyes? I want to know now. By-and-by will not be the least use. I remember when I was a child, if people told me I should have anything by-and-by, I never got it.'

'Good-bye, Celia dearest. John will write to your father.'

'Yes, and my father will keep the letter all to himself. When will you be back?'

'Soon, I hope; but I cannot say how soon.'

335

'Now, madam,' said the police officer, 'the time is up.'

Laura embraced her friend and stepped into the carriage. Her husband followed, then the detective, and lastly the faithful Mary, who had had hard work to get a couple of portmanteaus packed for her master and mistress, and a few things huddled into a carpet bag for herself. She had no idea where they were going, or the motive of this sudden journey. A few hasty words had been said to Trimmer, as to the conduct of the household, and that was all.

At the station Mr. Palby, the detective, contrived to secure a compartment for Mr. and Mrs. Treverton and himself. His subordinate was to travel with Mary in a second-class carriage.

'You needn't be afraid of his talking,' said Mr. Palby to his prisoner. 'Grummles is as close as wax.'

'It can matter very little whether he talks or not,' answered Treverton indifferently. 'Everybody will know everything in a day or two. The newspapers will make my story public.'

He thought with supreme bitterness how much easier it would have been for him to face this accusation as Jack Chicot than as John Treverton, *alias* Chicot; how much less there would have been for the newspapers to say about him, had he stood boldly forward at the inquest and faced his difficulty. About Jack Chicot, the literary Bohemian, the world would have been little curious. How much greater was the scandal now that the accused was a man of fortune, a country squire, the bearer of a good old name!

At five o'clock that winter afternoon the doors of the House of Detention closed upon John Treverton. There was some deference shown to the accused even here, and much consideration for the lovely young wife, who remained quietly with her husband to the last moment, and gave vent to none of the lamentations which were wont to disturb the orderly silence of those stony halls. Laura made herself acquainted with the rules and regulations to which her husband would be subject—the hours at which she would be allowed to see him, and then bade him good-bye without a tear. It was only when she and Mary were alone in the cab, on their way to the Midland Hotel, that her fortitude broke down, and she burst into convulsive sobs.

'Oh, please don't,' cried Mary, putting her friendly arms round her mistress. 'You mustn't give way, indeed you mustn't. It's so dreadful bad for you. Everything's bound to come right, ma'am. Look at master, how cheerful he is, and how brave and handsome he looked in that horrid place.'

'Yes, Mary, he pretended to be cheerful and confident for my sake, just as I try to keep myself calm in order to sustain him. But it is a mere pretence on both sides. I shall be a miserable woman until this inquiry is over.'

'Well, ma'am, of course it's an anxious time.'

'We have hardly a friend who can help us. What does Mr. Sampson know of criminal law? What does my husband know as to what he ought to do to protect himself in his present position? We are like children lost in a dark wood—a wood where there are beasts of prey that may devour us.'

'Mr. Sampson seems very clever, ma'am. Depend upon it, he'll know what to do. Lor', what a ugly place this London is!' exclaimed Mary, looking with astonished eyes at the architectural beauties of the Gray's Inn Road, 'everything so dark and smoky. Beechampton is ever so much grander.'

Here the cab turned into the Euston Road, and the palatial front of the Midland Hotel revealed itself in a burst of splendour to Mary's astonished eyes.

'My!' she exclaimed, 'it must be Buckingham Palace, surely!'

Her astonishment became stupefaction when the cab drove under the Italian-Gothic portico, and a liveried page sprang forward to open the door, and relieve the bewildered Abigail of her mistress's travelling bag. Her surprise and admiration went on increasing, like a geometrical progression, commencing above unity, as she followed her mistress across the pillared hall and up the marble staircase, to a corridor, whose remote perspective ended far away in a twinkling speck of gaslight.

'Gracious, what a place!' she cried. 'If all the hotels in London are like this, what must the Queen's palace be?'

The polite German attendant opened the door of a sitting-room, where a bright fire burned as if to welcome expected guests. He had softly murmured the words 'sitting-room' into Laura's ear as she crossed the hall, and she bowed gently in assent. No more was needed. He felt that she was the right sort of customer for the Grand Midland.

'Die pettroom is vithin,' he said, indicating a door of communication. 'Dere is also tressing-room. Dere vill pe a room vanted for die mait, matam, I subbose. I vill sent die champermait. Matam vill vish to tine?'

'No, thanks. You can bring some tea,' answered Laura, sinking wearily into a chair. She kept her veil down to hide her tear-stained cheeks. 'If a gentleman called Sampson should inquire for me in the course of the evening, please send him here.'

'Yes, matame. Vat name?'

'What man? Oh, you mean my own name. Treverton, Mrs. Treverton.'

She shuddered at the thought that in a few days the name might be notorious.

Mary ordered a dish of cutlets to be sent up with the tea, and presently she and the chambermaid were arranging Mrs. Treverton's bedroom, opening the portmanteau, setting out the ivory brushes and silver-topped bottles from the travelling bag, and giving a look of comfort and homeliness to the strange apartment.

Fires were lighted in the bedroom and dressing-room, and there was that all-pervading air of luxury, which, to the traveller of limited means, suggests the idea that, for the time being, he is living at the rate of ten thousand a year.

The evening was sad and weary for Laura Treverton. Now only was she beginning to realize the catastrophe that had befallen her. Now only, as she walked up and down the strange sitting-room, alone, friendless, in the big world of London, did all the horror of her position come home to her.

Her husband a prisoner, charged with the most direful offence man can commit against his fellow-man, to be brought, perhaps to-morrow, to face his accusers, and to have the details of his supposed guilt bandied from lip to lip to-morrow night, the subject of idle wonder and foolish speculations. *He*, her darling, degraded to the lowest depth to which humanity can fall! It was too horrible. She clasped her hands before her eyes, as if to shut out an actual scene of horror—the dock, the judgment-seat, the hangman, and the scaffold.

'My husband suspected of such a crime,' she said to herself. 'My husband, whose inmost thoughts are known to me; a man incapable of cruelty to the meanest thing that crawls.'

Sometimes, in the course of those slow hours, a sudden excitement took hold of her. She forgot everything except the one fact of her husband's position.

'Let us go to him, Mary,' she cried. 'Get me my hat and jacket, and let us go to him directly.'

'Indeed, ma'am, we can't get in,' remonstrated Mary. 'Don't you remember what they told us about the hours of admission? You were only to see him at a particular time. Why, they're all abed by this time, poor things, I make no doubt.'

'How cruel!' cried Laura; 'how cruel it is that I can't be with him!'

'If you go on worrying yourself like this, ma'am, you'll be ill.

You haven't eaten a bit since you left home, though I'm sure the cutlets was done lovely. Shall I order some arrowroot for your supper? Or a basin of soup, now? That would be more nourishing.'

'No, Mary, it's no use. I can't eat anything. How I wish Mr. Sampson would come!'

'It's almost too late to expect him, ma'am. I don't suppose he's left Hazlehurst. Perhaps he couldn't get away to-day.'

'Not get away!' echoed Laura. 'Nonsense! He would never abandon my husband in the hour of difficulty.'

The German waiter at this very moment announced, 'Mr. Zambzon.'

'I'm awfully late, Mrs. Treverton,' said the little man, bustling in, 'but I thought you'd like to see me, so I came in. I've engaged a room in the hotel, and I shall stay as long as I'm wanted, even if my Hazlehurst business goes to pot.'

'How good you are! You have only just come to London?'

'Only just come, indeed! I came by the train after yours. I was in London at seven o'clock. I've been with Mr. Leopold, the well-known solicitor—the man who's so great in criminal cases, you know,—and I've got him for our side. And I've been down to Cibber Street with him, and we've picked up all the information we can. The landlady's laid up with low fever, and so we couldn't get much out of her; but we've seen Mr. Gerard, and we know pretty well what he has to bring forward against us, and I think he'll be rather a reluctant witness. It's a pity that Mr. Desrolles is out of the way. We might have made something out of him.'

Laura turned to him with a startled look. Desrolles! That was the name by which her husband had known her father. He, to whom an *alias* seemed so easy, had been known in his London lodgings as Mr. Desrolles. And he had been in the house at the time of the murder.

'You have no fear as to the result, have you?' Laura asked Sampson, with intense anxiety. 'My husband will be able to prove himself innocent of this terrible crime.'

'I don't believe the other side will be able to prove him guilty,' said Sampson thoughtfully.

'But he may remain all his life under the stigma of this hideous suspicion. The world will believe him guilty, though the crime cannot be brought home to him. Is that what you mean?'

'My dear Mrs. Treverton, I am not clever enough or experienced enough to offer an opinion in such a case as this. We are only at the outset of things. Besides, I am no criminal lawyer.'

'What does Mr. Leopold say?' asked Laura, looking at him intently.

'I am not at liberty to tell you that. It would be a breach of confidence,' answered Sampson.

'I see. Mr. Leopold thinks there is a strong case against my husband.'

'Mr. Leopold thinks nothing at present. He has no data to go upon.'

'He must remember the report of the inquest, and all that was said in the newspapers.'

'Mr. Leopold thinks that of the newspapers,' exclaimed Sampson, snapping his fingers. 'Mr. Leopold is not led by the nose by the newspapers. He would not be where he is if he were that kind of man.'

'Well, we must wait and hope,' said Laura, with a sigh. 'It is a hard trial, but it must be borne. Will anything be done to-morrow?'

'There will be an inquiry at Bow Street.'

'Will Mr. Leopold be present?'

'Of course. He will watch the case as a cat watches a mouse.'

'Tell him that I should think half my fortune too little to reward him if he can prove—clearly and plainly prove—my husband's innocence.'

'Mr. Leopold won't ask for your fortune. He's as rich as——well, rolling in money. He'll do his duty, you may depend upon it, without any prompting from me.'

CHAPTER XL.

MR. LEOPOLD ASKS
IRRELEVANT QUESTIONS.

An inquiry was held at Bow Street next day. Several of the witnesses who had appeared nearly a year ago at the inquest were present, and much of the evidence that had been then given was now repeated. The policeman who had been called in by Desrolles, the doctor who had first examined the dead woman's wound, and the detective who examined the premises—all these gave their evidence exactly as they had given it at the inquest. Mrs. Evitt was too ill to appear, but her previous statements were read. There was one witness present on this occasion who had not appeared at the inquest. This was George Gerard, who had been subpœnaed by the prosecution, and who described, with a somewhat reluctant air, his discovery of the dagger in Jack Chicot's colour-box.

'This was a curious discovery of yours, Mr. Gerard,' said Mr. Leopold, after the witness had been examined, 'and comes to light at a curious time. Why did you not inform the police of this discovery when you made it?'

'I was not called as a witness.'

'No. But if you considered this discovery of yours of any importance, it was your duty to make it known immediately. You make your way into the house of the accused without anybody's authorization; you go prying and peering into rooms that have already been examined by the police; and you come forward a year afterwards with this extraordinary discovery of a tarnished dagger. What evidence have we that this dagger ever belonged to the accused?'

'There need be no difficulty about that,' said John Treverton, 'the dagger is mine.'

Mr. Leopold rewarded his client's candour with a ferocious scowl. Was there ever such a man—a man who was legally dumb, whose lips the law had sealed, and who had the folly to blurt out such an admission as this?

The magistrate asked whether the dagger could be found. The police had taken possession of all Jack Chicot's chattels. The dagger was no doubt among them.

'Let it be found and given to the divisional surgeon to be examined,' said the magistrate.

The inquiry was adjourned at the request of Mr. Leopold, who wanted time to meet the evidence against his client. The magistrate, who felt that the case was hardly strong enough for committal, granted this respite. An hour later John Treverton was closeted with Mr. Leopold and Mr. Sampson in his room at Clerkenwell.

'The medical evidence shows that the murder must have been committed at one o'clock,' said Mr. Leopold. 'You only discovered it at five minutes before three. What were you doing with yourself during those hours? At the worst we ought to be able to prove an *alibi*.'

'I'm afraid that would be difficult,' answered Treverton thoughtfully. 'I was very unhappy at that period of my life, and had acquired a habit of roaming about the streets of London between midnight and morning. I had suffered from a painful attack of sleeplessness, and this night-roving was the only thing that gave me relief. I was at a literary club near the Strand on the night of the murder. I left a few minutes after twelve. It was a fine, mild night—wonderfully mild for the time of year,—and I walked to Hampstead Heath and back.'

'Humph!' muttered Mr. Leopold, 'you couldn't have managed things better, if you wanted to put the rope round your neck. You left your club a few minutes after twelve, you say—in comfortable time for the murder. You were seen to leave, I suppose?'

'Yes, I left with another member, a water-colour painter, who lives at Haverstock Hill.'

'Good—and he walked with you as far as Haverstock Hill, I suppose?'

'No, he didn't. We walked to St. Martin's Church together, and there he took a hansom. He had no latch-key, and wanted to get home in decent time.'

'Did you tell him you were going to walk up to the Heath?'

'No, I had no definite purpose. I walked as far, and in whatever direction my fancy took me.'

'Precisely. Then your friend, the water-colour painter, parted from you at about a quarter-past twelve?'

'It struck the quarter while we were wishing each other good-night.'

'Within five minutes' walk of your lodging. No chance of an *alibi* here, I fear, Mr. Treverton; unless you met any one on Hampstead Heath, which in the middle of the night was not very likely.'

'I neither met nor spoke to a mortal, except a man at a coffee-stall near the Mother Redcap, on my way back.'

'Oh! you talked to a man at a coffee-stall, did you?'

'Yes, I stopped to take a cup of coffee at ten minutes past two. If the same man is to be found there he ought to remember me. He was a loquacious fellow, something of a wag, and we had quite a political discussion. There had been an important division in the House the night before, and my friend at the coffee-stall was well posted in his *Daily Telegraph*.'

Mr. Leopold made a note of the circumstance while John Treverton was talking.

'So far so good. Now we come to another point. Is there anybody whom you suspect as implicated in this murder? Can you trace a motive anywhere for such an act?'

'No,' answered Treverton decidedly.

'Yet you see the murder must have been done by some one, and that some one must have had a motive. It was not a case of suicide. The medical evidence at the inquest clearly demonstrated that.'

'You remember the inquest?'

'Yes, I was present.'

'Indeed!' exclaimed Treverton, surprised.

'Yes, I was there. Now to continue my argument; you, as the husband of the victim, must have been familiar with all her surroundings. You must know better than any one else whether there was any one connected with her who could have a motive for this crime.'

'I cannot conceive any reason for the act. I cannot suspect any one person more than another.'

'Are you positive that your wife had no valuables in her possession—money, for instance?'

'She spent her money faster than she earned it. We were always in debt. The little jewellery she had ever possessed had been pledged.'

'Are you sure that she had no valuable jewellery in her possession at the time of her death?'

'To my knowledge she had none.'

'That's curious,' said Mr. Leopold. 'I heard a rumour at the time of a diamond necklace, which had been seen round her throat two or three evenings before the murder, by the dresser at the theatre. Your wife wore a broad band of black velvet round her neck when she was dressed for the stage, which entirely concealed the diamonds, and it was only by accident the dresser saw them.'

'This must be a fable,' said Treverton. 'My wife never possessed

343

a diamond necklace. She was never in a position to buy one.'

'She may have been in a position to receive one as a gift,' suggested Mr. Leopold quietly.

'She was an honest woman.'

'Granted. Such gifts are given to honest women. Not often, perhaps, but the thing is possible. Her possession of that diamond necklace may have become known to the murderer, and may have tempted him to the crime.'

Treverton was silent. He remembered his wife's anonymous admirer, the giver of the bracelet. He had dismissed the man from his thoughts after his interview with the jeweller. No other gifts had appeared, and he had felt no further uneasiness on the subject.

'Have you thought of all the people in the house?' asked Mr. Leopold.

John Treverton shrugged his shoulders.

'What can I think about them? No one in the house could have had any motive for murdering my wife.'

'It is pretty clear that the murder was not done by any one outside the house,' said Mr. Leopold, 'unless, indeed, the street door had been left open in the course of the evening, so as to enable the murderer to slip in quietly, and hide himself until every one had gone to bed. At what time did your wife generally return from the theatre?'

'About twelve o'clock; oftener before twelve than after.'

'The murderer may have followed her into the house. She had a latch-key, I suppose?'

'Yes.'

'She may have been careless in closing the door, and left it unfastened. It is quite possible that some one may have entered the house after her, and left it quietly when his work was done.'

'Quite,' answered Treverton, with a bitter smile. 'But if we do not know who that some one was, the fact won't help us.'

'How about this man who occupied the second floor—this Desrolles? What is he?'

'A broken-down gentleman,' answered Treverton, with a troubled look.

He had a peculiar reluctance in speaking of Desrolles.

'He could not be anything worse,' said Mr. Leopold sententiously. 'This Desrolles was in the house at the time of the murder. Strange that he should have heard nothing of the struggle.'

'Mrs. Rawber heard nothing, yet she was on the floor below, and was more likely to hear any movement in my wife's room.'

'I should like to know all you can tell me about Desrolles,' said Mr. Leopold, frowning over his pocket-book.

Honest Tom Sampson sat and listened, open-eyed and silent. To him the famous criminal lawyer was as a god, a being made up of wisdom and knowledge.

'I can tell you very little,' answered John Treverton. 'I know nothing to his discredit, except that he was poor, and too fond of brandy for his own welfare.'

'I see,' answered Leopold quickly. 'The kind of man who would do anything for money.'

Treverton started. He could not deny that this was in some wise true of Mr. Desrolles, *alias* Mansfield, *alias* Malcolm. It horrified him to remember that this man was Laura's father, and that at any moment the disgrace of that relationship might be made known, should Desrolles' presence at the police court be insisted upon. Happily Desrolles was on the other side of the Channel, where only the solicitor who received his income knew where to find him.

Mr. Leopold asked a good many more questions, some of which seemed frivolous and irrelevant, but all of which John Treverton answered as well as he was able.

'I hope you believe in me, Mr. Leopold,' he said, when his solicitor held out his hand at parting.

'From my soul,' answered the other earnestly. 'And, what's more, I mean to pull you through this. It's a troublesome business, but I think I can see my way to the end of it. I wish you could help me to find Desrolles.'

'That I cannot do,' said Treverton decidedly.

'It's a pity. Well, good-day. The inquiry is adjourned till next Tuesday, so we have a week before us. It will be hard if we don't do something in that time.'

'The police have done very little in a twelvemonth,' said Treverton.

'The police have not a monopoly of human intelligence,' answered Mr. Leopold. 'We may do better than the police.'

Two advertisements appeared in the *Times*, *Telegraph*, and *Standard*, next morning:—

'DESROLLES—TEN POUNDS Reward will be given to anybody furnishing the PRESENT ADDRESS of Mr. DESROLLES, late of Cibber Street, Leicester Square.'

'TO JEWELLERS, PAWNBROKERS, &c.—LOST, in February, 187—, a COLLET NECKLACE of IMITA-

TION DIAMONDS.—Anybody giving information about
the same will be liberally rewarded.'

CHAPTER XLI.

MRS. EVITT MAKES A REVELATION.

Mrs. Evitt was very ill. It may be that a prolonged residence on a level with the sewers, and remote from the direct rays of the sun, is not conducive to health or good spirits.

Mrs. Evitt had long suffered from a gentle melancholy, an all-pervading dolefulness, which impelled her to hang her head on one side, and to sigh faintly, at intervals, without any apparent motive. She had been also prone to see all the affairs of life in their darkest aspect, as one living remote from the sun might naturally do. She had been given to prophesy death and doom to her acquaintance, to give a sick friend over, directly the doctor was called in, to foresee sheriff's officers and ruin at the slightest indication of extravagance in the management of a neighbour's household, to augur bad things of babies, and worse things of husbands, to mistrust all mankind, and to perform under her human aspect that ungenial office which the screech-owl was supposed to fulfil in a more romantic age.

She had always been ailing. She suffered from vague pains and stitches, and undefinable aches, which took her at awkward angles of her bony frame, or which wracked the innermost recesses of that edifice. She knew a great deal more about her internal economy than is consistent with happiness, and was wont to talk about her liver and other organs with an almost professional technicality. She was not an agreeable companion, but a long succession of lodgers had borne with her, because she was tolerably clean and unscrupulously honest. Upon this last point she prided herself immensely. She knew that she belonged to a maligned and suspected race; nay, that the very name of her calling was synonymous with peculation; and her soul swelled with pride as she declared that she had never wronged a lodger by so much as a crust of bread. She would let a mutton bone rot in her larder rather than appropriate the barest shank without express permission. Rashers of bacon, half-pounds of Dorset, lard, flour, eggs, were as safe in her care as bullion in the Bank of England.

George Gerard, to whom every penny was of consequence, had discovered this sovereign virtue in his landlady, and honoured her for it. He had suffered much from the harpies with whom he had dwelt in the City. He found his half-pound of tea or coffee last twice as long as in former lodgings; his rasher of bacon less costly; his mutton chop better cooked; his loaf respected. For him Mrs. Evitt was a model landlady; and he rewarded her integrity by such small civilities as lay in his power. What gratified her most was his readiness to prescribe for those ailments which were the most salient feature of her life. Her mind had a natural bent towards medicine, and she loved to talk to the good-natured surgeon of her disorders, or even to question him about his patients.

'That's a bad case of small-pox you've got in Green Street, isn't it, Mr. Gerard?' she would say to him, with a dismal relish, when she came in after his day's work to ask what she ought to do for that 'grumbling' pain in her back.

'Who told you it was small-pox?' asked Gerard.

'Well, I had it from very good authority. The charwoman that works at number seven in this street is own sister to Mrs. Jewell's Mary Ann, and Mrs. Jewell and Mrs. Peacock in Green Street is bosom friends, and the house where you're attending is exackerly opposite Mr. Peacock's.'

'Excellent authority,' answered Gerard, smiling, 'but I am happy to tell you I haven't a case of small-pox on my list. Did you ever hear of such a thing as rheumatic fever?'

'Hear of it,' echoed Mrs. Evitt rapturously. 'I've been down with it seven times.'

She looked very hard at him as she made the assertion, as if not expecting to be believed.

'Have you?' said Gerard. 'Then I wonder you're alive.'

'That's what I wonder at myself,' answered Mrs. Evitt, with subdued pride. 'I must have had a splendid constitution to go through all I've gone through, and to be here to tell it. The quinsies I've had. Why, the mustard that's been put to my throat in the form of poultices would stock a first-rate tea-grocer with the article. As to fever, I don't think you could name the kind I haven't had since I had the scarlatina at five months old and the whooping-cough atop of the measles before I'd got over it. I've been a martyr.'

'I'm afraid that damp kitchen of yours has had something to do with it,' suggested Gerard.

'Damp?' cried Mrs. Evitt, casting up her hands. 'You never made a greater mistake in your life, Mr. Gerard, than when you threw out such a remark. There ain't a dryer room in London. No, Mr. Gerard, it ain't damp, it's sensitiveness. I'm a regular sensitive plant; and if there's disease going about I take it. That's why I asked you if the small-pox was in Green Street. I don't want to be disfigured in my old age.'

Mr. Gerard looked upon Mrs. Evitt's ailments as in a large degree imaginary, but he found her weak and overworked, and gave her a gentle course of quinine, ill as he could afford to supply her with so expensive a tonic. For some time the quinine had a restorative effect, and Mrs. Evitt thought her lodger the first man in his profession. That young man understood her constitution as nobody else had ever understood it, she told her gossips, and that young man would make his way. A doctor who had understood a constitution which had hitherto baffled the faculty was bound to achieve greatness. Unfortunately, the good effect of Gerard's prescription was not lasting. There was a good deal of wet and foggy weather at the close of the old year and at the beginning of the new year; and the damp and fog crept into Mrs. Evitt's kitchen, and seemed to take hold of her hard-worked old bones. She exhibited some very fine examples of shivering—her teeth chattered, her complexion turned blue with cold. Even three-pennyworth of best unsweetened gin, taken in half a tumbler of boiling water, failed to comfort or exhilarate her.

'I'm afraid I'm in for it,' Mrs. Evitt exclaimed to a neighbour, who had dropped in to pass the time of day and borrow an Italian iron. 'And this time it's ague.'

And then, forcing the attack a little for the benefit of the neighbour, she set up one of those dreadful shivering fits, which rattled all the teeth in her head.

'It's ague this time,' she repeated, when the shivering had abated. 'I never had ague until now.'

'Nonsense,' cried the neighbour, with an assumption of cheerfulness. 'It ain't ague. Lord bless you, people don't have ague in the heart of London, in a warm, comfortable kitchen like this. It's only in marshes and such like places that you hear of ague.'

'Never you mind,' retorted Mrs. Evitt solemnly. 'I've got the ague, and if Mr. Gerard doesn't say as much when he comes home, he isn't the clever man I think him.'

Mr. Gerard came home in due course, letting himself in quietly with his latch-key, soon after dark. Mrs. Evitt managed to crawl upstairs with a tray, carrying a mutton chop, a loaf, and a pat of butter. To cook the chop had cost her an effort, and it was as much as she could do to drag her weary limbs upstairs.

'Why, what's the matter with you to-night, Mrs. Bouncer?' asked Gerard, who had given his landlady that classic name. 'You're looking very queer.'

'I know I am,' answered Mrs. Evitt, with gloomy resignation. 'I've got the ague.'

'Ague? nonsense!' cried Gerard, rising and feeling her pulse. 'Let's look at your tongue, old lady. That'll do. I'll soon set you on your legs again, if you do what I tell you.'

'What is that?'

'Get to bed, and stay there till you're well. You're not fit to be slaving about the house, my good soul. You must get to bed and keep yourself warm, and have some one to feed you with good soup and arrowroot, and such like.'

'Who's to look after the house?' asked Mrs. Evitt dismally. 'I shall be ruined.'

'No, you won't. I'm your only lodger just now.' Mrs. Evitt sighed dolefully. 'And I want very little waiting upon. You'll want some one to wait upon you, though. You'd better get a charwoman.'

'Eighteenpence a day, three substantial meals, and a pint of beer,' sighed Mrs. Evitt. 'I should be eat out of house and home. If I must lay up, Mr. Gerard, I'll get a girl. I know of a decent girl that would come for her vittles, and a trifle at the end of the week.'

'Ah,' said Gerard, 'there are a good many decent young men walking the streets of London, who would go anywhere for their victuals. Life's a harder problem than any proposition in Euclid, my worthy Bouncer.'

The landlady shook her head in melancholy assent.

'Now look here, my good soul,' said Gerard seriously. 'If you want to get well, you mustn't sleep in that kennel of yours down below.'

'Kennel!' cried the outraged matron, 'kennel, Mr. Gerard! Why, you might eat your dinner off the floor.'

'I dare say you might; but every breath you draw there is tainted more or less with sewer gas. That furred tongue of yours looks rather like blood-poisoning. You must make yourself up a comfortable bed on the first floor, and keep a nice little bit of fire in your room day and night.'

'Not in *her* room, Mr. Gerard,' exclaimed Mrs. Evitt, with a shudder. 'I couldn't do it, sir. It isn't like as if I was a stranger. Strangers wouldn't feel it. But I knew her. I should see her beautiful eyes glaring at me all night long. It would be the death of me.'

'Well, then, there's Desrolles' room. You can't have any objection to that.'

Mrs. Evitt shuddered again.

'I'm that nervous,' she said, 'that my mind's set against those upstairs rooms.'

'You'll never get well downstairs. If you don't fancy that first-floor bedroom you can make yourself up a bed in the sitting-room. There's plenty of light and air there.'

'I might do that,' said Mrs. Evitt, 'though it goes against me to 'ack my beautiful drawing-room——'

'You won't hurt your drawing-room. You have to recover your health.'

''Ealth is a blessed privilege. Well, I'll put up a truckle bed in the first-floor front. The girl could sleep on a mattress on the floor at the bottom of my bed. She'd be company.'

'Of course she would. Make yourself comfortable mentally and bodily, and you'll soon get well. Now, how about this girl? You must get her immediately.'

'I've got a neighbour coming in presently. I'll get her to step round and tell Jemima to come.'

'Is Jemima the girl?'

'Yes. She's step-daughter to the tailor at the corner of Cricket's Row. He's got a fine family of his own, and Jemima feels herself one too many. She's a hard-working, honest-minded girl, though she isn't much to look at. Her father was in the public line; he was barman at the Prince of Wales, and the stepfather throws it at her sometimes when he's in drink.'

'Never mind Jemima's biography,' said Gerard. 'Get your neighbour to fetch her, and in the meantime I'll help you to make up the bed.'

'Lor', Mr. Gerard, you haven't had your tea. Your chop will be stone cold.'

'My chop must wait,' said Gerard cheerily. And then, with all the handiness of a woman, and more than the kindness of an ordinary woman, the young surgeon helped to transform the first-floor sitting-room into a comfortable bedchamber.

By the time this was done Jemima had arrived upon the scene, carrying all her worldly goods tied up in a cotton handkerchief. She was a raw-boned, angular girl, deeply marked with the small-pox. Her scanty hair was twisted into a knot like a ball of cotton at the back of her head; her elbows were preternaturally red, her wrists were bound up with rusty black ribbon; but she had a good-natured grin that atoned for everything. She was as patient as a beast of burden, contented with the scantiest fare, invariably cheerful. She was so accustomed to harsh words and hard usage that she thought peo-

351

ple who did not bully or maltreat her the quintessence of kindness.

It was on the evening when Mrs. Evitt took to her bed, and the house was entrusted to the care of Jemima, that Mr. Leopold and Mr. Sampson came to make their inquiries at the house in Cibber Street. George Gerard saw them, and heard of John Treverton's arrest, with considerable surprise and some indignation. He felt assured that Edward Clare must have given the information upon which the police had acted; and he felt angry with himself for having been in some wise a cat's-paw to serve the young man's malice. He remembered Laura's lovely face, with its expression of perfect purity and truth; and he hated himself for having helped to bring this terrible grief upon her.

'There was a time when I believed John Treverton guilty,' he told Mr. Leopold, 'but I have wavered in my opinion ever since last Sunday week, when he and I talked together.'

'You never would have thought badly of him if you had known him as well as I do,' said the faithful Sampson. 'He has stayed for a week at a stretch in my house, you know. We have been like brothers. This is an awkward business, and of course it's very painful for that sweet young wife of his. But Mr. Leopold means to pull him through.'

'I do,' assented the famous lawyer.

'Mr. Leopold has pulled a great many through, innocent and guilty.'

'And guilty,' assented the lawyer, with quiet self-approval.

He was disappointed at not being able to see Mrs. Evitt.

'I should like to have asked her a few questions,' he said.

'She is much too ill to-night for that kind of thing,' answered Gerard. 'Her only chance of recovery is to be kept quiet; and I don't think she can tell you any more about the murder than she stated at the inquest.'

'Oh, yes, she could,' said Mr. Leopold. 'She would tell me a great deal more.'

'Do you think she kept anything back?'

'Not intentionally perhaps, but there is always something untold; some small detail, which to your mind might mean nothing, but which might mean a great deal to me. Please let me know directly I can see your landlady.'

Gerard promised, and then Mr. Leopold, instead of taking his departure, made himself quite at home in the surgeon's arm-chair, and stirred the small fire with so reckless a hand that poor Gerard trembled for his weekly hundred of coals. The solicitor seemed in an idle humour, and inclined to waste time. Honest Tom Sampson wondered at his frivolity.

The conversation naturally turned upon the deed which had given that house a sinister notoriety. Gerard found himself talking freely of Madame Chicot and her husband; and it was only after Mr. Leopold and his companion had gone that he perceived how cleverly the experienced lawyer had contrived to cross-question him, without his being aware of the process.

After this evening Gerard watched the newspapers for any report of the Chicot case. He read of John Treverton's appearance at Bow Street, and saw that the inquiry had been adjourned for a week. At Mrs. Evitt's particular request he read the report of the case in the evening papers on the night after the inquiry. She seemed full of anxiety about the business.

'Do you think they'll hang him?' she asked eagerly.

'My good soul, they've a long way to go before they get to hanging. He is not even committed for trial.'

'But it looks black against him, doesn't it?'

'Circumstances certainly appear to point to him as the murderer. You see there seems to be no one else who could have had any motive for such an act.'

'And you say he has got a sweet young wife?'

'One of the loveliest women I ever saw; I feel very sorry for her, poor soul.'

'If you was on the jury, would you bring him in guilty?' asked Mrs. Evitt.

'I should be sorely perplexed. You see I should be called upon to find my verdict according to the evidence, and the evidence against him is very strong.'

Mrs. Evitt sighed, and turned her weary head upon her pillow.

'Poor young man,' she murmured, 'he was always affable—not very free-spoken, but always affable. I should feel sorry if it went against him. It would be awful, wouldn't it?' she exclaimed, with sudden agitation, lifting herself up from her pillow, and gazing fixedly at the surgeon; 'it would be awful for him to be hung, and innocent all the time; and a sweet young wife, too. I couldn't bear it; no, I couldn't bear it. The thought of it would weigh me down to my grave, and I don't suppose it would let me rest even there.'

Gerard thought the poor woman was getting delirious. He laid his fingers gently on her skinny wrist, and held them there while he looked at his watch.

Yes, the pulse was a good deal quicker than it had been when he last felt it.

'Is Jemima there?' asked Mrs. Evitt, twitching aside the bed-curtain, and looking nervously round.

Yes, Jemima was there, sitting before the fire, darning a coarse gray stocking, and feeling very happy in being allowed to bask in the warmth of a fire, in a room where nobody threw saucepan lids at her.

George Gerard had rigged up what he called a jury curtain, to shelter the truckle bed from those piercing currents of air which find their way alike through old and new window frames.

Mrs. Evitt's thin fingers suddenly fastened like claws upon the surgeon's wrist.

'I want to speak to you,' she whispered, 'by-and-by, when Jemima's gone down to her supper. I can't keep it any longer. It's preying on my vitals.'

The delirium was evidently increasing, thought Gerard. There was generally this exacerbation of the fever at nightfall.

'What is it you can't keep?' he asked soothingly. 'Is there anything that worries you?'

'Wait till Jemima has gone down,' whispered the invalid.

'I'll come up and have a look at you between ten and eleven,' said Gerard, aloud, rising to go. 'I've a lot of reading to get through this evening.'

He went down to his books and his tranquil solitude, pondering upon Mrs. Evitt's speech and manner. No, it was not delirium. The woman's words were too consecutive for delirium; her manner was excited, but not wild. There was evidently something on her mind—something connected with La Chicot's murder.

Great Heaven, could this feeble old woman be the assassin? Could those withered old hands have inflicted that mortal gash? No, the idea was not to be entertained for a moment. Yet, stranger things have been since the world began. Crime, like madness, might give a factitious strength to feeble hands. La Chicot might have had money—jewels—hidden wealth of some kind, of which the secret was known to her landlady, and, tempted by direst poverty, this wretched woman might——! The thought was too horrible. It took possession of George Gerard's brain like a nightmare. Vainly did he endeavour to beguile his mind by the study of an interesting treatise on dry-rot in the metatarsal bone. His thoughts were with that feeble old woman upstairs, whose skinny hand, just now, had set him thinking of the witches in Macbeth.

He listened for Jemima's clumping footfall going downstairs. It came at last, and he knew that the girl was gone to her meagre supper, and the coast was clear for Mrs. Evitt's revelation. He shut his book, and went quietly upstairs. Never until now had George Gerard known the meaning of fear; but it was with actual fear that he entered Mrs. Evitt's room, dreading the discovery he was going to make.

He was startled at finding the invalid risen, and with her dingy black stuff gown drawn on over her night-gear.

'Why in heaven's name did you get up?' he asked. 'If you were to take cold you would be ever so much worse than you have been yet.'

'I know it,' answered Mrs. Evitt, with her teeth chattering, 'but I can't help that. I've got to go upstairs to the second-floor back, and you must go with me.'

'What for?'

'I'll tell you that presently. I want you to tell me something first.'

Gerard took a blanket off the bed, and wrapped it round the old woman's shoulders. She was sitting in front of the fire, just where Jemima had sat darning her stocking.

'I'll tell you anything you like,' answered Gerard, 'but I shall be very savage if you catch cold.'

'If an innocent person was suspected of a murder, and the evidence was strong against him, and another person knew he hadn't done it, and said nothing, and let the law take its course, would the other person be guilty?'

'Of murder!' cried Gerard; 'of nothing less than murder. Having the power to save an innocent life, and not saving it! What could that be but murder?'

'Are you sure Jemima isn't outside, on the listen?' asked Mrs. Evitt suspiciously. 'Just go to the door and look.'

Gerard obeyed.

'There's not a mortal within earshot,' he said. 'Now, my good soul, don't waste any more time. It's evident you know all about this murder.'

'I believe I know who did it,' said the old woman.

'Who?'

'I can remember that awful night as well as if it was yesterday,' began Mrs. Evitt, making strange swallowing noises, as if to keep down her agitation. 'There we all stood on the landing outside this door—Mrs. Rawber, Mr. Desrolles, me, and Mr. Chicot. Mrs. Rawber and me was all of a twitter. Mr. Chicot looked as white as a ghost; Mr. Desrolles was the coolest among us. He took it all quiet enough, and I felt it was a comfort to have somebody there that had his wits about him. It was him that proposed sending for a police-man.'

'Sensible enough,' said Gerard.

'Nothing was further from my thoughts than to suspect him,' pursued Mrs. Evitt. 'He had been with me, off and on, for five years, and he'd been a quiet lodger, coming in at his own time with his own key, and giving very little trouble. He had only one fault, and that was his liking for the bottle. He and Madame Chicot had been very friendly. He seemed to take quite a fatherly care of her, and had brought her home from the theatre many a night, when her husband was at his club.'

'Yes, yes,' cried Gerard impatiently. 'You've told me that often before to-night. Go on, for heaven's sake. Do you mean to say that Desrolles had anything to do with the murder?'

'He did it,' said Mrs. Evitt, whispering into the surgeon's ear.

'How do you know? What ground have you for accusing him?'

'The best of grounds. There was a struggle between that poor creature and her murderer. When I went in to look at her as she lay there, before the doctor had touched her, one of her hands was clenched tight—as if she had clutched at something in her last gasp. In that clenched hand I found a tuft of iron-gray hair—just the colour of Desrolles' hair. I could swear to it.'

'Is that all your evidence against Desrolles? The fact is strongly in favour of poor Treverton, and you were a wicked woman not to reveal it at the inquest; but you cannot condemn Desrolles upon the strength of a few gray hairs, unless you know of other evidence against him.'

'I do,' said Mrs. Evitt. 'Dreadful evidence. But don't say that I was a wicked woman because I didn't tell it at the inquest. There was nobody's life in danger. Mr. Chicot had got safe off. Why should I up and tell that which would hang Mr. Desrolles? He had always been a good lodger to me; and though I could never look at him af-ter that time without feeling every drop of blood in my veins turned to ice, and though I was thankful to Providence when he left me, it wasn't in me to tell that which would be his death.'

'Go on,' urged Gerard. 'What was it you discovered?'

'When the policeman had come in and looked about him, Mr. Desrolles says, "I shall go to bed; I ain't wanted no more here," and he goes back to his room as quiet and as cool as if nothing had hap-pened. When the sergeant came back half-an-hour afterwards, with a gentleman in plain clothes, which was neither more nor less than a

356

detective, them two went into every room in the house. I went with them to show the way, and to open cupboards and such like. They went up into Mr. Desrolles' room, and he was sleeping like a lamb. He grumbled a bit at us for disturbing him. "Look about as much as you like," he said, "as long as you don't worry me. Open all the drawers. You won't find any of 'em locked. I haven't a very extensive wardrobe. I can keep count of my clothes without an inventory." "A very pleasant gentleman," said the detective afterwards.'

'Did they find nothing?' asked Gerard.

'Nothing, yet they looked and pried about very careful. There's only one closet in the second-floor back, and that's behind the head of the bed. The bed's a tent, with chintz curtains all round. They looked under the bed, and they even went so far as to move the chimney board and look up the chimney; but they didn't move the bed. I suppose they didn't want to disturb Mr. Desrolles, who had curled himself up in the bed-clothes and gone off to sleep again. "I suppose there ain't no cupboards in this room?" says the detective. I was that tired of dancing attendance upon them, that I just gave my head a shake that might mean anything, and they went downstairs to the parlours to worrit Mrs. Rawber.'

Here Mrs. Evitt paused, as if exhausted by much speech.

'Come, old lady,' said Gerard kindly, 'take a little of this barley water, and then go on. You are keeping me on tenter hooks.'

Mrs. Evitt drank, gasped two or three times, and continued—

'I don't know what put it into my head, but after the two men was gone I couldn't help thinking about that cupboard, and whether there mightn't be something in it that the detectives would like to have found. Mr. Desrolles came downstairs at eleven o'clock, and went out to get his breakfast—as he called it,—but I knew pretty well when he went out of doors for his breakfast, he breakfasted upon brandy. If he wanted a cup of tea or a bloater, I got it for him; but there was mornings when he hadn't appetite to pick a bit of bloater with a slice of bread and butter, and then he went out of doors.'

'Yes, yes,' assented Gerard, 'pray go on.'

'When he was gone I put up the chain of the front door, so as to make sure of not being disturbed, and I went straight up to his room. I moved the bedstead, and opened the cupboard door. Mr. Desrolles had no key to the cupboard, for the key was lost when he first came to me, and though it had turned up afterwards, I hadn't troubled to give it him. What did he want with keys, when all the property he had in the world wasn't worth a five-pound note?'

'Go on, there's a good soul.'

'I opened the cupboard. It was a queer, old-fashioned closet in the wall, and the door was papered over just the same as the room. It was so dark inside that I had to light a candle before I could see anything there. There was not much to see at first, even with the candle, but I went down upon my knees, and hunted in the dark corners, and at last I found Mr. Desrolles' old chintz dressing-gown, rolled up small, and stuffed into the darkest corner of the cupboard, under a lot of rubbish. He had been wearing it only a day or two before, and I knew it as well as I knew him. I took it over to the window and unfolded it; and there was the evidence that told who had murdered that poor creature lying cold on her bed in the room below. The front of the dressing-gown and one of the sleeves were soaked in blood. It must have flowed in torrents. The stains were hardly dry. "Good Lord!" says I to myself, "this would hang him," and I takes and rolls the gown up tight, and puts it back in the corner, and covers it over with other things, old newspapers and old clothes, and such like, just as it was before. And then I runs downstairs and routs out the key of the closet, and takes and locks it. I was all of a tremble while I did it, but I felt there was a power within me to do it. I had but just put the key in my pocket when there came a loud knocking downstairs. From the time Mr. Desrolles had gone out it wasn't quite a quarter of an hour, but I felt pretty sure this was him come back again. I pushed back the bed, and ran down to the door, still trembling inwardly. "What the——(wicked word)—did you put the chain up for?" he asked angrily, for it was him. I told him that I felt that nervous after last night that I was obliged to do it. He smelt strong of brandy, and I thought that he was looking strange, like a man that feels all queer in his inside, and struggles not to show it. "I suppose I must put myself into a clean shirt for this inquest," he says, and then he goes upstairs, and I wonders to myself how he feels as he goes by the door where that poor thing lies.'

'Did he never ask you for the key of the closet?'

'Never. Whether he guessed what had happened, and knew that I suspected him, I can't tell—but he never asked no questions, and the closet has been locked up to this day, and I've got the key, and if you will come upstairs with me I'll show you what I saw that dreadful morning.'

'No, no, there's no need for that. The police are the people who must see the inside of that closet. It's a strange business,' said Gerard, 'but I'm more glad than I can say for Treverton's sake, and for the sake of his lovely young wife. What motive could this Desrolles have had for such a brutal murder?'

Mrs. Evitt shook her head solemnly.

'That's what I never could make out,' she said, 'though I've lain awake many a night puzzling myself over it. I know she hadn't no money—I know that him and her was always friendly, up to the last day of her life. But I've got my idea about it.'

'What is your idea?' asked Gerard.

'That it was done when he was out of his mind with *delirious tremings*.'

'But have you ever seen him mad from the effects of drink?'

'No, never. But how can we tell that it didn't come upon him sudden in the dead of the night, and work upon him until he got up and rushed downstairs in his madness, and cut that poor thing's throat?'

'That's too wild an idea. That a man should be raging mad with *delirium tremens* between twelve and one o'clock, and perfectly sane at three, is hardly within the range of possibility. No. There must have been a motive, though we cannot fathom it. Well, I thank God that conscience has impelled you to tell the truth at last, late as it is. I shall get you to repeat this statement to Mr. Leopold to-morrow. And now get back to bed, and I'll send Jemima up to you with a cup of good beef tea. God grant that this fellow Desrolles may be found.'

'I hope not,' said Mrs. Evitt. 'If they find him they'll hang him, and he was always a good lodger to me. I'm bound to speak of him as I found him.'

'You wouldn't speak very well of him if you had found him at your throat with a razor.'

'Ah,' replied the landlady, 'I lived in fear and dread of him ever after that horrid time. I've woke up in a cold prespiration many a time, fancying that I heard his breathing close beside my bed, though I always slept with my door locked and the kitching table pushed against it. I was right down thankful when he went away, though it was hard upon me to have my second-floor empty—and Queen's taxes, and all my rates coming in just as regular as when my house was full.'

Gerard insisted on his patient going to bed without further delay. She was flushed and excited by her own revelations, and would have willingly gone on talking till midnight, if her doctor had allowed it. But he wished her good-night, and went downstairs to summon the well-meaning Jemima, who was a very good sick nurse, having ministered to a large family of stepbrothers and stepsisters, through teething, measles, chicken-pox, mumps, and all the ills that infant flesh is heir to.

George Gerard communicated early next day with Mr. Leopold, and that gentleman came at once to Mrs. Evitt's bedside, where he had a long and friendly conversation with that lady, who was well enough to be inordinately loquacious. She was quite fascinated by the famous lawyer, whose manners seemed to her the perfection of courtesy, and she remarked afterwards that if her own neck had been in peril she could hardly have refused to answer any questions he asked her.

Once master of his facts, at first hand, Mr. Leopold called a hansom, and drove to the shady retreat where his client was languishing in durance. Laura was with her husband when the lawyer came. She started up, pale and agitated, at his entrance, looking to him as the one man who was to save an innocent life.

'Good news,' said Leopold cheerily.

'Thank God,' murmured Laura, sinking back in her chair.

'We have found the murderer.'

'Found him,' cried Treverton; 'how, and where?'

'When I say found, I go rather too far,' said Leopold, 'but we know who he is. It's the man I suspected from the beginning—your second-floor lodger, Desrolles.'

Laura gave a cry of horror.

'You need not pity him, Mrs. Treverton,' said Mr. Leopold.

'He's a thorough-paced scoundrel. I happen to be acquainted with circumstances that throw a light upon his motive for the murder. He is quite unworthy of your compassion. I doubt if hanging—in the gentlemanly way in which it's done now—is bad enough for him. He ought to have lived in a less refined age, when he would have had his last moments enlivened by the yells and profanity of the populace.'

'How do you know that Desrolles was the murderer?' asked John Treverton.

Mr. Leopold told his client the gist of Mrs. Evitt's statement.

Treverton listened in silence. Laura sat quietly by, white as marble.

'The young surgeon in Cibber Street tells me that Mrs. Evitt will be well enough to appear in court next Tuesday,' said Mr. Leopold, in conclusion. 'If she isn't, we must ask for another adjournment. I think you may consider that you're out of it. It would be impossible for any magistrate to commit you, in the face of this woman's evidence; but Desrolles will have to be found all the same, and the sooner he's found the better. I shall set the police on his track immediately. Don't look so frightened, Mrs. Treverton. The only way to prove your husband's innocence is to show that some one else is guilty. I wish you could help me with any information that would put the police on the right scent,' he added, turning to John Treverton.

'I told you yesterday that I could not help you.'

'Yes, but your manner gave me the idea that you were keeping back something. That you could—an' if you would—have given me a clue.'

'Your imagination—despite the grim realism of police courts—must be very lively.'

'Ah, I see,' said Mr. Leopold, 'you mean to stick to your text. Well, this fellow must be found somehow, whether you like it or not. Your good name depends upon our getting somebody convicted.'

'Yes,' cried Laura, starting up and speaking with sudden energy, 'my husband's good name must be saved at any cost. What is this man to us, John, that we should spare him? What is he to me that his safety should be considered before yours?'

'Hush, dearest!' said John soothingly. 'Let Mr. Leopold and me manage this business between us.'

CHAPTER XLII.

THE UNDERTAKER'S EVIDENCE.

'My father,' cried Laura, when Mr. Leopold had taken his departure, and she and her husband were left alone, 'my father guilty of this cruel murder! A crime of the vilest kind, without a shadow of excuse. And to think that this man's blood flows in my veins, that your wife is the daughter of a murderer. Oh, John, it is too terrible! You must hate me. You must shrink from me with loathing.'

'Dear love, if you had descended from a long line of criminals, you would still be to me what you have been from the first hour I knew you, the purest, the dearest, the loveliest, the best of women. But as to this scoundrel Desrolles, who imposed on your youth and inexperience—who stole into your benefactor's gardens like a thief, seeking only gain—who extorted from your generous young heart a pity he did not deserve, and robbed you of your money,—I no more believe that he is your father than that he is mine. While his claim upon you meant no more than an annuity which it cost us no sacrifice to give, I was too careless to trouble myself about his credentials. But now that he stands revealed as the murderer of that unfortunate woman, it is our business to explode his specious tale. Will you help to do this, Laura? I can do nothing but advise, while I am tied hand and foot in this wretched place.'

'I will do anything, dearest, anything to prove that this hateful man is not the father I lived with when I was a little child. Only tell me what I ought to do.'

'The first thing to be done is to go down to Chiswick, and make inquiries there. Do you think you could find the house in which you lived, supposing that it is still standing?'

'I think I could. It was in a very dull, out-of-the-way place. I can just remember that. It was called Ivy Cottage, and it was in a lane where there was never anything to be seen from the windows.'

'Very well, darling, what you have to do is to go down to Chiswick with Sampson—we can afford to trust him with all our secrets, for he's as true as steel—see if you can find the particular Ivy Cottage we want,—I dare say there are half-a-dozen Ivy Cottages in Chiswick, all looking out upon nothing particular,—and then discover all you can about your father's residence in that house, and how and when he quitted it.'

'I will go to-day, John. Why should Mr. Sampson go with me? I am not afraid of going alone.'

'No, dear, I could not bear that. You must have our good Sampson to take care of you. He is as sharp as a needle, and, in a country where he is not tongue-tied, will be very useful. He will be here in a few minutes, and then you and he can start for Chiswick as soon as you like.'

Half-an-hour later, Laura and Mr. Sampson were seated in a railway carriage on their way to Chiswick; and in less than an hour from the time she left Clerkenwell, Laura was looking wonderingly at the lanes with which her infancy had been familiar.

There had been great changes, and she wandered about for a long time, unable to recognise a single feature in the scene, except always the river, which looked at her through the gray mistiness of a winter afternoon, like an old friend. Terraces had been built; villas of startling newness stared her in the face in every direction. Where erst had been a rustic lane there was all the teeming life of a factory.

'Surely this cannot be Chiswick!' exclaimed Laura.

Yes, there was the good old church, looking sober, gray, and rustic as of old; and here was the village, but little changed. Laura and her companion rambled on till they left the new terraces and stuccoed villas behind them, and came at last to a bit of the ancient world, quiet, dull, lonely, as if it had been left forgotten on the bank of the swift-rolling river of Time.

'It must have been hereabouts we lived,' said Laura.

It was a very dreary lane. There were half-a-dozen scattered houses, some of which had a blind look, presenting a blank wall, pierced by an odd window and a door, to the passer-by. These were the more aristocratic habitations, and had garden fronts looking the other way. A little further on the explorers came to a square, uncompromising-looking cottage, with a green door, a bright brass knocker, and five prim windows looking into the lane. It was a cottage that must have looked exactly the same a hundred and twenty years ago, when Hogarth was living and working hard by.

'That is the house we lived in!' cried Laura. 'Yes, I am sure of it. I remember those hard-looking windows, staring straight into the lane. I used to envy the children in the house further on, because they had a garden—only a little bit of garden—but just enough for flowers to grow in. There was only a stone yard, with a pump in it, at the back of our house, and not a single flower.'

'Had you the whole house, do you think?' asked Sampson.

'I am sure we had not, because we were so afraid to take liberties in it. I remember my poor mother often telling me to be very quiet, because Miss Somebody—I haven't the faintest recollection of her name—was very particular. I was dreadfully afraid of Miss Somebody. She was tall, and straight, and old, and she always wore a black gown and a black cap. I would not for the world have done anything to offend her. She kept the house very clean—too clean, I've heard my father say, for she was always about the stairs and passages, on her knees, with a pail beside her. I have often narrowly escaped tumbling into that pail.'

'I wonder if she's alive still,' said Sampson; 'the house looks as if it was in the occupation of a maiden lady. I dare say my sister's house will look like that, when she has set up housekeeping on her own account.'

He lifted the brass knocker and gave a loudish knock. The door was opened almost immediately by a puffy widow, who had a chubby boy of three or four years old clinging to her skirts. The widow was very civil, and willing to answer any questions that might be asked her, but she could not give them the information they wanted. She begged them to come into her parlour, and she was profuse in her offer of chairs; but she was not the Miss Somebody whom Laura remembered.

That stern damsel, whose name was Fry, after occupying Ivy Cottage with honour to herself and credit to the parish for eight-and-thirty years, had been called to her forefathers just one little year ago, and was taking her rest, after an industrious career, in the quiet old churchyard where the great English painter and satirist lies. She had left no record of a long line of lodgers, and the amiable widow who had taken Ivy Cottage immediately after Miss Fry's death was not even furnished with any traditions about the people who had lived and died in the rooms now hers. She could only reiterate that Miss Fry had been a most respectable lady, that she had paid her way, and left the cottage in good repair, and she hoped that she, Mrs. Pew, would continue to deserve those favours which the public had lavishly bestowed upon her predecessor. If the lady and gentleman should hear of any party wanting quiet lodgings in a rural neighbourhood, within a quarter of an hour's walk of the station, Mrs. Pew would consider it a great kindness if they would name her to the party in question. She would have a parlour, with bedroom over, vacant on the following Saturday.

Sampson promised to carry the fact in his mind. Laura thanked the widow for her civility, and gave the chubby boy half-a-crown, a gift which was much appreciated by the mother, who impounded it directly the door was shut.

'Johnny shall have twopence to go and buy brandy snaps, he shall,' cried the matron, when her boy set up a howl at this blatant theft; and the prospect of that immediate and sensual gratification pacified the child.

'Failure number one,' said Sampson, when they were out in the lane. 'What are we to do next?'

Laura had not the least idea. She felt how helpless she would have been without the kindly little solicitor; and how wise it had been of her husband to insist upon Mr. Sampson's companionship.

'We are not going to be flummoxed—excuse the vulgarity of the expression—quite so easily,' said Sampson. 'Everybody can't be dead within the last seventeen years. Why, seventeen years is nothing to a middle-aged man. He scarcely feels himself any older for the lapse of seventeen years; there are a few gray hairs in his whiskers, perhaps, and his waistcoats are a trifle bigger round the waist, and that's all. There must be somebody in this place who can remember your father. Let me think it out a bit. We want to know if a certain gentleman who was supposed by old Mr. Treverton to have died here, did really die, or whether he recovered and left the place, as a certain party asserts. All the probabilities are in favour of the one fact; and we have only the word of a very doubtful character for the other. Let me see, now, Mrs. Treverton, where shall we make our next inquiry? At the doctor's? Well, you see, there are a dozen doctors in such a place as this, I dare say. At the undertaker's? Yes, that's it. Undertakers are long-lived men. We'll look in upon the oldest established undertaker in the village. If your father died in this place, somebody must have buried him, and the record of his funeral will be in the undertaker's books. But before I begin this business, which may be rather tedious, I should like to put you into a train, and send you back to London, Mrs. Treverton. A cab will take you from the station to your lodgings. You are looking pale and tired.'

'No, no,' said Laura eagerly, 'I am not tired. I had much rather stay. Don't think of me. I have no sense of fatigue.'

Sampson shook his head dubiously, but gave way. They went to the village, and after making sundry inquiries at the post-office, Mr. Sampson and his companion repaired to a quiet, old-fashioned looking shop, in whose dingy window appeared the symbols of the gloomy trade conducted within.

Here they found an old man, who emerged from a workshop in

the rear, bringing with him the aromatic odour of elm shavings.

'Come,' said Sampson cheerily, 'you're old enough to remember seventeen years ago. You look like an old inhabitant.'

'I can remember sixty years ago as well as I can remember yesterday,' answered the man, 'and I shall have lived in this house sixty-nine years come July.'

'You're the man for us,' said Sampson. 'I want you to look up your books for the year 1856, and tell me if you buried Mr. Malcolm, of Ivy Cottage, Markham Lane. You buried Mrs. Malcolm first, you know, and the husband soon followed her. It was a very quiet funeral.'

The undertaker scratched his head thoughtfully, and seemed to retire into the shadow-land of departed years. He ruminated for some minutes.

'I can find out all about it in my ledger,' he said, 'but I've a pretty good memory. I don't like to feel dependent upon books. Ivy Cottage? That was Miss Fry's house. I buried her a year ago. A very pretty funeral, everything suitable, and in harmony with the old lady's character. Some of our oldest tradespeople followed. It was quite a creditable thing.'

Sampson waited hopefully while the old man pondered upon past triumphs in the undertaking line.

'Let me see, now,' he said musingly. 'Ivy Cottage. I've done a good bit of business for Ivy Cottage within the last thirty years. I've buried—there—I should say a round dozen of Miss Fry's tenants. They was mostly elderly folks, with small annuities, who came to Chiswick to finish up their lives; as a quiet old-fashioned place, you see, where they was in nobody's way. First and last I should say I've turned out a round dozen from Ivy Cottage. It was a satisfaction to do things nicely for Miss Fry herself, at the wind up. She'd been a good friend to me, and she wasn't like the doctors, you know. I couldn't offer her a commission. Malcolm! Malcolm, husband and wife, I ought to remember that! Yes, I've got it! a sweet young lady, seven-and-twenty at the most, and the husband drooped and died soon afterwards. I remember. She had a very plain funeral, poor dear, for there didn't seem to be much money, and the husband was the only mourner. We buried him in rather superior style, I recollect; for an old friend had turned up at the last, and there was enough money to pay all the little debts and do things very nicely, in a quiet way, for the poor gentleman. There were only two mourners in his case, the doctor and an elderly lady from London, who followed in her own carriage. I remember the lady, because she called upon me directly after the funeral, and asked me if I was paid, or sure of being paid, as the deceased was her nephew, and she would be willing to perform this last act of kindness for him. I thought it a very graceful thing for the lady to do.'

'Did she give you her address?' asked Sampson.

'I've a notion that she left her card, and that I copied the address into my book. It would be a likely thing for me to do, for I'm very methodical in my ways; and with a party of that age there's always an interest. She might come to want me herself soon, and might bear it in mind on her death-bed. Well, now I've called upon my memory, I'll look at my ledger.'

He went to a cupboard in a corner of the shop, and took down a volume from a row of tall, narrow books, a series which comprised 'the story of his life from year to year.'

'Yes,' he said, after turning over a good many leaves, 'here it is. Mrs. Malcolm, pine, covered black cloth, black nails,——'

'That'll do,' interrupted Sampson, seeing Laura's distressed look at these details; 'now we want Mr. Malcolm.'

'Here he is, three months later. Stephen Malcolm, Esq., polished oak, brass handles,—a very superior article, I remember.'

'There can be no mistake, I suppose, in an entry of that kind,' asked Sampson.

'Mistake!' cried the undertaker, with an offended air. 'If you can find a false entry in my books, I'll forfeit five per cent. upon ten years' profits.'

'There can be no doubt, then, that Mr. Stephen Malcolm died at Ivy Cottage, and that you conducted his funeral?'

'Not the least doubt.'

'Very well. If you will get me a certified copy of the entry of his death in the parish register, I shall be happy to recompense you for your trouble. The document is required for a little bit of law business. Is the doctor who attended Mr. Malcolm still living?'

'No. It was old Dr. Dewsnipp. He's dead. But young Dewsnipp is alive, and in practice here. He can give you any information you want, I dare say.'

'Thanks. I think if you get me the copy of the register, that will be sufficient. Oh, by the way, you may as well find the old lady's address.'

'Ah, to be sure. As you are interested in the family, you may like to have it; though I dare say the old lady has gone to her long home before now. Some London firm had the job, no doubt. London firms are so pushing, and they contrive to stand so well with the medical profession.'

The address was found—Mrs. Malcolm, 97, Russell Square—and copied by Mr. Sampson, who thanked the old man for his courtesy, and gave him his card, with the Midland Hotel address added in pencil. The short winter day was now closing in, and Sampson felt anxious to get Mrs. Treverton home.

'I might have gone to the parish register in the first instance,' he said, when they had left the undertaker's, 'but I thought we should get more information out of an old inhabitant, and so we have, for we've heard of this old lady in Russell Square.'

'Yes, I remember spending a week at her house,' said Laura. 'How long ago it all seems! Like the memory of another life.'

'Lor', yes,' said Sampson; 'I remember when I was a little chap, at Dr. Prossford's grammar school, playing chuck-farthing. I've often looked back and wondered to think that little chap, in a tight jacket and short trousers, was an early edition of me.'

'You think the later editions have been improvements on that,' said Laura, smiling.

She was able to smile now. A heavy load had been suddenly lifted from her mind. What infinite relief it was to know that her father had never been the pitiful trickster—the crawling pensioner upon a woman's bounty—that she had been taught to think him. Her heart was full of gratitude to heaven for this discovery—so easily made, and yet of such immeasurable value.

'Who can that man be?' she asked herself. 'He must have been a friend of my father's, in close companionship with him, or he would hardly have become possessed of my mother's miniature, and of those letters and papers.'

She determined to go without delay to the house in Russell Square, in the hope—at best but a faint hope—of finding the old lady in black satin still among the living, and not represented by an entry in the ledger of some West-end undertaking firm, or by a number in the dismal catalogue of a suburban cemetery.

CHAPTER XLIII.

AN OLD LADY'S DIARY.

On the following afternoon Laura drove straight from the House of Detention to Russell Square. Her interview with her husband had been full of comfort. Mr. Leopold had been with his client, and Mr. Leopold was in excellent spirits. He had no doubt as to the issue of his case, even without Desrolles; and the detectives had very little doubt of finding Desrolles.

'A man of that age and of those habits doesn't go far,' said the lawyer, speaking of this human entity with as much assurance as if he were stating a mathematical truth.

Laura got out of her cab before one of the dullest-looking houses in the big, handsome old square—a house brightened by no modern embellishment in the way of Venetian blind or encaustic flower-box, but kept with a scrupulous care. Not a speck upon the window panes, not a spot upon the snow-white steps, the varnish of the door as fresh as if it had been laid on yesterday.

The door was opened by an old man-servant in plain clothes. Laura grew hopeful at the sight of him. He looked like a man who had lived fifty years in one service—the kind of man who begins as a knife-boy, and either stultifies a spotless career by going to America with the plate, or ends as a pious annuitant, in the odour of sanctity.

'Does Mrs. Malcolm still live here?' asked Laura.

'Yes, ma'am.'

'Is she at home?'

'I will inquire, ma'am, if you will be kind enough to give me your card,' replied the man, as much as to say that his mistress was a lady whose leisure was not to be irreverently disturbed. She was to be at home or not at home, as it pleased her sovereign will, and according to the quality and claims of her visitor.

Laura wrote upon one of her cards, 'Stephen Malcolm's daughter, Laura,' while the ancient butler produced a solid old George the Second salver whereon to convey the card with due reverence to his mistress.

The address upon the card looked respectable, and so did Laura, and upon the strength of these appearances the butler ventured to show the stranger into the dining-room, where the furniture was of the good old brobdingnagian stamp, and there was nothing portable except the fire-irons. Here Laura waited in a charnel-house atmosphere, while Mrs. Malcolm called up the dim shadows of the past, and finally came to the determination that she would hold parley with this young person who claimed to be of her kindred.

The butler came back after a chilly interval, and ushered Mrs. Treverton up the broad, ghastly-looking staircase, where drab walls looked down upon a stone-coloured carpet, to the big, bare drawing-room, which had ever been one of the coldest memories of her childhood.

It was a long and lofty room, furnished with monumental rosewood. The cheffoniers were like tombs—the sofa suggested an altar—the centre table looked as massive as one of those Druidic *menhirs* which crop up here and there among the wilds of Dartmoor, or the sandy plains of Brittany. A pale-faced clock ticked solemnly on the white marble chimney-piece, three tall windows let in narrow streaks of pallid daylight, between voluminous drab curtains.

In this mausoleum-like chamber, beside a dull and miserly-looking fire, sat an old lady in black satin—the very same figure, the very same satin gown, Laura remembered years ago; or a gown so like that it appeared the same.

'Aunt,' said Laura, approaching timidly, and feeling as if she were a little child again, and doomed to solitary imprisonment in that awful room, 'have you forgotten me?'

The old lady in black satin held out her hand, a withered white hand clad in a black mitten, and adorned with old-fashioned rings.

'No, my dear,' she replied, without any indication of surprise, 'I never forget anyone or anything. My memory is good, and my sight and hearing are good. Providence has been very kind to me. Your card puzzled me at first, but when I came to think it over I soon understood who you were. Sit down, my dear. Jonam shall bring you a glass of sherry.'

The old lady rose and rang the bell.

'Please don't, aunt,' said Laura. 'I never take sherry. I don't want anything except to talk with you a little about my poor father.'

'Poor Stephen,' replied Mrs. Malcolm. 'Sadly imprudent, poor fellow. Nobody's enemy but his own. And so you are married, my dear? Never mind, Jonam, my niece will not take anything.' This to the butler. 'You were adopted by an old friend of your father's, I remember. I went to Chiswick the day after poor Stephen's death, and found that you had been taken away. I was very glad to know you were provided for; though of course I should have done what I could for you in the way of trying to get you into an institution, or something of that kind. I could never have had a child in this house. Children upset everything. I hope your father's friend has carried out his undertaking handsomely?'

'He was all goodness,' answered Laura. 'He was more than a father to me. But I lost him two years ago.'

'I hope he left you independent?'

'He made me independent by a deed of trust, when I first went to him. He settled six thousand pounds for my benefit.'

'Very handsome indeed. And pray whom have you married?'

'My benefactor's nephew, and the inheritor of his estate.'

'You have been a very lucky girl, Laura, and you ought to be thankful to God.'

'I hope I am thankful.'

'I have often noticed that the children of improvident fathers do better in life than those whose parents toil to make them independent. They are like the ravens—Providence takes care of them. Well, my dear, I congratulate you.'

'God has been very good to me, dear aunt, but I have had many troubles. I want you to tell me about my father. Did you see much of him in the last years of his life?'

'Not very much. He used to call upon me occasionally, and he used sometimes to bring your mother to spend the day with me. She was a sweet woman—you are like her in face and figure—and she and I used to get on very nicely together. She was not above taking advice.'

'Had my father many friends and acquaintances at that time?' asked Laura.

'Many friends! My dear, he was poor.'

'Do you know if he had any one particular friend? He could not have been quite alone in the world. I recollect there was a gentleman who used to come very often to the cottage at Chiswick. I cannot remember what he was like. I was seldom in the room when he was there. I remember only that my father and he were often together. I have a very strong reason for wishing to know all about that man.'

'I think I know whom you mean. I have heard your poor mother talk of him many a time. She used to tell me all her troubles, and I used to give her good advice. You say you want particularly to know about this person.'

'Most particularly, dear aunt,' said Laura eagerly.

'Then, my dear, my diary can tell you much better than I can. I am a woman of methodical habits, and ever since my husband's death, three-and-twenty years ago last August, I have made a point of keeping a record of the course of every day in my life. I dare say the book would seem very stupid to strangers. I hope nobody will publish it after I am dead. But it has been a great pleasure to me to look through the pages from time to time, and call up old days. It is almost like living over again. Kindly take my keys, Laura, and open the right-hand door of the cheffonier.'

Laura obeyed. The interior of the cheffonier was divided into shelves, and on the uppermost of these shelves were neatly arranged three-and-twenty small volumes, bound in morocco, and lettered Diary, with the date of each year. The parliamentary records at Strawberry Hill are not more carefully kept than the history of Mrs. Malcolm's life.

'Let me see,' she said. 'Your father died in the winter of '56; your poor mother a few months earlier. Bring me the volume for '56.'

Laura handed the book to the old lady, who gave a gentle little sigh as she opened it.

'Dear me, how neatly I wrote in '56,' she exclaimed. 'My handwriting has sadly degenerated since then. We get old, my dear; we grow old without knowing it.'

Laura thought that in that monumental drawing-room age might well creep on unawares. Life there must be a long hybernation.

'Let me see. I must find some of my conversations with your mother. "June 2. Read prayers. Breakfast. My rasher was cut too thick, and the frying was not up to cook's usual mark. Mem.: must speak to cook about the bacon. Read a leading article on indirect taxation in *Times*, and felt my store of knowledge increased. Saw cook. Decided on a lamb cutlet for lunch, and a slice of salmon and roast chicken for dinner. Sent for cook five minutes afterwards, and ordered sole instead of salmon. I had salmon the day before yesterday." Dear me, I don't see your poor mother's name in the first week of June,' said the old lady, turning over the leaves. 'Here it comes, a little later, on the fifteenth. Now you shall hear your mother's own words, faithfully recorded on the day she spoke them. And yet there are people who would ridicule a lonely old woman for keeping a diary,' added Mrs. Malcolm, with mild self-approval.

'I feel very grateful to you for having kept one,' said Laura.

'June 15. Stephen brought his wife to lunch with me, by appointment. I ordered a nice little luncheon; filleted sole, cutlets, a duckling, peas, new potatoes, cherry tart, and a custard. The poor woman does not often enjoy a good dinner, and no doubt my luncheon would be her dinner. But my thoughtfulness was thrown away. The poor thing was looking pale and worn when she came, and she hardly ate a morsel. Even the duckling did not tempt her, though she owned it was the first she had seen this year. After luncheon Stephen went to the City, to keep an appointment, as he told us, and his wife and I spent a quiet hour in my drawing-room. We had a long talk, which turned, as usual, on her domestic troubles. She calls this Captain Desmond her husband's evil genius, and says he is a blight upon her life. He is not an old friend of Stephen's, so there is no excuse for that foolish fellow's infatuation. They met him first at Boulogne, last year; and from that time to this he and Stephen have been inseparable. Poor Laura declares that this Desmond belongs to a horrid, gambling, drinking set, and that he is the cause of Stephen's ruin. "We were poor when we first went to Boulogne," she said, with tears in her eyes, poor child, "but we could just manage to live respectably, and for the first year we were very happy. But from the day my husband made the acquaintance of Captain Desmond things began to go badly. Stephen resumed his old habits of billiard-playing, cards, and late hours. He had grown fond of his home, and reconciled to a quiet, domestic life. Darling Laura's pretty ways and sweet little talk amused and interested him. But after Captain Desmond came upon the scene Stephen seldom spent an evening at home. I know that it is wicked to hate people," the poor thing said, in her simple way, "but I cannot help hating this bad man."'

'Poor mother!' sighed Laura, touched to the heart by this picture of domestic misery.

'I asked her if she knew who and what Captain Desmond was. She could only tell me that when Stephen made his acquaintance he was living at a boarding-house at Boulogne, and had been living there for some months. He had spent a considerable part of his life abroad. He had nobody belonging to him, and he seemed to belong to nobody; though he often boasted vaguely of grand connections. To poor Laura's mind he was nothing more or less than an adventurer. "He flatters my husband," she said, "and he tries to flatter me. He is very often at Chiswick, and whenever he comes he takes my husband back to London with him, and then I see no more of Stephen till the next day, or perhaps not for two or three days after. He has what his friend calls a shake-down at Captain Desmond's lodgings in May's Buildings, St. Martin's Lane."'

'Aunt,' exclaimed Laura eagerly, 'will you let me copy that address? It might be of use to me, if I should have to trace the past life of this man.'

She wrote the address in a little memorandum book contained in her purse.

'My dear, why should you trouble yourself about Captain Desmond,' said the old lady. 'Whatever harm he did your poor father is past and done with. Nothing can alter or mend it now.'

'No, aunt, but as long as this man lives he will go on doing harm. He will go from small crimes to great ones. It is his nature. Please go on with the diary, dear aunt. You can have no idea how valuable this information is to me.'

'I have always felt I was doing a useful act in keeping a diary, my dear. I am not surprised to find this humble record of inestimable value,' said the old lady, who was bursting with gratified vanity. 'Where would history be if people in easy circumstances, and with plenty of leisure, did not keep diaries? I do not think there is any more about Captain Desmond. No; your mother tells me about her own health. She is feeling very low and ill. She fears she will not live many years, and then what is to become of poor little Laura?'

'Did you ever go to Chiswick, aunt?'

'Never, till after your poor father's death. I attended his funeral.'

'Was Captain Desmond present?'

'No; but he was with your father up till the last hour of his life. I heard that from the landlady. He helped to nurse him.'

'I thank you, aunt, with all my heart, for what you have told me. I will come and see you again in a few days, if I may.'

'Do, my dear, and bring your husband.' Laura shivered. 'I should like to make his acquaintance. If you will mention the day a little beforehand, I should be pleased for you to take your luncheon with me. I have the cook who roasted that duckling for your poor mother still with me.'

'I shall be pleased to come, aunt. We are in London upon very serious business, but I hope it will soon be ended, and when it is over I will tell you all about it.'

'Do, my dear, I am very glad to see you again. I dare say you remember spending a week with me when your mother died. I think you enjoyed yourself. This house must have been such a change for you after that poor little place at Chiswick, and there is a good deal to amuse a child in this room,' said Mrs. Malcolm, glancing admiringly from the monumental clock on the mantelpiece to the group of feather flowers and stuffed birds on the sepulchral cheffonier.

Laura smiled faintly, remembering those interminable days in that cheerless chamber, compared with which a dirty lane where she could have made mud pies would have been Elysium.

'I've no doubt you were extremely kind to me, aunt,' she said gently, 'but I was very small and very shy.'

'And you did not like going to bed in the dark; which shows that you have been foolishly brought up. Your mother was a sweet woman, but wanting in strength of mind.'

CHAPTER XLIV.

THREE WITNESSES.

In the forenoon of the following Tuesday John Treverton again appeared before the magistrate, at the Police-court in Bow Street.

The same witnesses were present who had been examined on the previous occasion. Two medical men gave their evidence as to the dagger, which had been sent to them for examination. One declared that the blade bore unmistakable traces of blood stains, and gave it as his opinion that steel once so sullied never lost the stain. The other stated that a steel blade wiped quickly while the blood upon it was wet would carry no such ineffaceable mark, and that the tarnished appearance of the dagger was referable only to time and atmosphere.

The inquiry dragged itself haltingly towards a futile close, when just as it seemed about to conclude, an elderly woman, wrapped in a thick gray shawl, and a cat-skin sable victorine, and further muffled with a Shetland veil tied over a close black bonnet, came forward, escorted by George Gerard, and volunteered her evidence. This was Mrs. Evitt, who was just well enough to crawl from a cab to the witness-box, leaning on the surgeon's arm.

'Oh,' said the magistrate, when Jane Sophia Evitt had been duly sworn, 'you are the landlady, are you? Why were you not here last Tuesday? You were subpœnaed, I believe.'

'Yes, your worship, though I was not in a state of health to bear it.'

'Oh, you were too ill to appear, were you? Well, what have you to say about the prisoner?'

'Please, your worship, he oughtn't to be a prisoner. I ought to have up and spoke the truth sooner—it has preyed upon me awful that I didn't do it—a sweet young wife, too.'

'What is the meaning of this rambling?' asked the magistrate, indignantly. 'Is the poor creature delirious?'

'No, sir, I ain't more delirious than your worship. My body has been all of a shiver—hot fits and cold fits—but thank God my mind has kep' clear.'

'You really must not tell us about your ailments. What do you know of the prisoner?'

'Only that he's as innocent as that lamb, yonder,' said Mrs. Evitt, pointing to a baby in the arms of a forlorn looking drab, from the adjacent rookeries of St. Giles's, which had just set up a shrill squall, and was in process of being evicted by a policeman. 'He had no more to do with it than that blessed infant that's just been carried out of court.'

And then, continually beginning to wander, and being continually pulled up sharp by the magistrate, Mrs. Evitt told her ghastly story of the handful of iron-grey hair, and the blood-stained dressing-gown, hidden in the closet behind the bed in her two-pair back.

'Which is there to this day, as the police may find for themselves if they like to go and look,' concluded Mrs. Evitt.

'They will take care to do that,' said the magistrate. 'Where is this Desrolles?'

'He is being looked for, sir,' replied Mr. Leopold. 'If your worship will permit, there are two gentlemen in court who are in possession of facts that have a material bearing on this case.'

'Let them be sworn.'

The first of these two voluntary witnesses was Mr. Joseph Lemuel, the well-known stockbroker and millionaire, on whose appearance in the witness-box there was a sudden hush in the court, and profound attention from every one, as at the presence of greatness.

Even that tag-rag and bob-tail from adjacent St. Giles's had heard of Joseph Lemuel. His name had been in the penny newspapers. He was a man who was supposed to make a million of money every time there was war in Europe, and to lose a million whenever there was a financial crisis.

'Do you know anything of this affair, Mr. Lemuel?' the magistrate asked, with an off-hand friendliness, when the witness had been sworn, as much as to say, 'It is really uncommonly good of you to trouble yourself about a fellow-creature's fate; and I want to make the thing as light and as pleasant as I can, for your sake.'

'I think I may be able to afford a clue to the motive of the murderer,' said Mr. Lemuel, who seemed more moved than the occasion warranted. 'I presented the unhappy lady with a necklace about a week before her death; and I have reason to fear that this gift may have been the cause of her terrible death!'

'Was the necklace of such value as to tempt a murderer?'

'It was not. But, to an uneducated eye, it appeared of great value. It was a gift which I offered to a lady whose talents I—as one of the outside public—enthusiastically admired.'

377

'Naturally,' assented the magistrate, as much as to say, 'Don't be frightened, my dear sir. I am not going to ask you any awkward questions.'

'It was a necklace I had bought in Paris, in the Palais Royal, a short time before. It was made by a man who had a speciality for these things. It would perhaps have deceived any eye except that of a diamond merchant, and might indeed have deceived a dealer, if he had judged by the eye alone. I gave fifty pounds for the necklace. It was exquisitely set, and really a work of art.'

'Did Madame Chicot suppose the stones were real?'

'I don't know, I told her nothing about the necklace. It seemed to me a suitable offering to an actress, to whom appearances are as important as realities.'

'Madame Chicot made no inquiry as to the intrinsic value of your gift?'

'None. It was offered and accepted in silence.'

'Is that all you have to say?'

'That is all.'

The next witness was Mr. Mosheh, the diamond merchant. His evidence consisted of a straight and succinct narrative of his interview with the stranger who offered for sale a set of imitation diamonds under the impression that he was offering real stones of great value.

'These crystals were some of them equal in size to the largest diamonds known in the trade,' said Mr. Mosheh. 'They would have been a tremendous haul for a thief, if they had been real.'

He gave the date of the man's visit, which was within a week of La Chicot's murder.

'Could you identify the man who called upon you with those stones?' asked the magistrate.

'I believe I could.'

'Was he the prisoner?'

'Certainly not. He was a man of between fifty and sixty years of age.'

'Has anybody a photograph of Desrolles?'

Yes, there was a photograph in court. Mrs. Evitt had furnished the police with two, which Desrolles had given her upon different occasions. One was in court, the other had been taken by the detective who was looking for Desrolles.

The photograph was shown to the witness.

'Yes,' said Mr. Mosheh, 'I believe that to be the same face. The man who came to me wore a large gray beard. All the lower part of the face was hidden, and the beard made him look older. I conclude that it was a false beard. But to the best of my belief that is the same man. The upper part of the face is very striking. I don't think I could be deceived in it.'

After this evidence Mr. Leopold urged that there was no ground for any longer detaining John Treverton. The magistrate, after some little discussion, agreed to this, and the prisoner was discharged.

CHAPTER XLV.

THE HUNT FOR DESROLLES.

When Desrolles left the village under the shadow of Dartmoor, after bargaining for a handsome annuity, he meant to enter upon a new and delightful stage of existence. The world was changed for him. Assured of a handsome income, he felt as it were, new born. He would rove, butterfly-like, from city to city. He would sip of one sweet, and then fly to the rest. All that was fairest upon earth was at his command. The loveliest spots in southern Europe should be the cradle of his declining years. He would leave off brandy, and live decently. Henceforward he would have a full purse, and freedom from care; for what tortures can conscience have in reserve for a man who has set it at nought all his life?

Mr. Desrolles considered Paris as the first stage in that voyage of pleasure which he had planned for himself; but once having entered Paris, with money in his pocket, and a sense of independence, all his schemes became as nothing when weighed against the fascinations of that wonderful city. He had spent some of his most reckless years in Paris; he knew the city by heart, with all her charms, with all her vices, all those qualities which she possesses in common with the courtesans who spring from her soil. Paris for Desrolles in his decline had all the delights she had offered him in his youth. She stretched out her many arms to detain and hold him like an octopus. Her life of the streets and the café, her dancing places—where the dancing began at eleven at night and ended only at some unearthly hour of the morning—her singing places, where bare-necked brazen women sat smiling in the glare of the gas—her wine shops at every corner—her billiard-rooms over every café—all these were charms which for Desrolles proved irresistible. There was an all-pervading note of dissipation in the place that delighted him. In London he had felt himself a scamp. In Paris he fancied himself little worse than his fellow men. There were differences perhaps; but only differences of degree.

Desrolles had come to Paris with the intention of curing himself of brandy. He carried out this resolve with laudable firmness. He cured himself of brandy by taking to absinthe. He entered Paris with

380

ninety-five pounds in his pocket, and a promise of a thousand a year. With the future so amply provided for, he was naturally somewhat reckless as to his expenditure in the present. He was not a man who cared for pomp or show. He had out-lived his taste for the refinements of life. With his purse full of money he had no inclination to put up at Meurice's or the Bristol. The elegant luxury of those establishments would have seemed *fade* to his perverted taste, just as brandy without the addition of cayenne pepper used to seem tasteless to a luckless English marquis, who burned life's brief candle at both ends, and brought it to speedy extinction.

Desrolles, like the hare, wound back to his old form. Years ago he had lodged in the students' quarter, and drunk at the students' cafés, and lost his money among those profane young reprobates from whom were to issue the future senators, doctors, and lawyers of France. The lodging had been dirty and disreputable twenty years ago. It was so much the more dirty and no less disreputable after the lapse of twenty years. But Desrolles was grateful to Providence and the Prefect of the Seine for having left his old quarters standing.

The house, beneath whose weather-worn roof he had spent such wild nights of old, had been spared from demolition by accident only, and was soon to be numbered with the things of the past. Its doom was fixed, it existed only on sufferance, pending the complete reconstruction of the quarter. A mighty Boulevard, marching on with progress as relentless as Juggernaut's car, had cut the narrow, dingy old street across, at right angles, letting daylight in upon all its shabbiness, its teeming life, its contented poverty, its secret crime, squalid miseries, and sordid vices.

The house in which Desrolles had lived had but just escaped demolition. It stood at the corner of the broad, new Boulevard, where mighty stone palaces were being raised upon the ashes of departed hovels. Its next door neighbour had been razed to the ground, and the gaudy papers that had lined the vanished rooms were revealed to the open day, showing how, stage by stage, the rooms had waxed shabbier, lower, smaller, till on the sixth story they had dwindled to mere pigeon holes. The ragged paper rotted on the wall; black patches showed where the fire-places had stood; and a great black column marked the course of a demolished chimney-stack. This outside wall had been shored up, but, even thus supported, the tall, narrow, corner house, contemplated from the street below, had an insecure look.

Desrolles was delighted to find his ancient den still standing. How well he remembered the little wine-shop on the ground floor, the bright-coloured bottles in the windows, the odour of brandy within, the blouses sitting on the benches against the wall, squabbling loudly over dominoes, or playing *écarte* with the limpest and smallest of cards.

He inquired in the wine-shop if there was *une chambre de garçon*—a bachelor's room—to be had upstairs.

'There is always room for a bachelor,' answered the buxom female behind the counter. 'Yes, there is a pretty little room on the fifth story, all that there is of the most commodious, *où, monsieur aurait toutes ses aises.*'

Desrolles shrugged his shoulders dubiously.

'The fifth story,' he exclaimed. 'Do you think my legs are as young as they were twenty years ago?'

'Monsieur looks full of youth and activity,' said the woman.

'Does La Veuve Chomard still keep the house?'

Alas, no. The widow Chomard had departed some nine years ago to the narrowest of houses in the cemetery of Mount Parnassus. The present proprietor was a gentleman in the commerce of wines, and also the proprietor of the shop.

That made nothing, Desrolles told the woman. All he wanted was a comfortable room on the first or second floor.

Unhappily the *chambrette de garçon* on the fifth stage was the only unoccupied room in the house, and after some hesitation Desrolles followed an ancient female of the portress species up the dirty old staircase, and into the chambrette.

'That gives upon the new boulevard,' said the portress, opening a small window. '*C'est crânement gai.* It is awfully lively!'

Desrolles looked down upon the broad new street, with its omnibuses, and waggons, and builders' trollies, circulating up and down—its monstrous scaffolding, and lofty ladders, and workmen dangling between earth and sky, with an appearance of being in immediate peril of death.

The room was small, but to Desrolles' eye it looked snug. There were comfortable stuff curtains to the mahogany bedstead, curtains to the window, a carpet on the red-tiled floor, a hearth on which a wood fire might burn cheerily, a cupboard for firewood, and a bureau with a lock and key, in which a man might put away a bottle or two for occasional use.

'It's an infernal way up,' he said. 'A man might as well live on the top of the gate of St. Denis. But I must make it serve. I am a staunch Conservative. I like old quarters.'

Of old the house had been free and easy in its habits. A lodger could come in at any hour he liked with his pass-key. Desrolles made an inquiry or two of the portress as to the present rule. He found that the old order still obtained. The present proprietor was *un bon enfant*. He asked nothing of his lodgers, but that they should pay him his rent, and not embroil themselves with the police.

Desrolles flung down the small valise which contained all his worldly gear, paid the portress a month's rent in advance, and went out to enjoy his Paris. That enchantress had him in her clutch already. He made up his mind by this time that he would defer his journey southward for a few weeks; perhaps until after the procession of the *Bœuf Gras* had delighted the lively inhabitants of the liveliest city in the world.

He went back to his old haunts, loved twenty years ago, and always remembered with fondness. He found many changes, but the atmosphere was still the same. Absinthe was the one great novelty. That murderous stimulant had not attained a universal popularity at the beginning of the Second Empire. Desrolles took to absinthe as an infant takes to the gracious fountain heaven has provided for its sustenance. He renounced brandy in favour of the less familiar poison. He found plenty of new companions in his old haunts. They were not the same men, but they had the same habits, the same vices; and Desrolles' idea of a friend was a bundle of sympathetic wickedness. He found men to gamble with and drink with, men whose tongues were as foul as his own, and who looked at life in this world and the next from the same standpoint.

His brutal nature sank even to a lower depth of brutality in such congenial company. Money gave him a temporary omnipotence. He was spending it with royal recklessness, believing himself secure against all future evils, when one morning chance flung an English newspaper in his way, and he read the report of John Treverton's first appearance at the Bow Street Police-court.

The paper was more than a week old. The adjourned inquiry must have been held a day or two ago. Desrolles sat staring at the page in a half stupid wonderment, his brain bemused with absinthe, trying to consider what effect this arrest of John Treverton might exercise upon his own fortunes.

There was no mention of his own name in the report. So far he was entirely ignored. So far he felt himself safe.

Yet there was no knowing what might happen. An investigation of this kind once commenced, might extend its ramifications in the widest directions.

'It is a pity,' Desrolles said to himself. 'The business was so comfortably settled. It must be the parson's son, that young coxcomb

I saw in Devonshire, who has set the thing moving again.'

His life in Paris suited him, it was indeed the only kind of life he cared for; yet so much was he disturbed by the idea of possible revelations to which this new inquiry might lead, that he began to consider the prudence of going further afield.

'America is the place,' he said to himself. 'Some sea-coast city in South America would suit me down to the ground. But that kind of life would only be comfortable with an assured income; and how am I to feel sure of my income if I leave Europe? As to Treverton being in trouble—I can afford to take that coolly. They can't hang him. The evidence against him is not strong enough to hang a mongrel dog. No, unless other names are brought up, the thing must blow over. But if I put the high seas between Mr. and Mrs. Treverton and me, how can I be sure of my pension? They may snap their fingers at me when I am on the other side of the herring-pond.'

This was a serious consideration, yet Desrolles had a lurking conviction that it would be wise for him to get to America as soon as he could. Paris might suit him admirably, but Paris was unpleasantly near London. The police of the two cities were doubtless in frequent communication.

He went to a shipping office, and got the time bill of the American steamers that were to sail from Havre during the next six weeks. He carried this document about with him for two or three days, and studied it frequently in his quiet moments. He knew the names of the steamers and their tonnage by heart, but he had not yet made up his mind to which vessel he would entrust himself and his fortunes. There was *La Reine Blanche*, which sailed for Valparaiso in a week's time. There was the *Zenobie*, which sailed for Rio Janeiro in a fortnight. He was divided between these two.

He told himself that he must have an outfit of some kind for his voyage. This and his passage would cost at least fifty pounds. Of the hundred which John Treverton had given him he had only sixty remaining.

'There will not be much left by the time I get to the south,' he said to himself. 'But I don't think Laura will throw me over. Besides, if the money is paid to my account in Shepherd's Inn—the Trevertons need never know my whereabouts.'

He made up his mind at last that he would go by the *Reine Blanche*, the ship which sailed earliest. He went to the Belle Jardinière, and laid out ten pounds upon clothing, and bought himself a portmanteau to hold his new garments. He called at the agents to take his passage and pay the necessary deposit, to secure his berth.

He had intended to go to the New World with a new name, but exhausted nature had required a good deal of stimulant after the purchase of the outfit, and by the time he reached the office Mr. Desrolles was, in his own phraseology, rather far gone. It was as much as he could do to reckon his money when he took a handful of loose gold and silver from his pocket. The clerk had to help him. When the clerk asked him his name, he answered without thinking—Desrolles; but in the next moment a ray of light flashed through the darkness of his clouded brain, and he corrected himself.

'Beg pardon,' he ejaculated, spasmodically. 'Desrolles a friend's name. My name's Mowbray. Colonel Mowbray, citizen, United States. Just finished a grand tour of Europe. 'Mericans very fond of Paris. Charming city. Good deal altered since my last tour—twent' years ago. Not altered for the better.'

'Oh, then your name is not Desrolles, but Mowbray,' said the clerk, scanning the American colonel somewhat suspiciously.

'Yes, Mowbray. M-o-w-b-r-a-y' answered Desrolles, laboriously.

He left the office, and being too far gone to have any definite views as to his destination, drifted vaguely to the Palais Royal, where he came to anchor at the Café de la Rotonde, and there called for the usual dose of absinthe, into which he poured half a tumbler of water, with a tremulous hand.

He fell asleep in the snug corner by the stove, and slept off something of his intoxication; or at least he awoke so far refreshed as to remember an appointment he had made with one of his new friends of the Quartier Latin, to dine at a restaurant on the Quai des Grands Augustins.

He had plenty of time to spare, so he sauntered round the Palais Royal, and stared idly at the shop windows, till he came to one where there was a great display of diamonds, when he recoiled as if he had seen an adder, and turned quickly aside into the gravelly garden, where he flung himself upon a bench, trembling from head to foot. 'Curse them,' he muttered, 'curse those shining shams. They have ruined me body and soul. I never took to drinking—hard—until after that.'

Beads of sweat broke out upon his contracted brow as he sat there, staring straight before him, as if at some horrid vision. Then he pulled himself together with an effort, braced his shattered nerves, and left the Palais Royal with something of the old 'long sword, saddle, bridle' swagger, which had been peculiar to him twenty years ago, when he called himself Captain Desmond, and had not yet forgotten his youthful days in a cavalry regiment.

He kept his appointment, treated his new friend like a prince, dined luxuriously, and drank deeply of the strongest Burgundy in the wine list, winding up with numerous glasses of Chartreuse. After dinner Mr. Desrolles and his guest repaired to a café on the Boulevard St. Michel, where there was a billiard table; and the rest of the evening was devoted to billiards, Desrolles growing noisier, more quarrelsome, and less distinct of utterance as the night wore on.

There were two things which Mr. Desrolles did not know; first, that his new friend was a distinguished member of the Parisian swell-mob, and was constantly under the surveillance of the police; secondly, that he himself had been watched and followed by an English detective ever since he left the Quai des Grands Augustins, which English detective knew all about Mr. Desrolles' intended voyage in the *Reine Blanche*.

Desrolles went home to his lodging, not too steady of foot, soon after midnight. He was prepared to encounter some slight difficulty in opening the door with his pass-key, and was pleased at finding that some other night-bird, returning to his nest a little earlier, had left the door ajar. He had only to push it open and go in.

Within all was gloom, save in one corner by the portress's den, where a glimmer of gas showed the numbered board whereon hung the keys which admitted the lodgers to their several apartments. But Desrolles knew every twist of the corkscrew staircase. Drunk as he was, he wound his way up safely enough, with only an occasional lurch and an occasional stumble. He managed to unlock the door of his room, after trying the key upside down once or twice, and making some circuitous scratchings on the panel. He managed to strike a lucifer and light his candle, leaning against the mantelpiece as he performed that feat, and giving a drunken chuckle when it was done. But his nerves must have been in a very shaky condition, for when a man, who had crept softly into the room behind him, laid a strong hand upon his shoulder, he collapsed, and made as if he would have fallen to the ground. 'What do you want?' he asked in French.

'You,' answered the intruder in English. 'I arrest you on suspicion of being concerned in the murder of La Chicot. You know all about it. You were examined at the inquest. Anything you say now will be used as evidence against you. You had better come quietly with me.'

'I don't understand you,' said Desrolles, still in French. 'I am a Frenchman.'

'Oh, very much of that. You've been lodging here three weeks.

You are known to be an Englishman. You took your passage to-day for Valparaiso. I called at the office to make inquiries an hour after you left it. No nonsense, Mr. Desrolles. All you've got to do is to come quietly with me.'

'You've got some one else outside, I suppose,' said Desrolles, with a savage glare at the door.

His expression in this moment was diabolical; a wild beast—a beast of a low type, not your kingly lion or your lordly tiger—at bay and knowing escape impossible, might so look; the thin lips curling upward above the long sharks' teeth; the grizzled brows contract-ed—the eyes emitting sparks of lurid light.

'Of course,' answered the man coolly. 'You don't suppose I should be such a fool as to trust myself in a hole like this without help. I've got my mate on the landing, and we've both got revolvers. Ah, none of that now,' ejaculated the detective suddenly, as Desrolles plunged his lean hand into his breast pocket. 'Stow that, now. Is it a knife?'

It was a knife, and a murderous one. Desrolles had it out, and the long-pointed blade ready, before his captor could stop him. The man sprang upon him, caught him by the wrist, before the knife could do mischief; and then the two closed, hand against hand, limb against limb, Desrolles wrestling with his foe as only rage and despair can wrestle.

He had been a famous bruiser in days of old. To-night he had the unnatural strength given to the overtasked sinews by a mind on the edge of madness. He fought like a madman: he fought like a tiger. There was not a muscle—not a sinew—that was not strained to its utmost in that savage conflict.

For some moments Desrolles seemed the victor. The detective had lied when he said that he had help at hand. The French police-man who had planned to meet him at that house at midnight had not yet come, and the Englishman had been too impatient to wait, be-lieving himself and his revolver more than a match for one drunken old man.

He did not want to use his revolver. It would have been a haz-ardous thing even to wound his man. It was his duty to take him alive, and surrender him safe and sound to be dealt with by the law of his country.

'Come,' he said, soothingly, having hardly enough breath for so much speech, 'let me put the bracelets on and take you away quietly. What's the use of this humbug?'

Desrolles, with his teeth set, answered never a word. He had got his antagonist very near the door; once across the threshold, a last vigorous thrust from his lean arms might hurl the man backwards down the steep staircase—certain death to the intruder. Desrolles' eyes were fixed upon the doorway, the door standing conveniently open. His bloodshot eyeballs flashed fire. It was in his mind that the thing was to be done. One more herculean effort, and his foe would be across the threshold.

Possibly the detective saw that look of triumph in the savage face, and divined his danger. However that might be, he gathered himself together, and with a sudden impetus, flinging all his weight against Desrolles, he drove his foe before him across the narrow room, hurled him with all his might against the wall, casting him loose for the moment, in order to grip him tighter afterwards.

But as that tall figure fell with terrific force against the gaudy-papered wall, there was a sudden crashing sound, at which the detective recoiled with a cry of horror. The frail lath and plaster partition split asunder, the rotten wood crumbled and scattered itself in a cloud of dust, half that side of the room dropped into ruin, as if the house had been a house of cards, and, with one hoarse shriek, Desrolles rolled backwards into empty air.

They found him presently upon the pavement below, so battered and disfigured by that awful fall as to be hardly recognizable even by the eyes that had looked upon him a few minutes before. In falling he had struck against the timbers that shored up the rotten old house, and life had been beaten out of him before he touched the stones below. It was a bad end of a bad man. There was nobody to be sorry for him except the detective, who had lost the chance of a handsome reward.

The Parisian journals next day made a feature of the catastrophe. 'Fall of part of a house in the Boulevard Louis Capet. Horrible death of one of the inmates.'

The English newspapers of a later date contained the account of the pursuit and arrest of Desrolles, his desperate resistance, and awful death.

EPILOGUE.

Mr. and Mrs. Treverton went back to Hazlehurst Manor, and there was much rejoicing among their friends at John Treverton's escape from the critical position in which the hazards of life had placed him. The subject was a painful one, and people in their intercourse with John and Laura, touched upon it as lightly as possible. Those revelations about John Treverton's first marriage, his Bohemian existence under an assumed name, his poverty, and so on, had created no small sensation among a community which rarely had anything more exciting to talk about than the state of the weather, or the appearance of the crops. People had talked their fill by the time Mr. and Mrs. Treverton came back, for they had spent a month at a Dorsetshire watering-place on their way home, for the benefit of Laura's health, whereby the scandal was stale and almost worn threadbare when they arrived at the Manor House.

Only one event of any importance had happened during their absence. Edward Clare—the poet, the man who sauntered through life hand-in-hand with the muses, dwelling apart from common clay in a world of his own—had suddenly sickened of elegant leisure, and had started all at once for the Cape to learn ostrich farming, with the deliberate intention of settling for life in that distant land.

'An adventurous career will suit me, and I shall make money,' he told those few acquaintances to whom he condescended to explain his views. 'My people are tired of seeing me lead an idle life. They have no faith in my future as a poet. Perhaps they are right. The rarest and finest of poets have made very little money. It is only charlatanism in literature that really pays. A man who can write down to the level of the herd commands an easy success. Herrick, if he were alive to-day, would not make a living by his pen.'

So Edward Clare departed from the haunts of his youth, and there was no one save his mother to regret him. The Vicar knew too well that John Treverton's arrest was his son's work, and treachery so base was a sin his honest heart could not forgive. He was glad that Edward had gone, and his secret prayer was that the young man might learn honesty as well as industry in his self-imposed exile.

To the exile himself anything was better than to see the man he had impotently striven to injure, happy and secure from all future malice. Weighed against that mortification the possible difficulties and hardships of the life to which he was going were as nothing to him.

The year wore on, and brought a new and strange gladness and a deep sense of responsibility to John Treverton. One balmy May morning his first-born son opened his innocent blue eyes upon a bright young world, arrayed in all the glory of spring. The child was placed in his father's arms by the good old Hazlehurst doctor, who had attended Jasper Treverton in his last illness.

'How proud my old friend would have been to see his family name in a fair way of being continued in the land for many a long year to come,' he said.

'Thank God all things have worked round well for us, at last,' answered John Treverton, gravely.

In the ripeness and splendour of August and harvest, when the heather was in bloom on the rolling moor, and the narrow streams were dried up by the fierceness of the sun, George Gerard came down to the Manor House to spend a brief holiday; and it happened, by a strange coincidence, that Laura had invited Celia Clare to stay with her at the same time. They all had a pleasant time in the peerless summer weather. There were picnics and excursions across the moor, with much exciting adventure, and some risk of losing oneself altogether in that sparsely populated world; and in all these adventures George and Celia had a knack of finding themselves abandoned by the other two—or perhaps it was they who went astray, though they always protested that it was Mr. and Mrs. Treverton who deserted them.

'I shouldn't wonder if we came to a bad end, like the babes in the wood,' protested Celia. 'Imagine us existing on unripe blackberries for a week or so, and then lying resignedly down to die. I don't believe a bit in the birds putting leaves over us. That's a fable invented for the pantomime. Birds are a great deal too selfish. No one who had ever seen a pair of robins fight for a bit of bread would believe in those benevolent birds who buried the babes in the wood.'

Being occasionally lost on the moor gave Celia and Mr. Gerard great opportunities for conversation. They were obliged to find something to talk about; and in the end naturally told each other their inmost thoughts. And so it came about, in the most natural way in the world, that one blazing noontide Celia found herself standing before a Druidic table, gazing idly at the big gray stones half embedded in heather and bracken, with George Gerard's arm round her waist, and with her head placidly resting against his shoulder.

He had been asking her if she would wait for him. That was all.

He had not asked her if she loved him, having made up his own mind upon that question, unassisted.

'Darling, will you wait for me?' he asked, looking down at her, with eyes brimming over with love.

'Yes, George,' she answered, meekly, quite a transformed Celia, all her pertness and flippancy gone.

'It may be a long while, dear,' he said gravely; 'almost as long as Rachel waited for Jacob.'

'I don't mind that, provided there is no Leah to come between us.'

'There shall be no Leah.'

So they were engaged, and in the dim cloudland of the future, Celia saw a vision of Harley Street, a landau, and a pair of handsome grays.

'Doctors generally have grays, don't they, George?' she asked, presently, *apropos* to nothing particular.

George's thoughts had not travelled so far as the carriage and pair stage of his existence, and he did not understand the question.

'Yes, dear, there is a Free Hospital in the Gray's Inn Road,' he answered, simply, 'but I was at Bartlemy's.'

'Oh, you foolish George, I was thinking of horses, not hospitals. What colour shall you choose when you start your carriage?'

'We'll talk it over, dearest, when we are going to start the carriage.'

Mr. and Mrs. Treverton heard of the engagement with infinite pleasure, nor did the Vicar or his easy-tempered wife offer any objection.

Before the first year of Celia's betrothal was over, John Treverton had persuaded the good old village doctor to retire, and to accept a handsome price for his comfortable practice, which covered a district of sixty miles circumference, and offered ample work for an energetic young man. This practice John Treverton gave to George Gerard as a free gift.

'Don't consider it a favour,' he said, when the surgeon wanted it to be treated as a debt, to be paid out of his future earnings. 'The obligation is all on my side. I want a clever young doctor, whom I know and esteem, instead of any charlatan who might happen to succeed our old friend. The advantage is all on my side. You will help me in all my sanitary improvements, and my nursery will be safe in the inevitable season of measles and scarlatina.'

Thus it came to pass that Celia, as well as John Treverton and his wife was able to say,

'But in some wise all things wear round betimes,
And wind up well.'

THE END.